# The King of Mirth

A JIM McGILL NOVEL

**Joseph Flynn**

Stray Dog Press, Inc.
Springfield, IL
2018

## PRAISE FOR JOSEPH FLYNN AND HIS NOVELS

"Flynn is an excellent storyteller." — *Booklist*

"Flynn propels his plot with potent but flexible force."
— *Publishers Weekly*

**The President's Henchman**
"Marvelously entertaining." — *ForeWord Magazine*

**Digger**
"A mystery cloaked as cleverly as (and perhaps better than) any John Grisham work." — *Denver Post*

"Surefooted, suspenseful and in its breathless final moments unexpectedly heartbreaking." — *Booklist*

**The Next President**
"*The Next President* bears favorable comparison to such classics as *The Best Man, Advise and Consent* and *The Manchurian Candidate.*"
— *Booklist*

"A thriller fast enough to read in one sitting."
— *Rocky Mountain News*

## BY JOSEPH FLYNN

**The Jim McGill Series**

The President's Henchman, A Jim McGill Novel [#1]
The Hangman's Companion, A JimMcGill Novel [#2]
The K Street Killer A JimMcGill Novel [#3]
Part 1: The Last Ballot Cast, A JimMcGill Novel [#4 Part 1]
Part 2: The Last Ballot Cast, A JimMcGill Novel [#5 Part 2]
The Devil on the Doorstep, A Jim McGill Novel [#6]
The Good Guy with a Gun, A Jim McGill Novel [#7]
The Echo of the Whip, A Jim McGill Novel [#8]
The Daddy's Girl Decoy, A Jim McGill Novel [#9]
The Last Chopper Out, A Jim McGill Novel [#10]
The King of Mirth, A Jim McGill Novel [#11]

McGill's Short Cases 1-3

**The Ron Ketchum Mystery Series**

Nailed, A Ron Ketchum Mystery [#1]
Defiled, A Ron Ketchum Mystery Featuring John Tall Wolf [#2]
Impaled, A Ron Ketchum Mystery [#3]

**The John Tall Wolf Series**

Tall Man in Ray-Bans, A John Tall Wolf Novel [#1]
War Party, A John Tall Wolf Novel [#2]
Super Chief, A John Tall Wolf Novel [#3]
Smoke Signals, A John Tall Wolf Novel [#4]
Big Medicine, A John Tall Wolf Novel [#5]

**The Zeke Edison Series**

Kill Me Twice, A Zeke Edison Novel [#1]

**Stand Alone Novels**

The Concrete Inquisition
Digger
The Next President
Hot Type
Farewell Performance
Gasoline, Texas
Round Robin, A Love Story of Epic Proportions
One False Step
Blood Street Punx
Still Coming
Still Coming Expanded Edition
Hangman — A Western Novella
Pointy Teeth, Twelve Bite-Size Stories

Published by Stray Dog Press, Inc.
Springfield, IL 62704, U.S.A.



Visit the author's web site: *www.josephflynn.com*

Flynn, Joseph
The King of Mirth / Joseph Flynn
374 p.
ISBN 978-0-9974500-5-7
ISBN eBook 978-0-9974500-4-0

Printed in the United States of America



PUBLISHER'S NOTE
This is a work of fiction. Names, characters, places, and incidents are either the product of the author's imagination or are used fictitiously; any resemblance to actual persons, living or dead, events, or locales is entirely coincidental.

*Book design by Aha! Designs*

# DEDICATION

In memory of Mary and John Coates.

## ACKNOWLEDGEMENTS

Catherine, Cat, Anne, and Susan do their level best to catch all my typos and other mistakes, but I usually outwit them. For this book, I've added the efforts of my Advance Reading Team. I thank them for their input and interest. Please be kind, if one or two tiny errors remain.

**AL**
**Reader Discretion Advised**
Contains Adult Language

# CHARACTER LIST

*[in alphabetical order by last name]*
**Gene Beck,** investigator for McGill Investigations
**Edwina Byington,** Patti's right-hand woman
**Haskell Carver,** head of security for Teagan Tobias
**Gabbi Casale,** partner in McGill Investigations
**Eloy Chavez,** Mexican drug lord
**Catherine Clarke,** daughter of Wallace Rhymes
**Jim McGill,** CEO, McGill Investigations
**Patti [Grant] McGill,** former President, head of Committed Capital
**Marlon Janeway,** client and brother of Alice Janeway
**Alice Janeway,** missing person
**Donald "Deke" Ky,** partner in McGill Investigations
**Daphna Levy,** Secret Service special agent
**Leo Levy,** Jim McGill's personal driver
**Dorie McBride,** Hollywood super agent
**Galia Mindel,** former White House Chief of Staff
**Frank Morrissey,** White House Chief of Staff
**Jean Morrissey,** President
**Fred Nakamura,** Keely Powell's samurai
**Maj Olson,** investigator for McGill Investigations
**Keely Powell,** investigator for McGill Investigations
**Yves Pruet,** partner in McGill Investigations
**Clint Rhymes,** son of Wallace Rhymes
**Cole Rhymes,** son of Wallace Rhymes
**Henry Rhymes,** son of Wallace Rhymes
**Wallace Rhymes,** stock broker
**Margaret "Sweetie" Sweeney,** McGill's longtime friend and conscience
**Tad Thacker,** environmental engineer
**Esme Thrice,** administrative director, McGill Investigations
**Teagan Tobias,** performance artist
**Lindsay Todd,** friend of Alice Janeway

# CHAPTER 1

***Tuesday, October 31, 2017***
***McGill Investigations International — Washington, DC***

Jim McGill and Margaret "Sweetie" Sweeney made Skype contact with Yves Pruet and Gabbi Casale of McGill's Paris office at nine a.m. Eastern Daylight Time. Paris was six hours ahead of Washington. So was Munich, Germany, where the last member of the video conversation, Marlon Janeway, lived.

Pruet and Gabbi looked to be in fine health. The same couldn't be said of Janeway. He looked pale even allowing for the fluorescent lighting he had at his location and the transmission of his image across thousands of miles. Beyond that, he wore a surgical mask over his nose and mouth. His eyes looked watery and were such a pale blue as to be almost colorless.

Janeway recognized the shock and concern evident on the faces of McGill and Sweetie. He managed a raspy laugh. "Not a pretty picture, am I?"

The idiom was pure American. But his voice had a hint of a German accent. McGill and Sweetie had been told by Gabbi that the man had been born and raised in North Carolina. So Janeway must have been overseas a *long* time.

Sweetie found her footing first. “What kind of illness are you suffering, Mr. Janeway?”

“Dengue fever. Made a business trip to Africa. Seems my bug spray wasn’t up to the job. Got a mosquito bite from a malignant critter.”

Okay, McGill thought, there was a hint of a Southern accent.

Poor guy.

Almost seeming to read McGill’s mind or at least the look in his eyes, Janeway said, “The doctors have told me not to give up hope yet. They have some very good medical people over here. On the other hand, I don’t feel I should start reading a long book. What I’d dearly like to do, however, is talk to my sister, Alice, one more time. Only I can’t find her.”

Pruet told McGill, “That is why M’sieur Janeway contacted us. I felt it would be more productive if he spoke to you directly.”

Let me get a good look at the man myself, McGill thought. Make it a whole lot tougher to turn down the case or say, “Maybe I can get to it a couple weeks from now.”

“Absolutely,” McGill said. “We’ll make time for you, Mr. Janeway. Call in staff investigators from other offices here in the States, if necessary.”

With just a hint of humor in his washed-out eyes, Janeway asked, “You’re not even going to ask if I can afford your services?”

McGill said, “I assume my colleagues in Paris already took care of that detail, but my partner, Ms. Sweeney, here, is our chief ethics officer. She’s already raised the subject of taking on some cases at compassionate rates or even *gratis.* You know, every so often.”

Janeway produced a dry chuckle. “I was just joking. I can pay your fees, which M’sieur Pruet and I did, in fact, discuss. I do approve of Ms. Sweeney’s idea, though.”

Sweetie offered a smile in reply.

“What can you tell us about your sister, Mr. Janeway?” McGill asked.

“She’s 12 years my junior, 28 years old, and my only sibling. Our parents are dead. I moved overseas 14 years ago. I’ve always felt a bit guilty about that."

The man's pale eyes filmed over with a sheen of tears, and he was silent for a moment.

"I kept in regular touch the first few years, at least once a month. Then my two children came along, and my contacts with Alice became more irregular and widely spaced. I never actually forgot about her. To the contrary, I think about her with a guilty conscience almost every day, but I never got around to writing or calling one-tenth of the times I thought I should."

Sweetie asked, "Was it hard for you to take your overseas job in the first place?"

Janeway coughed up another dry laugh. "Staying in Germany wasn't part of the plan when I left home. I was supposed to be gone only two weeks. Only, I did a terrific job, and I was offered a permanent position at almost double my pay back home. On top of that, I also met the woman who became my wife. Even so, I did my due diligence. I called my boss back home and asked what he thought. He said if I didn't take the job over here, he'd apply for it."

"Did you also check in with Alice?" McGill asked.

Now, the tears fell freely from Janeway's eyes. "I did. She said whatever made me happy would make her happy, too. Fourteen years old, and talking like that. So, I stayed, and one misbegotten trip to Africa many years later, here I am."

Janeway looked for a moment as if his summary had stirred up another memory, but it must have skipped on by because he didn't offer anything else just then.

"Tell us what you know about Alice's present situation," McGill said. "Where she lives, where she works, who some of her friends might be if you know that."

"She has a small house in Durham, North Carolina. I gave her the down-payment money, out of both generosity and guilt. She said she was going to repay me. I told her if she did that it would hurt my feelings. So she said she would make contributions to charity in my honor."

Janeway began to cry silently once more.

The others gave him a moment to collect himself.

Then McGill asked in a gentle voice, "Where does Alice work?"

Janeway blotted his eyes with a tissue that was handed to him by someone off-camera. To McGill, it looked like a woman's hand. The nails were trimmed closely. A nurse, maybe.

"Alice travels all over the country. The States, I mean. She's what I'd guess you'd call a Jill-of-all-trades for a performer named Teagan Tobias. Have you heard of him?"

"Sorry, no," McGill said. He turned to Sweetie.

She only shrugged in ignorance.

McGill asked his colleagues in Paris. Pruet was unfamiliar with the name.

Gabbi, an artist, knew more.

"I've read about him in the *New York Times International Edition*. He calls himself a performance artist. He does social satire with emphasis on his low opinion of most of humanity."

Janeway picked up that thread. "I've never seen any of the guy's work, but Alice tells me he gives voice to the legitimate gripes everyone encounters daily."

"Is Alice a hard-edged person?" McGill asked.

That drew a short, hoarse laugh from Janeway. "Anything but. My little sister is sweet, cheerful, generous." He caught himself before he started to weep again. "You know, thinking about it, though, she has a lot of legitimate complaints she could make if she felt like it."

"What kind of complaints, Mr. Janeway?" Sweetie asked.

"Well, basically, losing her whole family in a brief period. I left for Germany when she'd just started high school. She was a freshman at UNC when our parents died in a train derailment. Being isolated like that could make a person bitter."

"Didn't you come home for the funeral?" McGill asked.

Now, it was pain that filled Janeway's eyes as he gave a slight shake of his head.

"My parents died on the same day my first child, my son, was born. It was a horribly difficult delivery for both him and my wife.

Things were touch and go for both of them whether they'd survive for a week. I couldn't go. I told Alice what had happened, and she said I should be with my family. Alice has had way more than her share of grief."

It certainly seemed to McGill that Marlon Janeway also hadn't gotten off easy.

"Did you try to contact Mr. Tobias regarding Alice's whereabouts?" he asked.

For the first time, the man showed signs of anger. A good thing, McGill thought. You needed at least a bit of energy to produce hard feelings. Apathy would have been much worse.

"We spoke briefly. He acted as if his time was too valuable to give me more than the most clipped and concise answers. As if I was bothering him. He said he didn't know where Alice was. She was with the show for their last performance in Atlanta, but she didn't appear before the opening of the next stop in Washington, DC." Janeway pressed his eyes closed for a moment. Then he said, "The man told me if Alice called me, I should tell her if she didn't get back to work within the next few days she was fired. Then he hung up."

Sweetie shook her head. McGill remained stoic.

"I think that's all I can tell you," Janeway said. "I'm probably forgetting something. Not quite as sharp as I used to be."

McGill asked, "Do you know if Alice had any close friends in Durham? Someone she might have visited on the way to DC. A kindred spirit with whom she might share a confidence or a gripe about work?"

Janeway's head bobbed. "There must be someone like that. Alice is so easy to get along with; she has to have friends. Only I can't think of any names right now. I feel half-dead already."

"Mr. Janeway," McGill said in a curt, almost martial tone.

The man responded by blinking rapidly and saying, "Yes?"

"You have a lot to live for: your sister, your wife, your children. You fight just as hard as you can. Any doctor in the world will tell you that an indomitable spirit makes their treatments a lot more effective."

"I will, I will."

"You make sure you're still around when we find Alice for you."

A look of hope filled the man's eyes. "I will. Thank you."

Janeway nodded to the unseen person in his room, and he was disconnected from the group link-up.

At that point, Yves Pruet asked McGill, "Are you sure you will be able to make good on your promise, *mon ami?*"

McGill responded by making the Sign of the Cross.

No sooner had McGill invoked divine intercession than Esme Thrice buzzed him on the office intercom.

Sweetie gestured to McGill asking if she should end the Skype conference. McGill nodded. Sweetie waved a silent goodbye to Pruet and Gabbi; got a pair of quiet *au revoirs* in return.

"Yes, Esme?" McGill said.

"Someone here to see you, sir. No appointment, just a drop-in."

McGill and Sweetie looked at each other. They both heard the chill note of disapproval in Esme's voice. That was not like her at all, not without good reason, anyway. McGill said, "Ask the person to wait a moment. We have something we need to discuss with you."

"Yes, sir. I'll be right in."

She didn't take five seconds before entering the office and closing the door behind her. McGill gestured for Esme to take the open visitor's chair. Sweetie had moved back to that side of McGill's desk after the teleconference had ended.

"What's wrong, Esme? Whoever's outside offended you in some way?"

She took a deep breath and let it out slowly. "He introduced himself by saying, 'I remember you.' He was looking at my chest at the time."

"Creep," Sweetie said.

Esme nodded.

"Did he think he was being funny?" McGill asked.

"He always thinks he's funny. His name is Teagan Tobias. He's a performer."

McGill and Sweetie looked at each other. Neither of them believed the man's appearance was a coincidence, but McGill wanted to hear more from Esme before he spoke with Tobias.

"Is there anything more you'd be comfortable sharing?" he asked Esme.

Esme took a moment to cool down. "I saw his show years ago in New York when he was just getting started. I went with Cheryl, my then-fiancée at the time. We were thinking of getting married in one of the states that had legalized gay marriage before the Supreme Court lifted the ban nationwide. Massachusetts was the first state to allow gay people to marry, but that was done by a court order. Vermont was the first state to allow both civil unions and gay marriage by votes of the legislature. New York was the first state in which a Republican state Senate helped to pass a legalization statute after a previous Democratic state Senate had killed the bill."

"Huh," McGill said. "Didn't know that."

Esme smiled. "We extended our criteria a bit because Cheryl's a New York girl. Anyway, we were in Manhattan and decided to see Tobias' show, *Every Last Bastard in Town.*"

Sweetie guessed, "There was a dose of gay-bashing in the performance?"

"Actually, no. What ticked me off happened afterward. We saw the show in a little 99-seat theater. I think they called it an Equity-waiver place because you didn't have to use union people. After the show, Tobias came out to say thanks to the people who'd stuck around. He started asking for any gripes we had. You know, to see if he might be able to use them in his show."

"Pay-waiver material, huh?" Sweetie asked.

"Yeah, exactly. He wanted new story ideas for free. Anyway, he worked his way over to Cheryl and me, and he thought he was in heaven. We get that: guys imagining they might have a threesome with us. The ones who are even a bit perceptive understand right away why that's never going to happen, and they're nice about it. The jerks are slow to catch on and feel they have to insult us when they do."

McGill said, "Words to the effect that you don't know what you're missing."

"Yeah."

Sweetie followed up. "My guess is things got physical in a way he didn't expect. So, which one of you hit him?"

"Cheryl. She saw he was about to put a hand on me, somewhere it didn't belong, and kicked him hard on an ankle. He had to cancel his show for a week. We heard he was thinking about suing Cheryl, but we asked him if he wanted to have gay men and women picketing his show every night until he was forced to abandon it. The idea of the suit went away, but we heard he hired somebody to do security for him from then on."

Sweetie asked, "So where did you get married?"

"Vermont. It was lovely."

McGill wanted to know: "Didn't he recognize you when he showed up here?"

"He pretended he didn't. But he remembered. It wasn't just my boobs."

McGill said, "Good thing Cheryl wasn't visiting the office. She might've given him another kick for old time's sake."

Both Esme and Sweetie grinned at the thought.

"I think we've heard enough of Mr. Tobias' bio for the moment," McGill said. "Please show him in, Esme. Try not to trip him. It might be useful to hear what he has to say."

"I'll do my best," she said, her face hardening again.

Esme ushered Teagan Tobias into McGill's office without plunging a letter-opener into his back, but as she closed the door behind him she wrinkled her nose as if she'd sniffed a foul odor. Nonetheless, McGill welcomed the man. "Please have a seat, Mr. Tobias."

He gestured to the seat adjacent to where Sweetie sat but didn't offer a handshake.

Tobias' dark hair was neatly barbered. His eyes were a clear, pale gray. His other features were well proportioned and symmetrical. His sport coat, shirt, jeans, and shoes were business casual, well made and nicely fitted to an athletically slim body.

All in all, the guy looked like he might have just retired from the U.S. Olympic fencing team, might even have been a medalist. Silver, not gold, McGill thought. Tobias glanced at Sweetie briefly, and gave her a nod. Then he turned back to McGill.

"I have the feeling you already know why I'm here," Tobias said.

"I might, but why don't you tell me anyway?"

"Alice Janeway," Tobias said. "She hasn't shown up for work lately, is pretty damn close to getting fired."

"You'd like me to deliver a termination notice?" McGill asked mildly.

Tobias grinned. "Nice delivery. You ever perform onstage?"

"Got shot onstage once. Took a bullet for the maestro."

Tobias liked that, too. "Yeah, I read about that on the way over here. That and a bunch of other things. Anyway, I spoke to Marlon Janeway earlier this morning. So early by my schedule I was still asleep when he called. The only reason I answered was because I saw his last name on the caller ID and thought it was Alice calling."

"Mr. Janeway explained his reason for waking you?" McGill asked.

Tobias nodded. "He did. Said he might be dying and wanted to talk with Alice before he went bye-bye."

Sweetie had no trouble catching the performer's casually indifferent tone.

"You have no sympathy for the man?" she asked.

Tobias looked almost surprised to hear her speak. "None, and if you want to know why it's because the guy was never there for Alice when she needed him. He always had these perfectly reasonable excuses: his job, his wife, his kids. Okay, things happen, but every single time Alice could have used some help? The guy never stepped up once."

McGill glanced at Sweetie.

Neither had to say a word.

Both believed the man's indignation was real.

Of course, they didn't know if he was just a terrific actor.

"Did you ever come to Alice's aid, Mr. Tobias?" McGill asked.

"Damn right, I did. Lots of times. That's why I'm here right now."

"How's that?" Sweetie asked.

Once again, Tobias seemed surprised that she'd spoken. He told her, "Take a listen." Looking back at McGill, he elaborated, "Marlon told me he was going to call you. Your Paris office, anyway."

"We spoke directly," McGill said.

"Good. I imagine getting you started on looking for Alice must have cost him some money up front."

"It's the standard practice, yes."

"Did Marlon tell you he can pay your toll? I know that's probably a privacy issue with you, but what I'm getting at here is the man might not have the money he claims to have. No, that's not exactly right. He makes a very nice buck compared to most people. Thing is, though, in this particular household, Papa doesn't hold the keys to the treasury. Mama does, and she is one tightfisted *hausfrau*. Keeps a close watch on each and every one of the family's euros. Alice told me that, too. She might have an irrational love for her brother, but she's none too fond of Ms. Erika."

McGill said, "If that's, in fact, the case, Mr. Tobias, are you looking out for my best interests here? Advising me to get more than my usual advance?"

The performer cracked a smile. "No, not even close. My only concern is Alice. If the money from Germany gets cut off, I'll pick up the tab … if you can show me you're making real progress."

"Why us and not another detective agency?" Sweetie asked.

By now Tobias had gotten the drift that Sweetie was important enough to speak any time she felt so inclined, and McGill wouldn't cut her off. "Because I checked you out. Beyond the stories in the papers, on TV and online. I've got a researcher who works for me. He said your company is for real and it tends to get results."

"We do," McGill said, "but while we've taken on Mr. Janeway as a client, that doesn't mean we'd extend our services to you."

Tobias' mouth fell open, and then he laughed.

"You know, it's been a long time since anyone told me to buzz off. But why not? I do it to people all the time."

He got to his feet and added, "If you don't want my money, and I'm pretty damn sure you'll need it when old Marlon comes up dry, I'll give you a tip that might help you get where you need to go sooner rather than later. Is that okay?"

"That's fine," McGill said.

Tobias told McGill about a crazy guy named Tad Thacker who rushed backstage one night and tried to give Alice a ring with a great big diamond because she just had to marry him. They were going to spend the rest of their lives together. Tobias said, "What I was told, the ring would set back an average guy the better part of a year's pay."

"Alice called for help at that moment?" McGill asked.

"Didn't have to. My security chief, Haskell, didn't like the guy's looks from the jump. He was watching the whole thing and tossed the guy out while Alice stood there at a loss for words."

"Your man let the guy keep his ring?" Sweetie asked.

"Yeah."

"Who told you what happened?" McGill asked.

"Where were you when all this happened?" Sweetie added.

Responding in order, Tobias told them, "Alice and Haskell both gave me a rundown on what happened. I was in my dressing room with my earbuds in and Springsteen telling me about life in Jersey."

McGill followed up. "Did the guy persist?"

"Yeah, he did," Tobias said. "He had a front row center seat — something that's also fairly pricey — for my next performance. Alice had the foresight to think he might be in the house, and

Haskell and a couple members of his team hauled the guy away before I went on. Refunded his money and let him know that night was strike two. Strike three, Haskell told him, wouldn't be pretty. I didn't hear any further reports on the guy, but …"

Tobias looked at Sweetie. McGill thought maybe Tobias guessed she wouldn't care to hear profanity. That or possibly it was mentioned in some of the research he'd done and *knew* she didn't like vulgarities.

In any case, Tobias said, "Guys like Tad Thacker tend not to give up their obsessions easily, if at all. Alice accepted my offer to provide a personal bodyguard. That lasted for two weeks. Then she wanted to be on her own again. I suggested she leave her protection in place for a month, but she said no."

McGill asked, "How did you get the stalker's name?"

"Haskell grabbed the guy's wallet that first night to get a look at his driver's license. He took down the name and a street address in Portland. I didn't bring the address with me, but I can get it to you if you want."

McGill said, "That would be helpful. Do you have any photos of Mr. Thacker?"

Tobias nodded. "Haskell shot some with his phone. I can have him text you the pictures with the address."

"That would also be appreciated, thank you," McGill said.

Sweetie asked Tobias, "How did Mr. Thacker first become aware of Alice?"

"Alice told me that she asked Thacker the same thing. He said it was through *Playbill,* the theater magazine the ushers hand out before every performance."

"He saw a headshot of Ms. Janeway and a brief professional bio," McGill said.

"Yeah."

McGill added, "But Thacker's first meeting with her was the only one you know of?"

The question surprised Tobias. "Absolutely. No way Alice would have held back on me if anything else happened."

McGill paused for a moment and then asked, "How did Alice meet you?"

That made the man smile. He returned to his seat. "She stalked me, only in a socially acceptable way. I was performing in Raleigh, North Carolina, and she had the same kind of seat Thacker had, front row center. Only she had the same seat five nights in a row. That's not quite diamond-ring money, but for most people it'd mean giving up food for a month."

"You noticed her?" Sweetie asked.

Tobias shook his head. "Not when I'm in character and have the stage lights in my eyes. Haskell scoped her out. What he told me, though, was she didn't look the least bit threatening. Was perfectly behaved. Left promptly when the performance ended."

"So, then you were the one to make contact?" McGill asked.

Tobias nodded.

McGill followed up. "Why her as opposed to anyone else?"

"Well, in the first place, I've never been told anyone else has ever come to five consecutive performances of mine before, and Haskell told me something else that really grabbed me."

"What's that?" McGill said.

"Well, Haskell told me two things, actually. The first was that Alice seemed to get as big a kick out of all the various sketches, gags and jokes on the succeeding nights as she did on the first night, and she had a small notepad on her lap. She was making notes."

"Reviewers do that, don't they?" Sweetie asked.

Tobias shook his head. "They *dictate* their stories into recorders, at intermission and after the performance. People'd smack them upside the head, if they yapped during the show."

Both McGill and Sweetie could see that.

McGill had one more question. "How could Alice see what she was writing in a darkened theater?"

"Beats the hell out of me," Tobias said, "but she did. She showed me her notes when I invited her backstage after that final performance. Handwriting was neat as a pin, and, honestly, she struck me as too nice to work with a guy like me. The conversation got to the point where I was about to say, 'Nice to meet you. I'll leave some tickets for you the next time I hit town.' She could see that, too, but she didn't get needy or desperate or anything else. I had the feeling she was only going to stand up and say, 'It's been very nice meeting you.' So, I crossed up on her and said I wanted her to come work for me. You know what she said?"

McGill and Sweetie didn't.

Tobias told them, "I'll have to give my current employer two weeks notice."

McGill understood the implications of that. "She didn't give you any notice?"

"No."

"Would you really fire her?" Sweetie asked.

"Well, if she doesn't want to work for me anymore, that way she'd at least be able to collect unemployment compensation."

Tobias stood up and walked to the office door. He stopped and looked back at McGill and Sweetie. He told them, "I'm only half the SOB that I play on stage." Then he laughed. "Of course, there are moments when I might go as high as seven-eighths."

Sweetie gave it a slow three-count after Tobias had left and then asked McGill, "Do you think he has a car and a bodyguard waiting outside for him?"

McGill picked up his office phone. "I'll have Dikki take a peek and check the video."

Dikki Missirian, McGill's former landlord at his previous business address, was the building manager at his new location. Dikki's office looked out on the street opposite the front door. He also had video playback from the array of security cameras around the building.

Dikki reported quickly, "The gentleman flagged a passing taxi."

McGill had the response on speaker and thanked Dikki. He

then told Sweetie, "A man of the people despite his celebrity."

Sweetie laughed skeptically. "Yeah, sure. That seven-eighths of an SOB he mentioned? I bet it's closer to fifteen-sixteenths."

McGill said, "I'll defer to your judgment of personal decency, but I think you have something in mind that might only occur to a suspicious cop."

"I do," Sweetie said. "If Tobias thinks of this guy Tad Thacker as a legitimate threat to Alice Janeway, how come he isn't at least a little bit worried about himself, too?"

"You mean because a stalker might consider Tobias to be an obstacle between him and his object of desire?" McGill asked.

Sweetie said, "Worse than that. Thacker might think of Tobias as a *rival,* the only man in the world between him and the woman he can't live without."

McGill nodded. He'd seen obsessive characters before, more than a few. Some of whom had been other cops. But he'd never really understood fixation. For him, the attraction would have to be mutual, if it were to exist at all. Even so, he saw Sweetie's point.

"You're saying if Tobias considers Thacker to be a real threat, he should be more wary of possible trouble heading his way."

Sweetie nodded. "Yeah. Don't you think?"

"Not necessarily."

"Why not?"

McGill said, "For the simple reason that it never occurred to Tobias that someone as pathetic as Thacker could be a threat to him. Reduced to two words: male ego."

Sweetie sighed in disgust. "Just about anyone can manage a four-pound trigger pull. Shoot you dead before you can call him a sissy."

"As two people who have been shot, we both know that. Not everyone does. Worse, some guys do know but won't admit it."

"Men," Sweetie said.

"Come on now, Margaret," McGill said, "are you going to tell me women never practice denial?"

"No, I wouldn't do that."

"So what gender-neutral term can we agree on?"

*"People,"* Sweetie said.

McGill nodded. "That covers a multitude of sins."

***McGill Investigations International — Austin, Texas***

Maj Olson had been working with Gene Beck long enough — over a year now — that she was used to hearing him whistle his songs or other people's tunes most any time he wasn't eating, drinking or conducting a business conversation. He did, however, softly whistle even while taking an occasional catnap in the office.

Coming from anyone else, all of that whistling might have driven Maj crazy.

Not with Gene, though. He was to whistling what Andrea Bocelli was to singing.

Every note was perfect and nearly divine, a gift from above.

Gene's talent agent, Dorie McBride, had gotten two of his songs published in the past six months and they'd been recorded by top vocal artists in both the pop and country music fields. Both of Gene's tunes had hit number one in their respective recording charts.

Gene had taken his wife, Lissa, his darling young son, Cyrus, and Maj out to celebrate each time a song had made it to number one, and the second time that happened, while the missus was in the ladies' room changing kiddo's diaper, Gene had whispered to Maj how much money he'd earned.

"Good God," Maj had said, "why are you still doing anything but working on your music?"

Gene had told her, "I like my job. I like being out in the world, poking my nose into this place and that. It inspires me. If I just sat in a room trying to *think* up a song, that'd never work."

When Maj and Gene weren't working, they both liked to go out for a good run, five miles or so. Gene had been pleased to find out that Maj, a former college track athlete, could keep up with him.

She'd laughed and said, "Keep up with you? I've been taking it *easy* on you."

From then on, she'd set the pace.

Those were among the few times Gene didn't whistle: when he was breathless.

He was also silent that morning when Maj entered their office suite. Gene always beat her into work, and she didn't compete in that area. Gene had his office door closed, but Maj could hear an unfamiliar male voice speaking.

Maj tapped lightly on Gene's door to see if she needed to be in on the meeting.

Assuming Gene was talking to a prospective client.

He opened the door, gave her a discreet wink and said, "Come on in, partner."

A stocky silver-haired man in a western-cut suit got to his feet when he saw Maj. He gave her a nod and said, "Mornin', ma'am."

When Maj extended a hand and introduced herself, he shook it and added, "Wallace Rhymes."

Off the top of her head, Maj couldn't think of anything that rhymed with Wallace, but she knew better than to joke about someone's name, unless you knew the person well. Gene took his seat behind his desk. Maj and Rhymes used the guest chairs.

"Mr. Rhymes would like us to find a hat that was stolen from his collection," Gene said.

The idea that someone might collect hats struck Maj as odd, but it took all kinds. Considering what McGill investigators charged for their time, though, Maj said, "Must be one special hat."

"It is, Ms. Olson," Rhymes said, "a very special cowboy hat."

Having been born, raised and educated in the Northeast, Maj was still acculturating herself to Texas and other points south. It helped that her present hometown had the motto "Keep Austin Weird." Still, she'd seen enough of the Lone Star State to know that many Texans highly valued their cowboy heritage.

"It was once John Wayne's hat," Gene explained.

"Well, now," Maj said. "That's a hat of a different color, isn't it?"

"That's just the problem, ma'am," Rhymes said. "The color ain't true."

Maj understood intuitively. "Your hat was replaced by a knockoff."

Gene and Rhymes both nodded.

Gene handed a photograph to Maj and filled her in on the details.

"What you're looking at there is a cowboy hat with a six-inch crown and a pinch-front triangle crease. That was John Wayne's favorite style. The hat has a five-inch brim, a snakeskin band and the color is called silverbelly."

"Quite handsome," Maj said.

Rhymes nodded. "The Duke wore it in his very last film, *The Shootist.*"

Maj recalled that John Wayne's nickname was The Duke.

"That must add greatly to the hat's value," Maj said.

Gene said, "Mr. Rhymes appraises the hat at six figures."

Rhymes told Maj, "Auction values will go up and down as Western movies gain or lose favor. That doesn't matter to me. I love that hat. If none of my children care about having it, and I suspect they won't, I'm thinking of leaving it to the Smithsonian Institution. I've already received word the people there would be happy to put it on display, so the whole country could see it."

Wallace Rhymes fell silent, as if a new thought had just occurred to him.

Gene asked, "You've come up with something, sir?"

The old man shook his head. "Not anything helpful. I just thought maybe I'd give the Smithsonian some money instead of The Duke's hat. After you get it back for me, I mean."

"And what will you do with the hat then?" Maj asked.

"Well, it just came to me: Maybe I should be buried wearing it."

***McGill Investigations International — Washington, DC***

Among the many things McGill loved about the United States Constitution, he held the 22nd Amendment in especially high regard. That was the law that limited a president to being elected to no more than two terms. The Republicans had conceived of adding that restriction to the nation's founding charter when it looked like Franklin Delano Roosevelt might continue to be re-elected president for as long as he lived. Which, as it turned out, he had.

There had been no guarantee, of course, that Roosevelt would have won a fifth term, had his health allowed for such a possibility. Even so, the GOP hadn't wanted to take any chances that another Democrat might come anywhere close to FDR's record for longevity in office. So they pushed the 22nd Amendment through Congress in 1947, and it was ratified by three-fourths of the states by 1951, well within a proposed amendment's seven-year time limit.

In the inevitable way of things, the Republicans came to regret their success in amending the Constitution after Ronald Reagan had been elected and re-elected in the 1980s. While they didn't think Reagan might tie Roosevelt's record of being elected four times, they'd felt he'd have been a shoo-in for a third term. Despite signs of Reagan's serious mental slow-down in the latter two years of his second term, they were probably right.

McGill, on the other hand, was overjoyed that the 22nd Amendment hadn't allowed Patti Grant the opportunity of even considering a run for a third term as president. Now, McGill and Patti were private citizens again, and there were far fewer barriers to spending as much time together as they desired. So after McGill and Sweetie had met with Teagan Tobias, he'd picked up his phone, called his wife at Committed Capital, her new venture capital business, and asked, "How about we get together for lunch? I could use a bright woman's opinion on a matter of business ethics."

Patti said, "I thought that was Sweetie's role."

"It is, but I wouldn't mind a highly valued second opinion.

That and a little light banter, if you've got the time."

"I'll make the time, and it feels so good that I can say that now."

"I know," McGill said. "I feel the same way."

"I would like to skip the time-suck of going out to eat, though," Patti said. "Would you mind having lunch here?"

"What, at your desk?" McGill asked.

Patti laughed. "We could do that, if you like, but I'm pretty sure I can get a good table in the company dining room."

In the fashion of many modern, well-funded businesses, Committed Capital featured a variety of amenities, including a place to eat that would have drawn crowds if it were open to the public. In its planning stage, McGill had suggested that the menu include familiar fare as well as adventures in gastronomy.

"I can have a grilled cheese sandwich and a chocolate milkshake?" McGill asked.

"You tell me, Big Boy. How's your waistline doing?"

"I'd tell you, but I saw you peeking just this morning."

They both laughed and agreed to dine together in an hour.

***Committed Capital, Inc. — Washington, DC***

The nameplate outside Patti's office suite read Patricia McGill. She'd also instructed Ace Cole and Daphna Levy, the new Secret Service special agents she shared with Jim, to address her by the family name of her second husband. She used the McGill name for her new business purposes as well.

She'd begun to consider making the name change in the final year of her presidency. It had been fitting, she'd thought, to keep Andy Grant's surname when she first ran for president, not all that long after Andy had died. She'd also been elected to the House of Representatives as Patricia Grant. Once she'd become president, it never would have done for her to run for a second term under another name. New Coke had shown the foolishness of rebranding a winning name.

Still, she'd thought about making the change during the final year of her second term. There would have been no personal downside to doing so. She never could decide, though, if it might have hurt Jean Morrissey's chance to become the second female president.

Damn flighty women. They can't even figure out who they are, much less run the country.

Patti Grant could easily imagine members of the GOP and True South saying words to that effect.

Now, however, with Jean in the Oval Office, she thought that changing her name might help her to recede from the public spotlight, lessening the chances of being compared to her successor for good or ill. Much more important, she'd hoped the change would bring her even closer to Jim, and that seemed to have worked.

He hadn't made a big deal out of it, only saying, "I can't possibly love you more than I already do, but I've never felt more honored."

Of course, he'd said that while holding her in his arms, and the kiss he'd given her was unlike any she could remember before or since. That heartwarming reminiscence was interrupted by Edwina Byington buzzing Patti to announce an incoming phone call.

"Galia Mindel would like to speak with you, Mrs. McGill."

Patti had brought Edwina along with her from the White House.

Discarding the usual protocol, Edwina hadn't addressed Patti as Madam President even once since leaving the Executive Mansion. Edwina had decided if you were going to move on in life, then you had to make the appropriate adjustments. Patti had never considered the matter, but she'd immediately felt Edwina was right. Welcoming her new title — Mrs. — would help to ground Patricia McGill in her new reality.

"Please connect me with Galia," she said.

"Yes, ma'am."

Edwina put the call through, and Patti said, "Galia, it's so good to hear from you. How are things in New York?"

Patti hadn't spoken to her former chief of staff since Galia had resigned not long before Jean Morrissey had been elected. Galia had feared at the time that her years of collecting embarrassing intelligence on opposition politicians might be exposed and used to damage Jean's election chances and soil Patti's reputation. Both concerns had turned out to be, thus far, needless worries.

Any exposure of Galia's treasure trove of personal and political misbehavior might have destroyed large swaths of both parties. The other side of the aisle had reckoned correctly that if those to the left of the political center were smeared, those to the right would be afforded the same treatment. Then the only remaining political parties would be Cool Blue and True South.

There were times, however, when Patti thought that might not be a bad idea.

Get rid of the old power centers with all their baggage and start fresh.

But she didn't bother herself, not directly, about politics anymore.

Galia told Patti, "New York is even more expensive than Washington, and Manhattan is *so* much more congested. I can't step out of my building's front door without catching a whiff of the onion bagel some passerby just ate."

Patti laughed. "That's probably more of a problem in some neighborhoods than others."

"Hah," Galia said. "If it wasn't bagels, it'd be black bean chilaquiles."

"Well, New York is a global magnet, and people have to eat."

Galia moved on from food. "I'm getting in my boys' hair, too. They love me, of course. Their kids and wives like me, but only up to a point. And I promised them, and myself, that I'd never become a Nagging Nana, but I can't help myself. I see *hundreds* of ways I could make each of them so much more efficient, more productive, more —"

"Perfect?" Patti asked.

After a moment's silence, Galia said, "If anybody else asked that,

I'd have to say no, they're perfect already. Just the way I raised them to be. Or instructed them to be, if we're talking grandchildren and in-laws."

"There's something more, isn't there?" Patti asked.

"Yes … they pooled their money, the grown-ups. Well, maybe the grandkids chipped in, too, for all I know. They bought me a ticket."

"A flight to outer space?" Patti heard a laugh laced with sorrow. "I was kidding, Galia."

"Well, they weren't. They bought me a ticket for a cruise … *around the world.* Five months long, I'd be gone."

"Jim and I —"

"Were gone six months, I know. But the two of you are married and still in love. This cruise is for 'single ladies and gentlemen of a certain age.' I can only imagine the horrors. But you know how competitive I am. I'd be out-hustling all the other old dames for the least worst old goat on the boat. Probably some guy who smelled only mildly of cough syrup and liniment. And then, as we're nearing home and my boys can see me from the dock, I'd throw myself overboard, screaming at them, 'See what you made me do.'"

Patti did her best not to laugh.

She didn't quite succeed.

To make amends, she asked, "How may I be of help, Galia?"

"You brought Edwina with you, so I can't be your secretary. How about I become the person who brings you coffee?"

"I don't drink coffee, as you well know."

"Tea, then. You do like that."

"We'll find something for you, Galia. Meaningful work. At an appropriate salary, with benefits."

"Have I ever told you I love you like a daughter?"

"I'm not sure that's wise. You're not old enough, and I never got along with my own mother. But I won't send you out to sea."

"There might still be one hitch we have to think about," Galia said.

Patti knew just what Galia meant, and replied, "Your house in

Dumbarton Oaks. Right next to the one Jim and I bought. You still own it. We'll all be neighbors: you, me and Jim."

"Yes, that."

"He's coming here for lunch today," Patti said. "I'll talk to him."

McGill joined his wife in the Committed Capital dining room at the appointed hour. There were two walls of windows, one looking out on the street, the other on the building's central courtyard. Diners had two modes of service available: self and table. If you liked to be waited on, you were expected to tip appropriately. Generously, even, if you were having a good day. Woe betide the stingy individual for he had one foot out the door, even if he didn't know it yet.

That had happened only once in the company's first year in business — the wait-person not just being under-tipped but stiffed entirely — and it was already part of Committed Capital lore that the offender was gone by the end of the week.

McGill always tipped generously, but that day he chose to carry both Patti's lunch and his own to their table overlooking the courtyard. Presenting the missus with her order, ginger and carrot soup, three breadsticks and a glass of Gewurztraminer, he sat down with his still sizzling grilled cheese sandwich and a frosty chocolate milkshake.

McGill raised his glass and said, "To us."

Patti touched her glass to his and said, "To us."

They sipped their beverages and Patti added, "You just wanted to fetch our lunches so people will think you always wait on me."

The dining room was about two-thirds full, but as far as McGill could tell, without doing an obvious scan of his environs, most people were tending to their own dining companions and conversations. The other diners had also allowed the boss and her mate elbow room of at least three tables.

"I didn't notice anyone sneaking a peek at us," McGill said.

"They try not to be obvious."

"So we could play footsie under the table, and nobody would blink?"

"Most likely."

"I'll have to come here with you more often," McGill said. "See how far we can push the bounds of decorum."

"You're shameless, Jim."

"Hungry, too." McGill started in on his sandwich while it was still hot.

Patti took her cue, and they ate in companionable silence, affording the time to let a minor emergency intrude, as one so often did whenever two people wanted to have a bit of time to themselves. The outside world, however, remained peaceful.

Finishing his sandwich with gusto and a last sip of his milkshake, McGill dabbed his mouth with a napkin and asked Patti, "Have you ever heard of a guy named Teagan Tobias?"

She nodded.

The affirmative answer impressed McGill. "I should have known."

Patti cast her gaze about the room, and then whispered to McGill, "This may come as a surprise to you, but since leaving politics, I've taken to reading the Entertainment section of the *Post*."

McGill smiled. "Really?"

"Yes. If you can work actively in a field related to your old profession, I can at least read the scuttlebutt about mine."

McGill asked, "Are you disappointed that the PBS series Dorie McBride wanted you to introduce didn't work out?" Dorie had been Patti's old talent agent in Los Angeles.

"A little bit, yes. I was looking forward to that, actually."

"But you're still happy working at Committed Capital, right?"

"Definitely," Patti said. "We'll do many good things here, and maybe one or two great things. Even so —"

"Would you want to do another movie?"

"No, nothing like that. But something small, smart and factual, television of some sort, I think that might interest me."

"Okay," McGill said, "I'll see if I can find something like that as a Christmas gift."

Patti squeezed his hand. "You'd have to become the executive producer of the show. That might cause you to compromise your principles."

"I'll bring Sweetie with me for ethical protection."

"Well, that would certainly be a first for television."

"Meanwhile, back to Teagan Tobias. He came to see me today, offering help in finding a woman who works for him, well, who's still under contract. She's also the sister of the paying client who wants to find her."

Patti frowned. "You suspect foul play?"

"I don't know what to suspect yet. I do know that my client, Marlon Janeway, is in precarious health. He'd like to speak with his missing sister, Alice, at least one more time. I urged him to be strong, but I'm not sure my exhortation is a match for dengue fever."

Patti squeezed McGill's hand. "Oh, my, the poor man. Do you think you'll be able to find his sister in time?"

McGill sighed. "Given the circumstances of that moment, I all but promised that I would. Now, just the idea makes me cringe, but I still think it was the right thing to do at the time."

"Me, too."

"Yeah?" McGill asked.

Patti nodded. "People can be tenacious, even under the worst circumstances, when they have a reason to hang on. I don't know how all this will turn out, but I think you've bought yourself a bit more time than you'd have had otherwise."

McGill was happy to hear Patti verbalize what he'd been thinking.

She took the next step, too. "What kind of help did Teagan Tobias offer?"

"He gave me someone who's at least a reasonable facsimile of a suspect. Someone who might have grabbed Alice."

"That's good, isn't it?" Patti asked.

McGill said, "In both police work and politics, information is only as good as the source who provides it. What can you tell me about Teagan Tobias, whether it comes from the *Post* or anywhere else?"

McGill took a look around to make sure there was no chance anyone might overhear the discussion he and Patti were having now. He needn't have worried. The dining room had emptied out except for them.

Nobody told the boss she had to get back to her desk.

McGill silenced the notifications on his phone so he wouldn't be bothered.

Patti said, "According to the story in the *Post,* Teagan Tobias used to be a copywriter at a New York City ad agency. He won a few awards, but wasn't setting the ad world on fire. One day, his boss, a creative director, came into Tobias' office. He tossed a print ad that Tobias had written on his desk. Just about every word had been crossed out with a red pencil."

"Ouch," McGill said. "Doesn't exactly sound like constructive criticism."

"Not at all. Making matters worse, the boss turned on his heel without an explanatory word and started to leave Tobias' office."

"And that was when things got interesting," McGill guessed.

Patti nodded. "They certainly took a turn toward the dramatic. Tobias didn't bother to read any of the creative director's criticisms. He balled up the sheet of paper and threw it at the back of his superior's head. Only the man had heard the paper being crumpled and turned around just in time to get hit right between the eyes with his wadded-up critique."

McGill grinned, thinking maybe Tobias had a redeeming quality or two.

Patti continued, "That was when the fight started. At least, that was when the creative director started throwing punches. Tobias swore under oath at a civil suit he filed that he never threw a punch or tried to kick his adversary, but he did duck and dodge the other guy's attack. And it came out that witnesses looking on from the office doorway saw the creative director break both of his hands when he failed to hit Tobias but connected with a wall behind him. The boss did similar damage to a foot when he hit the wall with a misplaced kick."

"I have to think that Tobias got fired, though," McGill said.

"He did, and that was when he took his antagonist and the ad agency to court. They were sued, respectively, for attempting to cause great bodily harm and maintaining a hostile workplace. Tobias' lawyer was a bulldog. He subpoenaed the witnesses to the fracas and used threats of bringing perjury charges against them if they didn't testify honestly."

McGill asked, "How much money did Tobias get?"

"Undisclosed, but probably substantial, as he claimed no other ad agency in town would hire him after the incident. In any case, it was more than enough for him to do a small stage production of a show he wrote called *Every Last Bastard in Town*."

"Yeah, Esme went to see that. I like the title," McGill said, "but Tobias must have had more than one grievance to write an entire show."

"Oh, yes. The first show ran for an hour. It was mostly a monologue, a rant against people Tobias felt had wronged him. At just the right moments, though, other actors, playing the roles of malefactors, would appear onstage."

McGill said, "Sure, gotta have bad guys. Women, too?"

Patti nodded. "Mr. Tobias possesses an equal opportunity ire."

"Needless to say, the fall guys and gals were less than physically attractive."

"Trolls one and all, except for the treacherous beauties, of course."

"All of them getting their just desserts, no exceptions," McGill said.

"Yes. The *Post* says, even his comely foes are brilliantly cast as looking like people you'd love to hate, and they all get what they have coming. Some critics with a degree of sensitivity have called Tobias out for appearance bias and off-handed cruelty. Nonetheless, he was packing 'em in."

"None of Tobias' critics have penned their objections in red ink and tossed them on his desk?" McGill asked.

Patti smiled. "I suppose there might be some risk in doing that."

"Just how much box-office success has Tobias enjoyed?"

Patti said, "He seems to have tapped into a deep vein of personal resentment among the theater-going public. His show is now called *Every Last Bastard in the World.*"

McGill nodded. He'd certainly had his share of gripes before going to work for himself. Still, he said, "The trick to doing a show like *Every Last Bastard* must be balancing cruelty with catharsis."

"Maybe you should see it for yourself, Jim. Teagan Tobias' show is running in town right now."

"That's a good idea. We can make a night of it."

Patti shook her head. "Not me. I still draw too much attention. My presence might even affect the presentation of the material. If Tobias or someone else in the cast spots me and there's any good improv talent onstage, I might become a subject of the performance."

McGill hadn't thought of that. "Probably be a good idea to keep it from Tobias that I'm in the house. I could buy a ticket somewhere near the back of the room through a broker."

"Take Daphna to the show with you," Patti said. "People will look at her, not you."

"I'm not as pretty as a Secret Service agent?" McGill asked.

"Of course, you are. Just not as young and pretty."

McGill had to laugh.

"What are you doing to find Alice in the meantime?" Patti asked.

McGill sighed. "The usual for something like this. Checking all the hospitals and morgues between Atlanta and here. Sweetie volunteered to take the first shift."

On that cheerful note, Patti told him, "I talked with Galia Mindel this morning."

***Sixth Street — Austin, Texas***

"That's a different one, isn't it?" Maj Olson asked Gene Beck.

She meant the tune he was whistling. The two of them were walking along Sixth Street, home of Austin's music row. They'd parked Maj's car a couple blocks up the street. When they worked a case together, they'd alternate driving duty. That day, Gene had asked Maj if she'd mind taking the wheel. He thought there might be a new song in the mail from his muse.

Something marked special delivery.

Not that Gene couldn't drive and compose at the same time. Still, splitting his attention between the two tasks was likely to diminish the quality of each one. It'd be a shame to lose a great tune by paying strict obedience to traffic laws. On the other hand, it wouldn't do to come up with a modern masterpiece at the cost of plowing into a pedestrian.

As they neared their destination, Gene had asked Maj to pull over. He thought walking would help him finish his song. Never one to hinder the advance of popular culture, Maj had parked the car.

She'd asked her question only after Gene had stopped both whistling and walking.

They'd come to a halt in front of the music club that was their destination. The sign out front said Hell's Belle and below that the message Hot Licks All Night Long.

Maj thought Gene's melody was distinct from most of his other work. Something new.

"Yeah, it might be the beginning of an unexplored direction," Gene said. He tapped his right foot on the sidewalk and bobbed his head for a moment. "Okay, I've got it now."

Maj knew he meant that he wouldn't forget the melody or even a note therein.

There were times when Maj felt humbled — even as someone who held an Ivy League doctorate — in the face of genius. Not that Gene ever thought of his gift as such or let it swell his head. He opened the door to the club for Maj and said, "After you, ma'am."

Stepping inside, Maj saw an auburn-haired woman maybe ten years her senior standing behind the far end of the bar, reading glasses at the tip of her nose. Her attention was focused on a sheaf of old-fashioned computer print-outs. She used the pen in her right hand to tick off items that caught her attention.

The bar ran parallel to the wall on the left for about two-thirds the length of the room. A string of four-chair tables occupied the right side of the space. The tables stopped just short of a small bandstand projecting from the back wall. Four narrow doors stood between the far end of the bar and the bandstand. They were labeled: His, Hers, Mine and Kitchen.

The only natural light entered the bar through the front window. A soft incandescent glow came from ceiling canisters above the bar. The woman looked up from her paperwork and took notice of the two people standing just inside the entrance.

"No need to be shy," she said. "If you want a drink, you're in luck. If you want food, you're not. Kitchen doesn't open for another hour."

Maj and Gene walked over and stood in front of the woman.

Maj started to say, "Actually, we're looking for—"

Gene lightly put a hand on Maj's shoulder, cutting her off. "We're looking for someone who wouldn't mind giving me an honest opinion of a little melody that just came to me."

The woman took off her reading glasses, put them on the bar and asked Gene, "Haven't I seen you somewhere?"

"I don't believe we've met," Gene said.

She looked him over and took notice of his wedding ring, and the fact that Maj wasn't wearing one. Still trying to figure them out, she asked Gene, "You want to audition to play in my place?"

"No, ma'am. I'd just like your opinion, and then my friend and I would like a beer, of course." Gene put a twenty on the bar.

The woman took it and asked, "You're going to sing a cappella? The two of you?"

"Just me," Gene said, "and I won't be singing, just whistling."

"Whistling?" she echoed, and then a light came on in her eyes. She had at least heard of Gene somewhere around town. "Okay, you go right ahead."

Gene tried out the tune he'd just conceived.

His whistling was pitch perfect, as always. Within 10 seconds, the woman was smiling and keeping the beat by tapping her hand on the bar. By the time Gene finished, he'd earned her applause.

"You think it's all right?" Gene asked.

"All right? It's too damn good for the likes of this place," she said, "and you, I've heard about you. The guy who runs all over town whistling like a bird, if birds knew how to write music. I half-thought you were just some story people passed around. A tall tale of sorts."

"No, ma'am," Gene said.

The woman behind the bar looked at Maj. "I've also heard he's been running with a woman lately. Is that you?"

Maj said, "Yes."

"Does he whistle all the time the two of you are running?"

"Unless I set the pace too fast."

The woman laughed, liking that idea. Then she let her good feelings slip away and asked, "What do you two really want? Twenty bucks is more than enough for a couple of beers, but it won't buy much in the way of information. Not that I have any to offer anyhow."

Maj asked, "Are you Catherine Clarke?"

"Yes. No harm admitting that."

"Is Wallace Rhymes your father?" Gene asked.

She hesitated before answering.

Gene said, "We'll take that as a yes. He said you weren't happy with him."

Catherine slapped the twenty down on the bar and pushed it toward Gene.

"What the hell do you two want?"

Maj told her, "We're looking for John Wayne's hat."

"Damn," Catherine said, "I always wondered if it would come to that one day."

***Committed Capital, Inc. — Washington, DC***

Sitting in Patti's office now, McGill just sighed. He couldn't even work up the exasperation to curse. Not after Patti had told him that Galia's sons wanted to send her on a lonely-hearts cruise around the world. Just the idea was enough to make him shudder.

He told Patti, "When I was a kid and didn't want to eat something Mom had fixed for dinner, my father would tell me, 'If you get hungry enough, you'll eat it and like it.' I couldn't argue with his logic, but I was counting on Mom not to let things go that far."

"And she didn't let you down," Patti said.

"Of course not. But if you put Galia on a boat for five months, she might get desperate enough to marry some guy who's the equivalent of cold meatloaf."

Patti said, "Galia told me she might jump overboard just as the ship comes back into view of her sons."

For just a moment, McGill thought Patti was giving him a way out of his predicament.

Then his conscience made him concede, "No, we can't let her do that."

"Good of you to say."

The urge to fight hadn't gone out of McGill entirely. "Okay, I can see Galia has to get out of New York, at least for the time being, and she does just happen to have a house right next to ours, but do you have to give her a job here, too?"

"She needs to work; that's what she does. The lack of meaningful employment this past year is probably why she drove her sons crazy."

There were times when McGill hated unassailable logic.

You couldn't argue with it; you could only pout.

And for anyone older than five, pouting never looked good.

"Don't despair," Patti told him. "I've been thinking I could use Galia as a scout."

McGill perked right up. "You mean like a sports team's scout? Beating the bushes from Podunk to Poughkeepsie for undiscovered talent?"

"Don't get too carried away. I'm not talking about sending Galia to the sticks or having her spend all her time on the road, but it would make sense to have her visit high-tech hubs here in the U.S., and in Europe and Asia, to see if there are any projects we would want to finance. Air travel, lodging and meals would be first class, of course. I could see her being out of town for as much as a quarter of the year."

McGill would have preferred six months to three.

Patti continued, "Of course, with the constraints of the White House no longer weighing upon me, you and I could take more frequent vacations, not that we'd want to do a six-month expedition again any time soon. But you do have several offices of your own firm now, and you've told me you're thinking of adding London and Berlin to your roster. So you might choose to make the occasional business trip of your own."

Between spending leisure time with Patti and doing his own business travel, McGill could imagine his Galia-free time expanding to six months. The other half of the year wouldn't involve constant contact. He could suck it up and make the best of the situation.

He told Patti, "Those are some negotiating skills you learned during your time in government."

"I'll even throw in a back rub tonight, while you tell me one of your police adventures, but until then don't lose your grumpy mood entirely. It might be just the lens you need to watch *Every Last Bastard in the World.*"

Patti had gotten two tickets at the back of the house for that night's performance with just one phone call. Private citizen now or not, money still talked. McGill would reimburse her and write off the cost as a business expense. He had just gotten up and kissed Patti goodbye when her phone chimed.

She said, "A text from Daphna. She wants to know what she should wear tonight."

McGill said, "Sporty casual with easy gun access. In case I really dislike the show."

***University Hospital — Charlottesville, Virginia***

Teagan Tobias had no trouble finding Alice Janeway. He knew where she was all along. Alice had collapsed right in front of him, less than an arm's-length away, in his Charlottesville, Virginia boutique hotel suite. Being gifted with fast-twitch muscles as well as a quick wit, Teag had caught Alice before she hit the floor. That had kept her from suffering any damage to her skull or neck but, man, she just went lights out and he hadn't been able to revive her.

He was the one who strained what felt like every muscle in his back. Alice wasn't even a bit overweight, and he was more than a little strong. Even so, she'd gone from apparently running on all systems to dead weight in the blink of an eye. The result, Teag imagined, would be like catching a 130-pound bag of sand dropped from five-feet-eight inches in the air.

A call to 911 and an ambulance ride to the nearby major university hospital had been the start of a scene out of … well, if Edvard Munch had worked in video instead of oils, that would have pretty much captured it. Screaming arguments between Teag and the medical staff, near mayhem between him and the hospital security guys, and futile exhortations for someone, *anyone,* to bring Alice back to sentient life.

The madness had started when Teag denied that Alice had medical insurance coverage, even though he provided it. Teag was thinking ahead to what looked like an even grimmer time. Wearing an Atlanta Braves baseball cap and sunglasses despite the late night hour, Teag had taken $30K in hundred-dollar bills out of a gym bag and given it to some hospital billing flunky, saying, "This woman gets every damn thing she needs, no questions asked, no price is too high. You understand what I'm saying?"

The implicit threat of violence in his voice had made the message crystal clear.

Fat lot of good either money or mayhem might have done.

A doctor who looked like a Doogie Howser stand-in came to see if Teag could provide any medical history for Alice that might give the other docs, presumably the ones past puberty, a clue as to what they were confronting and just maybe how they might treat it.

Teag knew where he should have gone right from the start. Instead, trying to deny what he feared, he ran through a list of routine childhood illnesses Alice had told him about over the years they'd worked together. Then when he could avoid it no longer, he got to the heartbreaker.

"She also had encephalitis," he told the kid doctor.

Doogie's jaw dropped. He knew Teag shouldn't have held back on that.

Teag didn't give the kid time to complain. "She became comatose back then as a result. Whole damn thing was caused by a fucking mosquito bite. But that was years ago when she was a kid, even younger than you."

The young doctor didn't hear the implied insult. He ran off to share the news. Teag sat in a waiting room for what seemed half of his life. He bore his fear, hate and discomfort without complaint. He was a shit, and he knew it. He'd just been lucky enough to figure out a way to spin his anger and rage into gold.

But what the hell had Alice ever done to deserve being on the brink of death again?

Nobody stepped forward with an answer, but it wasn't hard to guess.

He was responsible for Alice ringing the Reaper's doorbell right now. Being exposed to his shows all these years, internalizing all the bile he spewed, filtering it through that unflappable kindness of hers, refusing to pass any of his crap on to anyone else, it had finally overcome her. How could it not?

Three doctors finally came to see him. He had to look and smell like shit by then, but they were kind to him. The oldest guy, white-haired, squatted in front of him. Held it without even a creaking joint. Pretty impressive for an old bugger.

He didn't have Teag's name, so he only said, "We're sorry, sir. We did everything we could."

"She's dead?"

The doctor shook his head. "Not yet. She's still with us, but her brain function has declined throughout the night. We thought she might not make it until this morning, but she stabilized just recently."

"Any chance for recovery?" Teag asked in a flat voice.

"Not in the experience of any physician in this hospital or those of other colleagues we contacted. We're very sorry, but we don't expect her to live much longer."

The old doc stood, as if that was that.

"Hospice?" Teag asked.

"If that's what you prefer, certainly."

Without any further questions to answer, the doctors expressed their regrets as a group and left. Left standing in front of Teag was the guy from the billing department. There was a balance to be paid.

Teag said, "Get my friend down here, have an ambulance waiting to take my friend where we want to go next and you'll get your money."

The billing guy preferred to be paid up front.

Teag lowered his sunglasses just enough to show his eyes.

The billing guy changed his mind.

***Old Dominion Palliative Care — Richmond, Virginia***

The hospital episode happened a week ago.

Now, Teag looked at Alice lying on the bed in her hospice suite and thought she was nearly as white as the sheet and pillow on which she lay. Many people in hospice settings simply rested on single beds, juiced to the eyes with painkillers. The whole point was to let go peacefully. Alice, on the other hand, was wired to an array of monitors, IV-lines, and a catheter. The monitors measured her remaining brain function, and the IVs provided life-sustaining fluids and nutrients. The catheter carried away waste.

She was registered at the facility under the name of Barbara Lipman, the one teacher in all of Teag's years of education who could take whatever sass he threw at her and give it back tenfold. As far as Teag was concerned, Ms. Lipman was his muse.

Alice, on the other hand, just let whatever crap Teag threw at her slide on by. Teag never could get Alice to lose her cool, and in the beginning he had tried. He'd overload her with work, he'd yell at her, threaten to fire her, and nothing ever rattled her.

Her silent "fuck off" was a potent weapon.

Blue-blood Brits even had a name for it: mute insolence.

Teag didn't know if Alice could enter some kind of Zen state of mind at will or what. When she didn't want to get ruffled, though, there was no way in the world anyone could aggravate her. Hell, if everyone could be as imperturbable as Alice, Teag wouldn't have an act anymore.

The crazy thing was, Alice *loved* it when Teag pounded lumps on other people.

That was what had made her attend those five consecutive performances in Raleigh. She had the whole show memorized by the third viewing, and she still laughed like a madwoman. It was her distinctive giggles and guffaws that first caught Teag's attention onstage. He wanted to know who she was and had Haskell pinpoint her for him.

It took him their whole first year of working together before he gave up trying to figure Alice out: how she never let any direct criticism bother her, but loved it when he carved up other people. He finally just came right out and said, "You seem to be the sweetest person I know, but you have a sense of humor about other people that's just as mean as mine. What is it with you, Alice? You have a split personality or something?"

She'd been standing in his dressing room in San Francisco when he'd put that question to her. She took a seat and cupped her chin in one hand, thinking. "I just might have a little Sybil in me. So it could be a multiple-personality thing. I love the way you cut through all that BS other people think is important. I just try to keep that same kind of crap from ever bothering me."

She made it seem so simple, Teag thought. Good thing for him most people weren't so self-aware. "Well, you do a helluva job with both parts, Alice. There are times when you shrug off one of my rants so easily I think I'm losing my touch."

He'd no sooner said that than she gave him a smile so cute that a young Shirley Temple would have killed for it. "Oh, no, Teag, you're still a total asshole. Never worry about that."

His mouth fell open, and two seconds later he enjoyed the best laugh of his life.

Alice gave him a wink and walked out of his dressing room.

The bad thing about that moment was it gave Alice the idea *she* could be funny.

That raised the only real point of contention between them. Alice knew she'd struck gold with her dig at him. So she started dropping hints that maybe she could do a little writing for Teag. That led to the idea she might even join him onstage.

That wasn't going to happen. The only people who ever got to stand in the footlights with him all played the same role: maddening fools. He didn't see using Alice in that way. He'd never thought of exploiting her in any way, never once made a move on her. Not that he didn't think she was attractive. She was, in a way that didn't need a lot of makeup and high-end hairdos to bring out.

Thing was, Teag liked heavy artifice.

For one night or maybe two, never more than three.

Alice had been with him for years now. He *valued* her, as much as he could hold anyone in high esteem. There had been times, of course, when he thought of trying to get her into his bed, but he knew if that happened it would change everything. He'd wind up firing her within a month. That was just who he was.

So, instead, she became the woman who kept his shows running smoothly.

Leaving him to be the star, the caustic wit who skewered all the fools in the world.

There was one other thing that both of them agreed on. It came up one night after everyone else had left a theater in Bloomington, Indiana. That was the night Alice first told Teag about her bout with encephalitis as a kid and the coma she'd lapsed into as a result.

She'd said, "It's a good thing to eat vegetables; it's a bad thing to become one."

Another line Teag had liked.

"So, what's your point?" he'd asked.

"If I were ever to be kept alive by machines again, with no hope of waking up, will you please pull the plug on me? If you'll do that for me, I'll do that for you if things work out the other way around."

"Deal," Teag said on the spot.

What he didn't say was she wouldn't be the first person he killed.

He also hadn't mentioned that in a rare moment of magnanimity he'd decided to grant one of Alice's requests and just maybe part of another. Next year's show would have a new, recurring character added to the cast. Alice would become Teag's "Nagging Conscience," i.e. the biggest pain in the ass he'd ever known. He'd write the part, but if Alice had something good to offer, an insight into character or a killer line or two, he'd let her have that writing credit.

Only look what the hell had happened now.

Alice was nine-tenths dead, and Teag never bet against the odds.

That was one of the reasons he'd gone to visit McGill. To see for himself if the great detective appeared to live up to his press clippings. Teag had the distinct feeling he did, only McGill looked a bit older than expected. Still good for his age, but he wasn't a kid anymore. If it came down to a fight between them, and McGill didn't get off a lethal first shot, Teag felt sure he'd come out on top.

It would have been better if McGill had agreed to let Teag pay his tab if Frau Janeway cut off the cash from that direction. If Teag were picking up McGill's invoices, he'd have had the right to ask for progress reports. Now, that was a nonstarter. What he had to do was steer clear of McGill, but appear to be agreeable if the guy came to him looking for help.

Teag had also decided he'd have to be slicker about doing in Alice, too, if things came to that. He wouldn't be able to just — oops — kick all of her electrical connections out of the wall socket. That crap wouldn't play at all. What he'd need to do was … hire a hacker to take down the entire hospice's power for a good half-hour.

Good-bye, Alice, and probably half the other hospice residents.

He could live with that.

He'd have to put the hired hacker down, too. Also not a problem.

But tonight wasn't the night. He bent over Alice and lightly pressed his lips to her forehead. One of the monitors said her body temperature was 96°, but she already felt damn cold to him. Maybe she'd just kick off on her own. Save him a lot of hassle.

But he didn't want that to be his parting thought for Alice.

So he said softly, "Have to go, babe. Got a show to do tonight."

### *Hell's Belle — Austin, Texas*

Catherine Clarke reclaimed the twenty-dollar bill from Gene and tapped two mugs of Lone Star beer for him and Maj Olson. She pointed them to a nearby table. She took her eyeglasses and computer printout into the space adjacent to the bar with the door labeled "Mine." When she came back out, Maj noticed that she'd brushed her hair while in her office. She also had a bottle of Virgil's Root Beer in hand. Private stash. She joined the two private investigators at the table.

"I never drink alcohol in this place unless there's a damn good reason to either celebrate or honor someone's memory. The last time was when Molly Ivins passed away. I still mourn losing her and Ann Richards, especially with the two of them leaving us in successive years."

Catherine took a hit of her root beer.

"Hell, the way important Texas women were dying, I thought I might be next."

She laughed to let her guests know she was joking.

"So is Daddy fixing to die?" Catherine asked.

"He looked fairly vital to me," Maj said.

"I thought so, too," Gene added. "Why would you think otherwise, Ms. Clarke?"

"Because you said you're looking for that silly damn hat he bought years ago. John Wayne, the eternal cowboy and *pater familias*. You're familiar with both meanings of that title, aren't you?"

Gene, not a Latin scholar, glanced at Maj, and she supplied the answer.

"Father of the family is the primary translation," she said, "but it can also mean the owner of the family estate."

"Exactly. In Daddy's case, both definitions apply but it's the money that matters here. He told his four kids, me and my three brothers, he'd let us know who was going to get control of the family business by passing on John Wayne's hat to the chosen one before he left us to be with Jesus. That's why I thought he might be nearing the end."

"You've lost contact with your father?" Maj asked.

Catherine smiled without any warmth. "Our relationship wasn't misplaced; I severed it. Haven't seen or talked with Daddy in almost ten years. I'm more than a little surprised you're here to talk to me."

"He gave us your name, address and phone number, Ms. Clarke," Gene said. "You're still important enough to him to know where to find you."

She sighed. "I'd say his interest is more proprietary than paternal."

"And being anyone's property is an idea you'll have no part of," Maj said.

"Exactly."

"Did you tell your father you have no interest in John Wayne's hat or anything else he might leave to one of his children?" Gene asked.

Catherine clasped her hands together in an almost prayerful manner, leaned forward and looked at Maj and then Gene. "Here's how things stand with me and my father. He paid for four years of tuition and fees at Rice University for me. Even though my college days were quite some time ago, that was still a tidy sum. I paid him back every last penny. Then I saved up and bought this place, all on my own. Nobody else contributed a dollar. I'm hardly making a fortune here, but I get by. I like the people who come here and all the live music I get to hear. I'm happy. I don't want a penny of my father's money, and I certainly don't want John Wayne's hat."

Gene let a beat of silence pass.

Maj intuitively felt the next reply should be his.

He said, "Your father told us he just might decide to be buried in that hat."

Catherine laughed and shook her head. "Just goes to show how stubborn he and I both are. I told Daddy I'd pass on any money he gave me to the Democratic Socialist Party. That'd give heart attacks to half of his golfing buddies and most of their wives, but probably hardly any of his pals' mistresses."

Gene and Maj looked at each other.

Then Maj said, "Might any of your brothers have taken the hat, if not to stake his own claim then to deny the mantle falling to one of the others?"

That idea also made Catherine laugh. "Okay, here's how my family sets up. My brother Henry and I are fraternal twins. Cole and Clint, two years younger than Hank and me, are identical twins. If someone asked which one of us is the evil twin, you know, like in the movies, all four of us would be in the running."

"Except you told us you don't care about your father's money,"

Gene said.

"I don't," Catherine replied. Then she added with a wicked smile. "Still, if I'd ever had the thought that taking that stupid hat would cause Daddy to pitch a fit, maybe even blow a gasket, I might have stolen it just to be mean."

"Did you take it?" Maj asked.

Catherine shook her head. "But you know what? I think I'll see if I might find it before you two do. Dude it up like it might belong to a gay *caballero* and then give it back. See if Daddy still wants to be buried in it."

In the same gleeful spirit of family discord, Catherine was only too happy to give her brothers' addresses and phone numbers to Gene and Maj. Just as her father had said she would.

Before the investigators could depart, Catherine also told Gene, "Hey, let me know if you record that song you whistled for me. I'd like to hear it again. You know, orchestrated."

***Paxton-Carter Theater — Washington, DC***

Leo Levy dropped McGill and Special Agent Daphna Levy off at the theater fifteen minutes before showtime. Patti had purchased McGill's armed and armored black Chevy from the federal government for her husband. She'd said she would feel more at ease about his well-being knowing he continued to have a rolling fortress as his personal wheels.

Respecting his wife's wish, but curious nonetheless, McGill had asked Patti, "How much did that car set you back?"

"Not quite as much as a fighter jet, but close," she'd told him.

"Remind me to give you a foot-rub tonight," he'd replied.

That evening was the first time Leo and Daphna had met. Given the family name they shared, they discussed the possibility of kinship. They agreed to pursue research into the matter.

Entering the theater, Daphna told McGill, "I like Leo. He's a good guy, and I can tell already he must be a fantastic driver. He makes that car move like Fred Astaire on a dance floor."

McGill smiled, liking the simile. "He is good."

"He's also the first Jew I ever met with that kind of accent."

"You mean a Dixie twang?"

"Yes."

"He comes by it honestly. It's part of his charm."

McGill wondered if his Secret Service bodyguard was developing a crush on his driver. There had to be at least a 30-year age difference … but who was he to interfere with other people's personal lives? Except for those of his children, of course.

They found their seats in the middle of the last row of the mezzanine. There was no chance that Teagan Tobias would be able to peer through the stage lights and see them. Problem was, there were two characters seated in front of McGill and Daphna wearing top hats and tails. Not that *Every Last Bastard in the World* was the kind of performance requiring formalwear.

Not that *any* staged entertainment called for wearing high hats indoors.

McGill and Daphna looked at each other. Without a word passing between them, they agreed to let Daphna play the hard-ass. She leaned forward, tapped each of the two clowns on a shoulder. She whispered something McGill couldn't hear.

He had no trouble hearing their laughter.

They turned to look at McGill and Daphna.

McGill was surprised to see that one of the dandies was female. Both of them wore smirks of self-satisfaction and looked more than mildly intoxicated. Possibly from an illegal substance. Always a handy lever for a cop to manipulate. McGill no longer had police powers, of course, but Daphna had the full backing and authority of the federal government.

The two goofs got in the first words, though.

The guy looked at McGill and said in a bad try at an English accent, "Sorry if we're blocking your view, old man. We have rare scalp conditions, Darleen and me. Must keep our heads warm or we act out. Do all sorts of mischievous things."

Darleen giggled and nodded as if she'd be only too happy to show them.

There was no question in McGill's mind now that the two of them were drunk or stoned, but he didn't smell alcohol. Marijuana was legal in DC, other than on federal property, but McGill didn't catch the scent of pot either. That meant the two fools had to be stoned on some prohibited pharmaceutical.

Daphna had come to the same conclusion and looked at McGill to see how far he wanted her to go.

"Show them your badge, Special Agent," he said.

Despite the two goofs' buzz, Daphna's job title caught their attention, but their faces showed doubt, as if McGill might be spoofing them. Then Daphna pulled out her badge and gave them a good long look. At that point, fear crept into their eyes.

McGill didn't want to terrify them. A little cooperation was all he required.

Without any further debate or tomfoolery.

He said, "Special Agent Levy is with the Secret Service, as you can see from her badge. That's part of the Treasury Department. She could arrest you for suspicion of illegal drug use and turn you over to the Metro PD. Then she might put in a request to the IRS, also part of the Treasury Department, to have your parents' tax returns audited to make sure they aren't the ones supplying your illegal drugs."

People in adjoining seats were following the drama now.

A few of them recognized McGill.

One guy told the two clucks, "Don't you fools know who you're messing with? He's the damn president's henchman."

McGill corrected the man. "The former president's henchman. Now, my friend and I are just trying to make sure we can see the show."

Daphna pulled her coat back so the idiots could see the handcuffs clipped to her belt.

McGill thought that was appropriate; flashing her gun would

have been going too far.

A canned announcement came over the theater's P.A. system reminding everyone that recording that night's performance by photography, video or audio devices was strictly prohibited, and the show would begin momentarily.

The two jokesters turned their faces toward the stage and sank low in their seats with their hats now on their laps. That was fine, but McGill noticed that at least half-a-dozen people had their phones pointed at him and Daphna.

They did the only thing they could.

Smiled for the cameras and waited for the house lights to go down.

***Backstage at the Paxton-Carter Theater***

Teagan Tobias got ready to step onstage. Nobody ever dared to bother him at this moment. To do so would have resulted in an immediate boot off the show's payroll. That and an earful of high-volume profanity. There were times when Teag thought such behavior might actually be a good way to start a show: deliver an offstage rant to let the audience know what was coming.

A test of that proposition had yet to occur.

Tonight, his own mind was messing with him. He couldn't find his native rage. That was exceedingly rare. According to his parents, he'd been born with a short fuse. The shrink his mother had taken him to see at age seven had called it an oppositional defiant disorder. The symptoms, both Teag and Mom had been told, were a quick loss of temper, disobedience at home and school, and ignoring or rebelling against rules.

Despite hating the therapist on sight, Teag thought she'd nailed his behavior. He'd even liked the acronym for his diagnosis: ODD. Being odd suited him. Normal kids, he thought, were just good little sheep, being herded this way and that by parents, teachers and even the occasional lurking pedophile.

Nobody had ever tried to get a hand down Teag's pants, though. Even as a child, his snarl was enough to keep most adults at a distance. If they didn't take that hint, he wouldn't hesitate to bite someone who persisted in annoying him. That behavior, of course, constituted a crime: assault and battery.

The assault was the fear the victim felt; the battery was the physical contact.

Very few young children were actually prosecuted in court for biting someone, but as a kid grew older, bigger and more likely to do great bodily harm, the chances of a criminal charge resulting in incarceration increased. The shrink had warned Mom about that, and referred her to a specialist who might work with Teag more effectively.

Yeah, right. Even way back then Teag had seen the woman was afraid he'd bite her.

Going to the specialist, though, would have taken a big chunk out of Dad's income. So after Teag had come home from the shrink that day and Mom had shared the story, Dad had sat at the kitchen table and crooked a finger at Teag, beckoning him to come close. Staying perfectly in character, Teag remained right where he was, several feet away.

Dad hadn't yelled, only said, "Mom tells me that you've started biting people again, along with all the other crap you pull. So here's the thing: I'm going to let you bite my hand as hard as you can."

Teag smelled a rat. His father saw Teag's suspicion and grinned.

"I'm glad you're no dummy. You think I'm going to hit you when you bite me, right?"

Teag nodded. He was wondering if he should start running right now. He didn't, but only because he knew Dad would catch him.

His father said, "This bite is free. You can do it, and I'll let you. No punishment."

Teag was still suspicious, but his father held out his hand, palm down and sideways to his son. "Go ahead, bite me."

Suspicion continued to linger in Teag's mind, but the proffered hand was magnetic. He inched toward it. As he drew near, his father told him, "Just the meat of the hand, not the little finger. If you bite the finger, I will hit you. Hard enough to make your head spin."

Dad's warning tempered the appeal of biting his hand, but not enough to stop Teag.

He lunged and sank his teeth into the palm and back of Dad's hand. He clamped down with as much pressure as his young jaws could manage. His teeth broke the skin of Dad's hand. He tasted his father's blood on his tongue.

His mother was horrified, but Dad just sat there as if he was waiting for a phone call. Teag's jaws ached before he finally gave up and released his father's hand. Teag thought now was the time he'd catch a beating for what he'd done.

But Dad only said to Mom, "Marguerite, will you please fill a large bowl with ice cubes and cold water?"

Teag's mother complied even though it was clear she hadn't understood the request. For his part, Teag had the uneasy feeling Dad might drown him right there in the kitchen. Push his face into the bowl until he couldn't hold his breath any longer. But he didn't do that.

He only got up from his chair, walked over to the kitchen's swinging door, swung it closed and pointed to the wall he'd just exposed.

"See that wall?" he asked Teag.

Fearing but not understanding what would come next, Teag nodded.

Dad said, "You just got the last free bite you'll ever have. If I ever hear you've bitten Mom or anyone else, this is what I'll do to you."

Throughout all the years that followed, Teag still couldn't recall seeing the punch his father threw; it was that fast. But he certainly heard it. It even felt to him as if the whole house shook. The hole in the wall looked as if a cannon ball had hit it.

Dad's hand was now bleeding from the knuckles as well as from where Teag had bitten it. If Dad felt any pain, Teag couldn't see it. He just sat down and put the hand in the bowl of ice-water Mom had set on the kitchen table.

"We'll just leave that hole there," his father told Teag. "Cover it with the door when company comes over. But anytime you feel like biting someone or even just giving Mom a hard time, you take a look at that hole. Because my next punch will be all yours. Do you understand?"

Even at seven years old, Teag did. He nodded.

"Good boy. If you can trust me, I'd like to give you a hug now."

Teag interpreted that as an order and complied.

He felt the immense strength in his father's arms and upper body as they encircled him, and he was shocked when Dad gently kissed the top of his head. "Give your mother a kiss, too."

Teag obeyed, and then looked back to see what command he had to follow next.

"Why don't you go lie down on your bed?" Dad said. "Just close your eyes. If your head is spinning, see if you can let it settle down. Can you do that for me?"

Teag nodded and ran from the room.

In later years, he'd heard from Mom the conversation in the kitchen that had followed.

"You think that will work?" she'd asked her husband.

"I hope so. If it doesn't work, we might need to have him locked up."

"So we'll leave the hole in the wall?"

"Oh, yeah."

"Would you really hit him?"

"Not that hard … but hard enough."

That was what had stayed with Teag throughout his life: The threat had been real.

It was too late to settle the score with his father now. He was dead, and even if the terror the old man had instilled in him had made Teag a socially viable individual, he still hated him for filling him with a sense of vulnerability he'd never been able to shake. Then again, thinking of Dad now gave him the energy he needed to go onstage in exactly the right frame of mind.

As he stepped into the spotlight, thinking that he might put one over on McGill added a bounce to his step.

McGill and Daphna watched along with the rest of the audience as Teagan Tobias stepped onstage from the wings at stage right. As he appeared, another player came into view from the opposite side of the stage. This second player was a guy who had his eyes glued to an iPhone he held in one hand.

A projected image of a busy block in what appeared to be Midtown Manhattan served as a backdrop. A cacophony of internal combustion engines, horns, hip-hop snippets and a helicopter passing overhead created an immediate sense of high tension. Something bad was about to happen.

Teag looked across the expanse of the stage and saw he was on a collision path with the guy coming toward him. He took a step to his left. The idiot with his eyes on his phone inadvertently drifted a step to his right. Not breaking stride, Teag shared a look of disgust with the audience and took a step to his right to avoid contact.

The guy with the phone guffawed at something he saw and took a step to his left, putting him back in line again to bump into Teag.

In a stage whisper, Teag said, "Sonofabitch."

Upping his game, Teag faked taking a step to the right and then moved back to his left. Feeling he'd solved his problem, he shared a wink with the audience. They laughed.

On cue, the guy with the phone laughed, too. He'd just seen something so hilarious it made him bend over and then spin in a circle … one he didn't fully complete, leaving him in line with Teag as he started forward again.

"Asshole," Teag called out in a voice that filled the theater.

Only the other guy didn't hear him because he wore earbuds blocking out the world.

His hands dangling and clenched in front of him, Teag strode forward in a straight line, as if he were going to charge right into the bastard. Only he didn't. Still fifteen feet distant from his nemesis, he faked going left, right and left again, ending up on the same line where he started.

Laughing once more at something on his phone, but seeming to mock Teag at the same time, the other guy mirrored Teag's moves perfectly. Seeing that there would be no escaping the devil, Teag shared a maniacal, murderous grin with the audience. Then he raised his hands in a position to strangle the oncoming bastard, squeeze the life out of him. Teag threw his head back, and now he was the one laughing.

Only before he could commit murder, throngs of other workaday drones stormed onstage from both wings. Teag and his arch-enemy got lost in the jostling crowd. Moments later the mob cleared, leaving only a thoroughly rumpled and disheveled Teag behind.

He looked at the clenched hands he still held in front of him.

Then, defeated, he let them drop to his sides.

He reached into his coat and took out a phone, plugged a pair of buds into his ears, started to laugh and moved on. Only a guy, going the other way, stepped out of a shadow and banged into Teag.

"Watch where you're going, asshole," the guy said.

Teag tripped the guy as he tried to storm past.

Gave him a kick in his heinie to help send him on his way.

Alone on the stage, Teag unplugged his earbuds and looked at the audience.

"I gotta start telecommuting," he said.

***Dumbarton Oaks — Washington, DC***

On the drive home from the theater, McGill asked Daphna, "What did you think of the show?"

After making sure McGill was safely ensconced in the backseat of his car, Daphna had sat up front with Leo. "I have mixed emotions," she said.

"Which are?"

"Well, maybe it's because I'm the child of immigrants, but I think a lot of Americans, the ones whose families have been here a long time, complain *way* too much."

Leo responded to that sentiment by clearing his throat.

"There are exceptions, of course. I was speaking generally. I've only heard stories from my parents, but they told me about what they had to put up with before coming to this country. Living as Jews in Egypt was no bed of roses."

"Musta provided some strong motivation to move on," Leo suggested.

Daphna nodded. "You're right. All the adversity compelled them to look elsewhere, to do whatever it took to come here. Even so, my baseline for what I let bother me is higher than most people I know. Despite all that, I'm enough of a child of this country that … well, I thought a lot of what Teag Tobias had to say was funny, and much of it rang true."

The show had interspersed incidents akin to the opening scene with monologues by Teag that examined the fine points of everyday hassles with a plaintive tone and a sharp wit. The finale was the revenge of the guy whom Teag had booted in the butt in the opening scene. He'd organized a gang that wore leather jackets bearing the name Bad Ass Bankers. They chased Teag, surrounded him, and pummeled him.

Teag cried out as if he was taking a real beating. After he produced several piteous moans and shrieks, the assailants began to have second thoughts, voiced worries about their legal exposure and whether they might be arrested or, even worse, sued for damages. They wondered aloud if they might help their case by calling for an ambulance.

They decided that was too big a risk.

Instead, they stepped back and offered Teag a stock tip in return for his silence.

Lying on the stage, he took the deal.

The stage lights faded and that was it.

"What'd you think, Boss?" Leo asked McGill.

"It wasn't bad," McGill admitted.

"I think you laughed more than I did," Daphna told him.

"Might have."

"You get any insights into him and Alice Janeway?" Leo asked.

"I don't know yet. Teag Tobias told me he hadn't let Alice Janeway do any of the writing for his shows, but I thought some of the best punchlines showed a woman's sensibilities."

Daphna said, "Like the time he'd thought he'd gotten lucky with that woman who tried to get him drunk on Pinot Grigio so she could seduce him. Only she'd matched drinks with him and fell in love with Ernest and Julio Gallo instead of him."

"Yeah, like that," McGill said. "If a guy had written that scene, he'd have had them drinking whiskey, not wine. She'd have fallen in love with Old Grand-Dad. At least it seems that way to me."

"I'm more partial to bourbon myself," Leo said.

"What's the point, who wrote what?" Daphna asked.

McGill told both of them, "I'm just trying to get a feel for things. Sweetie and I have put the word out to every hospital and morgue we found listed between Atlanta and DC. It was an email blast and so far we haven't heard of Alice showing up anywhere. It's still early, as we've only heard from 20% of the places we queried, but most of those were the major hospitals and morgues in towns with more than 100,000 people. It's possible something unfortunate, but not fatal, could have happened in some out-of-the-way burg, but I'm already getting a bad feeling about this situation."

"Do you think Alice is dead and buried in a forest somewhere?" Daphna asked.

"That or some two-digit IQ hillbilly has her tied up in his shack," Leo added.

McGill had been thinking of such misfortunes in generalized terms.

Now, he had specific images in his mind.

He said, "Let's try to be hopeful as long as we can."

## CHAPTER 2

***Wednesday, November 1, 2017***
***McGill Investigations International — Austin, Texas***

The prior evening, Maj Olson, a creative thinker, came up with an idea. Gene Beck found it so appealing he gave it a whistle of appreciation. "Yes, ma'am, let's do that. We'll still have to talk to the Rhymes brothers in person, but adding a digital component to our investigation couldn't hurt."

Maj had thought of distributing wanted posters online. Feature a prominent, beautifully lighted photo of Wallace Rhymes' John Wayne hat sitting front and center. Below it, a bold-faced headline said: $1,000 reward for the return of this hat. In smaller type directly below the headline, the body copy read: If you know who took this hat or simply wish to return it anonymously, contact McGill Investigations International, Austin, Texas.

A phone number and an email address were provided.

Maj used her computer skills to put the digital poster together, and they put it up on several social media sites.

As it was John Wayne's hat they were trying to find, both detectives felt that surely the Duke would appreciate using the modern-day equivalent of cowboy media to get his chapeau back. Wallace Rhymes had already been informed that incidental expenses would be added to his invoice. He'd replied, "Spend whatever it takes. I've checked out the two of you and your boss. I know you'll do right by me."

Both of the P.I.s had found it interesting that *they* had been investigated. It gave them an insight into their client's character. He was a careful man. Honest, too. He knew that as someone in his late 70s, he occasionally got a bit forgetful. He'd told them that sometimes it slipped his mind that he'd left his wallet and driver's license at home when he got in his car to go somewhere. One time, he'd even forgotten he should have been wearing his glasses when he was behind the wheel, but he hadn't yet reached the end of his half-mile long driveway before he'd recognized that mistake and corrected it.

Despite those occasional lapses, he told Gene and Maj that he was sure he'd worn John Wayne's hat outside of his house only on special occasions.

"When was the last time that occurred?" Maj asked.

"Independence Day."

"So the Fourth of July."

Rhymes shook his head. "*Texas* Independence Day, March 2, 1836, the day the Republic of Texas declared its independence from Mexico."

"Was your family here back then?" Gene asked.

"No, sir," Rhymes told him. "But the first time I set foot here, I knew I'd come home."

That sentiment made Maj wonder if Rhymes had any Native Americans, Latinos, or African Americans working for him. People who mightn't hold Rhymes' romanticized views of either John Wayne or the Old West but still held legitimate access to his grounds or even his house. She decided to save that question for later. She didn't want the client to think she was casting aspersions on any of his cherished beliefs. Or the people who worked for him either.

Gene and Maj were on their way out of the office that morning to go talk with the Rhymes brothers when the sight of the empty desk in the reception area stopped both of them. They'd promised each other to find someone to handle the clerical end of the office, but neither had made good on the pledge. They were about to swear once more that the task would be completed soon when a young man entered their office suite.

He reminded Maj of John Sebastian, the lead singer of The Lovin' Spoonful, as seen on her parents' album covers. The guy who had just stepped into their workplace was also too young to have seen the band perform in person.

"Help you?" Maj asked.

"You come about the reward?" Gene added.

"To answer both your questions," the guy said, "I hope you can help me, and, yes, I came after I saw your reward offer online this morning. My name's Kyle Tompkins. I'm a reporter for the *Austin Journal*. I'd like to do a story about your search for the cowboy hat."

Maj and Gene looked at each other, silently weighing the positives and negatives.

The extra exposure might help them get the hat back more quickly.

Or it could flood them with a river of false leads and waste their time.

Kyle Tompkins understood their dilemma intuitively. He said, "We've got a circulation of just about 100,000 readers, and I think a story like this would be read by almost everybody who picks up a copy of the paper. With your $1,000 reward, a lot of people would be inclined to provide all sorts of leads, absurd or not, just for the slightest chance to get the money. I could act as your filter. I'd provide you with all the leads, of course, but categorize them, so you don't waste too much time on the farfetched possibilities."

Maj and Gene looked at each other.

"Up to you," Gene told her, "if you want to be our contact person with Kyle here, it's okay by me. But I think I'll stick to talking to people in person."

Starting with the Rhymes brothers, Maj understood.

While Maj was thinking about what to do, Kyle told her, "I've read your book, Ms. Olson: *Stealing the Chief.* Thought it was great. Exciting and very well written. Gave all the details a reader needed without wasting a word."

Maj's book about finding and recovering the stolen Santa Fe Super Chief with John Tall Wolf had reached the top ten of the *New York Times* non-fiction list. The advance and the royalties from the book had provided Maj with a substantial nest egg. Her publisher had extended her an open invitation to submit a new manuscript whenever she wanted.

The only problem with that was she hadn't had any comparable adventure to pen.

She was impressed, though, that Kyle had read her book.

Still, she said, "The *Journal* comes out once a week on Fridays, right? And this week's paper has already gone to bed, or can you still find room for a new story?"

Kyle looked at his phone to see what time it was. "If you can give me the go-ahead, I can get a few paragraphs and a photo of the hat into the print edition. I can flesh out the story in the online edition. Depending on how your investigation goes, I'll do the follow-up in both editions."

Maj looked back at Gene to make sure he was still on board.

He nodded.

"Okay," Maj said. "You've got yourself a story."

"Great. Let me start with a quick question. Like a lot of people who grew up around here, I've seen my share of cowboy movies, and the hat you're looking for strongly resembles one I remember from *The Shootist.* Are you looking for John Wayne's hat?"

Maj and Gene shared a glance.

Neither of them wanted whoever had the hat to either keep it or to demand a higher reward.

Maj told Kyle, "Let's just say we're interested in finding a genuine piece of Americana."

### *McGill Investigations International — Washington, DC*

"Did you like the show?" Teag Tobias asked.

The phone call reached McGill's office at nine a.m. He wouldn't have thought Tobias would even be awake at that hour. Didn't theater people dine out and party late after a performance? He couldn't really say, but he was more than a little surprised that Tobias knew he'd been in his audience last night.

So how did he know? The answer came to him a heartbeat later.

"The two jokers in the top hats," McGill said.

"Yeah, them," Tobias agreed. "What else you got?"

McGill pushed his line of thought a bit further. "The house was almost sold out, just a few empty seats here and there. You didn't think I'd be alone, so you didn't bother with single-seat possibilities. You had all the likely spots covered, and you, what, passed out more top hats or other obstructions?"

Tobias chuckled. "You're pretty good."

McGill added, "At least one or two of the people taking photos or videos of me with their phones were working for you, too."

"*Very* good. I was disappointed to see that Madam President —"

"She no longer uses that title," McGill said.

"Okay. Your lovely wife then. I was sorry to see she didn't accompany you, but the young lady who was your guest was also quite attractive. Is it possible someone that fetching actually does protective work for the Secret Service?"

"I'm too discreet to say," McGill replied.

"Sure. So back to my original question. What did you think of the show?"

"I liked it more than I thought I would."

"That's good. So what didn't you like?"

"The beats mostly."

A moment of silence ensued, followed by Tobias saying, "You mean the vocal pattern of my monologue or the content of the material?"

"Both. What seemed funny at first became predictable by the second half of the show. Beyond that, some of the commentary was just too mean for my taste. Sure, some people are just horrible excuses for human beings. Cops see that all the time. But we see amazingly unexpected examples of kindness and even self-sacrifice, too. I kept waiting for one of those moments to come in your show, but it never did."

"Maybe that hasn't been my experience," Tobias said.

"My sympathy, then. Strictly as a peanut gallery observation, though, I think it would help your act. A little more empathy from the crowd would only make it easier to identify with your moments of outrage. Make it more powerful."

After a long beat, Tobias said, "I didn't know you were a shrink."

"I'm not," McGill said, "just a guy who keeps his eyes open and mind in gear. So what can I do for you, Mr. Tobias?"

"I just thought, if it's not too much to ask, that when you find Alice, I'd appreciate it if you told her I'd really like to talk with her, if she feels okay about doing that."

"Are you still thinking about firing her?" McGill asked.

"Not so much. What I'm thinking now is expanding her role in the show. If we can reach a happy medium and she's still interested."

For the moment, McGill lapsed into silence.

"You still there?" Tobias asked.

"Yeah."

"You hear anything from Frau Janeway yet?"

"No," McGill said.

"If she finds out how her money's being spent, you will."

"Have you ever met the woman?" McGill asked.

"No. Everything I know about her I've heard from Alice, and she's the only person I've ever heard Alice badmouth."

McGill thought about that, and he told Tobias, "You know, there are a few things you might do to help, other than front any money."

"What?"

"My colleagues in Europe were unable to get a recent photograph of Alice. If you have one, I'd appreciate if you could text or email a copy to me."

"You'll have a photo five minutes after we're done talking."

"Good. I'd also like a photo of Tad Thacker, and I'd like to speak with your security director, Mr. Haskell."

"Haskell is his first name. Haskell Carver. He played middle-linebacker for the New Orleans Saints for part of one season. Looked like he was going to make all-pro in his rookie year, but the ligaments in his right knee got turned into macramé."

"Sorry to hear that."

"Yeah, it's the shits, but like I told him, better to have your knee scrambled than your brain."

McGill laughed.

"You thought that was funny?" Tobias asked.

"Yeah," McGill said. "That line showed both acid and empathy. Pretty much the kind of balance I was talking about earlier."

***Department of Natural Resources — Portland, Oregon***

Tad Thacker worked as a wildlife biologist for the Oregon Department of Natural Resources. Almost from birth, Tad had been more fascinated by animals than he was with most people. More often than not, even as an adult, he found wildlife to be more comprehensible than his fellow human beings. Blessed with loving and somewhat indulgent parents, he'd had dogs, cats, birds and aquaria of fish at home to keep him company.

To a large extent, the company of species other than his own provided all the emotional support, except for parental, that Tad had needed. He was neither shy nor reclusive. He played well with others at school, but he simply hadn't felt the need to form close attachments to his classmates.

By the time Tad had reached middle school, his father had thought that the camaraderie of a sports team might be helpful for purposes of socialization as well as physical development. Only Tad chose to go out for the track team. That might have fit in with

Dad's plan except Tad had opted to run long distances and, as fate would have it, he left everyone else far behind.

Normally, being a champion athlete brought with it the opportunity for social contact with all of one's peers, male and female, and that was just what happened, but not in the usual way. Having been taught humility by his mother, Tad insisted on sharing credit for all of his victories with his coaches, teammates, teachers and the student body at large.

As a result, he was loved by everyone but intimate with none.

Tad was just different but fortunate enough to be admired, not ridiculed, by his peers and the adults in his life. He eventually became an all-state runner in high school, but didn't quite hit the mark of a potential Olympic gold medalist, and that was the caliber of runner that earned scholarships at places like Stanford and UCLA.

Mom and Dad had brought up those schools, thinking a milder climate like California's might somehow lead to warmer social companionship for their son. Instead, he attended the University of Oregon, made the track team and became one of the Ducks, as the university's sport teams were nicknamed. Tad also ducked most of the social opportunities at the school. He was more than happy with his studies in wildlife biology. He couldn't have imagined a better profession for himself than studying the behavior of animals and managing their habitats.

Upon graduating with honors and making use of a contact provided by the track team's head coach, Tad landed a job with the state's Department of Natural Resources. Its mission statement was to safeguard the beauty and wonders of the forests for future generations. Even better, the forests also had wonderful running paths.

Tad might have settled into his job and other circumstances for life. He could have seen himself wandering off into the trees in his final days, sitting down and leaning back against a tree until he breathed his last. He'd be too emaciated by then to make a decent meal for any scavenger. He'd simply decompose and whatever useful nutrients remained would become part of the ecosystem.

He was perfectly at peace with those prospects for his future … until Greg, the guy who worked next to him, left a *Playbill* for *Every Last Bastard in the World* out and open on his desk. Tad had seen live theater before; his parents had taken him, saying it would be good cultural exposure. It had been all he could do to sit still for two or more hours, trying to laugh in the right places and not be more than a half-beat behind in his applause.

He hadn't gone to see live entertainment or even a Hollywood movie since starting college.

It bothered him far more than it should have to see the *Playbill* open on the desk next to his. It was a distraction. If Greg were in the office, he would have asked him to close it, please. But Greg was out having lunch with his fiancée.

Hoping he wasn't making too great a social error, Tad reached out to pick up and close the offending publication. He would have liked to put the thing into one of Greg's desk drawers so he wouldn't have to look at it at all. Only he felt sure that would be too great a trespass. He decided he would simply turn it face down on the desktop and ignore it.

He picked up the magazine with his left hand, and that was when his whole life changed. He caught sight of a photo of a young woman. Someone who looked exactly like the only girl who'd ever made Tad's heart beat faster than a finishing kick in a close race. His breath caught in his throat, and without conscious thought, he opened the *Playbill* wide and centered it in his field of vision.

The name beneath the young woman's photo said: Alice Janeway.

She was pretty, had shoulder-length brown hair, dark eyes and a bright smile.

Alice had a purity to her that he'd only noticed before in one person. The first and only true love of Tad's life, Jenny Nyland. Just like Jenny, Alice was neatly groomed and conservatively dressed. The light in her eyes, the glow of her skin and the gleam of her smile left him speechless. It was as if he could see her soul, maybe even a soul reborn, both ideas strange notions for a guy who'd stopped going to church in his teens.

He knew he had to meet Alice Janeway.

So he did something he'd never done before.

Committed a petty theft.

He stole Greg's Playbill and hid it in his car.

***McGill Investigations International — Austin, Texas***

"You want to say it or should I?" Kyle Tompkins asked Maj Olson.

The two of them had stayed behind at the office while Gene Beck left to go talk with Henry Rhymes, Catherine Clark's twin, and the eldest of the Rhymes brothers. Not that Gene had mentioned where he was going to Kyle.

"Say what?" Maj asked.

The two of them sat in Maj's office. She'd decided she wanted to ask him a few questions before she answered any of his queries. See how they might fashion a way of working together that pleased all involved.

Kyle told Maj, "Nine out of ten people I meet who are over 30 and have parents in their 50s or older, tell me I look a great deal like an old-time rock singer," Kyle said.

"You mean John Sebastian."

"Bingo. Now that we have that out of the way —"

"No, no. Since you brought it up, are you at all musical?"

Kyle did a finger roll on Maj's desk and said, "I play a fair piano. Had classical training courtesy of my parents. Sneaked off to an AME church in town that combines traditional hymns with contemporary gospel songs. Both styles are backed by a former blues pianist who left the bottle and nightclubs behind when he found Jesus. Despite my being white and wet behind the ears, he gave me lessons in return for making contributions to the church."

"You put money in the collection basket?" Maj asked.

"That and helped with some janitorial work."

"You still play?"

Kyle nodded. "When I'm not busy setting the world of small circulation journalism on fire."

Addressing that point, Maj asked, "Do you know how to keep a secret … at least for a little while?"

"I don't usually make any promises that extend past my next deadline, but under certain circumstances, for some people, I might make an exception."

"Are you saying you can be bought?" Maj asked.

"Not with money or party favors, but give me the chance to turn a good story into a great story, and I can be patient for a little while. So who is it you'd like to know if I know?"

"You'd have to wait until Gene and I wrap up this investigation before submitting your story. Or else you'll have to settle for the suitable-for-children version of what happens."

Kyle grinned. "I don't write for *Nickelodeon Magazine*."

Maj thought for a moment. "So file other stories for grownups the next two weeks. Can you live with that?"

"I'd prefer not to … and I could always start looking into things myself. Do some *investigative* journalism, you know."

"You could, but you'd be up against two pros who are backed up by a whole network of other pros. You might come out ahead, but chances are you won't, and you'll have no chance at all that we'll ever give you another story."

"You said you would just a little while ago," Kyle reminded her.

Unruffled, Maj replied, "Things change."

The reporter sighed. "Okay, two weeks. Starting right now. So, once more, who is it you'd like the scoop on?"

Maj had wanted to ask Kyle what he might know about Catherine Clark.

Now, though, she had just come up with another idea.

"Not who, where. As in where do I find the best country-and-western venues in town? Those performers like to wear cowboy hats, don't they?"

Kyle Tompkins winced. He should have thought of that right off.

He wondered if Maj Olson was starting to affect his professionalism.

***Galia Mindel's House — Washington, DC***

Galia had the time to have the plastic dust covers removed from all the furniture in her Washington house, but she'd yet to order any groceries online. So she put in a delivery request for two ginger chicken quinoa bowls from Commissary DC for her and Patti. Then Frank Morrissey, Galia's successor as White House chief of staff, called and said he'd like to meet with her. Frank knew whenever anyone important came to town.

Galia felt flattered that she was still thought of as someone who mattered. She'd shared a treasure trove of political secrets with Frank. Undoubtedly, he hoped she had learned something new to pass on to him. You could never have too much dirt on your political enemies. With Frank joining the party, Galia ordered a Tuscan Beef Burger for him.

Showing that he was still operating at the top of his game, Frank picked up Patti at her office, on the way to Galia's house, and had Patti speak to President Jean Morrissey en route. It was the first time the two women had spoken since Jean's inauguration. Both of them considered it important to maintain the appearance that Jean didn't need any coaching from her predecessor.

Nonetheless, both the GOP and True South kept pushing at the idea that the only thing that would save the Republic from disasters of all sorts would be to elect a conservative man the next time around. That would be the opposition's unceasing drumbeat until Election Day 2020.

Galia's guests and their catered meals arrived within a heartbeat of each other. Forsaking formality, they decided to eat and talk in the kitchen. Galia and Patti drank San Pellegrino sparkling water; Frank went with a Schweppes ginger ale.

Nobody wanted any alcohol-induced fuzziness to cloud their

thinking.

"Well, here we all are once more," Patti said. "Jean sends her regards, Galia."

"My best to Madam President, too," Galia told Frank.

He nodded to indicate he'd pass along Galia's regards.

Galia asked Patti, "How did Mr. McGill take my news?"

Without saying a word, the look on Frank's face clearly asked, "What news?"

Both women took in the silent inquiry but each had a bite to eat before answering.

Patti said, "Yum." Then she told Galia. "Jim was surprised he's going to be your neighbor, but he let me persuade him that living next door to you wouldn't be entirely awful."

Galia laughed. "Has he ever confided to you that he sometimes regrets saving my life?"

"No. He still gets Christmas cards from your boys and the grandkids. They warm his heart."

"Sure, my kids make him feel good, but I still give him heartburn."

Patti said, "I think, if anything, he might feel you took up too much of my time."

With a clear note of indignation, Galia said, "That was what the job demanded."

After downing a sip of ginger ale, Frank said, "Byron DeWitt feels the same way about me."

"See," Galia said.

"But now you'll be working for me again," Patti told Galia.

"This job can't be as intense as the presidency … can it?"

"No, and it will definitely be different for you."

Galia didn't like the sound of that. Frank looked on with silent interest.

"What's that mean?" Galia asked.

Patti told Galia of the plan to have her scout the world for a third of each year looking for people with brilliant ideas in which Committed Capital might invest — and that all of Galia's flights and accommodations would be first class.

Both women noticed that Frank's eyes brightened upon hearing that news, but Galia had reservations, to put it mildly.

"That's almost the same idea my sons had for me," she said.

"No," Patti said in a soft but firm voice, "this *won't* be a lonely-hearts cruise. This will be serious business, looking for and sometimes finding, big ideas that will bring jobs and prosperity to our country. If we do this right, you and I will be remembered for more than our White House years. Without advocating gender bias, I also thought you might keep a special eye out for female innovators. The next Marie Curie might get her start because Galia Mindel discovered her brilliance."

The flattery was transparent, but that idea did seize Galia's imagination.

Even Frank applauded it. "Bravo, you've still got it, Mrs. McGill."

The fact that Patti had adopted the McGill surname wasn't a state secret, but it had yet to become a staple of either traditional or social media. Even so, Frank knew about it. Both Patti and Galia were pleased that Jean Morrissey was being so well served by her chief of staff.

Galia said, "Okay, Frank, tell us why you invited yourself to this little chat."

He got straight to the point. "Jean told me that she's mentioned to both of you that she's going to serve in the White House for only one term, and she might even resign after two years in favor of Vice President Dick Bergen."

Patti and Galia nodded.

Frank said, "Well, with the GOP and True South advancing the theme that women can't be trusted to serve successfully as president, the two years and done option is out the window."

"Is she going for two full terms?" Galia asked.

"One term for sure. A second term is up for discussion with Byron. At the moment, the thinking is if things are going well in the country and it looks like Bergen is better than even money to win the presidency, she'll bow out. If it looks like she'll need to run for a second term to keep the other side out of the White House … I think she'll bite the bullet and do it."

"It's none of my business," Patti said, "but how might that affect things between Jean and Byron?"

"If you mean might a divorce sink any plan for a second term, no. Jean told me Byron would campaign at her side, if that's what she chooses to do. After a second win … I'm pretty sure he'd move back to California."

"He was slotted to head Jim's office in Los Angeles," Patti said.

"You might give him a heads-up on that," Frank said. "From what I've heard, Ms. Rebecca Bramley is doing quite well out there."

Both women kept straight faces, but each was impressed by the depth and breadth of Frank's knowledge.

Patti said, "Rebecca is hoping to open an office in Toronto eventually."

Frank shrugged. "People plan, God laughs, and there's work to do in the meantime."

"Speaking of which," Galia said, "what do you have in mind for Mrs. McGill and me?"

Looking at Patti, Frank said, "What I'd like you to do, Mrs. McGill, and Jean agrees with me on this, is to defend your time in the White House, at the times and places, and in the manner of your choosing, but not too infrequently. Remind people that you did a damn fine job for the country in the face of a determined opposition. Rebut clearly the idea that women are not up to the job of being president and doing it well."

Patti said, "Jean will be speaking up for her own stewardship at the same time?"

"Not at exactly the same time. We wouldn't want either of you to step on the other's message. The ideal would be the equivalent of a one-two punch. Stagger the bastards with the first blow, knock them down with the second. If necessary, I can quietly coordinate things."

Patti nodded, liking the idea. "Jean should take the lead the first time out. After that, we can work out different patterns."

"You won't have any trouble with Mr. McGill?" Frank asked.

"No. I'll have to talk with Jim about this, but as we all know he's not one to shy away from a fight."

"Good."

"And what do you want from me?" Galia asked him.

Frank laughed. "I'm sure you know I want to hear any deep, dark secrets you've uncovered since leaving the White House, but now I'm interested in something else, too."

"What?"

"Well, Mrs. McGill is offering you a job to gather commercial intelligence from all over the world. I thought that would be a perfect cover and dovetail beautifully with you becoming the White House's unofficial, unacknowledged master foreign agent, collecting who knows what interesting and even vital political nuggets. Do you think you might enjoy that, Galia?"

Both Frank and Patti had their eyes on Galia.

Neither of them was surprised to see a smile form on her face.

### *McGill Investigations International — Sausalito, California*

Keely Powell was the first person to arrive in daylight at the relatively small Northern California office of the McGill investigative empire. She and her husband, Ron Ketchum, both formerly of the LAPD, worked the firm's investigations in Northern California, Oregon, Washington State and the Mountain West. Their office manager, Fred Nakamura, was a veteran of Force Recon, one of the United States Marine Corps special operations capable forces.

During Fred's time in uniform, Force Recon's missions were deep reconnaissance and direct action. Unlike their Navy brethren in the SEALs, the Marine special operators had yet to achieve a ubiquitous profile in popular culture. Fred liked it that way.

Without inspiring a bit of doubt in either Keely or Ron, Fred had informed them that he was the direct descendant of a long line of samurai warriors. He'd joined the Marines, he told them, because they had the only special forces unit that had agreed to let him take a katana — a samurai sword — on his missions.

Fred had arrived at the office well before dawn as he did every morning, checked for messages and left that day's flower arrangement on Keely's desk for her to appreciate and contemplate. Then he departed for nearby Mount Tamalpais to meditate as the sun rose.

That pre-dawn morning, he'd also left a note on Keely's desk.

It was written in both Japanese kanji and English.

*Call McGill-sama.* The suffix meant a person of higher rank than oneself.

Fred was teaching Japanese to Keely. The culture as well as the language.

Ron, just then, was dropping off their son Matt at pre-school or Keely would have had him on a conference call when she called McGill. It was always good to hear from the boss, and Ron enjoyed talking with him. It continued to inspire both of them that a former street cop had managed to marry someone who became president of the United States.

More than likely, something like that would never happen again.

Still, associating with someone like McGill made them both think they might get lucky, too, in some almost magical way.

When the call went through, she said, "This is Keely Powell, sir. I got a message to give you a call."

"If you remember, Keely, you and I were in the same shootout in Washington. After that, I think I said everyone involved can call me Jim."

"I do remember … Jim. Thank you. It's just that I'm studying Japanese these days, and I think that's put me in a more formal frame of mind. But I'll remember. What can I do for you, Jim?"

"The latest report I received from your office says both you and Ron recently finished a case. Are there any other obligations on your schedules at the moment?"

"All's quiet on the western front right now, but that usually doesn't last long."

"I'm glad to hear business is good. California still has reciprocity with Oregon about PIs working in each other's states, right?"

"We do."

"Great. I'd like you or Ron, your choice, to fly up to Portland and take a look at a man named Tad Thacker. He works for the state's Department of Natural Resources."

"Any particular angle to take on this guy?" Keely asked.

"A woman named Alice Janeway has gone missing. She works, or worked, for a performance artist named Teagan Tobias. Alice was last seen in Atlanta. Thacker, at least momentarily, became obsessed with Ms. Janeway. He tried to give her an engagement ring backstage after a performance by Tobias in Portland; said they were going to spend the rest of their lives together. She'd never met him before, and he was escorted out. The next night he showed up at another performance in a front-row center seat. He was tossed out of the theater before the show started. He hasn't pestered Ms. Janeway again, that we know of, but most of these guys aren't quitters."

"No, they're not," Keely agreed. "How long ago did this happen?"

"I checked on that this morning. It was six months ago, back in May."

Thinking about that, Keely said, "I'm surprised the guy was able to restrain himself that long. Most of these creeps don't have that kind of impulse control."

"Not unless they've been busy working out some elaborate plan," McGill said.

"Oh, hell, let's hope it's not that."

"It occurred to me," McGill said, "that somebody who's not in touch with reality might like to take his object of desire home, show her what she's been missing. That might involve a lot of moving parts, transporting her from one side of the country to the other."

"Yes, it would. Was she working when she went missing?"

"She was present at Tobias' closing performance in Atlanta two weeks ago. There was a scheduled week off between shows, but she didn't show up for the first week of shows here in D.C. It could be she just got tired of working for Tobias; they'd had some professional disagreements. She might be down in the Caribbean soaking up the sun. When someone like Thacker might be involved, though, we've got to locate her, whatever the situation is."

Keely said, "What if Thacker has left his job or is taking some vacation time himself? He might have her and be anywhere by now."

"If it comes to that, we'll see about mounting a company-wide effort. Of course, if we find anything to suggest it's an actual kidnapping, we hand everything we have to the FBI posthaste."

"Right."

"Had you ever heard of Teagan Tobias before now, Keely?"

"The name sounds familiar, but with work and Matt being only recently potty-trained, Ron and I don't get out a lot."

"Tobias is on YouTube. Fly up to Portland and take a look at his act on the way. Let me know what you think, okay?"

"Sure. Do Alice and Tobias have a personal relationship?"

"He said it was cordial but strictly professional at first, but then, as I mentioned, things got more complicated. She wanted more involvement in his act. He refused to do that, but he gave her more money. Now, he seems willing to relent on her creative ambitions, too."

Keely said, "Sounds screwed up, but not too different from a lot of stuff Ron and I saw in Los Angeles with movie people."

"Did you run into any star-stalkers out there?"

"Oh, yeah. Most of them were fairly pathetic, susceptible to being scared away, but some of them … damn it, people died at their hands. If you don't remember the names of any of the victims, they're easy enough to find online."

"Maybe you should take Ron with you."

"It's his week for primary parent duty. My shift starts next Monday."

McGill said, "I've seen how tough you are, Keely, but be careful, okay?"

"Yeah, I'll take our office manager, Fred, with me."

"The guy who took my phone message? He sounded very … gentle."

Keely laughed. "Don't let his good manners fool you, Jim. He's a Marine *and* a samurai."

"Whoa," McGill said, "that should be enough. Let's hope so, anyway."

***Rock Creek Park — Washington, DC***

Before saying hello or even introducing himself to McGill, Haskell Carver said, "I voted for your wife both times she ran for president."

The guy knew how to make a good first impression, McGill thought.

"Kind of you to say," he replied, extending a hand. "I'm Jim McGill."

Haskell shook hands and gave his name. "I told my little girl she could be president someday, too, if that's what she wants. She's only five, so that doesn't mean too much to her now, but she'll remember what I said and understand when she gets older."

"Always good to plant the right seeds early," McGill said.

After speaking with Keely Powell, McGill had called Haskell and asked if he might take Teagan Tobias' security chief to lunch. It had been Ace Cole's turn to bodyguard McGill that day, but he had left the Secret Service special agent back at the office. McGill had told Patti there'd be times like this.

Haskell had said, "If it's all the same to you, I'd like to go to Rock Creek Park and get a run in. Are you up for that?"

The day was mostly cloudy, but the temperature was in the mid-50s.

For someone who grew up in Chicago, that was balmy for autumn.

"Sounds good," McGill said. "How far do you want to run?"

"I use three miles as a starting point. I'll do at least that much, but I won't do more than five miles. Don't want to overexert my football knee."

"I'm fine with either three miles or five," McGill said. "I usually run the Mall, but a change of scenery might be nice."

They met at the intersection of Tilden Street and Beach Drive NW to run the Southern Section of the Rock Creek Trail. The course was paved and mostly flat. It shared space with a bike path, and for the most part the path ran along its namesake creek. More than a few of the trees and shrubs were still in leaf, and on a workday, for most denizens of the town, foot traffic was light.

All in all, it was a pleasant place to push back against the effects of time and gravity.

"Are you up to talking as we run?" Haskell asked.

"If you don't do better than six-minute miles, yeah," McGill said.

McGill saw that Haskell no longer looked like a middle linebacker. In a sleeveless T-shirt and running shorts and shoes, he was tall with well-defined musculature, but he was also lean. Looked like he hadn't consumed an unnecessary carbohydrate for years. The lack of any spare weight probably made things easier on his surgical knee.

Haskell said, "Six-minutes a mile? I usually do seven."

"Then we can have a nice chat," McGill replied, taking off.

He wasn't sure Haskell hadn't been putting him on about running at a slower pace, but there was no question McGill had at least fifteen years and maybe twenty on the other guy. He also noticed Haskell didn't strain in the least to make up the distance of McGill's surprise start.

"Teag told me you'd have questions about Tad Thacker," Haskell said. "Is that right?"

"That's part of what I have in mind."

"What else?"

"I'm also curious about what you think of your boss?"

Haskell showed McGill a wicked grin, and McGill wondered if

that was the way he'd looked when he was about to level a running back or a receiver on the football field.

The security chief said, "I signed what you call a non-disclosure agreement with Mr. Tobias. It says if I talk out of turn I can be fired, sued, maybe even taken out and shot."

"That last part seems a bit harsh," McGill replied.

"I asked for extra life insurance, so they deleted that one."

"Still, you can't talk about your boss."

"Well, that's an interesting question. My mother and father worked for a community newspaper in Philadelphia. Dad was an editor; Mom was a copy-editor. They taught me to read things *closely.* That applied to schoolbooks first, of course. But when it looked like I was going to make the NFL — a choice Mom hated — they told me I had to read all the fine print in my contracts, too."

"A skill you put to use when Teag Tobias hired you?" McGill asked.

Haskell nodded. "My contract and non-disclosure agreement with him say insofar as speaking to either traditional or popular media goes, I can't say if he so much as farts after eating beans. But I checked before coming to see you today. There's no language restricting my speaking freely to a private investigator with Mr. Tobias' permission. Which I asked for and received. The only limits on what I can say, as I see it, are my senses of employee loyalty and personal discretion."

"Seems reasonable," McGill said. "So can you tell me what you think of Teagan Tobias? I ask because my first and second impressions weren't that great."

The two men ran a good quarter-mile before Haskell replied.

"I like him more often than not," he said, "but when I don't like him, I wonder if I should have ever liked him at all. There are times he makes me laugh hard enough to shake head to toe — which isn't great for my knee. There are other times I think he's just cruel, and I want to punch him. I can still throw a good punch, too. All in all, I can live with him."

McGill thought about what he'd just heard. He was curious

about how much Haskell got paid and how that affected his feelings, but he'd save that for later, if he brought it up at all.

Taking a different direction, he asked, "Have you had to deal with many people who hate either Tobias or his act?"

"Some of each; some who hate both. He got threatened by these gay ladies once. That was when he hired me, right after that."

McGill smiled. "One of those ladies works for me now."

"Yeah?"

"Yeah. She said Tobias pretended at my office that he didn't remember her."

"That's BS. From what I've seen of Teag, he never forgets anyone who ticks him off."

"Who else?" McGill said. "I mean, are there any people he or you thought were genuine threats to his well-being?"

"Three. Two guys and another woman. We relayed those threats to a dude who used to assess that kind of thing for the Secret Service. He agreed they were real."

McGill found that very interesting. "What's his name? The former Secret Service guy."

"He's not going to talk to you about Teag."

"That's okay. I just want to see if the people I know in the Secret Service think he's good."

Haskell nodded. "That's reasonable. His name's Waylon Jakes."

"So what happened with these three real threats?"

"Nothing yet. They're all still hanging fire out there. Keeping us on our toes."

"How many people does Tobias have working security for him?"

"Me, two other guys and a woman."

"Has he ever tried to hit on the woman?"

Haskell laughed. "You'd do better trying to get on the sweet side of a buzz-saw."

"Do you and your people work shifts?" McGill asked. "Cover the man around the clock?"

"We work shifts, but there are times Teag tells us all to knock off for a while. That's when he's working and touring. When he takes a break, he's out there all on his own. Even now, in the middle of a tour, he'll tell me he needs some time to himself. And whatever he wants, he gets. You aren't planning to do him in, are you?"

McGill took the question as facetious but the look on Haskell's face was serious.

Seeing that, he said, "No, I have no ill intent. I don't understand, though, how a guy can just ignore multiple serious threats whenever the mood strikes him."

"Neither can I. Whatever any of us on the security team thinks of the man, he pays all of us nice money. We'd hate to lose our jobs just because he misread Greta Garbo and starts spouting, 'I want to be alone.'"

"Greta didn't say that?" McGill asked.

"She said, 'I want to be *let* alone.' In other words, don't bother me."

McGill thought: This guy really does pay attention to detail.

"What can you tell me about Tad Thacker?" McGill asked.

"That dude? He wasn't interested in Teag at all. He lost his heart to Alice, the poor fool."

"She didn't like him or doesn't like guys in general?"

Haskell gave that a moment's thought. "I never got the vibe that she's a ladies' lady, but I never saw or heard of her dating a guy either. Can't really tell you who or what warms her heart. I can say for sure she doesn't like to be rushed by some dude who pops up out of nowhere."

"I was told Thacker didn't take the hint right away," McGill said. "Came to the show the night after you'd escorted him out. Did he try to call or write to Alice after that?"

"If he got her phone number somehow, I wouldn't know about that unless she told me. She didn't say anything about getting any unwanted calls or texts."

"She never seemed to be unusually anxious, even if she didn't let on that something was wrong?"

It looked to McGill as if Haskell had started to shake his head but stopped himself.

"She was worried about something?" McGill asked.

"I'm not sure, but … You ever whack your ulnar nerve?"

McGill said, "My funny bone? Sure. Plenty of times."

"So you know how that tingles, and sometimes you shake your arm to make it feel right."

"Uh-huh."

Haskell said, "Well, there were a few times, maybe four or five, the week before Alice left, that I saw her shaking her left arm just that way. Only I never saw her bump into anything."

McGill processed that information. "You think she might have been getting sick?"

The former football player produced a dry laugh. "Listen, between my personal experiences and what I learned from teammates, I can tell you a fair bit about orthopedic medicine. Neurology, on the other hand, that's not my specialty. Beyond funny bones, I mean."

"Fair enough," McGill said. "Let's get back to Thacker for a minute. How did he react the two times you gave him the heave-ho? Did he make any threats against you, Alice or even Tobias? Did he show or voice any rage?"

Haskell shook his head. "No. He went quietly both times. Backstage, he seemed genuinely puzzled that things didn't go the way he'd planned. Like, maybe, Alice hadn't read her copy of a script he'd already memorized. When we hauled him out of his seat the next night, I thought he was going to cry, but he didn't fight or even fuss."

"How did he look?" McGill asked. "Maybe heartbroken?"

"You know, you just put your finger on it. That's exactly the right word. I should've thought of it. Only how can your heart break over someone you don't really know?"

McGill replied, "How can you fall in love with someone you've never met?"

They came to the end of their run at the Memorial Bridge. Five miles. Both of them were damp with sweat but neither felt tired. Leo was waiting for them in the Chevy. McGill asked Haskell,

"How many photos did you take of Thacker?"

"Between the two nights: thirteen. Still have them on my phone. I can text them to you."

"I'd appreciate that."

McGill gave Haskell a lift back to his car and got the photos of Tad Thacker from him.

***Rhymes & Associates Architects — Austin, Texas***

The architecture firm of Henry Rhymes & Associates, AIA, had its offices on San Jacinto Boulevard not far from Voodoo Doughnut V, a 24-hour cash-only donut shop that kept Rhymes and his staff fueled when working late hours. If he or his people felt the need to stretch their legs rather than distend their mid-sections, a stroll to the landmark statue of Stevie Ray Vaughn and back would add a mile to their Fitbits.

When Gene Beck walked into the firm's reception area he saw a comely young woman who looked barely old enough to be a high school graduate. The nameplate on her desk said Lisette. She was on the phone with someone, but she had the multi-tasking skills to spot Gene, give him a smile and hold up an index finger to signal she'd be with him in just a minute.

Didn't even take that long. She wrapped up the call and said, "May we design something for you, sir?"

Got right to point, Gene thought. He liked that.

Struck a chord with him, too. The money he'd been making from his songwriting had him thinking of moving out of his rental house and buying something nicer. "Now that you mention it," he said, "that's a possibility. Assuming you do residential as well as commercial work."

Lisette said, "Mr. Rhymes told me if a pharaoh ever walks through the door let him know we do pyramids."

Gene laughed and said, "Don't think I need anything that fancy. Just something for my wife, my son and me. Might like to have a recording studio on the premises, though."

Her eyes got big and she smiled. "Are you a musician?"

"Songwriter."

"That's even cooler. Have you done anything I might know."

Gene told her the titles of his two hit songs.

"That was you? I *love* those songs." She sang the opening line from each one. Had a decent alto voice, too.

"I didn't write the lyrics," Gene said, "but I do have another line of work."

"What's that?"

"I'm a private investigator." He handed Lisette a business card. "Catherine Clarke sent me. I'm looking into Mr. Wallace Rhymes' missing hat."

"You write songs *and* do investigations?"

"I enjoy a good run, too. You think Henry Rhymes might agree to give me a few minutes?"

Lisette said, "Let me buzz him. I'll mention you might need a new house. You know, just in case he's not impressed by private eyes."

Gene grinned. He really liked this kid. Given her sharp wit, he revised his estimate of her age to a bit over 21 … maybe a week or two. She buzzed the boss, told him who would like a minute or two of his time, and the reasons why.

She got an affirmative reply and told Gene, "Go through the door behind me, turn right and it's the office at the end of the hall."

Gene gave her a salute and followed instructions.

Just so there was no confusion, Henry Rhymes was waiting for Gene in his office doorway. He had the same height as his father, about six-two, with the same solid build, minus the extra weight of Wallace Rhymes' late-in-life passivity. The younger man looked like he still hit the gym. He had a good grip, too, when he shook Gene's hand.

"My sister, Catherine, told me you or your associate, Ms. Olson, might be coming to see me, Mr. Beck. Come on in."

Gene followed him into his office and immediately noticed the hat hanging at a jaunty angle from a hatrack in the corner of the office to his right. Unless he was mistaken —

Henry Rhymes saw his interest and said, “Catherine told me you’re looking for Dad’s hat; there it is. Sorry to cut into your revenue, but some problems resolve themselves easily. Would you like to sit down and hear a short, boring story or just take the hat back to Dad?”

Gene looked at the architect. “I’m fond of stories, even the brief ones.”

He sat in a guest chair placed opposite the man’s desk. Rhymes took a deep breath and let it out before he got going. “My mother died from complications of childbirth right after Clint and Cole were born. The doctors never said as much, but I’ve come to think that delivering twins a second time was just too much of a strain for her heart. The poor thing stopped and the medical team couldn’t revive her.”

“My sympathy to you and your siblings,” Gene said.

“Yes, well. We sure could have used some. Catherine came to blame Dad, Clint and Cole for our mother’s death. More so when she was younger, but still a little, I think. Once my younger brothers came to understand their older sister’s feelings, they turned things around on her. They blamed Catherine and me for being born first. If our parents had just skipped us and gone straight to them, they said, everything would’ve been fine.”

Gene said, “That must have been tough on everyone. How did your father handle it?”

“Well … I guess this story is longer than I first thought. Maybe I’ve compressed it in my mind as I’ve gotten older. Dad was born in Massachusetts; Mom was the native Texan. Dad wasn’t in the oil business; he didn’t raise cattle. He was a stockbroker, and a damn good one.”

“Massachusetts, huh? He sure lost *that* accent,” Gene said.

“Mom’s kin were Texas pioneers. Dad worked real hard to fit in, including learning to speak Texan. But his ancestors landed in Rhode Island while it was still a British colony and later moved a bit north to the Boston area."

Gene said, "I'd say he *mastered* the local lingo."

"Well, living in the state for over 60 years might explain that. In his only act of rebellion, that I've ever heard of, Dad decided to go to college at UT instead of Harvard. But he wasn't so foolish as to do anything like becoming an English major. He studied business both as an undergrad and in graduate school. Maybe he chose to come to Texas because it's a place where people are proud if they make a lot of money. They don't talk about it in whispers. Anyway, he met Mom in school, and that's where he learned all about Texas history."

"So your father became fascinated by local folkways as a result of meeting your mother, is that right?" Gene asked.

Rhymes hesitated and then sighed. "To the degree necessary to ingratiate himself to his new in-laws, he acculturated. But he got into cowboy collectibles *after* Mom died. It's easy to think, and maybe even true, that it was his way to try to hold onto his memories of their younger days, when he actually first wore a cowboy hat. What's also true is his emotional availability to his children became scarce. He seemed to be occupied by his work and decades of quiet mourning for the wife he lost.

"He always provided for us materially, up to the point we got our college undergraduate degrees. He told us by then we should be able to fend for ourselves. Catherine, Clint and I took advantage of getting a free ride through college, though Catherine paid him back. Cole took a one-time payment of $100,000 instead of college tuition to get his rodeo career underway."

"How'd that go?" Gene asked.

"Quite well, until he broke too many bones to continue. By then, maybe through some paternal gene of Yankee shrewdness, he'd managed to save and invest wisely enough to buy a large cattle ranch with his twin brother. Clint went to Texas A&M and got a degree in agricultural economics. The two of them are the real cowboys in the family."

Gene said, "Does that give them any edge with your father?"

Henry Rhymes laughed. "If my father doesn't remind one of us kids it's our turn to pay for dining out with him, that's a big show of affection. He's pretty egalitarian about that and other outlays of his cash. None of us can complain, though. He pushed us in directions that led to comfortable lives, minus Cole's arthritis from all the bone fractures. I suppose Catherine's situation is somewhat more tenuous than what us three brothers have, but people in Austin like their beer and their music, and that's not likely to change. So, she should be all right, too."

"Tell me if I'm going too far here," Gene said, "but how would you say your father is doing mentally these days."

"That is pretty snoopy, but that's your job, isn't it?" Rhymes asked. "The only reason I'll answer you is because I can see how it's relevant. He's slowing down, mentally and physically. There are moments he doesn't mind that. He's told me he's sure my mother will be there to greet him when he goes … but sometimes he can get annoyed with himself whenever he's forgetful."

Henry Rhymes pointed to the cowboy hat hanging on the rack.

"He forgot that the last time we went out to dinner."

"Was it Texas Independence Day?" Gene asked.

Rhymes grinned and asked, "How'd you know?"

"Your father told my partner and me he wears that hat only on special occasions."

"That's right. Anyway, it was my turn to pick up the check, so he said thank you and good-bye, leaving it on the chair next to where he sat. He was gone by the time I got my credit card back. I thought I'd just keep the hat until the next time we go out to eat, but if he misses it, you can return it to him."

Gene said, "Thank you. I will. I'll tell him you kept it safe for him."

"That's fine. Or you can tell him you solved the mystery and be his hero."

On Gene's way out of the architectural firm with Wallace Rhymes' hat in hand, Lisette, the receptionist, handed him a business card with her name and phone number on it.

She'd written on the reverse side: *Call me if you ever need help.*

***Hill Country — Georgetown, Texas***

After Maj Olson sent reporter Kyle Tompkins on his way, she called Wallace Rhymes and asked if she might pay a visit to his home and take a look around. He didn't ask the obvious question: "You think I just mislaid my hat?" He only said, "Of course, look around, talk to my housekeeper, have an ice tea on the house."

"Thank you. Gene and I also had an idea that might help us get your hat back, but we want to run it past you first." She told Rhymes of the plan to post an online photo and description of the hat — without mentioning the John Wayne provenance — and offer a $1,000 reward for information leading to the hat's return.

After a short pause, Rhymes said, "My only concern about that is you might be flooded with shabby imitations."

"We'll have your photo for comparison, and we won't bother you with anything that doesn't look like a match."

"All right then. I don't suppose it could hurt."

"Good. I'll see you within an hour."

"I won't be here," Rhymes said, "but I'll leave word to let you see whatever you want. An old coot like me doesn't have any racy secrets to hide."

Maj chuckled politely. "Are you coming into Austin, sir?"

"No, I'm going out to do a little *plein air* painting: hills, streams, clouds and sky."

"Oils?" Maj asked, inquiring about his painting preference.

"Pastels," he replied.

The fact that Rhymes painted at all came as a surprise to Maj. Pastels only added to the revelation. If she'd had to guess any artistic inclinations he might have, she'd have said it would be casting bronze in the likenesses of cowboys, Indians and cavalrymen.

Frederic Remington revisited.

Pastels just showed how people could surprise you.

Rhymes' home in Georgetown, Texas, was 30 miles outside of Austin: a hop-skip-and-a-jump commute by Texas standards. Rhymes gave her clear directions and told her she'd be there in little more than the wink of an eye. Maj's Porsche Cayenne SUV was fast, but she didn't think the trip would be that quick. Then again …

The Texas Transportation Commission had set 85 MPH speed limits on some roadways, after traffic engineering studies, but many a Texan drove as if he or she was on an autobahn: pedal to the metal and don't bother me about no arithmetic. After getting a feel for the state, Maj had bought the Porsche for keeping up with traffic as much as anything else.

She drove to Georgetown at what she estimated the tolerance of the Texas Highway Patrol to be on a day with clear and dry weather conditions. Even so, by the time she arrived, she assumed her client was off on his painting jaunt.

She steered the Porsche onto the Rhymes' half-mile-long driveway. The new client's mansion sat on 100 acres, complete with a burbling spring. It had been bought back in the days before housing developments with far smaller lots had sprouted in the Hill Country like so many wildflowers. Georgetown itself was known as the Red Poppy capital of the state, and the bright flowers planted throughout the town proved the point.

The driveway continued straight past the house, presumably to a garage out back, and also branched to the right to form an oval in front of the house. Maj brought the Porsche to a stop opposite the double-door entrance. One of the doors opened before she could get out of the car.

A middle-aged Latina wearing what Maj thought of as a pale blue housekeeper's frock and black rubber-soled shoes stood in the opening. She offered her guest a small smile, but her posture was tense, almost apprehensive. Given her druthers, Maj thought, the woman would have stepped back inside, closed the door and pretended nobody was home.

Walking toward her, Maj smiled and gave a friendly wave. "Hi, my name is Maj Olson. I work for Mr. Rhymes, too."

The woman looked at the gleaming Porsche and drew the obvious inference: Rhymes paid some people a whole lot better than others. Presumably, there were other privileges that also accrued. Deference must be paid.

"*Sí, señora.* I am Solana. I manage the house for *Señor* Rhymes."

"*¿Estaría más cómodo hablando español?*" Maj asked. Would you be more comfortable speaking Spanish?

Apparently not, as Solana stiffened visibly.

Maj had studied Spanish in both high school and as a college undergrad, but her command of the language was far from polished. Whenever native speakers conversed rapidly, she had a hard time keeping up. She had learned a good trick, though, from her first boss with the Amtrak cops.

Ask the question she'd just put to Solana. If the other person *thought* you spoke her native tongue, she wouldn't try to put something past you in Spanish. She'd be stuck trying to tell her story in her second language, English, where *you* would have the advantage in spotting a lie.

Of course, if you became truly fluent in another person's language, then you let her think you didn't know a word of it, and she might blab something useful right in front of you.

"No, no, Miss Olson," Solana said, "let us speak English."

Maj might have said, "*Cómoda deséa.*" As you wish.

But she said, "Sure, we can do that. May I step inside?"

Solana swung the door open and made way for Maj to enter. Befitting a big house, the entryway was large and the rooms within view looked to be built on the same scale. Still, there was no sense of grandiosity, no vaulted ceiling that served no purpose other than providing space for an immense chandelier that might kill a dozen people if it ever fell.

There was more than enough space to be comfortable, but that was it. The furnishings looked high end but unostentatious. The paintings on the walls were signed W. Rhymes for the most part. And, son of a gun, the man could really paint.

Maj had always thought of pastels as a gauzy medium, perfect for daubers who'd never learned draftsmanship and probably didn't have much composition skill or a color sense either. Now, she scolded herself for holding such a misbegotten prejudice. She'd have been delighted to own any of Wallace Rhymes' paintings.

The prize of the collection was right there where you walked into the house. It was a portrait of a beautiful young woman, and Maj knew immediately she must have been Catherine Clarke's mother. The hair, eyes, and other features were all but identical. The skin tones were luminous. More than just masterful artistry, the portrait was clearly a work of love.

"Beautiful," Maj said.

Solana only nodded. "What would you like to see, Miss Olson."

Maj looked at her and said, "The whole place, top to bottom."

***Portland, Oregon***

Having been a cop with the LAPD for twenty years, engaging in scuffles with dirt-balls of all sizes, shapes, colors and genders, and never needing to be admitted to a hospital, Keely Powell didn't often think of herself as someone who required backup. Then again, the world seemed to be changing.

Her experience as a cop had never included being in a firefight like the one Jim McGill had brought back to mind.

A squad of bad guys had been firing automatic weapons all the hell over the place. That place had been the fanciest neighborhood in the nation's capital, for God's sake. People liked to compare all sorts of civil disruptions to being "like a war zone." Keely had never been in military combat, but she thought that day in Washington had been a reasonable facsimile.

She'd even asked her traveling companion, Fred Nakamura, about that on the flight up to Portland. Fred didn't pay much attention to current events and hadn't seen any images of the ambush on Wisconsin Avenue. Keely found an online video for him.

Fred paid close attention and offered his opinion. "More like a terrorist operation than clear-cut urban combat. If you're trying to take, retake or defend a city, you don't have civilians calmly strolling down the street never thinking their next step might be their last. The good guys, the bad guys and everyone caught in between are hyper-vigilant."

"Okay, but still," Keely said.

"It was a domestic terrorist attack," Fred insisted, but he allowed, "it's fair to think of it as being close to a military operation. Both require planning, well-armed personnel and a readiness to kill. By the way, it looks like you and your people did a highly respectable job, taking down the attackers, suffering no KIAs, and limiting harm to the incidentals."

"Incidentals?" Keely asked.

"People in the wrong place at the wrong time."

"Wouldn't they normally be thought of as innocent bystanders?"

"Never met anyone not wearing baby diapers who was totally innocent. Even toddlers start trying to put one over on Mom and Dad."

Thinking of her son, Matthew, Keely couldn't argue with that.

Upon reflection, she felt glad to have Fred on hand.

Even if flight restrictions kept him from bringing his samurai sword along.

Upon landing and deplaning, Keely found a quiet nook in the airport and called Portland Police Bureau Commander Jackie Jessup. As Keely had mentioned to McGill, California and Oregon had reciprocity in allowing licensed investigators from the neighboring state to work in each other's territory. Even so, Keely wanted to interview Tad Thacker at his workplace, if possible.

Putting a potential suspect in a corner at his job tended to produce quicker, more honest results in Keely's experience. If nothing else, the embarrassment of being confronted by the police in front of one's co-workers made the subject of the investigation more motivated to end the experience as quickly as possible, and with a minimum of fuss. Make it look like the whole thing was one big misunderstanding.

To do what Keely had in mind, all the proprieties would have to be observed. The subject's superior would be contacted first. A private space for the interview would be obtained to keep the subject's level of embarrassment manageable. Keely would conduct the questioning in a quiet but serious voice. Fred's stern presence looming in the background would convey the gravity of the situation.

None of that would be possible without, at a minimum, the consent and assistance of the local police and the interview subject's work supervisor. Private investigators couldn't simply enter private property, and certainly not state property, and start questioning people. If a P.I. was stopped at the front door of someone else's property and told to get lost, he or she had better do just that or face a loss of license and possible jail time.

That was why Keely called Commander Jessup.

Back in the days when both women were detectives in their respective departments, Keely had received a call from her colleague in Portland. A dirtbag named Edgar Tinley with a long history of thumping people on the head with beer bottles had upped his game to gashing his girlfriend with a hatchet. He'd only gone so far as to break the skin and terrify the poor woman, but he'd said if she didn't both put out for him and cook his favorite meals on demand, he'd cut off her arms and legs. Maybe her head, too, if she put him in a really bad mood.

Jessup had involved Keely because: "Edgar told his girlfriend he was going down to California to see his brother and get some sun. When he gets back, he said, his girlfriend had better have her head on right or she'd lose it. We have a warrant out on this guy, but he's supposed to be somewhere on the beach in L.A. County. Thought you should know since you have all those great looking women down there, and for all we know Edgar has his hatchet with him. If you catch him before he does any damage in your state, I'd be happy to come down, take custody of the turd and bring him back home."

Jessup emailed mugshots and descriptions of Edgar Tinley to Los Angeles. Keely coordinated the search with the L.A. County

Sheriff's Department, and within two hours the forces of law and order arrested the wanted man in the midst of committing the crime of public urination on Zuma Beach.

"How'd you get him so fast?" Jessup asked when Keely called her with the news.

She said, "He was the only guy on the beach wearing a plaid flannel wetsuit, and he had his wienie wagging in the wind. Not that it was terribly noticeable, but cops down here, we have sharp eyesight."

Jessup laughed and uttered the words nobody ever forgot: "I owe you one."

So when Keely told her old friend that she and her associate were in town and could use a little help in the way of influence and maybe a warm, uniformed body from the local cops, Jessup didn't even need to be reminded that it was time to repay Keely.

"I'm dressing better than ever these days," Commander Jessup said. "Can't remember the last time I put on a uniform, except for ceremonial occasions. But I bet I can get you in to see anyone you want to see in town. So who're you looking at?"

Keely gave her Tad Thacker's name and place of employment.

"What'd he do?"

Keely told Jessup about Thacker's impromptu and totally unwelcome proposal of marriage to Alice Janeway.

"Okay, let me see if I got this right," Jessup said. "This lady, Alice Janeway, was last seen by her boss two weeks ago in Atlanta, didn't show up for work in Washington, D.C. a week ago, and was seriously hassled by this Thacker guy here in Portland six months ago."

"I had to check back with Mr. McGill on that last point, but he confirmed that, yes. Thacker made his move in Portland when Teag Tobias was doing his show here."

After thinking things over for a moment, Jessup said, "I'd be doubtful about all this if Thacker had let a year or more go by without doing anything, but six months, that still seems to be within the realm of possibility. It'd give him time both to bring his feelings to a boil and concoct some damn fool plan."

"Pretty much the way I feel, too," Keely said. "So you'll help us?"

"Us?" Jessup asked.

"I brought my office manager with me."

The police commander laughed. "Really? Well, you'll have to explain to me how these private sector jobs work."

"Glad to," Keely said. "You want to drive your own car or should we swing by and pick you up?"

"What kind of car did you rent?"

"Cadillac Escalade."

"Damn, girl, come and get me. You'll have to tell me about all the other perks you get. Meanwhile, I'll call the Department of Natural Resources and see if I can set up an interview with Don Juan Thacker. If he's not around, we'll talk to any co-worker who knows him. Oh, and by the way, this makes us even for Edgar Tinley."

"He's still locked up?"

"Yes, he is."

Keely said, "Good. Let's hope this one works out the right way, too."

***The White House — Washington, DC***

The uniformed Secret Service officers at the White House recognized McGill's Chevy the moment it stopped at the Southeast Gate. They also remembered Leo but pretended not to know McGill. The duty sergeant asked, "Who's that you got with you, Leo?"

Leo played along. "Hitchhiker I picked up. Says he's got some real good ideas to share with the president."

"Him and a million others," the sergeant said. "He looks a bit shady to me."

McGill lowered his window and said, "Do I have the time to get some popcorn, Mike, before the headliners come on?"

"You know my name, sir?"

"Yours and your people's, too. I believe you're all on my Christmas card list."

The sergeant smiled, dropping the act. He saluted and his officers followed suit.

"Yes, sir. Christmas, birthdays and every other special occasion. You didn't miss one in eight years living here, and we haven't forgotten that. Welcome back, Mr. McGill. SAC Kendry is waiting for you. You know the way to her office."

"I do, but my money says Elspeth will be waiting for me at the door to the building."

An hour earlier, McGill had decidedly mixed feelings about putting in a call to the White House and asking for a favor. He'd thought his connections to the pinnacle of power in the country had been put behind him. That hope had been dashed when he'd been unable to get through to Celsus Crogher, his one-time nemesis and the former head of the president's security detail. Celsus, wonder of wonders, was out of the country on vacation with his wife, Merilee, and their son, Patrick, so named in Patti's honor.

Even without that bow to his wife, McGill told himself he couldn't interrupt the family's getaway just to ask Celsus' opinion of Waylon Jakes, the former Secret Service special agent who did threat evaluations for Teagan Tobias.

With Celsus out of the picture, that left Elspeth Kendry, the current head of presidential protection, for him to call upon. In the old days, he could have simply picked up a phone and asked to see her. That was, have her come to him. But those days were over. Now, he had to go to her, if she'd agree to see him.

Determining even that much would require an intermediary.

Not President Jean Morrissey, of course. Her time was too valuable to arrange small favors for a past tenant of the White House. Well, for him anyway. Patti would be another matter, but

McGill wasn't about to bother her either. He called Jean's brother, Chief of Staff Frank Morrissey, and was pleased that Frank took his call.

"Mr. McGill," Frank said, "good to hear from you."

Sounded like he meant it, too, McGill thought. Then he heard why.

The new chief of staff told McGill, "I had the pleasure of speaking with President Grant and Galia Mindel earlier today."

"You did?" McGill asked.

"Yes, at my predecessor's house. I heard she'd come back to town and decided to drop in. That was forward of me, no doubt, but the job often requires as much. I was surprised and pleased to find President Grant was already there."

That came as news to McGill, too. He'd have to see if Patti volunteered that tidbit to him.

"I'm sure you all had a lot to talk about," McGill said, "and I won't be bold enough to ask what the topics of conversation were. Instead, I'll inquire if I might have a small favor, totally unpolitical in nature."

"Always happy to help a friend," Frank said.

McGill and the chief of staff had gotten along, but friendship was an overstatement. It also implied a return of favor would be claimed someday. As long as it was in proportion, McGill decided he could live with that.

"I'd like to have maybe ten minutes of Elspeth Kendry's time, if she has it to spare, and she wouldn't mind talking with me."

McGill's relationship with Elspeth had been agreeable more often than not, but it had also had a tense moment or two.

Frank didn't see any problem, within the bounds McGill had mentioned.

"I won't ask what you want," he said, "but SAC Kendry will have to decide if it's appropriate to help you."

Frank was finessing things here, McGill understood. He wanted to be able to collect a future favor, but he also wanted to be outside the blast zone if something blew up in McGill's face. Elspeth could be sacrificed, but he, and certainly the president, had to be above reproach.

"That's fine," McGill said.

"Hold the line, please. I'll contact SAC Kendry and get right back to you."

Took less than a minute. "How soon can you be here?" Frank asked. "SAC Kendry's free for the next 45 minutes. After that, she's tied up for the rest of the day."

McGill replied. "Leo can get me there in 15 minutes."

Actually, he made it in twelve.

"Mr. McGill, good to see you again, sir."

"You, too, Elspeth."

She stood behind her office desk. Hadn't bothered to meet McGill at the door. Elspeth's secretary had shown McGill in. He shook Elspeth's hand and declined the offer of something to drink. Elspeth thanked her secretary and dismissed her. McGill and his hostess took their seats.

He said, "I won't ask, but I hope Frank Morrissey didn't take you away from anything to see me."

"I won't tell you if he did, but I can say the chief of staff and I understand each other quite well. We're pretty much cut from the same cloth."

"Stylish and tough as nails."

Elspeth didn't respond verbally but the corners of her mouth turned up.

McGill said, "I've come to get your opinion about someone who might have a bearing on a case I'm working. That is, assuming you even know him, of course. His name is Waylon Jakes."

Elspeth's eyes narrowed and she squeezed the padded arms of her chair.

McGill went with the obvious response. "You know him, but don't think of him fondly. If I've got that right, I apologize. I didn't know of any past connection."

Elspeth closed her eyes and maybe counted to ten, McGill thought.

That was as far as he'd gotten before she looked at him again.

"You really don't know him?" she asked.

"Heard his name for the first time this morning. Got it from a private sector bodyguard named Haskell Carver. For what it's worth, Haskell seems like a nice guy."

"Jakes isn't."

McGill gave it a beat. "I told Frank Morrissey that my agenda has nothing to do with politics. I'll tell you I'm not interested in anything that has to do with either past Secret Service operations or you personally. I was told Jakes did three threat evaluations for a man who employs a woman who might be missing. The only thing that interests me is whether you think Jakes does a good job in that capacity. If it turns out that's so, I'll need to see if there's any connection between the possibly missing woman and the people who made the threats."

Elspeth leaned forward and put her hands on her desk.

"Was the missing woman also the subject of threats?" she asked.

"Not that I've heard. The target, to my knowledge, is a man named Teagan Tobias. The woman works for him. It's still a possibility she just took off somewhere on her own. But if she didn't, hurting her would be a good way to hurt Tobias."

"Is the woman his wife?"

"No. They collaborate professionally."

"How long has she been gone?" Elspeth asked.

"She's a week overdue for work; hasn't been heard from in two weeks."

"The collaboration has been successful, at least professionally?"

"Yes, but … not as fulfilling as the woman thought it could be."

Elspeth sat back and thought about that. Then she told McGill, "Jakes is a good threat evaluator. If he sees something bad coming, he's not imagining it."

"Thank you, Elspeth. I appreciate your taking the time to see me."

He started to get up, but Elspeth raised a hand to stop him.

"I'll tell you something I think, too. If the woman you're looking for left of her own volition, she'd have sent some kind of message by now. 'Sorry, I just can't hack it anymore.' Or 'I'm sitting here in paradise, and you're not. Fuck you.' She'd have said something."

McGill asked, "You think she's dead?"

"That or wishing she was," Elspeth said.

McGill was on his way out of the building, lost in thought, navigating the corridors from memory, when he heard a voice call out to him. "Mr. McGill, it's so good to see you … but you're looking pale again."

Focusing on the moment, McGill saw the White House physician, Dr. Artemus Nicolaides. He said, "Pale even for an Irishman?" It was an old joke they shared.

"Well, maybe not that chalky. I think I can see the tinge of a fading tan."

The two men shook hands and the physician said in a serious tone. "You and the president are feeling well? You're not skipping your annual examinations just because Patricia has left office?"

Nick was among those people who'd been asked to address the former Chief Executive by her first name. Thing was, McGill couldn't remember if he had a check-up scheduled, and he hadn't heard if Patti had seen her doctor lately.

The situation was as plain to Nick as a *Washington Post* headline.

He shook his head and gently took McGill's arm. "Come with me. I'll give you my ten-minute office special. No charge."

McGill let Nick lead him down the hallway. The physician's quarters were nearby and McGill thought it wouldn't hurt to get a quick once-over. He felt sure he was in good health, but this way he'd have grounds to ask Patti if she had a checkup scheduled.

"I did a five-mile run this morning," he told Nick as they entered the doctor's office. "Averaged just over seven minutes per mile while carrying on a conversation."

Nick nodded. "That's very good, but the human body is more than a heart and two lungs. Take off your jacket and shirt and sit on the table."

McGill did as he was told. Nick took his patient's blood pressure, found it to be within normal limits. Approved of the heart rhythm he listened to. He checked out McGill's eyes, ears, nose and mouth. They all passed muster as well.

"Any problems with urination or bowel movements?" Nick asked.

McGill shook his head.

"Good. You remember those polyps in your colon you had removed?"

"I was anesthetized at the time, but I haven't forgotten being wheeled into the O.R."

"You are not quite 50 years old yet, but I think it would still be a good idea for you to have a colonoscopy. Better safe than sorry."

McGill was about to protest, but he thought better of it. He wanted to have as many more good years with Patti and his kids as he could. He wanted to be there for Sweetie and all the other people he either loved or had working for him. So why put up a fuss?

"You're right, Nick. Should I use the same doctor as last time?"

"I'm sorry to say he's passed away."

"That guy? He was younger than me."

"He was also a mountain-climber, and he took a fall."

McGill winced, but he appreciated Nick skipping the opportunity to tell him not to take any foolish chances with his life.

"I can give you the name of someone good," Nick said.

Those words sparked a memory for McGill. He recalled Haskell Carver telling him that Alice Janeway had acted like she'd whacked her funny-bone. On more than one occasion.

He said, "Nick, I recently heard about a woman who seemed to have a tingling in either her left arm or hand. Maybe both. What kind of a condition might that indicate?"

"How old is this woman?"

"Twenty-eight."

"Would you know if she was being treated for cancer? Chemotherapy is notorious for causing neuropathy."

"I didn't hear any mention of that, and I don't think she could have done her job if she was being treated in that way."

Nick scratched the back of his head, as if that would aid his thought process. "There are viral and bacterial infections that can cause this symptom. Epstein-Barr virus for example. Leprosy or diphtheria might also be a cause. Then there's HIV or possibly an inherited disorder."

McGill said, "So, in any case, this could be a symptom of something serious."

Nick nodded. "It's certainly something you'd want a physician to evaluate. This woman is someone you know personally, my friend?"

"She's someone I'm looking for," McGill told him.

Nick replied, "Don't take any chances. Find her as quickly as you can."

***Portland Police Bureau/Department of Natural Resources — Portland, Oregon***

Keely Powell and Commander Jackie Jessup of the Portland Police Bureau hugged each other upon making their re-acquaintance. Fred Nakamura offered the commander a polite but subtle bow. His gesture was returned in a like manner.

"Is either of you carrying a weapon?" Jessup asked.

"C'mon, Jackie," Keely said. "We know better than that. Oregon doesn't recognize any other state's concealed carry permits. Heck, Fred even left his samurai sword at home. Of course, there's no concealing that thing."

The commander gave Fred an appraising look. "Samurai sword,

huh? Well, I don't want anyone losing his head on my watch — not without my say-so, anyway. Still, I'm glad you two are observing all our legal niceties. You want me to drive that rich man's truck over to the Department of Natural Resources?"

"Only if you're thinking of buying one and want to do a test-drive," Keely said.

Fred shook his head. "Not even. I'm the only driver listed on the rental agreement. Wouldn't want to break any rules."

Jessup laughed. "Amazing he can say that with a straight face, but rules are rules."

The two women sat in the backseat so as not to trifle with Fred's driving prerogative.

"I got in touch with a woman named Marlys Reed at DNR," Jessup told Keely. "She's Tad Thacker's boss. He's an environmental engineer; she's one, too, plus she has a Master of Public Administration degree. I've got an MPA myself, but I think my curriculum must've been a bit different from hers."

Keely laughed. "Yeah, DNR people probably don't think they're the heroes we cops do."

"Maybe just champions of another stripe," Jessup said. "Be a hell of a world without trees, clean air and water."

"Okay, point taken," Keely said.

Even Fred nodded, without ever taking his eyes off the road.

Jessup said, "Anyway, I told Ms. Reed the story about her boy Tad and Ms. Alice Janeway. She wasn't amused by Tad's approach to romance. Said if he'd tried that kind of thing with a co-worker she'd show him the door, and put a boot to his backside to make sure he left quickly. She said Tad will be waiting for us. If Tad wants, she'll stay and be his witness to the proceedings. If he wants to talk to us without her around, that's okay, too. As long as we fill her in afterward. If he refuses to talk at all, he'll be put on paid leave and maybe face a disciplinary hearing for bringing discredit to the reputation of the DNR."

"Maybe?" Keely asked.

Commander Jessup grinned. "Well, sweetpea, the great state

of Oregon can't just take the word of a California P.I. The DNR would have to do its own investigation before coming to a swift and righteous decision."

Keely sighed. "Sheesh, that due process stuff, you never know where it'll turn up."

Tad Thacker knocked twice, politely, on his superior's office door two minutes after Keely and Jessup had introduced themselves to the DNR supervisor, Marlys Reed. Fred had stayed with the Cadillac, at Keely's suggestion. Her revised opinion was Fred's presence might intimidate Thacker, put him ill at ease and maybe even make him clam up.

"I might keep him from shooting somebody, too," Fred suggested.

Jessup pushed her suit coat back, revealing her duty weapon. "I've got that covered."

Fred didn't argue. He knew women could get testy if you even hinted they weren't cold-blooded killers.

After meeting her visitors, the only question Marlys Reed had for them was, "This ring Thacker tried to give the woman, was it … substantial?"

Keely said, "I didn't get a detailed description, but in context it was big enough to scare her."

"Right." She picked up the phone on her desk and made the call. "Thacker, come see me in my office immediately."

She hadn't delivered the summons with either a shout or a snarl, but the chill tone used to convey those words made both Keely and Jessup wonder how many former DNR workers had heard the same thing on their last days of employment.

After Thacker knocked on the door, Reed used the same voice to say, "Come in."

The door opened but Tad Thacker didn't step inside the office immediately, as if he preferred to hear any bad news from a distance.

Marlys Reed wasn't having any of that. "Jesus Christ, Tad, this is a meeting, not an execution. Get in here and close the door behind you."

He stepped inside, but left the door open, and jumped an inch or so into the air when he noticed Keely and Jessup sitting in the guest chairs to his left. While he was still trying to work out what the presence of strangers meant, Marlys told him again, "Close the door."

Tad clearly didn't like that, but he did as he was told.

Marlys introduced the visitors to him. "The lady to your immediate left is Commander Jackie Jessup of the Portland police. Next to her is Ms. Keely Powell, a private investigator from California. Ladies, this is Tad Thacker, environmental engineer."

Thacker processed the intros sequentially. Looking at Jessup and Keely, he said, "I didn't do anything wrong." Turning to his boss, he asked, "You sure I'm not being fired?"

Marlys said, "Nobody's accusing you of a crime, Tad, but these ladies have brought me some disturbing news about you. It will be in the interest of keeping your job if you answer their questions directly and honestly. Some of what you have to say may be embarrassing to you, and if you choose, I'll step out of the office, and you can speak to them directly. I will, however, ask them for a summary when all of you are finished. I don't think I'll need specific details, just a … a broad recap of your discussion. So would you like me to stay or leave?"

Tad turned to look at the two visitors.

Jessup told him, "We have no reason at this moment to think you've committed any crime, Mr. Thacker. It may even be that you might help us solve one. You think you could do that?"

Keely added, "You don't even have to talk to us at all. You can walk back out that door right now, if you like. Only that would make us wonder why you don't want to cooperate."

The implicit threat in Keely's words scared Thacker, but the fear was quickly replaced by a moment of epiphany. He knew what the two unfamiliar women wanted. He turned to look at his supervisor and could tell she knew what they wanted, too. What he couldn't work out just then was what his best course of action was.

Marlys narrowed his options. She said, "All right, *I'll* make a decision. I'm going to step out for a bit. I suggest again that you answer any question these women have for you, and do so honestly. In my opinion, as the supervisor of this department, that would be in your best professional interest."

Keely kept a straight face, but she thought Reed's message was pretty damn diplomatic for one engineer speaking to another. The supervisor stepped out of her office and closed the door behind her. Thacker looked at the two remaining women.

Jessup said to him, "Why don't you take a seat, Mr. Thacker?"

The only one available belonged to his boss.

The look in his eyes said he wasn't about to sit there.

Jessup smiled and got up. She sat in Marlys Reed's chair. "I'm comfortable sitting behind a big desk. You sit beside my friend, Keely, Mr. Thacker. Go ahead; she doesn't bite."

He eased sideways onto the empty chair.

He leaned toward the door in case he needed to make a break for it.

Jessup looked at Keely and asked, "You see the light go on in Mr. Thacker's eyes?"

Keely nodded. "He knows why we're here."

Thacker looked from one woman to the other, trying to see if he was being tricked.

Keely added, "It was probably the only time in his life he did anything like that."

"You think?" Jessup asked. "My guess is he tried something like it in, say, high school."

Thacker's face turned red.

"Is that right, Tad?" Keely asked. "Was there a girl … You know what? I think I understand now. There *was* a girl in your past, and she reminded you of Alice Janeway."

"Is that right, Mr. Thacker?" Jessup asked. "Alice looks like someone else?"

Tad's eyes started to fill with tears.

Keely sighed. "Life can be a bitch, can't it? The girl in your past found someone else."

Tad shook his head. In a whisper, he said, "No, she died."

That sent chills through both women, thinking what it might mean.

Portland being her jurisdiction, Jessup asked, "*How* did she die, Mr. Thacker?"

Tears streaming down his cheeks now, he said, "The tour bus went off a mountain road in Italy. The driver had been drinking."

The memory clearly drew on a well of sorrow that still pained Thacker, but the two women felt a sense of relief. Each of them had thought that someone who grew up to become any kind of an engineer might know how to sabotage a bus. They seriously doubted, though, that a young Tad had known how to inebriate a working bus driver.

With tears running down his cheeks, Thacker said, "Eight of my classmates died. One of the moms was a travel agent, set up the trip at a discounted price for anyone in my class who wanted to go. *I* wanted to go, but even with the cheap price my family couldn't afford it."

"Other friends died, too?" Keely asked.

"Three more besides Jenny."

Jessup said, "I'm sorry to have to bring this up, Mr. Thacker, but did Jenny return the affection you felt for her?"

He smiled through his sorrow. "Yeah, she did. Most of the kids couldn't figure it out. I mean, I was smart. I'm not ugly. I just couldn't … maneuver through social situations like the other kids. They got along — or dissed — each other without having to give it a moment's thought. I had to plan every step I made."

He covered his face with his hands. The two women let him have a moment.

Looking at Jessup again, he told her, "Jenny wasn't like the other kids. She was kind. I think I became a charity case for her at first, but then she got to know me a little and liked me for who I was. I tried not to think things might go farther eventually, but I couldn't help myself."

Keely asked, "Did you ever do or say anything to put her off in any way?"

Thacker turned to her. "No, never. I was just thinking, hoping, dreaming. I *really* wanted to go on that trip with her. I was the only one who didn't go who showed up at the bus that took the others to the airport. I wanted to say goodbye and tell them to have fun."

"Did you say those things, Mr. Thacker?" Jessup asked.

He nodded.

"Everyone appreciated your sentiment?" Keely followed up.

"They did. Jenny's mom, Mrs. Nyland, was one of the chaperones. She gave me a big hug. The guys who went shook my hand. The girls hugged me, too, and Jenny … she gave me a kiss."

Before his grief could overcome him again, Jessup said, "So how did you come to see a photo of Alice Janeway?"

"There was a picture of her in *Playbill.* A guy in the office had a copy on his desk for *Every Last Bastard in the World.* I saw Alice's photo in a side-story, and I immediately felt it must have been Jenny's doing that I saw that picture. She wanted me to meet Alice, wanted us to be together. I felt the same way."

"But Alice didn't share that feeling," Keely said.

Thacker only shook his head, keeping his eyes down.

"I was foolish, deceiving myself," he said, "acting like a high school kid again." He looked up. "I've really made a lot of progress since I was a kid, but seeing Alice's picture … I ran right out and bought an engagement ring without ever thinking how crazy that was."

Keely said, "You came back to the theater the following night, Mr. Thacker, after you had some time to think about things."

He took and released a deep breath, wiped the tears from his eyes. "I read the review of the show, how Mr. Tobias lashes out at people who make him angry. I could understand that. The newspaper story also said he was very funny. There are times, almost every day, when I wish I could laugh more. Knew how and when to do it. So, I went to see the show, but they wouldn't let me stay."

"Did that make you mad, Mr. Thacker?" Jessup asked.

"Yeah, it did. But then it made me laugh, too. I thought I should send a letter to Teag Tobias and tell him what happened. Maybe he could use it in his show."

"Did you do that?" Keely asked.

He shook his head. "I was going to send an apology to Alice Janeway, too, but I didn't do that either. It would have been too painful to explain myself."

Keely and Jessup looked at each other, silently asking if they bought everything Thacker had told them. They exchanged small nods. Still, Jessup had one more question.

"Mr. Thacker, have you done any traveling in the past month?"

He shook his head. "Just to work and back. I was offered a ticket to a Seahawks game in Seattle, but I didn't go. I like watching football, but the stadium up there gets too loud for me."

Keely stood up and extended her hand to Thacker. He rose to take it.

"Thank you for your time, Mr. Thacker. We appreciate your talking to us, and please accept our condolences for the loss of your classmates."

He bobbed his head in appreciation, and then he asked, "Alice is okay, isn't she?"

Keely took a beat before saying, "My client is someone who's concerned about her well-being."

A look of sorrow came into Thacker's eyes, but he only nodded and left the office.

Marlys Reed returned and Jessup gave her a summary of the interview.

Keely got a confirmation that Thacker hadn't missed any work in the past month.

***Wallace Rhymes' House — Georgetown, Texas***

Maj Olson had told Solana, Wallace Rhymes' housekeeper, that she intended to search the place from top to bottom. That was actually the reverse of how she began her efforts. She started in the basement and worked her way up. Solana accompanied Maj downstairs and showed her how to use the mansion's intercom system.

"You and I will be the only ones here until *Señor* Rhymes returns home from his painting," she said. "If you need my help, you push the button and I will come."

She pushed an intercom button to demonstrate.

Maj got the feeling that, the basement aside, Solana didn't want her wandering through the house by herself. "Does Mr. Rhymes stay away long when he paints outdoors?"

From the look Solana gave Maj, the investigator felt her question had been deemed impertinent.

"Is not for *me* to ask," Solana said. Meaning Maj shouldn't either.

Undaunted, Maj said, "Okay, but don't you know from experience how long he tends to stay out?"

Maj could see Solana wanted to say no, only she suspected her denial wouldn't be believed. So instead of lying, she gave the fuzziest possible reply: "Is different every time."

Maj had showered that morning, so she felt certain it wasn't her body odor that was offending Solana so seriously. Maj didn't know what the problem was, but the woman was beginning to tick her off. "So Mr. Rhymes could be gone anywhere from minutes to hours? Maybe even days?"

Solana understood Maj was mocking her.

That only worsened her mood. So she repeated. "You push the button if you need me. Then I come." And only then was the implication. Solana started to go, but then she turned back. "My suite is on the top floor. Is private. *¿Comprende?*"

"How will I know which part of the floor is yours?"

"*All* of it," Solana said.

"*Okay,* your quarters are off limits. Makes my job that much easier."

*Sotto voce* but still perfectly audible, each woman said, "Bitch."

Solana climbed the stairs to the first floor, leaving Maj alone. So be it, Maj thought, as she started to search every nook and cranny big enough to hide John Wayne's pretty old hat. She looked anywhere an elderly man might have taken it off, set it down and forgotten all about it.

The basement had a polished cement floor that was largely covered by thick rectangular black rubber mats. The ceilings were high compared to most below ground spaces Maj had seen and had recessed lights. Outside of the area apportioned to the house's HVAC and laundry facilities, the remainder of the space was an open floor-plan that was set aside for athletic endeavors that included ping-pong, pool and martial arts.

Photos on the wall area adjacent to a judo mat showed the Rhymes offspring, in younger years, each clothed in the white gi worn in Japanese martial arts. One shot had the kids lined up, standing next to a man who must have been their *sensei.* He wore a black belt. So did Catherine Clark, who looked to be about 15. Her fraternal twin, Hank, standing next to her had a brown belt. The younger identical twins, Clint and Cole, had purple belts.

Three other pictures showed Catherine tossing each of her brothers to the mat. A final photo showed all three boys piling on Catherine at the same time. Her *sensei* looked on as if he expected her to overcome all of them.

Studying that last picture, Maj tried to decide if it was posed all in fun. She thought maybe. Then again, it might be her brothers were giving her what they considered to be well-deserved payback. A girl showing them up? Well, they'd show her.

Thinking about the meeting she and Gene had with Catherine, though, Maj remembered the story of the Rhymes siblings blaming each other for their mother's death. That would be something that might have felt real while they were very young, but not likely as they'd matured.

They looked competitive but not hostile in the photos, and that's no small tribute to a man who'd raised four kids without a wife. Having hired help and plenty of money to spend would have made things easier, but giving the kids a moral grounding and an emotional balance, that would still be a big job for a single parent.

Chauvinist that she was, Maj felt the task would be harder for a man than a woman.

Failing to find the missing hat in the basement, Maj moved upstairs. The floor plan on the ground level included a living room, a library, a home office, an artist's studio with a north-facing skylight, a family room with a huge flat screen television and a high-end stereo system, two dining rooms: one casual and relatively small; one formal and large, a very big kitchen and two powder rooms.

Maj combed through all of them, looking into every space in which the missing hat might have been misplaced. She took into account Wallace Rhymes' height and how high he might have reached if for some reason he'd been standing on a chair. She looked low as well as high, in case the old man had been moving about on his hands and knees for some reason.

With Maj working from one room to the next, Solana stayed one jump ahead of her, as if they were two pieces in some oversized board game. The queen of the third floor didn't say a word to Maj nor did the detective speak to her. Even in the silence, though, their mutual antipathy seemed to grow.

By the time Maj finished examining the main floor of the house, she was thirsty. She didn't presume to raid her client's refrigerator, but she'd already learned which kitchen cabinet held drinking glasses. She chose a mid-sized glass and filled it with cool water from the sink. Solana was eyeing her from one of the room's two entrances.

"Are you finished?" the housekeeper asked.

Maj shook her head and said, "One time I was looking for a stolen train. I had to look through several states to find it, but with some good help I did. You understand what I'm saying?"

Solana understood well enough to give Maj a dirty look and

walk away.

She'd no sooner departed than the thought hit Maj: It's more than personal dislike; this woman had something to hide. Damn, had she stolen the hat? If so, why? Long-term employment with Wallace Rhymes had to be more valuable to her than even the $100,000 the hat might fetch.

Of course, if she could have both …

Maj rinsed out the drinking glass she'd used and put it in the dish drain. She went upstairs, and looking behind her she saw that Solana was no longer tailing her. Instead, the housekeeper had anticipated Maj. Solana was sitting on a chair in front of a door at the far end of the second- floor hallway. Her legs were crossed at the ankles and her arms were folded across her chest.

Her body language was clear: *You won't get past me without a fight.*

Maj wasn't about to go that far, but if she ever bumped into Solana on a street corner, and there were no cops around, the two of them might have a frank discussion. The kind punctuated with punches and kicks. Maybe even a tooth or two on the sidewalk.

The three bedrooms on the left side of the hallway were furnished for boys: Texas Rangers pennants and posters, a basketball signed by Hakeem Olajuwon, a baseball signed by Nolan Ryan, a signed poster of Tuff Hedeman riding a bull at a rodeo.

Maj was no judge of sports collectibles, but she got the feeling that all of the inscribed memorabilia were worth a pretty penny. That made her think that if a thief had slipped into Wallace Rhymes' house — or even knew someone who worked there — he would have taken more than a cowboy hat.

Maybe that was reason enough to think Wallace Rhymes had mislaid his chapeau outside of the house. But if that innocent explanation was the case, why the hell was Solana behaving so defensively? Even without a clear answer, Maj felt the woman was definitely hiding something.

Was the housekeeper Rhymes' secret sweetie? Their boudoir was one floor up? Had Solana felt entitled to some additional off-the-books compensation?

Maj searched the bedrooms on the other side of the hallway. Catherine's room held no sports paraphernalia. Popular culture was more her thing, especially in the area of music. A framed poster of The Highwaymen held pride of place. It was signed by all four members: Johnny, Waylon, Willie and Kris. Kristofferson also had a solo poster, also signed, and a copy of his handwritten lyrics to "Sunday Mornin' Comin' Down."

Maj looked closer at the song lyrics. Damn, she thought, if that was the original rendering, it had to be worth a small fortune. She wondered why Catherine didn't keep the thing at her club.

Wallace Rhymes' bedroom was twice the size of the others. No sports or music nicknacks here, only a half-dozen paintings done by the man himself, and Maj's opinion of his work continued to grow. He'd done portraits of his four children, another of his late wife and a pastoral setting that might have come from somewhere on his land, but also might have been an imagined slice of heaven.

What all of the bedrooms had in common was that none of them held the missing hat.

Maj had searched high, low, and in between with no luck.

With Solana's quarters off limits, that meant … Maj needed a really big ladder.

### *McGill Investigations International — Washington, DC*

McGill and Sweetie sat in his office talking about the status of the "Where's Alice?" investigation thus far.

"I called Waylon Jakes, despite Haskell Carver's warning that he wouldn't talk to me and the look in Elspeth Kendry's eyes that said she wouldn't mind shooting Jakes," McGill said.

"And you found him perfectly charming?" Sweetie asked.

"Nah. He did come across as a jerk: sour, short-tempered and superior."

"He showed no deference to your formerly prominent position?"

McGill grinned. “Not a bit. That was okay, but if he’d gotten any surlier I might have liked to break his nose on general principles.”

“You ruffian,” Sweetie said with a smirk.

“Yeah, that’s me. Anyway, Jakes did spit out that he no longer works for Tobias. He said Tobias refused to implement any of his suggestions to keep himself safe. That being the case, Jakes stopped working for him. Said he didn’t want to be blamed if Tobias got killed due to his own stupidity.”

“Did Jakes say anything about the nature of the threats or give you the names of the people making them?” Sweetie asked.

McGill shook his head. “The only thing he’d tell me was the threats are real. Haskell Carver didn’t go into detail either. He only said they came from two men and a woman.”

Sweetie mulled the situation for a moment. “Maybe the hostility has more to do with business matters than the material Tobias uses in his act.”

McGill said, “Hadn’t thought of that, but, sure, money causes lots of problems. What kind are you thinking of?”

“Well, Tobias doesn’t use any elephants in his act that I know of, but he is running a traveling circus, isn’t he?”

“There are clowns certainly, if only to serve as the butts of Tobias’ jokes and rants,” McGill agreed.

Sweetie said, “Okay, so let’s take a speculative look at some of his overhead. He has to pay for the theaters he uses. Then there are the people who do the lights, sound system, ticket-taking and security. All backstage people, like Alice Janeway, are on the payroll, and maybe some of those people, if not all, make union wages.”

“There’s also advertising, travel, lodging and meals to pay for,” McGill said. “Now that you’ve brought up money, I wonder what the guy’s break-even point is.”

Sweetie nodded. “I’m also wondering how well his show has been doing the last year or two. We might try to find out if he’s been making his nut. If he hasn’t, maybe he doesn’t think he has the time to worry about someone punching his ticket or at least considers death threats as secondary problems."

"I can ask Patti to call Dorie McBride, ask her how artistically successful and financially healthy Tobias is, but …"

"What?" Sweetie asked.

"But I'm starting to revise my thinking about the overall situation. The way Teag Tobias performs, and probably the way he runs the business end of his operation, he's likely to be the personal magnet of any tangible hostility. I don't think anyone who hates him would get much satisfaction from attacking someone he employs. After all, if he's the SOB he plays onstage, he might just laugh off someone else taking a fall."

Sweetie considered McGill's notion and nodded.

"I think you're right. So, if that's the case, we're still left with our central question."

"Yeah," McGill said. "Where's Alice?"

***Wallace Rhymes' House — Georgetown, Texas***

In the unlocked garage behind Wallace Rhymes' house, along with a black Chevy pick-up truck, a silver Lincoln MKZ and a gorgeous racing green MGA roadster, Maj Olson found what she needed: a telescoping aluminum ladder. Thanks to her background as a collegiate athlete, she'd maintained a regular and vigorous exercise routine. Gene Beck had added to her fitness repertoire with some of the drills he'd learned in special forces training.

She had no trouble lifting the ladder, carrying it to the back of the house and silently propping it up directly beneath a third-floor window. Pushing it up to full extension presented two problems: could she do it quietly — no metal-on-metal shrieking — and could she do it without scarring the outside brickwork?

There was only one way to find out. Exerting great care and as much lift as her muscles could manage she began to push the ladder's extension upward from its base frame. Happily, that went far more easily than she would have thought. No high-pitched noises to attract Solana, no gouges in any bricks. Still, there remained one essential concern: Would the darn thing take her as high as she wanted to go?

The idea, of course, was to get a peek in the housekeeper's hidden realm. Even if Solana's relationship with Wallace Rhymes was perfectly platonic, that didn't mean she mightn't have taken advantage of the old man and swiped his hat. Would he even suspect the woman of treachery? Likely not, if he hadn't seen any evidence of a character defect in the past. If Rhymes was also a gentleman, as Maj felt he was, he'd never dream of searching the woman's quarters.

In fact, likely as not, Rhymes wouldn't even believe Maj if she told him she'd spotted the hat in Solana's quarters. He might be far more upset that Maj had peeked through a window. With that in mind and not knowing when Rhymes might return, Maj put her muscles into raising the last section of the extension.

It stopped just short of one of Solana's windows. Maj saw she should be able to peer through the glass by standing two or three rungs below the top of the ladder. Thank God for three things: no shade was pulled down on the window; she was not afraid of heights, and she had the climbing talents of a young simian.

Remembering that she'd need to document anything she saw, Maj put her phone in her jacket pocket for easy retrieval. She took a quick look around, said a brief prayer that neither Solana nor Rhymes would see what she was doing, and started climbing. She scurried upward as if the devil was chasing her, warning that you don't get out of hell that easily, but she still had the time to form an idea for a less dangerous alternative should she ever need to snoop a house's upper reaches again.

Keep a drone with a camera and a relatively silent motor in her car.

Meantime, the low-tech approach got her the look through Solana's window that she'd wanted. Better yet, she had a view of Solana's bedroom. The housekeeper was commendably tidy. Her bed was neatly made. No clothing was draped over a doorknob. A pair of slippers was tidily placed at the foot of the bed.

Unfortunately, John Wayne's hat wasn't left sitting in the middle of Solana's bed or atop her dresser. It might've been in the room's closet, but that door was closed. For a reckless moment, Maj considered seeing if she could lift the lower half of the window and creep inside. Take a good look around all of the housekeeper's personal domain.

It wasn't so much her conscience as the fear of dire consequences that told her: *No damn way you do anything that stupid.*

Maj sighed. She'd done a lot of work for nothing … but then she saw the hat. It had been there all along. Not on the bed or the dresser but in a framed photograph that hung on the wall directly opposite her vantage point. The subject of the shot was an elderly Latino with a prominent belly. From the ground up, he was wearing cowboy boots, blue jeans, a Western shirt and John Wayne's hat.

All of that and a beaming smile.

Making sure she didn't fall, Maj eased her phone out of her pocket. She had to get a picture or five of that photograph. Her iPhone had a 12-megapixel camera, and there was adequate sunlight in the room, without reflecting directly off the window, to get some good shots. Not wanting to stint on her effort, she clicked off *ten* shots from different angles to improve her odds of getting something good.

Maj had just finished and was about to slip the phone back into her jacket pocket when a voice from below said, "Having fun up there?"

Maj missed putting the phone in her pocket as she turned her upper body to see who'd caught her. The phone fell. Wasn't a chance in hell it'd survive a fall from that height. Of course, she wouldn't do too well, either, if she took a spill. So she took the prudent step of securing her position before worrying about anything else.

Turned out the phone didn't break at all.

Gene Beck, standing below, caught it.

Maj also didn't come to grief. Instead of falling, she quickly slid down the frame of the ladder. Her shoes protected her feet from any abrasions. Her bare hands didn't fare quite as well. She'd given herself bright red welts on each of them.

"Damn, that hurts!"

"You find the hat?" Gene asked.

"Didn't you hear what I said about my hands?"

She held them out in case he'd missed seeing the wounds.

Gene said, "I've got some disinfectant in my car. You'll be fine."

Gene found the photos on Maj's phone, stared at them and, inevitably, whistled.

"Well, look at that." He scanned each shot a second time.

Looking on, Maj was pleased with her work, but she told Gene, "Let's put that ladder back fast."

"Don't hurry on my account," a voice said.

Maj and Gene turned their heads and saw Wallace Rhymes.

Solana stood next to him pointing a damning finger at Maj.

***McGill Investigations International — Washington, DC***

Sweetie left McGill to go to her own office and call her husband, Putnam Shady. Putnam, through his association with billionaire Darren Drucker, had gained insights into the finances of the pluperfectly wealthy. Both Sweetie and McGill felt sure that Teagan Tobias didn't qualify for that stratospheric realm of riches, but it was possible Tobias had brushed up against — or pissed off — someone in that class.

In either case, it was possible an interested or offended party had made discreet inquiries about Tobias' place among society's elite. To wit, who had the bigger fortune?

It was always reassuring to the immensely wealthy to learn they were running at or near the head of the pack. Joy might also be found in discovering that someone else's fortune might be measured in piddling millions. Teag Tobias' net worth might barely rise even to that level, but there was no downside in Sweetie asking Putnam to see if he could find out anything on the performer's financial situation.

McGill had decided that he'd have to speak directly with Tobias tomorrow morning. Knowing that three people actually meant to do him harm, possibly even kill him, just might mean that anyone working for the man might become collateral damage. Yes, Tobias might not be upset by someone else's death, but if the message, "You're next," was included in the murder, that could put Tobias off his game, harm the quality of his act, and he wouldn't like that.

McGill took the chance that Dorie McBride would take a direct call from him, not needing any intercession on Patti's part. Maybe the fact that one of his investigators, Gene Beck, was also a client of hers would work in his favor. Apparently, something did. The legendary Hollywood super-agent answered on the first ring.

"Mr. McGill, how nice to hear from you," she said effusively.

McGill was no sucker. He knew immediately that Dorie was playing some angle.

"If you've got another project for Patti," he said, "you'll have to speak with her directly."

There was a moment's silence. McGill interpreted it as Dorie recalculating a new approach to whatever it was she wanted. "Well, I have any number of interesting possibilities for Patricia. I just need to see which one might best appeal to her, and would fit in with the important work she already has at hand."

McGill understood perfectly. Dorie didn't have anything in mind for Patti. Something else, related to him, had stoked her fires. It took only a heartbeat for him to make the jump: Caitie. Had she come up with —

"You've read Caitlin's magnificent new screenplay, of course," Dorie said.

McGill hadn't. Even so, he said, "How is it you've read it, Dorie?"

There was just a half-beat of embarrassed silence before the doyenne of L.A. show biz said, "Well, you know, of course, I have friends almost everywhere. One of them in Paris passed the word to me."

"Have you actually read the script, Dorie?"

A slightly longer silence followed. “No, but I trust my friend in Paris completely. Not only that, but others in town, L.A. I mean, have also heard the same raves. A bidding war is about to break out any second now. I just hope to have a fair chance at presenting the advantages I might offer to Caitlin as her representative.”

McGill wondered if the script was just a gag his youngest child had concocted as a giggle. If it really existed, he thought he’d have heard about it through the family grapevine. Given that he’d intended to ask a favor from Dorie, he decided to play along.

“Well,” McGill said, “you’ve done well by Gene Beck.”

“And that’s just the beginning for him,” Dorie agreed.

“I could mention that to Caitie,” McGill said.

“I’d be so grateful if you did.” Then, knowing one hand always washed the other, she asked, “Is there anything I might do for you in return?”

“You know, Dorie, it just so happens that there is.”

He asked her to give him the lowdown on Teagan Tobias’ standing as a showbiz figure, both critically and financially. She agreed immediately, not even asking why he wanted to know. It wasn’t hard for her to guess that it had to do with a case he was working.

“Is there anything else?” she asked.

McGill decided to take a shot in the dark. “Have you ever heard of Alice Janeway?”

Dorie sounded embarrassed when she said, “No, I’m afraid not.”

She was clearly hoping she hadn’t slipped and failed to take note of an up-and-comer.

“Alice works backstage for Teagan Tobias. As far as I know, she has no performing, writing or directing credits, but she’s hoping for a breakthrough. If she’s out in L.A. knocking on doors, I’d appreciate knowing about it.”

“There’s no end to *hopefuls* out here,” Dorie said.

McGill told her, “I know, but if you could ask around about Alice, that’d be a big help to me — and you did ask if there was anything else you might do for me."

Dorie understood perfectly. "If she's out here, I'll find her and let you know. What was her name again?"

"Alice Janeway."

"Oh, dear. She'd have to change that."

Tell it to Meryl Streep, McGill thought.

He said goodbye to Dorie and then sent a text to Caitie in Paris.

*Ma chère enfant, téléphone-moi.* My dear child, call me.

*Immédiatement.* Immediately.

Caitie had warned him about using Google translations, but he thought this message was pretty clear, even if linguistically amiss.

The phone on McGill's desk rang, and for a split-second McGill thought he'd nailed it. Then he saw Keely Powell was calling.

McGill picked up. "All's well, Keely?"

"If you mean were there hassles of any kind, no. Everything's good."

"Glad to hear it. So what did you learn?"

"A friend of mine on the Portland cops and I had a sit-down with Tad Thacker at his place of employment. In his boss's office, in fact. She offered Thacker the choice of her leaving or staying for the interview. When he didn't decide right away, she left it to me and my friend, Commander Jackie Jessup, to speak with Tad."

"Please give the commander my thanks for her help," McGill said.

"I will, and I'm also buying her dinner tonight on the company tab."

"That's fine. So what did you learn about Mr. Thacker."

"He hasn't missed a day of work in over three years, hasn't been out of state this year."

McGill said, "So, if Alice Janeway was abducted, he didn't do it personally. Does he seem like a guy who might hire someone else to grab her?"

"Not at all, Jim."

Keely gave McGill the sad story of Tad Thacker losing his teenage crush and said, "That's why he got miles ahead of himself when he showed up with a ring for Alice."

"Poor guy," McGill said, "but at bottom your cop instincts say there's no way he'd do anything to hurt Alice?"

"No, I don't see it, not at all. His boss, Marlys Reed, says he contributes to any good cause his colleagues pass the hat for, and Commander Jessup says he doesn't have so much as a parking ticket to his name. All that being the case, I have to think there goes your only suspect if something bad did happen to this woman."

"Not necessarily," McGill said. He told Keely about the three people who'd threatened Teag Tobias' life. "Maybe one of them thought of Alice as a way to hurt Tobias, though I don't see that myself."

Keely said, "I'll take your word for it, but it still might be a possibility."

"A slim one, but maybe. Thanks for doing good work in a hurry, Keely. Give my regards to Ron and Matt when you get home."

"Will do."

"Hey, one more thing," McGill said. "Did Tad Thacker ask why you were questioning him about Alice?"

"He asked if she was all right. I told him our client was concerned with her welfare. Didn't think it would be a good idea to get specific."

"Wise choice. Thanks again." McGill said goodbye and ended the call.

Caitie's call reached McGill the moment he hung up.

"What's up, Dad?"

"Tell me something, kiddo. Have you written a new screenplay?"

After a moment of silence, McGill's youngest said, "Damn."

"Is that a yes damn or a no damn?"

"It's a yes."

"Are you happy with both your effort and the result?"

McGill heard a glee-filled giggle. "Yeah, it's great. How'd you know about it?"

"Dorie McBride told me. She said a bidding war is about to start."

"What?"

Having been married to a former actress for a decade, McGill knew more about the movie-making process than your average P.I. That included protecting your intellectual property. So he asked, "You've secured your copyright for the screenplay, right?"

"Oh, yeah, Dad. *Absolument.* I've registered my script with the U.S. Copyright Office, the Berne Convention for the Protection of Literary and Artistic Works here in Europe, and Writers Guild of America, West, in L.A."

"That's my girl," McGill said with pride.

"How'd Dorie McBride know, though? I don't get that."

"My dear, someone somewhere ratted you out. Dorie wants to represent you, but call Patti to see what she has to say about hiring an agent."

"Right. That's what I was thinking. I still find it hard to believe anyone knows about me. It's not like you and Patti are still in the White House."

McGill said, "I think that's something that might haunt all of us for quite a while."

***Wallace Rhymes' House — Georgetown, Texas***

Wallace Rhymes looked at the hat Gene Beck had brought to him from Henry Rhymes' office. He rotated it in his hands and then put it down. "It's a very nice piece of work, but still a knockoff. Something I use for informal occasions, like having dinner with one of my children. I just hadn't gotten around to picking it up, after forgetting it that night at dinner with Henry."

Rhymes had convened a meeting in his home office. He sat behind his desk with the air of a judge. The three people sitting before him — Gene, Maj and Solana — all worked for him. He couldn't sentence them to lengthy prison terms, but he could fire one or all of them, give negative reviews to the Austin business community and make future employment difficult for each of them.

Well, for Solana anyway.

The private investigators had James J. McGill behind them. McGill had his wife and one of the world's larger fortunes behind him. Even so, Rhymes didn't think McGill would like one of his people coming off like a sneak-thief trying to climb into the private quarters of Rhymes' housekeeper.

"Who wants to say their piece first?" Rhymes asked.

Maj and Gene looked at each other and nodded, silently agreeing they'd let Solana speak first. The housekeeper wanted none of that. She told Rhymes, "Ask them what they were doing."

"All right," he said. "Ms. Olson, Mr. Beck, please give me a status report on your investigations."

Gene took the verbal baton. "Well, sir, Ms. Olson and I spoke to your daughter, Catherine. In our mutually considered opinion, she has no interest in your cowboy hat, John Wayne provenance or not."

Rhymes offered a small smile, "She's a pistol, that one, as independent as a firecracker on the Fourth of July. What else?"

Gene said, "On my own, I spoke with Henry, Clint and Cole. Henry also showed a lack of desire for the hat. Clint and Cole both said they'd like to have it, but they didn't want to threaten the bond between themselves by one of them having the hat while the other didn't. They admitted they're trying to think if a sharing plan might be devised. They feel a third party might be necessary to guarantee fairness, but they don't know who that person might be."

"I didn't know that," Rhymes said, "that my younger sons might like it."

Solana seemed to shrink in her chair upon hearing that news.

Rhymes couldn't help but notice his housekeeper's reaction, but he turned his attention to Maj. "What do you have to say for yourself, Ms. Olson? Did you think a forgetful old man might've mislaid his hat in his own house? Thought you could clear things up right quick."

"That was one of the two ideas I had in mind, sir. The other one was maybe your eyesight isn't what it once was."

"What do you mean?" Rhymes asked.

"Well, I know from experience in my own family that people's perception of colors can change as they age. You told Gene and me that you knew your hat had been replaced by a knockoff because the color wasn't true to the original hat."

"That's right," Rhymes said.

"Among other things, I wanted to see how Gene and I saw the knockoff's color compared to a photo of the original. I thought of that, and maybe you had misplaced the genuine article. Only I couldn't find either hat, the original or the knockoff, anywhere from your basement to the bedrooms upstairs. The only place I didn't check was Solana's suite, and she made it very clear to me that she didn't want me poking around up there. She even sat on a chair in front of the door to her quarters to block the way."

Rhymes cast a glance at the housekeeper who continued to shrink.

Turning to Maj, he said, "So you took it upon yourself to haul a ladder out of my garage and have a look anyway."

"Yes, sir. I hate leaving a job half-finished."

That made the old man grin. "Me, too. You didn't nick the paint on any of my cars, did you?"

"No, sir."

"Well, that's a point in your favor, anyway. Were you able to make any significant discovery before you were so rudely interrupted?" Rhymes asked.

Maj nodded. She also clenched her hands, which were stinging intensely now.

"You hurt yourself?" Rhymes asked.

Maj nodded. "Sliding down the ladder in the hope of making a quick getaway." She showed him the red welts on the palms of her hands.

The old man sighed through a thin smile. "My children often inflicted their own punishments while making mischief." He nodded toward a door to his left. "There's a powder room behind that door, as you surely know by now. In case you didn't look for my hat in the medicine cabinet, there's a package of antiseptic towelettes in there. Also, a bottle of aloe vera lotion to help relieve your pain. Go tend to your hands; we'll wait."

Maj thanked him and went into the powder room.

Solana looked as if every second of delay in learning her fate was torture.

Gene took the opportunity to begin whistling "The Blue Danube Waltz."

Rhymes was immediately taken by the performance. Solana looked like she was more in the mood for Del Shannon's "Runaway" than the work of Johann Strauss II. After a moment or two, Rhymes politely clapped his hands for Gene's musical interlude, and Maj returned.

"What, if anything, do you have to show for your snooping efforts, Ms. Olson? Mr. Beck has been stalling for you quite nicely just now."

Gene handed Maj's phone back to her, the incriminating hat photos already cued up.

Maj gave the phone to Rhymes and said, "There are several shots to examine, sir. You'd know better than us if the gentleman in the photographs is wearing your hat."

Rhymes scanned one shot after another.

Solana seemed to sink more deeply into her chair with each flick of his wrist.

When Rhymes finished a second pass through the images, he handed the phone to Maj.

"That gentleman in the pictures is Ernesto Fuentes, Solana's father, the man who kept this property in such lovely shape before he retired two years ago. Went back home to Mexico, didn't he, Solana?"

Without looking at Rhymes, she nodded.

"How is your father, now? Enjoying good health, I hope."

Now, the housekeeper looked up. "He is dead."

"I'm sorry to hear that," Rhymes said, the expression on his face substantiating his words. "He was a good man. How is it you have a picture of him wearing my hat?"

Tears sliding down her cheeks now, Solana said, "He loved you, *señor*."

"And I had a deep affection for him, too," Rhymes replied.

"He also loved your hat, and knowing it once belonged to a famous movie star."

"I remember letting him try it on once," Rhymes said. "It was a good fit."

"He never forgot that kindness, *señor*, and when I heard he was dying —"

"And having heard me complain that none of my children cared about it — or so I thought — and with my trying to think of a fitting way to pass the hat on, so to speak, you came up with your own idea: Send it to your father, and replace it with a knockoff."

Solana lowered her head, but only for a moment. "I didn't send it to my father only to wear while he was alive."

"What do you —" Then Rhymes understood what Solana meant. "Your father was buried wearing my hat?"

Wearing a brave face now, Solana nodded.

To which Gene replied, "She's lying."

***Department of Natural Resources — Portland, Oregon***

Marlys Reed was looking at her reduced office budget for the coming year — set by the great minds of the state legislature, the bastards — and wondering whether she'd have to neglect Mother Nature's well-being or cut her staff by a head or three. It would be an evil choice either way. She couldn't see bringing herself to stint on any of the conservation projects on the department's drawing boards. Nor did she want to let any of her people go. They were all smart, hard-working and deeply committed to preserving as much of the natural world as humanly possible.

There'd been great hope in the state that legalizing the recreational use of marijuana would bring in enough tax money to pave the city streets with gold and keep the rest of Oregon green. Sure enough, there'd been a spike in revenue, but people couldn't stay stoned all the time and the "grass tax" hadn't provided as much money as euphorically had been predicted.

The people who'd touted the revenue estimates should have been drug-tested.

With her dilemma unresolved, Marlys thought maybe the thing to do would be to lay off the first three people who popped into her office that day. Let fate decide who got canned. If she didn't have the stomach to do that, maybe she should just quit and let someone else do the dirty work.

She could scoot to Washington State, maybe get a job up there.

Those people seemed to enjoy their marijuana more.

Maybe their state budget didn't require "reductions in force."

A knock at Marlys' door brought her back to the notion of firing the first three people who came calling on her. That'd be just the thing if there were three of them together right now. She could swing the axe and … no, she couldn't.

She only said, "Come in."

The door opened and Tad Thacker stepped in. "You have a minute, Marlys?"

"Sure, Tad, have a seat."

He closed the door behind him and sat.

"Is this about the interview with the police officer and that private investigator?" Marlys asked. "I hope you can understand why I felt it was important to help find a woman who might be missing."

If Tad filed a complaint against her, maybe she would be the one looking for a new job.

Tad nodded. "I agree, it was important. I'm not bothered by that. It did surprise me, though. Being questioned about Alice made me think of Jenny again, and that's always painful."

Marlys knew that story; everyone in the office did.

"Sure, I'm sorry about that. Quite a coincidence the two of

them looking so similar."

"Yeah. Anyway, it sort of got me reviewing my life and one of the things that came to mind is I haven't taken any vacation time in years."

"Let me check," Marlys said. She brought up her computer and punched in Tad's name. Her eyes went wide when she saw the relevant number. "You're right. You've got 40 days, eight weeks of vacation time, accrued. So you'd like to take some of it?"

"Maybe all of it," Tad said.

Marlys was tempted to ask where the heck he'd go for two months, a Tibetan monastery? Spend all his time meditating and chanting "Ommm." Then she had an insight; she knew what Tad wanted to do. He was going to *look* for Alice Janeway. If the cops and the P.I. didn't find her, maybe he would.

She thought that was more than a little loony, but it was also sweet. Charming even that a mild-mannered naturalist could see himself as a hero riding to the rescue. Saving the day when the professionals couldn't.

Of course, if Tad fell flat on his face and became a public laughingstock doing so … well, that might be cause for dismissal, reducing her need to let someone else go. On the other hand, if by some miracle, Tad became a hero, it wouldn't look good for the powers that be to can him or any of his colleagues, if Tad stuck up for them. Which he would.

Marlys said, "Tad, you've earned that time off. If you need all of it, take all of it."

"Starting tomorrow?" Tad asked.

"If that's what you want, sure."

Tad stood and extended a hand to Marlys. "Thank you."

She shook it, knowing she was a hypocrite. "You're welcome."

After Tad had departed, Marlys wondered if she should give that local cop, Jessup, a heads-up that Tad would be playing detective … but Tad hadn't come right out and said that. She just felt he'd do that.

Hell, she knew that was *exactly* what he was going to do.

Now, the cops and that P.I? They could find that out for themselves.

***Wallace Rhymes' House — Georgetown, Texas***

"What did you just say, Mr. Beck?" Wallace Rhymes asked Gene.

Without hesitation, Gene told him, "Your housekeeper is lying, sir."

"And how do you know that?" Rhymes' tone implied that Gene's answer had better be both clear and persuasive. That, or he and Maj would have their services terminated forthwith.

Gene said, "Government training, sir. Special forces and then something a bit darker I'm not supposed to talk about."

The other three people in the room looked closely at Gene. Maj had heard of Gene's training by the Air Force Special Operations Command, but she hadn't heard of any *darker* operations. She decided to say nothing about that for the moment.

Rhymes was not as reticent. "Are you saying you were CIA or something like that?"

Hearing that, even as speculation, made Solana squirm in her chair.

"I really can't say, sir," Gene told Rhymes. "What I can talk about, though, is one of the patterns of deceit I was taught to recognize. Solana didn't once admit that what she did was wrong. She reminded you of the bond of affection you felt for *Señor* Fuentes. Then she played a sympathy card by telling you that he'd died."

"I asked her how Ernesto was doing," Rhymes replied.

"Yes, you did, sir, and may I ask, have you put that same question to her any other time in the recent past?"

"Yes, of course, every week or so I'd ask how Ernesto was getting along."

Gene turned to Solana. "How long ago did your father die?

Please don't lie. I'll find out the actual date with very little trouble."

The housekeeper looked daggers at Gene, but when he didn't let that bother him, she broke down and cried, hanging her head and covering her face with her hands.

Gene told Rhymes, "She was saving the news of her father's death, sir, in case she needed it for just this kind of situation. Assuming he really is dead."

Raising her head and dropping her hands, Solana spat, "He *is* dead!"

Gene continued unruffled, "Anyway, building a rapport with the questioner, reminding him of emotional ties, is supposed to make a false confession easier to accept while avoiding a true response. In this case, Mr. Rhymes, you made things even easier by supplying the answer for Solana. You suggested that her father was buried with the hat. She was happy to go along, if that was what you wanted to think had happened."

The housekeeper's rollercoaster of emotions hit another peak of anger.

She snarled at Gene, "That was what was *supposed* to happen … my father being buried wearing that hat."

In a quiet voice, Wallace Rhymes asked, "What really happened, Solana?"

Solana dropped her head and answered in a whisper no one could hear.

Even so, it was clear to Wallace Rhymes that someone he'd once regarded as extended family had deceived him. In a harsh voice he said, "Speak up, woman!"

She looked at him with tears streaming down her cheeks. "Your hat was stolen … twice."

The situation was becoming clearer to the old man. "You took it the first time. Why'd you do that?"

"*Señor,* as you already said, you told me yourself none of your children wanted it."

Rhymes sighed. "Apparently, I was wrong about that."

"Yes, but neither of us knew better, and my father dearly loved that hat. He said the one time you let him try it on, the hat gave him a whole new way of seeing the world. Made him feel almost as if he was a king, not just someone who toiled for others."

Rhymes' face sagged, his anger dissipated with sadness taking its place. "Ernesto never told me that. I always thought he liked working here."

"He did," Solana said. "You are both kind and generous. But the time he put that hat on his head, he imagined for the first time in his life what it would be like to own such a place as this. He told me this himself."

"Ernesto wrote me that he'd saved enough money to buy his own ranch down in Mexico," Rhymes said.

"He did," Solana told him. "It is a pretty place but humble compared to here, maybe a tenth the size of this one. It was his dream come true, only the dream wasn't as grand as he thought it would be."

Solana clearly shared her father's disappointment, and felt the pain of his death.

That and the regret for the second theft, the nature of which she'd yet to reveal.

Maj supplied another missing element. "You thought your father would feel better about his circumstances if he had John Wayne's hat to wear."

Solana nodded. She looked at Rhymes. "We both thought no one here wanted it. So where was the harm?"

Rhymes didn't have an answer to that, except, of course, for a violation of trust.

Now, Gene asked the pertinent question. "Do you know who took the hat from your father?"

Solana nodded. "Eloy Chavez."

Neither Maj nor Rhymes recognized the name, but it struck a chord with Gene. He took out his phone and accessed a search engine he was no longer supposed to use. He entered the name Solana had just mentioned.

"Well, hell," he said. "Is this the guy?"

Keeping hold of his phone he showed a photo to Solana. Fear entered her eyes and she nodded. Gene let Maj and Rhymes take a look, and he put the phone back in his pocket.

He said, "Chavez is one of the bigger drug bosses south of the Rio Grande. He must've taken a liking to the hat. But my question is, how'd he hear about it?"

Solana's face sagged with regret. "My father talked about the hat one too many times. Word reached Chavez. He showed up at my father's rancho himself. He told my father that he was a much better choice to wear John Wayne's hat than an old man who'd toiled for gringos and now had just a speck of land to call his own. He said he'd buy the hat from my father or he would just take it from him and kill him and his three children. My two brothers in Mexico and me here in Texas."

"So your father sold the hat?" Maj asked.

"No, he *gave* the hat to Chavez. Said it would be his honor to do that. He did the best he could to protect his children … but he'd told me how wearing that hat had made him feel: like a once poor man who had miraculously risen in the world. As soon as the hat was gone, though, his soul began to shrink within him. My brothers told me his end came fast."

Solana looked as if her future might be brief, too.

Still, she managed to say to Rhymes. "I am sorry for what I did, *señor.*"

Rhymes nodded and turned to Gene and Maj. "You two think you can get my hat back?"

Gene said, "Would you settle for getting Eloy Chavez?"

Maj gave her partner a dubious look. "You really think we can work in Mexico?"

Gene said, "No, you never want to fight the other guy's fight. You make him deal with you on your own terms. We get Chavez to come here."

Rhymes said, "You do that, and I'll make sure he rots in a Texas prison for the rest of his miserable life. I'd like to have my hat back, but I'll settle for Chavez's head."

"What's the plan for *any* of this?" Maj wanted to know.

Gene told her in a word, "Disinformation."

***Dumbarton Oaks — Washington, DC***

"And how was your day, dear?" McGill asked Patti when she arrived home shortly after he had.

Both McGill and Ace Cole had checked the house's security system to make sure it was functioning properly and hadn't been hacked or otherwise trifled with. They'd also done a quick search of the place just in case someone who was really good at getting past electronic safeguards was lurking under the marital bed or in the master shower stall.

All was well, and since McGill had shown both of the former First Couple's Secret Service special agents, just the previous week at the Federal Law Enforcement shooting range in Cheltenham, Maryland, that he could still shoot fast and straight, Ace had bidden McGill goodnight.

Despite all that, when Daphna Levy arrived with Patti, she asked McGill, "You and Ace checked the premises, right?"

"Sure did," McGill said. "We were quick about it, so Ace had the time to do a little dusting and polishing, too."

Patti grinned, but Daphna only asked, "You checked the grounds, too?"

"You mean the backyard? Ace said he'd do that on his way out."

"I'll double-check," she said.

"Fine," McGill said.

"Thank you, Daphna," Patti added.

Once she'd gone, McGill gave the missus a kiss.

Then he asked, "Are there really still loons out there who mean to do you or me harm?"

She nodded. "So Elspeth Kendry tells me, but only after I asked."

McGill said, "Not that I'd wish such creeps on anyone, but hasn't the threat-focus shifted to Jean Morrissey by now?"

"The vast majority, certainly," Patti said, "but there are obsessive types who hate leaving a job undone."

McGill sighed. "Crazy and compulsive, now there's a combination for you. So did you hear from Caitie?"

Patti beamed at McGill. "She's going to leave all of us in the dust before long. Did she tell you the storyline of her screenplay?"

"Terrible father that I am, I focused on making sure she didn't get robbed of her creation. That and getting the right agent."

Patti gave him a peck on the cheek. "Well, that's important, too, but I thought she might have mentioned that you inspired her story idea."

"*What?*" McGill asked. Elaborating, he added, "How?"

"You were sitting with Caitie in a hospital waiting room in South Dakota. Remember now?"

McGill did. "I asked her if she took a taxi from Minnesota, putting it on her credit card."

"And then?" Patti asked.

"She came up with the idea of a young woman in New York City using a taxi to follow a guy all the way across the country. She said the guy was a grad student. I said he was a traffic engineer. As I remember things, Caitie thought that was *fresh*."

"Fresh enough to create a new nightmare character. A *highly disturbed* civil engineering prodigy has it in mind to call attention to the nation's infrastructure crisis by blowing up bridges, tunnels, highway interchanges and whatnot that are about to fall down anyway due to neglect, and if that doesn't get the government to start working on infrastructure repair, he intends to bring down the Golden Gate."

McGill shivered at the thought that his daughter could conceive such a plot.

"You want to know the kicker?" Patti asked.

"The good guys don't win? Or you can't even tell who the good guys are?"

"You'll have to read the script to find out all that. What I meant, though, is that Caitie gave you a co-writing credit."

McGill's jaw dropped. "Can she do that?"

Patti nodded. "She said you came up with the idea of putting the taxi on a credit card and imagined the object of the pursuit as an engineer."

"I did, but I was just spitballing."

"That can be a highly paid profession in L.A. and a lot of other places. People come to Committed Capital and pitch ideas every day. I don't see how you can refuse Caitie honoring your contribution. Not without putting a seriously big dent in your relationship to Caitie."

McGill sighed. "All I can say is if we win an Oscar, she's going to do all the talking."

Patti laughed. "That won't be a problem for Caitie."

McGill moved on to domestic matters.

"It's my turn to cook tonight," he said.

"A good thing for both of us," Patti replied.

"I was thinking of something relatively fast and simple. How about some BLTs, followed by a helping or two of fresh-from-the-oven apple crumble for dessert, washed down by our adult beverages of choice?"

"Champagne?"

"I was thinking of beer, but I can go with bubbly."

"I'll peel the apples," Patti said. "Maybe even slice them, add the cinnamon and sugar. Cooking was never really my thing, but I think I could become a decent pastry chef."

McGill grinned. "Words every man would love to hear from his mate."

Sharing another kiss sent them on their way to the kitchen.

McGill had the sandwiches, flutes and a bottle of champagne on the kitchen table in short order. The apple crumble had ten minutes to go in the oven, but its aroma was already mouthwatering. Especially paired with bacon. McGill and Patti raised their glasses and toasted each other: family, friends, country and the hope for a better world.

McGill opened the dinner conversation by saying, "I dropped

in at the White House today."

Keeping a straight face, Patti asked, "Forgot your White Sox cap in your old closet, did you?"

"I'd never make a mistake like that," McGill said. "The team is rebuilding, and things are starting to look good for the future."

Patti said, "There's a worry off my mind."

"I called Frank Morrissey before I stopped by, just to make sure I wouldn't interrupt anything important."

"Always good to be considerate."

Seeing he wasn't going to get anywhere by being indirect, McGill said, "Frank told me he dropped in unannounced at Galia's house this morning and was pleased to find you were there, too."

"I was. Would you care to hear about any of our topics of conversation?"

"Well," McGill said, "as long as you're not dealing in state secrets anymore ..."

Patti's face gave her away. It wasn't that she avoided looking at McGill or compressed her lips. It was, rather, a complete lack of facial animation. It had been the better part of a year since he'd seen Patti put on the presidential poker-face.

"Cripes," McGill said, "Frank didn't want you to do something for the government, did he?"

Patti got up from the table. "Be right back. Time to take the crumble out of the oven."

McGill didn't say a word. Instead, he speculated. Had Frank asked Patti to troubleshoot some foreign trouble-spot? Or maybe act as the U.S. spokesperson at the U.N. for some important issue? Worse, Frank might've asked Patti to do fundraising for someone who was politically compatible but personally objectionable.

Patti came back to the table with two steaming plates of crumble.

She placed one in front of McGill. "Give it a minute before you eat."

"Sure. So what did Frank want?"

Patti took her seat and a moment to reply. "How much do you know about the extent to which Galia helped me during my presidency?"

McGill said, "I *know* only as much as you told me. I made private guesses about a lot more. I don't think Galia actually went out and threw somebody off a bridge for you, but I wouldn't be surprised if she'd considered doing that or its equivalent. I also think she took satisfaction in being, what, the president's badass?"

"Well, you already had the henchman spot filled, but you're essentially right. What Frank asked her to do, and you must keep this to yourself, is to act as his unofficial spy both here at home and abroad."

"Uh-huh," McGill said, "that's one shoe dropped, but I have the feeling there's another."

"When Frank heard that I intend to use Galia as a global scout for new investment opportunities, he said that would be the perfect cover for Galia's spy work."

McGill sat back in his chair. The crumble had cooled enough to sample. He picked up his fork and took a bite. So simple a confection, but so good. Frank's plan was simple, too, but it also might be less pleasing in its results.

That forced McGill to say, "I don't think you can do it. If anything went wrong and the connection to your company was revealed, the negative publicity would be the death of Committed Capital. For that matter, if things went really badly, it could be the end of Galia, too."

"You honestly think so, Jim?"

"I don't doubt Galia could come out on top in any political knife-fight, but what we're talking about here could be the real thing. Let's remember she didn't do too well when John Patrick Granby tried to garrote her in the White House Press Room."

McGill had to intervene, saving Galia's life in the nick of time.

A shiver ran through Patti. "I saw the video of that attack just once; I couldn't bear a second viewing. I kept thinking: What if you hadn't been there? What if Granby had somehow smuggled a gun into the press room? You and Galia might both be dead, along with any number of others."

McGill hadn't taken his thinking as far as that last point.

Still, he used it to buttress his argument. "So there's no question: You won't go along with Frank Morrissey's scheme. It's too dangerous for everyone who'd be involved."

"Yes, you're right. I'll have to talk with Jean, though, tell her I regret being unable to help Frank with the idea he raised this morning. The tricky part will be holding the details back and suggesting she speak to her brother if she needs the particulars."

"That's a good approach," McGill said. "Let her decide if it's smart for her to know."

"Exactly. But the problem remains that if I hire Galia and have her travel abroad, how will I know if she doesn't work for Frank, anyway, behind my back? She seemed really excited about the idea."

McGill thought for a moment. "Show her the video of Granby choking the life out of her. If there's any chance that isn't scary enough to change her mind, let her find another job."

Patti took a deep breath and exhaled slowly. "I'd have to watch it with her, but I'll do that for Galia."

McGill squeezed her hand. "Tell her I won't be there if something like that happens again."

Patti sighed and asked, "And how was your day, dear?"

McGill said, "The guy we thought might be stalking Alice Janeway was a false alarm. On the other hand, there are three people who've made credible death threats against Teag Tobias, and it's possible, if not yet likely, that one of them might have grabbed Alice as a proxy for hurting him."

Patti pushed her portion of apple crumble to McGill.

"Finish mine, too, and let's go upstairs."

McGill never argued with directives like those.

Just before McGill drifted off to sleep, Patti already dozing next to him, a thought entered his mind. It was inspired by Caitie's generosity, including him in the authorship of her screenplay. Teag Tobias had told McGill that Alice wanted to contribute to the writing of his show. What if he'd relented, even just a little, and maybe a single line of dialogue that Alice had contributed got one of the bigger laughs of the night? Maybe Alice thought she should get public credit for her contribution, but Tobias said, "No way."

How might something like that be resolved?

McGill couldn't honestly say. It seemed melodramatic to think Tobias might … what? Get rid of Alice? Make her disappear? He couldn't buy that, at least not yet. Still, no one seemed to know where Alice was. McGill thought maybe what he should do was call Caitie. See what she thought his next move should be.

Before he did that, though, he decided he should take a long look at just who Teagan Tobias was. Do a character analysis. He made a note to that effect. Then he fell asleep.

***Old Dominion Palliative Care — Richmond, Virginia***

Teag Tobias had canceled his show that night due to "a sudden illness." Disappointed fans were offered their choice of a full refund or the same seats at a make-up show that would be tacked on to the end of the run in Washington. It was also mentioned that as compensation for the inconvenience they'd suffered, Teag would do a Q&A at the end of the replacement show.

They could bitch at him then for getting sick.

If that didn't satisfy the bastards, Teag thought, screw 'em.

He entered the hospice where Alice was vegetating. He hated to think of things that way, but that was the verb that came to mind. He found dismal consolation in the fact that due to the assistance of elaborate bio-engineering her face was still warm to the touch. That semblance of life made the notion of pulling her plug even harder.

What really worried him, though, was an idea that almost

made him really sick. That was the perception that his act was starting to wear thin. He tried to tell himself that his usual vituperative energy was down just a bit. The phrasing of his insults had become, what? Repetitive? God, if that was the case, he'd have to freshen up the whole show.

Only, how many ways were there to criticize people or bitch at the world at large?

The vocabulary was pretty well set, and anybody who was beyond middle school had already heard every curse word in the book. Shock value diminished with each repetition. Unless … the anger and bile came from a new and unexpected source.

If you heard a cop or a construction worker get vulgar, well, that was to be expected.

But if Miss Goody Two-shoes started spitting fire …

Well, brother, then the shock effect would be back. So would the laughs. The nervous energy, too. What venom might the little Kewpie doll spout next? People would be dying to find out. On the edge of their seats waiting to hear. And every seat in the house would be filled.

Tobias stroked Alice's cheek.

"Come on, sweetheart, open those pretty green eyes. Daddy needs you. Wake up and all your dreams will come true. You'll get to write and perform after all. You'll be a star."

He glanced up at the monitor that measured brain activity.

His words hadn't caused a ripple.

Trying a different angle, Tobias told Alice, "You know, there are other little sweethearts out there. You don't have a corner on the market. It might take me a while to replace you, but I bet it could be done. Find someone who can both write and perform. If I want, I bet I can find someone who can do both those things and is named Alice, too. Even if she isn't, though, I'd bet she'd change her name to Alice for the right money."

The monitor continued to show the real Alice remained unimpressed.

In a rational frame of mind, Tobias might have acknowledged

Alice was incapable of any response. She wasn't ignoring him, even if that was how she was making him feel. Thing was, he'd always had a helluva time trying to ignore any perceived slight, real or imagined.

He took a step back from Alice's bedside.

Wouldn't do to slap Alice. She wouldn't feel it, as far as he could tell. Also, it wouldn't look good at all if some hospice staffer walked in and found him beating her.

In a soft voice, Tobias told Alice, "I really need you, babe. Come on, wake up."

Now, Tobias was thinking of the criticism McGill had given him:

*What seemed funny at first became predictable … the commentary was just too mean … some people are just horrible … but we see amazingly unexpected examples of kindness and even self-sacrifice, too. I kept waiting for one of those moments to come in your show, but it never did.*

In the moment, Tobias had shrugged that off. What the hell did McGill know? *Something* was what. His damn words kept echoing in Tobias' head like a church bell that wouldn't stop ringing. He heard them more clearly than ever as he looked down at Alice.

Tobias thought he wouldn't even have to hire a hacker to short-out Alice's life-support system. All he'd have to do would be stop paying for all the machines that kept her breathing, fed and hydrated. He had no legal obligation to provide that money.

If he said, "That's it for me," somebody else would have to pick up the tab.

Only he'd bet nobody would do it for long.

Then it'd be, "So long, sweetheart."

He'd be free to go off on his merry way. Except he didn't think his act would outlive Alice by much more than a year. More and more people would get to the point McGill had seen right off. Eventually, if he didn't find any redemptive point of view and the humor to go with it, he would be finished.

Sure, he could cast someone else as his foil, someone who saw hope in the bleakest of moments, and that someone could be a fetching young woman just like Alice, only she wouldn't *be* Alice. Crazy as the idea seemed to Tobias at the moment, he knew it *had* to be Alice — and no one else — or he was finished.

He stepped back to Alice's bedside and stroked her cheek again.

"Whatever you want, Alice, I'll give it to you. Just wake the hell up, okay?"

On his way out, Tobias made sure Alice's account was current.

## CHAPTER 3

***November 2, 2017***
***McGill Investigations International —Washington, DC***

Sweetie walked into McGill's office that morning and told him, "Teagan Tobias hasn't cracked the top one percent of richest Americans yet, and won't anytime soon, but by most people's standards he's doing very well."

"How well?" McGill asked.

Sweetie nodded and took a seat. "His stage show is just one of his revenue streams. He's done TV work domestically and online whiskey commercials in Japan. He does five-minute weekly commentaries on a syndicated radio program. He has a popular, monetized website. He's written three books — published in hardcover, paperback and audio — and he's even talking to some money-people about becoming a partner in a new motion picture production company."

McGill whistled. "A little bile goes a long way. No, that's not accurate. He's got a *lot* of ill-will, and the wit and vocabulary to make a fair number of people laugh at his black humor. You got all your information from Putnam?"

"Yeah. Took him about ten minutes, once he got a spare

moment. Sometimes it scares me how easy it is to find out what we used to think of as private matters."

"Then again," McGill said, "that's helpful to people in our business."

"Yes, it is, but I'm starting to think every investigative body, private or public, should have a chief ethics officer."

McGill said, "I won't argue with that, but I won't hold my breath either. Did Putnam give you a figure for Teag's net worth?"

"An educated guess: just north of $50 million."

There had been many times when such a sum of money would have boggled McGill's mind. After having Patti whisper into his ear what her fortune was, his perspective had changed. Tobias was far wealthier than most people would ever be, but he was a shoe-shine boy compared to the mega-rich.

One thing was certain about people on any point of the big-bucks spectrum, though: None of them ever wanted to see their fortunes dwindle.

So McGill asked Sweetie, "You think having Alice say adios to Tobias might possibly cost him a nice chunk of money or at least keep him from grabbing a bundle he could have had with her help?"

Sweetie mulled that two-part question for a moment. "I think that would be more of a question for someone on the showbiz side of things.."

"Yeah," McGill said. "I've got Dorie McBride working on that. She should be getting back to me today, I think."

"Oh, yeah," Sweetie asked. "Since when does she carry water for you?"

McGill said, "Since she thinks it's in her interest."

He told Sweetie about Caitie's screenplay, and the writing credit she'd extended to him.

Sweetie smiled ear to ear. "Good for her. Maybe you'll give me your autograph one day."

"The guff I take, even from my oldest friend," McGill said.

"It only makes you stronger," Sweetie replied.

"Right."

"Trust me on this. I've read the stories of all the martyrs. None of them even said 'ouch,' and they all made it to heaven."

McGill said, "I'll try to bear that in mind."

"Getting back to business, I was thinking I might go down to North Carolina, see if Alice has any old college chums who stayed local and might have gotten a picture postcard from her, if she's taken a vacation somewhere nice. What's the town where Alice went to school?"

"Chapel Hill," McGill said. "That's a good idea. She might even be staying with an old friend, if she just wanted a bit of refuge. There wouldn't be any public record of that. I'll have Leo give you a ride down there. He speaks the language."

Sweetie knew what McGill meant. Leo had the right accent, knew all the local figures of speech, looked natural saying "y'all." He'd even make the right hand gestures when words wouldn't suffice. All of those things were advantages. People were always more forthcoming with one of their own.

Sweetie said, "The way Leo drives, I wouldn't be away from home much longer than if I flew. Putnam will be happy to spend a little more time with Maxi, but what about you? Who's going to drive you around?"

McGill said, "It's been a long time since I've driven regularly, but I still know how a steering wheel, an accelerator and a brake pedal work."

"Glad to hear it, but you're overlooking one little detail."

"What?"

"If I take your car and driver, what will you use for wheels?"

"Damn," McGill said. Talk about overlooking the obvious.

Then he remembered that not only did he have a healthy bank account, his company provided cars or transportation subsidies to all of its senior investigators. The prospect of buying his own set of wheels, one in which he'd do his own driving, almost made him feel giddy.

"I'll buy a car," McGill said.

Sweetie saw the pleasure in his smile, didn't blame him a bit.

Even so, she had a suggestion. "I don't worry about you getting a Lamborghini or something crazy like that, but why don't you ask Leo, before he and I hit the road, what he might recommend?"

McGill knew that Leo's idol, stock-car racing legend Richard Petty, had won many of his big races driving Plymouths and Oldsmobiles. Leo spoke of those cars like long-lost loves. That was fitting as none of them was in production any longer. Still, McGill was sure Leo would have some solid advice for him.

Once McGill had figured out just what kind of car he wanted, that was. Two-seater or four. Better be four in case he had occasion to take all three of his kids somewhere. Of course, if he wanted to take Patti, too, and maybe at least one Secret Service agent … cripes, was he looking at a station wagon?

"Why are you shaking your head?" Sweetie asked him.

"Just trying to make adjustments to new realities," McGill said.

Maybe he'd better try renting a few cars before he made a purchase.

Esme Thrice buzzed McGill. "Mr. McGill, there's someone here to see you. He doesn't have an appointment, but he says he might have some information that could help you with a case you're working."

McGill and Sweetie exchanged skeptical looks.

"What case?" McGill asked.

He heard Esme repeat the question. Then she said, "Alice Janeway."

Sweetie got to her feet, and McGill gave her a nod.

She stepped out of the office to back up Esme, if necessary.

"What's this person's name?" McGill asked.

Esme said, "Tad Thacker."

***The White House — Washington, DC***

Former President Patricia Grant (now Patti McGill) ate breakfast that morning with current President Jean Morrissey in the

Family Dining Room at the White House. Patti had arrived in a Secret Service SUV with tinted windows that Jean had sent for her. Patti had worn a head scarf, sunglasses and a navy blue trench coat. She didn't tarry getting into the vehicle or entering the Executive Mansion.

It was possible a sharp-eyed reporter might have seen her — recognized her — but it wasn't likely. There was no compelling reason for the secrecy, but in the history of the presidency, former presidents returned to their erstwhile seat of power only for ceremonial occasions. They didn't drop in just to chat.

Then again, there'd never been two consecutive female presidents before.

Collegial conversation might become a useful exercise.

Jean was waiting for Patti with a pot of mint tea heated to just the right temperature for sipping. The two women embraced, and Jean stepped back wearing a smile. "You've added some muscle, Madam President," Jean said.

"And you've maintained yours, Madam President," Patti replied. "No small feat while doing your job."

"I'm trying to keep up with Byron. His recovery continues to amaze me, and himself. He's even taken up jumping rope. I don't want to discourage him, but there are times I worry more about him breaking his neck than going to war with Russia."

Patti asked, "We're going to war with Russia?"

"Not anytime soon, but I wouldn't mind getting into a good hockey fight with that goon in the Kremlin."

Patti grinned. "Well, you've got a good six inches in height on him."

"I bet I'm stronger, too, and I don't ride horses topless."

Patti laughed, "Probably a wise political choice."

"I'd lose the Betty Crocker moms for sure, but they don't vote for me anyway. Damn, it's good to see you here again, Patti."

The new head butler, Tennyson, knocked and entered the room.

"Breakfast, Madam President." Turning to Patti, he added, "So nice to see you again, Madam President."

Tennyson had been the second-in-command to Blessing, the former head butler who now worked for the McGills at their Dumbarton Oaks house. It looked as if Tennyson had brought the entire kitchen staff with him, all of whom also remembered Patti with fondness.

President Morrissey told the crowd, "Mrs. McGill was never here this morning, please remember that, but thank you all for stopping by."

Tennyson nodded and the others followed suit.

Crepes, fresh fruit, orange juice and coffee were added to the teapot on the dining room table. The staff withdrew, and Jean turned to Patti, gestured her to a seat and took her own. "This visit is all about some scheme Frank has concocted, isn't it?"

Patti took a bite of a crepe and said, "Delicious, and yes, it is."

Jean sighed. "He tries his damnedest to help me. By and large, he succeeds, too. I'd never have gotten to the governor's mansion in Minnesota, much less here, without him. But I know he must've gone too far for you to be here. What does he want you to do?"

"One of the few things I can't afford to do: put the reputation of Committed Capital at risk." Patti told Jean of her idea to use Galia as a global scout for new high-tech projects her company might fund, and how Frank wanted to use that job as a cover for Galia to do political spying for him.

That idea stopped Jean cold, her forkful of honeydew melon halfway to her mouth. "Damn, I have to say I *like* that idea."

"It does have potential merit. She might learn what hostile or even friendly nations might be planning that isn't in our interest. The downside, though, could be awful. Jim thought about the damage it might do to Committed Capital if Galia was found out, and he also pointed out that there might well be personal — physical — danger for Galia if things went really wrong."

Jean sighed and nodded.

Just as her predecessor had, Jean read her daily briefing. She learned, often in more detail than she'd cared to know, the cruel fates that could befall employees of the U.S. government serving abroad. Even minor State Department employees were prized kidnapping targets for terrorists and hostile intelligence services. If the woman who'd been the chief of staff to a former president were suspected of doing anything that even resembled spy-craft while traveling in foreign lands, well, grabbing her at the first opportunity would be all but obligatory.

Just think of the secrets that might be squeezed, perhaps literally, from her.

Galia had to know everything, and perhaps more, than the former president knew.

And Galia would never be able to withstand harsh interrogation.

President Jean Morrissey felt sure her brother Frank had realized all that, but from his point of view it would be worth the risk. After all, giving your life for your country was the stuff of heroes. Better yet, learning the bad guys' evil plans, saving your country from disaster and getting away clean was the fabric of legends.

Who was to say a Jewish grandmother couldn't be such a hero?

Only the former president and her henchman didn't think that was how things would work out for Galia. The current president, damnit, had to agree with them. The likelihood of disaster was greater than the possibility of success.

"I'll tell Frank to go back to the drawing board," Jean told Patti.

"I'm sorry, Jean. I didn't want to come here to spoil your day."

The president laughed. "You know we don't need friends for that. Not when we have Congress to do the job."

"Right. But I did come up with an idea that might perk you up a bit."

"What's that?" Jean asked.

"I'm going to suggest to Galia that she start a website, one that's friendly to our side of the political spectrum. I even know someone who might provide the seed money for such a project."

Jean smiled. "Said benefactor to remain nameless."

"Anonymous and well-shielded by any number of cutouts. My

thinking is Galia still has endless contacts and sources in town. She might turn up all sorts of important stories that someone who didn't—"

"Also have a connection to a White House VIP, who shall also remain nameless, for the most inside of her scoops. You think that would keep Galia productively occupied?"

Patti nodded. "I do. Political skulduggery is more Galia's game than the real thing."

"I agree, but if Galia already sees herself as Mata Hari, will she go along?"

Patti said, "We'll remind her that the real Mata Hari was executed by a firing squad."

***McGill Investigations International — Austin, Texas***

"You want me to use my own newspaper to lie to our readers?" Kyle Tompkins asked Maj Olson.

She and Gene Beck had invited the reporter from the *Austin Journal* back to their offices. They were using Gene's space for the meeting. He'd put up a couple of framed photos of famous Country & Western recording artists who'd covered a couple of his songs.

The singers had signed their names and expressed their appreciation of Gene's work, one of them saying, "Gene, if you're not the best tunesmith in the business already, you're gonna get there fast." Kyle read that sentiment twice before turning to Gene and asking, "Is that for real?"

Gene didn't take offense. He said, "I can make a phone call right now, and you can ask the lady yourself if she was just trying to make me feel good."

Showing a reporter's natural skepticism, Kyle said, "Yeah, I'd love to speak with the woman. I'm a big fan of hers."

Letting Gene and Maj know that he'd recognize an impostor, if they were trying to put one over on him. Even the slightest hesitancy in making the call would show they were trying to fake him out. But there wasn't any stalling. Gene just took out his phone and made the call.

"Hi, Alison, it's Gene … Well, not at this very minute, but you know how it is. Inspiration might strike at any moment. Listen, if you've got a moment, I've got a young fellow here who'd love to just say hello. Is that okay? For what? Yeah, absolutely. You get the first listen to my next song. Hold on just a second now."

Gene extended his phone to Kyle with a hand over the speaker.

"Be nice now," he told the reporter, "and don't take up too much of the lady's time."

Kyle nodded and took the phone.

"Hello, my name's Kyle Tompkins. I … Yes, ma'am, I am a fan. What? My favorite? Actually, I love the way you cover Paul McCartney's song, 'I Will.'" Kyle listened, and giggling like a kid, he covered the phone's speaker and told Gene and Maj, "She says Paul likes her cover, too." Returning to his conversation with the singer, Kyle said, "I just happened to see your photo in Gene Beck's office and the inscription you wrote to him. I said it sure would be cool if I got to talk with you sometime. What? You'll be coming back to Austin soon? If Gene would like to bring me along, I'd be welcome backstage. That'd be great, only I have to tell you, I am a reporter." Kyle laughed at the reply. "Yes, ma'am, I'll be sure to have my rabies shot first. Thank you for taking the time to talk with me. Good-bye."

Looking starry-eyed, Kyle handed the phone back to Gene.

That was when Maj told Kyle how she and Gene would like him to help them. Brought him back to earth like he'd fallen off a tall building. It took him a beat before he got out the question about lying in his own newspaper.

"The boy might have a point," Gene told Maj. "His paper probably won't reach the guy we want to see the story, anyway."

Kyle Tompkins became indignant upon hearing that. "We might not have the circulation of the *American-Statesman,* but we reach the people who matter most: young people with disposable income they spend like crazy."

The reporter crossed his arms in front of his chest as if ready to counter any rebuttal.

"Yeah, yeah, Anglo yuppies who read the paper on their phones," Gene said, "but how do you do with the ethnically diverse communities in town?"

Kyle's self-embrace slackened slightly.

"We do better with white folks, I have to admit," he said.

"Not so much with Latinos?" Maj asked.

"Actually, better with them than the African-American community. They're our second-biggest demographic and growing slightly faster than our number of white readers."

"They have more of a cross-over with the cowboy milieu than the black folks have?" Gene asked.

Kyle said, "I guess. I never thought of it that way before, never heard cowboy and milieu used in the same sentence either. So just what the heck is it ..."

Maj and Gene hadn't told Kyle just what kind of lie they wanted him to publish, only asked how he felt about the proposition generally.

Kyle put two and two together and got: "John Wayne. Is this about that missing John Wayne hat?"

Letting that question hang in mid-air, Maj asked one of her own. "Your paper's Latino readers, do they ever pass any stories along to family members back in Mexico?"

The reporter found that question interesting, and thought about it for a moment. "You know, I recall a few letters to the editor from people south of the border. Usually when some yahoo up here has ranted about shutting off immigration. I don't know if ... well, yeah, I do. I was going to say I can't think of any other topic that would draw a response from Mexico, but there was a story in our paper about Willie Nelson saying onstage that he'd like to play with Javier Bátiz someday. That got a *lot* of feedback from Mexico."

"I can see that," Gene said.

Maj couldn't. "Who's Javier Bátiz?"

She'd asked Kyle, but he handed the question off to Gene.

He said, "He's the godfather of rock 'n' roll in Mexico. Down there, he's called *El Brujo Del Rock,* the Warlock of Rock. He was the biggest early influence on Carlos Santana's playing."

Knowing all that earned Gene credibility points with Kyle.

Still, the reporter asked, "What's all this got to do with me lying in my paper, risking not just my job but my entire career?"

Gene looked at Maj, and she gave him a nod.

"What we're looking for, Kyle," Gene said, "is a way to sucker a major Mexican narcotics trafficker into coming up here to Austin. You think you could have some fun writing that story?"

The young reporter's mouth fell open.

After a moment's thought, he managed to say, "I don't know if I should run for cover or … wait a minute. *This* is tied into John Wayne's missing hat?"

Both Maj and Gene nodded.

"Damn," Kyle said. "Forget about second-tier newspapers. If I can't get a book-*and*-movie deal out of this, shame on me. I'm in."

***McGill Investigations International — Washington, DC***

Tad Thacker sat in one of McGill's visitor chairs and Sweetie sat in the other. The environmental engineer from Oregon looked from one of his hosts to the other and back.

In a soft, measured voice, Tad said, "I am in no way dangerous to either of you or anyone else." He paused to consider his words. "No, that's not entirely true."

In an equally dispassionate tone, McGill asked, "Who might consider you a menace, Mr. Thacker?"

The guest from Oregon answered with his own question. "Did your associate, Ms. Powell, give you my background?"

"As much of it as she was able to learn on short notice," McGill said. "Once we learned you hadn't left your home state in the relevant time period, we didn't investigate further."

"But she told you about Jenny Nyland dying, didn't she?"

"Yes, she did. Must have been a heartbreaking situation for everyone involved."

"It was. Still is for some of us," Thacker said. "To answer your question, if I find out something bad has happened to Alice — though I still haven't heard what your concern about her is — I might not find the self-restraint to … keep myself out of trouble."

Sweetie said, "From what I heard of Keely Powell's report, I understand that you came to realize your sentiment for Ms. Janeway was off the mark, to put it mildly."

Thacker nodded. "Yes, I saw that within a few days. I accepted that Alice wasn't Jenny, and there was no reason why Alice should think of me as anything but a frightening stranger."

McGill nodded. "Good thinking, Mr. Thacker. So why do I have the feeling you've got something more to tell us?"

Thacker gave McGill a thin smile. "Because you're good at your job, I guess. There is more. I'd like to give you something, but I need to reach in my pocket to do it. It's just a thumb-drive. Is it okay if I fish it out slowly?"

McGill and Sweetie answered simultaneously: "Slowly."

Thacker brought the thumb-drive out a millimeter at time and dropped it on the desk in front of McGill. "I never saw Alice again after that first night; I never went to another Teag Tobias performance after the following day. I realized and accepted that my behavior had been improper."

"But?" Sweetie asked.

Thacker said, "But I was curious. I wanted to know if there was more than just a physical resemblance between Jenny and Alice. There was no harm in that. Jenny was dead and Alice would never know. So I did some online research. Quite a lot of it, actually."

Disturbed now, McGill asked, "But you never attempted to contact Ms. Janeway again?"

Thacker shook his head. "Not even once. Not in any fashion. It was just a matter of curiosity, and possibly a way to see how Jenny's life might have gone had she lived."

"What did you find out, Mr. Thacker?" Sweetie asked.

He smiled sadly. "Based on what I knew personally about Jenny, and what I learned about Alice, there was maybe a fifty percent overlap. There were also distinct differences. I put my analysis, and all the information I'd gleaned about Alice, on that thumb-drive. I wanted you to have it. I thought it might be helpful to you."

McGill and Sweetie exchanged a glance.

McGill said, "Thank you, Mr. Thacker. I also appreciate your restraint in not asking the nature of the case we're working."

"You're welcome," Thacker said, and got to his feet.

Sweetie said, "You're not going home, are you, Mr. Thacker?"

He shook his head. "Could've just sent the thumb-drive to you express delivery, if that's what I had in mind."

"So what are you going to do?" McGill asked.

"I'm not certain. There was nothing I could have done to prevent Jenny's death. I was just a kid at the time. But if Alice is in trouble, and I have to assume that's why someone came to you, I just feel … I feel like I can't just sit by. I have to do something."

McGill said, "Mr. Thacker, our powers as licensed private investigators are limited by law. Generally speaking, evidence of a crime discovered by a private citizen is admissible in court, unless you tick off the judge. Then the appeals process can drag on for half of eternity, and if you committed a crime to obtain evidence, say illegally entering someone's premises or stealing a person's property, you can be arrested and prosecuted. You realize that, right?"

Thacker nodded. "Yeah, I do. That's why if I legally find any relevant information I'll share it with you. I read as much as I could find out about you on the flight east, Mr. McGill. I know you don't have any problem working with the police and federal officers. That's fine with me. I'm just trying to lend a hand. I owe that much to Jenny. Thank you for your time, sir."

He got to his feet, gave a nod to Sweetie and left.

Thacker seemed like a perfectly reasonable and competent fellow.

Except he had admitted he might do harm to anyone who hurt Alice.

Before McGill and Sweetie could begin to discuss Tad Thacker's sudden presence in the case, Esme buzzed McGill. "A phone call from Germany, sir."

"Marlon Janeway?" McGill asked.

"A Mrs. Erika Janeway," Esme responded.

The client's wife. McGill took the call. He was told in short order that there would be no further payments made on the matter her husband had initiated. If the services already rendered exceeded the amount her husband had paid, the issue would have to be settled in a German court.

The woman had begun her spiel without a *hallo* and ended it without an *auf wiedersehen.*

Well, Teagan Tobias had warned McGill about her.

***En Route to The Paxton-Carter Theater — Washington, DC***

Leo Levy drove McGill and Special Agent Ace Cole to the theater where Teagan Tobias was performing the final five days of his show's Washington, DC run. Sweetie remained at the office to view the material on the thumb-drive Tad Thacker had given them. She would plug it into a stand-alone laptop that was isolated from the company's network.

Both McGill and Sweetie had become computer savvy enough to suspect that Thacker, nice fellow though he seemed to be, might still try to pull a fast one and hope they would plug his thumb-drive into their computer system and give the guy from Oregon access to all their confidential files. Actually, it was Caitie McGill who'd warned her father about such a ploy and how to defeat it. She and a friend had used such a trick in a screenplay they'd written.

Not the current one to which McGill was listed as a co-author.

McGill had checked out the feasibility of Caitie's ploy with

Patti's data operations manager at Committed Capital, a former high-ranking official at the NSA. He'd told McGill, "You, as a happily married man, sir, don't need to worry, but most guys should be more careful about sticking third-party hardware into their data systems than where they stick their other hard thing."

The security exec had delivered his caveat with a straight face, so McGill had accepted it that way. He moved on to another concern, automotive transportation.

"Leo, I'd like you to drive Sweetie down to North Carolina. You okay with that?"

"Sure, boss. It's always good to go home. When do Ms. Sweeney and I leave?"

"The two of you should talk and work out the time."

Ace Cole asked McGill, "You're going to have Special Agent Levy or me drive you around in one of our SUVs?"

The rolling fortresses the Secret Service used, he meant.

McGill shook his head. When Cole started to object, McGill held up a hand.

"I've decided it's time I had my own car again. What would you recommend, Leo?"

From the grin on his face, Leo thought that was a good idea. "Foreign or domestic?"

McGill cut off another attempt by Cole to object and said, "I'm open to either."

"But not a one-of-a-kind machine like this vehicle," Leo said.

"No, something right off the assembly line."

"A stock car." Leo's smile broadened.

"Yes."

Ace slumped back in his seat, scowling and saving his fire for later.

"Has to be fast, maneuverable and damn dependable," Leo said.

"All of those things," McGill said. "It can be stylish, but shouldn't be *too* eye-catching."

"Right. Maybe even a little understated so the speed comes as a surprise."

McGill nodded. "Yeah, that'd be good."

"There's one big point to consider here, boss."

"What's that?"

"Thinkin' about what you want, you might wind up with a car that's *too* fast for you. Both off the startin' line and at the top end."

Ace Cole allowed himself a barked laugh.

McGill didn't rebuke him. The guy was only trying to do a difficult job, but he was beginning to remind McGill of a younger Celsus Crogher.

"How about this, Leo?" McGill asked. "You can put me through whatever training and tests you think appropriate, and I'll buy something that fits within my limitations."

"That's reasonable," Leo said. He glanced at Ace and threw him a bone by asking, "You got any suggestions?"

"Uh-huh," the special agent said. "Let him buy an M-1A2 Abrams."

That was the U.S. Army's main battle tank. Had a 120 mm cannon and a .50 caliber machine gun. Carried a crew of four, so McGill could bring all his kids. But it weighed 68 tons, had a top speed of only 42 miles per hour, and came with a $6.2 million price tag.

Leo laughed.

McGill asked, "Is the ammo additional?"

Cole muttered, "My idea's no crazier than yours."

McGill sighed. He didn't see a family resemblance between the young agent and Celsus Crogher, but they were definitely kindred spirits. Only Celsus had mellowed with time. Well, McGill wasn't about to go through the ordeal of lugging around another Secret Service hard-ass again. He'd ask Patti if she wanted to keep the kid as her full-time bodyguard. McGill thought he could live with Daphna Levy. If Patti didn't want Ace Cole, he'd have to go.

Leo pulled up in front of the theater, and sensing the vibe in the car asked McGill, "You carrying, boss?"

"No. I didn't feel particularly threatened this morning."

"You want Billy Joe or Little Minnie?"

Billy Joe was Leo's Smith & Wesson Bodyguard, a long-barreled .38 revolver; Little Minnie was a small Smith & Wesson Shield .40 caliber semi-auto.

McGill shook his head. He'd already gone running with Haskell Carver without carrying a weapon. The chance that he'd need a firearm inside the theater was minuscule.

"I'll be fine," he said.

Cole said, "I'll be there right next to you."

"No, Ace, you won't. Take the rest of the day off."

"I can't do that."

"Sure, you can," McGill said. "Leo, give him cab fare."

"What?" Cole said. "You're *dismissing* me?"

McGill said, "I am. We're not suited for each other."

The young special agent had his own thoughts about that, but he was wise enough not to give voice to them. He only said, "I'll call for my own ride."

"Fine," McGill said, "maybe there's a tank handy."

"Boss," Leo said, "humor me and take Little Minnie."

McGill nodded and accepted the compact semi-automatic, sticking it into a coat pocket. He got out of the car. The doors to the theater were locked, but there was a bell to press. McGill did so, and a moment later Haskell Carver appeared and let him in.

Leo watched from his spot at the curb until McGill disappeared inside.

Ace Cole walked down the block with his phone pressed to his ear.

Leo took his iPad from the glovebox and started researching cars for McGill.

***McGill Investigations International — Washington, DC***

Sweetie had just loaded Tad Thacker's thumb-drive into the isolated laptop when Esme buzzed her. "Ms. Sweeney, I have a call for Mr. McGill from the Austin office. Should I put it through to

Mr. McGill's mobile or would you like to take it?"

"Is it Gene or Maj calling?" Sweetie asked.

"Both of them."

"Sounds serious. I'll take it. Can I patch Jim into the call if he needs to hear from them?"

"Yes, ma'am. If you need any help with that, let me know."

"Thanks, Esme. Put them through to me."

She did, and Gene said, "Ms. Sweeney, this is Gene Beck. I'm here with Maj Olson."

"Hello," Maj said.

"Hello to both of you," Sweetie replied. "Something big going on?"

Gene said, "Might well be. We've come up with an idea to lure a major foreign drug trafficker here to Texas. We're about ready to run with it and —"

Maj jumped in. "We thought it might be a good idea to check in with you or Mr. McGill first."

Sweetie laughed dryly. "Yeah, that's a fair assumption. How about a little background on the situation?"

The partners from the Texas office took turns filling her in on Wallace Rhymes' missing John Wayne cowboy hat and how it wound up in the hands of Mexican drug boss Eloy Chavez.

"We think we've got a pretty good way to lure Chavez up to Texas," Gene told Sweetie.

Maj filled Sweetie in on the plan to use Kyle Tompkins' blog to make it look like Chavez got a knockoff of the John Wayne hat, not the real thing.

"We wanted to use Kyle's column in the *Austin Journal* to plant the false story," Maj said, "but we couldn't do that. It'd hurt the paper's reputation, but there's a link to Kyle's blog in the paper, and Kyle says everybody who reads the paper knows he saves the really juicy stuff for his blog."

"Okay," Sweetie said, "so if the lure works, what do you see as the problems? I've got my own ideas, but I'd like to hear yours."

Gene replied, "A guy like Chavez will have to personally

confront the people who made a fool out of him, but no way will he come to the U.S. alone. He'll have a posse with him. Not one so big he'll attract attention crossing the border, but big enough to stack the deck in his favor. They'll probably come in ones or twos and then regroup on our side of the border."

Maj added, "Also, before he comes to the U.S., he'll probably look to hurt or kill the two Fuentes brothers still living in Mexico and Solana Fuentes here in Texas. Gene and I have even considered the possibility that Chavez might even have Ernesto Fuentes' body dug up and desecrated. So we've taken steps to see none of that happens."

Sweetie said, "Good, and what kind of law enforcement reception party would you have waiting for these bad guys?"

Gene told her, "Our client, Wallace Rhymes, would like it to be strictly Texas Rangers and himself. He said he'd personally like to plug Chavez right between the eyes. Rhymes is a stock-broker pushing 80 years old, but down here you never know. He could well mean it. I suggested we'd also better have some DEA people on hand."

"Absolutely," Sweetie said. "If foreign drug dealers and killers enter the country, you've gotta have some feds on hand. They'd sulk if they weren't invited. You'll especially need them if you're looking for U.S. sanctuary for the Fuentes family. And tell the client that your company's chief ethics officer doesn't approve of taking mortal vengeance. Certainly not for a hat, even if it once did belong to John Wayne."

"Otherwise, we have your approval?" Gene asked.

"Yours and Mr. McGill's," Maj added.

"Let me talk with Jim and one of us will get back to you. Don't go ahead with your plan until you hear from us. Hold off discussing this with the Texas Rangers and the DEA, too."

"You think we'll get a go-ahead, though, right?" Gene asked.

Sweetie told him, "I can't say for sure, but I will tell you both Jim and I enjoy a good sting operation."

### *The Paxton-Carter Theater — Washington, DC*

Haskell Carver had the use of an office backstage that seemed barely big enough to have the oxygen for him and McGill to inhale at the same time. Even so, there was a second guest chair available if someone else cared to join them.

"Pretty close quarters in here," McGill said.

Haskell nodded. "Yeah, but it's a step up from the old days. You know, when I had to change into my Superman duds in a phone booth."

McGill grinned. "That was you, huh?"

"Well, before my football injuries piled up, that's who I thought I was."

McGill moved on to the business at hand. "I spoke briefly with Waylon Jakes. He confirmed that he considers the people who made the death threats to Teagan Tobias to be serious in their intent. He didn't provide any specific details, though. He only said I'd have to take that up with Tobias."

"He's just next door, in a considerably larger space, if you want to ask him."

"I will," McGill said. "I want to get their names and home addresses, if available. But how about you tell me what their plans for killing the man are?"

Haskell paused to reflect for a moment. "Well, as long as you're gonna find out anyway, the two guys both said they plan to shoot Teag. The woman didn't specifically say she would kill him, only cut off both his legs and then shit on his head. Everybody considers the double amputation as likely to be fatal."

"Gruesome as well," McGill said, "but was the threat truly serious?"

"She sent a photo of herself holding a chainsaw. The thing was running. You could tell by the way the edges of the blade were blurred."

McGill thought about that for a second. "If you're holding an activated chainsaw, it would be really tough to take a selfie."

"Yeah, well, even crazy people have friends."

"True," McGill said, "but the friend would have to be crazy, too, if he or she knew that the photo would be used as part of a death threat. On the other hand, if the photographer had been given a false, innocuous reason for taking the picture, you'd have yourself a possible lead."

Haskell smiled at McGill. "I like that. You are some kind of detective."

"The private and costly kind. I have to assume the photographer's name doesn't appear on the front or back of the print, but was there a manufacturer's name?"

"What kind of manufacturer?" Haskell asked.

"The kind that makes photographic paper," McGill said. "The use of high-quality paper to make the print might narrow things. Then you can look at the resolution of the photo, its depth of field, the composition of the person and the saw, the use of light and shadow, the color saturation, if the picture wasn't shot in black and white. Technique can be as telling a signature as a name."

"Wow. You know all that stuff, huh?" Haskell asked.

McGill said, "You work as a cop long enough, there's no end to the things you can learn. May I ask you something you might have observed and thought about?"

"What's that? I mean, you can *ask*, but I won't guarantee an answer."

"Fair enough. Here's what I'd like to know. Has Alice Janeway's absence put Tobias off his game in any way, and if Alice doesn't come back, might her absence wind up costing Tobias money in one way or another?"

The big security man gave McGill a long look. It wasn't threatening in any way; it was an assessment of the man who'd asked him not just one question but two. After a 10-second study of McGill, Haskell got up from his chair and went to the door. He opened it, leaned out and looked both ways. Listened as hard as he looked, it appeared. Then he reentered the small space and closed the door behind him. Took his seat again.

In a quiet voice, Haskell said, "The only credit for any writing in the show goes to Teag. Originally, he didn't even want any names used for any of the other people who appear on stage with him. Only he couldn't get anyone good who'd go along with that idea. So those people do get name credit in the Playbill. But as far as writing goes, Teag is the one and only, except ..."

Haskell looked at the door, leaned toward it and seemed to be listening again for the sounds of anyone approaching. He righted himself and turned back toward McGill. In a soft voice, Haskell said, "I've overheard some of the arguments Teag and Alice have had about writing. From what I could tell, Teag never gave an inch about writing the whole show himself ... but I've noticed some small changes in Teag's monologues."

"Like what?" McGill asked.

"I can't really put it into ... well, yes, I can. It's the *words* he's been using lately. Most always, in the past, Teag's words fell into one or two categories: the knife or the whip. He was always slashing or thrashing somebody or something. Lately, this past tour anyway, he's added ... damn, I guess you'd call it a tickle. Something that makes you laugh without anyone having to suffer for it, except for maybe Teag himself. You ask me, he gets some of his biggest laughs that way now, and thinking about it, I think that new approach had to come from Alice."

"Even if she hasn't gotten any credit for it," McGill said.

Haskell nodded. "Yeah, that's right. So, if I'm right about all this, yeah, Teag will miss Alice in more ways than one. She might have been the one to show the way forward. Keep things going for the long term."

The big man realized the subtext of his words and shook his head. "Shit, I hope she's all right. All our jobs might depend on her."

***Committed Capital — Washington, DC***

Edwina Byington buzzed Patti in the CEO's office. "Ms. Mindel is here to see you, Mrs. McGill."

"Please send Galia in, Edwina. No interruptions, please."

Other than emergency calls from Jim or their kids.

The same exceptions as when Patti had worked in the Oval Office.

Galia strode in, and Patti knew immediately that she wouldn't be breaking any unwelcome news to her former chief of staff. The storm cloud that stretched across Galia's brow said she already knew what was coming. That and she was far from pleased by Patti's decision.

Galia stood in front of Patti's desk, not quite glaring at her but coming damn close.

"Would you care to sit, Galia?" Patti asked.

"I don't plan to stay that long."

"All right."

"Frank Morrissey called me, after the president spoke to him."

"After I spoke to Jean," Patti said.

"That's right. In all the years I worked for you, I never asked for any special favors, but —"

Patti held up a hand like a traffic cop. "You did ask for a favor, after your children wanted to put you on a slow boat to a December romance, and I agreed to help. When Frank Morrissey intruded on our arrangement … well, I've never promised Frank anything."

Galia Mindel never wept, at least that anyone had ever seen. Still, her emotions were raw, and her eyes glistened. Most likely, she'd assert, with a sheen of acid not tears. "Damn it, Patricia, I could have succeeded at both jobs. You of all people should know that. I helped to make you president."

"Yes, you did," Patti said, "and that earns you a return of favor, but not a blank check."

Galia turned on her heel to leave.

Until Patti added, "Now, who taught me that favor-yes, blank check-no calculus?"

The question hit Galia like a rock between the shoulder blades. She tensed and stopped dead in her tracks. So Patti threw two more queries her way. "Do you think I'd deny you something just to be cruel? Have you ever seen me act that way?"

Galia turned, and now the acid began to leak from her eyes.

"Why couldn't you just have some faith in me?" she asked.

"Please sit down, Galia."

The former chief of staff didn't want to yield an inch, but when she saw Patti's eyes had misted, too, she gave in and sat.

"What I'm about to tell you," Patti said, "might send you running out of this office, cursing my name and swearing never to return." She took a beat of silence before adding, "And that wouldn't even be the part that bothers me most."

Despite her distress, Galia couldn't repress a smile. "No? What would be the worst part?"

"All on my own, the moment I heard Frank Morrissey raise his idea, I thought, 'I can't have Galia use my new company as a front for spying.' If that secret ever got out, that would be the end of Committed Capital, and I'd never get a chance to start over without suspicions arising that I was up to something duplicitous again."

"I wouldn't get caught. I can do this," Galia asserted once more.

Patti shook her head. "You also told me to beware of people who promise the world when they can't even deliver a cold-water walk-up in a bad part of town."

"Me and my big mouth," Galia said, showing no humor at all.

"You told me that was your mother's expression," Patti reminded her.

"Dead thirty years and the woman still haunts me."

"Okay, Galia, here comes the hard part. When I talked to Jim about all this last night, he said you don't have what it takes to handle the nasty, physical part of a job like the one Frank suggested. He said there's always a risk it could turn brutal, and you wouldn't know how to respond."

Galia's face turned to stone. "I'm stronger than Mr. McGill thinks."

"Jim reminded me of your encounter with John Patrick Granby in the White House Press Room."

Reflexively, Galia's hands went to her throat, reliving the horror of being choked to death. She realized what she was doing and forced her hands onto her lap. She met Patti's gaze and then looked down at her hands, as if they might act on their own again.

Patti said, "I didn't want to do it, but I thought I'd better look at the video of that awful day. My original idea was to show it to you. You've never seen it, have you?"

Keeping her eyes down, Galia shook her head.

"Good," Patti said. "It wouldn't be helpful to you at all. But I felt I had to see it, and Jim said he'd watch it with me. He'd never seen it before. After he watched it, though, he brought up a point I'd never have thought of, and I doubt you would either."

"What?" Galia said, still not meeting Patti's eyes.

"Well, as horrible as it sounds, Granby wanted a good look at you as you died. He thrust his head over your right shoulder as he choked you. Jim said if you knew some basic self-defense and had the mental fortitude not to freak out, all you'd have had to do to get free would be to hook your right thumb backward and straight into Granby's right eye. Jim said it was right there within easy reach, and you could have popped the eye out of his head like a seed from a watermelon, and Granby would have dropped the garrote like it was on fire."

A shudder passed through Galia, and now she looked up. "I didn't know that. How could I know that? How could I *do* that?"

"That was Jim's point. You couldn't and you didn't, but if you put yourself in the wrong situation, and Frank Morrissey can't guarantee that you won't, well then, where will you be?"

Galia didn't answer. She only got to her feet and crossed to the door to Patti's office. Looking back, her mouth moved as if she was going to say something, a rationalization perhaps, a reason why things would never get to that life-or-death point again, but not a word escaped her. The former White House chief of staff turned away, opened the door, and left.

Leaving Patti to wonder if she'd been wrong.

Maybe not showing the video to Galia had been a terrible mistake.

***The Paxton-Carter Theater — Washington, DC***

"You were talking to Haskell, weren't you?" Teagan Tobias asked.

McGill had stepped next door to Teag's dressing room.

The door had been open, so McGill had said, "Knock-knock."

Now, McGill took Teag's question as the opening to a conversation, so he stepped inside and helped himself to an available chair. "Yeah. You have that little closet next door bugged?"

Tobias offered a bleak smile. "No need; the walls are thin. Didn't catch the topic under discussion, but I recognized the voices. You care to fill me in? You know, since I'm the guy picking up Haskell's salary."

"Fair enough," McGill said. "Tad Thacker has nothing to do with Alice's absence. One of my people went up to Oregon and spoke to him and his boss. Tad hadn't set foot out of Oregon for the past year when he was interviewed."

McGill didn't mention that Tad was now in Washington, DC. Or had been earlier that morning. There was actually no telling where he might be at that moment.

"You didn't just take his word for that alibi, I hope," Teag said.

"His boss confirmed it. Said Tad had no absences from work and a record as a conscientious employee and all-around good guy."

"When he's not proposing to a woman he'd never met before."

McGill told Tobias the tragic story of Jenny Nyland.

To McGill's mild surprise, Tobias seemed to experience a moment of limited empathy.

"Really?" Tobias seemed to understand Tad's pain. Then he added, "His high school girlfriend looked like Alice, and she wasn't *way* out of his league?"

McGill added the grace note to the story: Jenny's parting kiss to Tad.

Tobias sighed, and a look of genuine pain filled his eyes. "Sonofabitch, that truly sucks. I can actually understand now why the poor sap acted the way he did."

McGill hadn't thought of Teagan Tobias as someone who could feel, much less understand, another person's pain. That was certainly out of character with the role he played in his show.

"I spoke on the phone with Waylon Jakes," McGill said. "He thinks the threats on your life are genuine, and some people I also talked with said Jakes is good at such evaluations. I was talking with Haskell just now about getting more information on the three people who threatened you. He told me there were two men and a woman, but he didn't give me any names or other personal information. That's what I need from you now. These people have to be checked out thoroughly and as soon as possible."

Teag frowned. "Why? They're after me, if you believe them, which I don't. They have no interest in Alice. They're not relevant."

McGill took a long, silent look at Tobias.

"What?" the performer asked when his patience with McGill's stare expired. "Even if I've got my head up my ass about my personal exposure here, what's that got to do with Alice?"

"Where'd you grow up?" McGill asked.

"Brooklyn. What the hell has that got to do with anything?"

McGill said, "Most people around the country, when they think of New York City, they're thinking about Manhattan, as they've seen it on TV and in the movies. They don't think about the other boroughs."

Injured homeboy pride now showed in Tobias' face. "Maybe they don't know jack about some of the other boroughs, but if they aren't total gomers they've at least heard of Brooklyn."

McGill nodded. "That's a fair assessment, I think. Being a

Chicago cop for 20 years, I had occasion to meet colleagues from other cities, including New York cops who worked in Brooklyn. They told me some pretty hairy tales about everyday street crime there, and lunatics on the loose, and the organized crime families based in Brooklyn."

"Yeah, you've got all that in Brooklyn," Tobias said.

"So, if you know all that, how come it never occurred to you that some SOB looking to hurt you might go after someone close to you? Seems like that would be something natural to suspect. But maybe you're just so egocentric it never crossed your mind."

For the first time in their brief acquaintance, Tobias seemed, to McGill, to be embarrassed. He explained it by saying: "Now you know just what kind of a prick I can be. Complete with moments of being a total dumbass. Christ, why didn't I think of that? You want to screw me, you could go after Alice. I've got my bodyguards. These days, what's Alice got for protection? Not a damn thing. Shit."

Tobias hung his head and covered his face with his hands.

McGill studied him. He thought he'd heard both pain and fear in the man's voice. His emotions seemed both appropriate and genuine … but he wondered once again: Just how good an actor was Teagan Tobias?

After what McGill estimated to be close to a minute, Tobias looked up. He glanced at McGill and then took out his phone and tapped a single key: speed dial. "Haskell, it's me. Yeah, I was just talking with him … No, that was okay, what you told him. I want you to give him everything we have on those three creeps who threatened to kill me. Yeah, *all* of it. I'll send him right over."

Tobias ended the call without saying goodbye.

He looked at McGill. "I've got to pull myself together before the show tonight. I'm going to need some time alone. If you want to talk to me, that'll have to wait until tomorrow morning."

He thought for a moment and added, "Not too early tomorrow morning — unless it's good news about Alice."

McGill stood up. "Okay, we'll do things that way."

Tobias added, "Close the door on your way out, will you?"

***En Route to McGill Investigations International — Washington, DC***

McGill had Leo take him back to the office, but not before he went back to Haskell Carver's cubbyhole, asked for and received copies of every security incident involving Teagan Tobias in the past twelve months. Printing out copies of the events took fifteen minutes. In addition to the three *serious* threats on Tobias' life, there were another eight warnings of murder deemed to be people just spouting off. In Boston, though, there had been an actual crime charged: attempted assault with deadly weapons. Two fools in the audience at one of Tobias' shows threw ten D-cell batteries at the stage from their balcony seats.

None of them had found the mark, but the nitwits had even more projectiles to hurl. Only Haskell's suspicion of the pair had prevented a further barrage. He hadn't liked their looks when he'd seen them enter the theater. He and another security heavyweight had decided to keep an eye on the potential trouble-makers. They'd pounced before Tobias could be hit.

Haskell told McGill that he had to restrain his colleague from tossing one of the cretins over the balcony railing.

"Only got him to stop by saying the idiot might land on some innocent person below," Haskell said. "That was the same rationale I'd told myself just a moment earlier."

Hearing all that, McGill asked the security chief, "Would you say Tobias is street-smart?"

"Hell, yes. Maybe even street-brilliant. His old man was a small-time accountant, but Teag hinted to me a couple of Daddy's clients were these guys." Haskell pushed the tip of his nose to one side.

Bent nose. Shorthand for a mafioso.

"Did Tobias ever make fun of any of those people?" McGill asked.

Haskell laughed. "He never said, but my guess is hell no. He'd know better."

McGill had found all that very interesting.

Skimming Haskell's print-outs on the ride to his office, McGill thought that definitely one and possibly two of the eight death threats against Tobias that had been written off as nothing but talk should be given greater credence. The performer's street-smarts must be slipping. Either that or Haskell had overestimated Tobias' savvy.

When McGill finished his reading, Leo asked, "How do you feel about foreign cars, boss?"

"Open-minded," McGill said. "Isn't Mercedes making cars in this country?"

"SUVs and a couple other models in Vance, Alabama. BMW has a plant in Spartanburg, South Carolina. Lots of Asian car companies have assembly lines all across the country. But what I'm thinking about is a German car built in Germany. For you, I mean."

"Sure, I'd consider it," McGill said. "I imagine you've got something relatively fast in mind."

"Zero to 60 in 4.5 seconds. I think you should be able to handle that."

"I appreciate your confidence." In fact, McGill thought that kind of acceleration was more than fast enough for anyone who wasn't a professional race-car driver.

Leo said, "Okay, then. I'll do a little more research."

He pulled into the garage at McGill International, and the boss went upstairs.

***McGill Investigations International — Washington, DC***

Sweetie waved McGill into her office when he got back to headquarters.

"What's up?" he asked.

"Were you a John Wayne fan?" Sweetie asked.

"A fan of his movies?"

"What else did he do?"

McGill said, "He was pretty far to the right politically, a fan of Richard Nixon. Defended him even after the Watergate scandal blew up."

"Jim, we were just little kids when that happened. How do you know about all that?"

"My dad was a precinct captain for the other side," McGill told Sweetie.

"He was?"

"Yeah. Anyway, Nixon was a bogeyman in our house. But I take it you were talking about John Wayne's movies."

"Yeah, did you like any of them?"

"I really liked *The Quiet Man*."

"Yeah, well, that was set in Ireland. How about all the cowboy movies he made?"

McGill said, "Not so much. What's going on here? The Wayne estate has a job for us?"

Sweetie told him, "It's more tangential than that, but it involves John Wayne. Sort of."

She briefed him on the case that the Austin office had taken and where things stood at the moment. "So what do you think, Jim? Should we be part of a plan to sucker a big Mexican drug dealer into a trap in Texas?"

Sweetie, of course, had mentioned that sworn federal and state officers would be involved.

McGill said, "The DEA will want to run the show once they hear of the idea and … that's probably for the best. A low profile on our part would probably lessen the chance of any comeback at us."

"I thought about that, too. We wouldn't want to put our role in any TV ad for the firm."

McGill laughed. "I didn't know we did *any* advertising."

"We don't. Of course, we could just tell the client down in Texas: 'Tough luck. Some modern-day *bandito* stole your cowboy hat? Live without it.'"

McGill asked, "Would that be the ethical thing to do?"

"People's lives matter more than a hat, and you didn't like the guy's movies anyway. Still, it doesn't feel right just to back off from a challenge."

"Call Gene and Maj back and tell them I said to sit tight tonight. We'll have a decision for them tomorrow morning."

Sweetie nodded. "Okay."

"That way we can each think about it some more, and get wise advice from our respective spouses."

"That's a good idea, but I'll have to phone Putnam. I'm going to North Carolina with Leo, remember?"

"Leave tomorrow," McGill said. "Get a good night's sleep at home. I'll see if I can get in touch with Byron DeWitt in the morning. Maybe as a former Deputy Director of the FBI, he'll have a suggestion how we might best handle the federal end of things, if we go ahead."

"Sounds good," Sweetie said. "Byron might even know some DEA honcho who *likes* John Wayne."

Before leaving for home himself, McGill stopped into Deke Ky's office on the first floor of McGill's headquarters building. Deke could have had an office up on the third floor with McGill and Sweetie. As a senior member of the firm, responsible for East Coast investigations from Washington, DC through Maine, he'd have been entitled to that perk. Only Deke had wanted a measure of relief from the scrutiny he'd have gotten up on the third floor.

McGill thought that was reasonable; he respected independence.

He knocked on Deke's office door and waited for permission before entering.

"How's it going?" he asked Deke as he stepped into the office.

"Good. Just wrapping up a case."

"What was it?"

"An economist at the Federal Reserve Bank had car trouble. So his wife drove him to work and picked him up afterward. On the way home, they got a text that their son had been taken to a hospital after being injured during a high school basketball practice."

McGill took a seat, and said, "An economist whose son is a jock?"

"Supposed to be a smart jock, captain of the team."

"Okay, so Mom and Dad rush to the hospital, and …?"

"The kid isn't there. They were pranked, and Mom's car was burgled."

"Let me guess," McGill said. "The thief wasn't after Mom's purse. So what did Dad have with him? Something, I hope, he at least locked in the trunk."

"Yeah, that's where it was: a report on an upcoming monetary policy the Fed is going to implement. Apparently, there are tech-savvy creeps who could have used the report's information to get an edge on futures trading."

McGill smiled and said, "I like your use of the conditional tense. That tells me the bad guys' plan was foiled."

"It was," Deke said. "Three guys are locked up right now, and two are running, but I don't think they'll get far."

"Good. So why did the aggrieved party turn to us rather than the FBI or the SEC or whoever?"

"The dad was once the professor of a Georgetown student named Abigail McGill."

"Ah," the proud father said.

"Also he wanted his missing report retrieved before he talked to his bosses and offered his explanation and, if necessary, his resignation."

"So how did you retrieve the report?" McGill asked.

Deke said, "I started at the beginning: Dad's car being on the fritz. The victim didn't think that someone might've sneaked into his garage and sabotaged it."

"But you did," McGill offered with a smile. "So who had the video camera that captured the bad guy's smirking face?"

"Actually, he was wearing one of those Guy Fawkes masks. Problem with that was, it must've kept him from seeing in detail what he needed to see while he was working on the car. So he lifted the mask, and that was that as far as seeing his mug. There was a disguised camera right there in the garage. Two more closed circuit cameras on nearby houses caught the van that the bad guys used."

"They didn't even think to steal license plates for the vehicle?" McGill asked.

"They did. Took them from a neighbor directly across the street from where they were living."

"Geniuses," McGill said.

"Lazy," Deke countered. "Anyway, I called the Metro cops and Treasury agents after I made sure the thieves were home. The cops secured the block and the feds broke down the front door to the house."

Deke smiled after sharing that last tidbit.

McGill had no doubt Deke would have loved to be on the entry team.

"So the good guys retrieved the stolen report?" he asked.

"Yeah."

"Good work, Deke."

"Thanks. You think we should give Abby a referral fee?"

McGill laughed. "I'll take her to dinner. That should do. You can come along for a free meal, too, if you like."

Deke shook his head. "Not necessary. Just doing my job."

"I admire your work ethic … so much I'd like you to take on something else."

"What?"

"You remember NYPD Detective Lily Kealoha?"

A spot of red appeared on each of Deke's cheeks. He'd been more than a little smitten by that particular member of New York's Finest.

McGill was kind enough not to comment on the blush.

"I do," Deke said.

"I was thinking of asking if she might do a little moonlighting for us. Nose around Brooklyn and see what she might find out about the early years of one Teagan Tobias. See if he might've had any trouble with the local cops and get a general impression of what he was like as a young man."

"I could do that myself," Deke said.

"Okay, if your schedule allows, go for it."

"Yeah, it does. Still, it wouldn't hurt to have some help from local law enforcement."

McGill nodded. "Your call. You know what your budget is. If getting a little extra help works within those numbers, it's fine by me. Just be advised, I'd like the information sooner rather than later."

"Of course," Deke said. "I'll leave for New York right away. Call Detective Kealoha en route."

"That's the spirit," McGill said.

For Deke's sake, he only hoped Lily hadn't found a new boyfriend.

***Chapel Hill, North Carolina***

Lindsay Todd was caught with curlers in her hair when the doorbell rang. She wasn't expecting her date for another 10 minutes. She was nervous as it was. She couldn't let him see her like this, but if he had to ring the doorbell more than twice before she could ditch the curlers and brush her hair, he might write off the whole evening and scoot.

A recent Ph.D. in American Literature, Lindsay had landed a tenure-track teaching slot at UNC. She'd been over the moon about that stroke of good fortune. The only thing that could make it better would be if she found a beau in a similar professional spot at one of the two other major universities in the Research Triangle: Duke or N.C. State.

Looking for a mate at her own university just seemed too claustrophobic. There were sports rivalries, of course, between UNC and the other two nearby universities, but she didn't give a fig about organized athletics. That made her something of an odd duck in the Triangle, and it might put off some guys, but she liked to run, and once they got a good look at her legs and other attributes, they'd be the ones saying, "Rah, rah, sis boom bah!"

Not that she was looking for someone who was interested only in appearances. She wanted a complete and compatible relationship. Someone with whom she could share the joys and aggravations of working in higher education. Someone who could discuss the events of the day in an informed and incisive way. So, telling herself there was no real downside, she'd signed up for membership on a very special dating site: Summa Cum Wednesday.

Limited to people with doctorates who didn't mind mangling their Latin a little, it was a way to meet bright young men and women, none older than 35, and get together with others of their kind mid-week when nearby restaurants typically had their dinner specials. The members of SCW got to meet with prospective sweethearts, chat knowledgeably, eat inexpensively, and reflect on Thursday whether there might be a Friday or Saturday encore.

All of that sounded delightful to Lindsay, only her date was too early.

It was all her fault, though. She'd opted to let the guy pick her up at home rather than meet him at the restaurant. God, she hoped he didn't turn out to be a creep. With a second ring of the doorbell, Lindsay decided she had to go to the door in her curlers.

Maybe that would be a good test of the guy's sense of humor.

A tale to be told to future children years from now.

In fact, the caller wasn't even her date.

Tad Thacker stood in front of her. He took note of her intermediate state of dress, nothing risqué but still not how he'd expected to be greeted, and blushed. Standing there with half of her head in curlers, wearing a housecoat, and, oh God, did she still have the Sally Hansen Bleach on her upper lip, Lindsay blushed, too.

She still had the presence of mind to demand of the untimely visitor, "Who *are* you?"

Tad managed to offer his name and say, "I'm looking for Alice Janeway."

Then he offered Lindsay a handkerchief. Seeing it was clean she accepted it, not knowing how she should put it to use. The guy who'd called himself Tad gestured at his own upper lip. Lindsay understood immediately and blushed more furiously than she had the first time. She had forgotten the Sally Hansen Bleach and immediately wiped it off her face. Wondering what to do next, she handed the handkerchief back to Tad What's-his-name.

That was when she saw her actual date had seen the whole burlesque act. He was early, too, and he looked like a man who was grateful that he'd just avoided a head-on collision. He gave Lindsay a little wave and said, "Maybe another time."

Probably not any time short of Judgment Day, she thought as he hurried away.

Furious, Lindsay growled at Tad, "Let me know when I can wreck your life at the most inconvenient possible time."

She stepped back into her apartment and was closing the door when Tad said, "I'm sorry, but I really am looking for Alice Janeway."

The door slammed shut before he got Alice's family name out.

But not before he'd again mentioned her given name.

Lindsay opened the door a crack. Peeking out, she asked, "You're not some sort of creep, are you? A stalker or anything like that."

"No."

"A bill collector?"

"No."

"A jilted boyfriend?"

"No. I think Alice might be in trouble. I'm trying to help."

The door opened another inch. The concern in Lindsay's voice was clear when she said, "Why would you think Alice is in trouble?"

"Because a private investigator and a police officer came to my place of employment and asked me about her."

The opening of the door narrowed, might have closed completely except Tad added, "I spoke with James J. McGill earlier today. His company is conducting the investigation."

"*The* James J. McGill, the one married to the former president of the United States?"

"Yes. Listen, I understand that I came at a very bad time, but I'd really like to speak with you. You were Alice's friend, right?"

"I *am* Alice's friend. We haven't spoken for a few months, but we're still friends."

"That's good. I saw a nice restaurant about a mile down the road."

"Benjamin's."

"Yes, that's it."

"It's a nice place, but it's not cheap. Most people around here say the name is double entendre."

"Sorry," Tad said.

"What it means is dinner for two will set you back a Benjamin, a hundred-dollar bill."

"That's all right with me. Listen, bring a friend with you. If you know a police officer bring him or her along. Dinner's on me."

Lindsay opened the door wide enough to poke her head out.

"Why do you think Alice is in trouble?"

"I wasn't told so by the people who questioned me, but I think she's gone missing."

A new reason for fear creased Lindsay's face. "That'd be awful, but why do you care? Do you know Alice?"

Tad said, "I'll be at Benjamin's for the next hour or so. I'll tell you why I'm interested, if you come."

"And bring a friend, right?"

"Absolutely. Anyone you like. I'm really sorry I messed up your plans."

Tad turned and left, sticking his handkerchief back in a pocket.

***Dumbarton Oaks — Washington, DC***

The lights were on at the new McGill manse when Leo pulled up with McGill in the backseat of the Chevy. Already parked in the driveway was one of the distinctive black armored SUVs that the Secret Service and other government entities used to transport poohbahs who might draw hostile shouts, hurled rocks or even gunfire.

"Looks like you've got company, boss," Leo said. "Mrs. McGill is still using government wheels and drivers?"

"She is, but that's not her ride."

Leo was about to ask how McGill knew that — high-end government vehicles tended to be clustered within the same model year, and all of them were black — but he decided to take another look at the SUV. He saw the distinction. The vehicle parked in McGill's driveway was clean but it didn't gleam. A light coat of dust had settled over it. Leo suspected the former president's ride was polished daily not just washed following inclement weather.

"Secret Service?" Leo said.

McGill sighed, knowing he had provoked this situation.

"Yeah," he said, "unless the Girl Scouts have up-armored their cookie sales."

Leo grinned. "Well, whatever's waitin' for you in there, take it like a man."

"Do my best, Leo."

"Hey, boss, how're you gettin' to the office in the morning?"

McGill said, "Maybe I'll buy a Metro pass."

Leo was tickled by the idea of McGill using public transportation.

Only because he didn't know his boss had ridden the CTA in Chicago for years.

"Well, good luck with that. Ms. Sweeney and I will see what I can find out down home."

"Thanks, Leo. Good hunting."

McGill exited the car and took his key out to open the front door as he approached his house. Leo motored off behind him. Before McGill got within an arm's-length of the portal to his home, the door opened. Patti was there, looking at him with an expression he knew well: the forbearance of a saint with an almost inaudible sizzle of underlying pique.

Her greeting to him was a peck on the cheek, not a kiss on the lips.

The angle of that platonic hello allowed McGill to see that Elspeth Kendry stood fewer than ten feet behind Patti, holding an attaché case. McGill was half-tempted to give the missus a pat on her backside. That image of marital familiarity might jar Elspeth, possibly throw some mental sand into the gears of whatever security lecture she was about to deliver. Instead, McGill opted for decorum and taking his scolding like a man, as Leo had suggested.

Also, he knew full well there wasn't a wife in the world who liked to be used as a comic prop.

He felt, though, that putting an arm around Patti's shoulders was within bounds — and also suggested that whatever slight differences of opinion might exist between the two of them, in the end marital unity would prevail. At least, McGill hoped so.

He told Elspeth straight out, "It just wasn't working out with Ace and me."

McGill felt somewhat reassured that Patti didn't try to slip away from him.

"Yeah, he feels the same way," Elspeth told McGill.

McGill nodded. Knowing that the sentiment was mutual reassured him.

"That's good," he said, "but we both know that my sending him packing made it easier for him to tell you that."

Elspeth nodded. "Special agents can't pick and choose their assignments, that's true. But there are a couple things that might not have occurred to you, sir."

McGill thought to say she could call him Jim, but the mood didn't seem right.

All he said was, "What might those things be?"

"What's most important is that you are unanimously considered the most difficult package in the history of the Secret Service." Package meaning a protected person. "And that challenge has only increased now that you have left the White House."

That evaluation surprised McGill, the emotion showing on his face.

Patti only rolled her eyes. McGill let his arm slide off her shoulders.

"Look, Elspeth ..." He paused to marshal his thoughts. "I've never been anything but polite, at a minimum, with the Secret Service. I'm not and never have been a First Lady; I can't be judged as a presidential spouse by the standards my predecessors have set. That would be not only unfair but also unrealistic."

McGill caught hold of another thought to buttress his argument. "I've heard that Byron DeWitt is doing remarkably well with his recovery."

Patti nodded and said, "The president told me as much today."

McGill smiled at her, appreciating the support. Looking back at Elspeth, he said. "Okay, then, Byron is the second male presidential spouse. More than that, he's a former deputy director of the FBI. Once he's back to full speed, does the Secret Service think he's going to meekly submit to any guidelines that were laid out for, say, Lady Bird Johnson?"

Elspeth looked as if she'd just been hit by a headache of McGill's conjuring.

Seeing her reaction, McGill said, "You hadn't thought of that? Well, get ready. You'll have your hands full with him. You probably won't even bother worrying about me anymore."

Elspeth was about to reply, quite possibly to say she didn't *worry* about him at all; her only concern was meeting her professional responsibilities. But McGill had another inspired thought, and cut off any reply with a raised hand.

He said, "If you think Byron or I are a tough cover, how would you deal with someone more like yourself? Another woman president, this one who has had her *own* law enforcement background, maybe even as a federal officer. Elspeth, what kind of a protection detail would you accept if you were the next president?"

That notion stopped SAC Kendry cold. For just a second, her mouth moved, but no words came out. McGill stepped into the verbal void, "I'm sorry, Elspeth. I'm not trying to make your job impossible; I just hoped to make you see things from my point of view. That and let you know more changes will be needed, with Byron DeWitt if no one else, and sooner rather than later."

"Thank you for that," Elspeth said, sounding not the least bit grateful.

She extended the attaché case she'd been holding to McGill.

"These are the current threats against your life, the ones the Secret Service considers credible."

McGill accepted the case, surprised by its heft.

Elspeth turned to Patti and said, "Good to see you again, Madam President. You have a lovely home here."

Looking at McGill she added, "Be well."

***Benjamin's Restaurant — Chapel Hill, North Carolina***

Lindsay Todd decided to meet Tad Thacker unaccompanied. She'd debated the wisdom of doing so. Yes, there was some risk in meeting an unfamiliar man alone. Only that was exactly what she'd planned to do with her original date for that evening. With that fellow, she'd even agreed to let him come to her apartment. What was to say he mightn't have pushed his way inside the premises and initiated a night of horrors.

Well, she had checked out his credentials before she'd agreed to the date. He had earned his doctorate with honors. He had already established a promising record of publications. He was likely making more money than she was, having a year's head-start on the path to pedagogical prominence. But, what the hell, all that didn't mean he mightn't be a creep or even a monster.

On the other hand, Tad Thacker, a complete stranger, seemed to present himself as a caring person. Lindsay could see in his eyes that he was genuinely worried about Alice, and now so was she.

Lindsay and Alice had been friends since their freshman year of high school. Then after Alice lost her parents, and her brother moved to Germany, they became closer to sisters. Alice moved into the Todd house to live with Lindsay's family. There had never been any talk of adoption, but Jerry and Lee Anne Todd had treated Alice like she was their third daughter, not a charity case.

Lindsay and her younger sister, Caroline, had done the same.

Alice had left school after getting her master's degree in secondary education. She was happy to teach at the high school level. It had looked to Lindsay as if Alice would become the beloved principal of some high-achieving school before she was through. Beyond that, Alice was a self-taught drama coach. She led two ambitious productions at her school every year, while Lindsay was still sweating out her qualifying exams and then working on her dissertation.

Alice had always found time to help Lindsay fight through the doubts that she'd ever get her doctorate or find a teaching slot at a school that wasn't Podunk U. After getting the job offer from UNC, Lindsay thought she and Alice would be the best of friends right through the time they became old widowed ladies, and then one of them would lead the way to their divine reward and the other would follow close behind.

Only Alice had gone to see Teagan Tobias when he came to Raleigh, and then went back every day for nearly a week. Lindsay couldn't understand it. She thought Tobias was just plain mean, even disgusting at times. And then, wouldn't you know it, Alice went to work for the dreadful creature. Took right off and traveled with him all over the country.

At first, Lindsay had felt more than a little revolted thinking Alice was sleeping with that vile creature, but Alice had disabused her of that notion. Said she'd never slept with Teag, as she called him. Not even once.

"Then what is the attraction?" Lindsay demanded. "Is it money?"

"I do make more than I'd ever earn teaching high school," Alice said. "I probably make more than you'll ever take home from UNC."

That shocked Lindsay.

"But what it really gives me," Alice said, "is the vicarious pleasure of seeing someone really just letting his anger fly in any damn direction he pleases. The first time I saw that, it was a revelation. The second time, it became a drug. I couldn't get enough."

Lindsay was struck dumb. Alice had never been anything but polite and pleasant while living with the Todd family. Her parents had absolutely fallen in love with Alice. So much so there had been a time when Lindsay and Caroline had felt jealous.

It took all of two seconds for Lindsay to think of the answer to the question that popped into her mind: What do you have to be so angry about? Losing her own mother and father at the same time, for one thing. Having her brother find a new life almost at the very same time, for another.

Yes, living with the Todds had been about as soft a landing as anyone could ask for, but that hadn't made the loss Alice had experienced any less traumatic. She hadn't been raised either to complain or show anger, but that didn't mean she couldn't enjoy the company of someone who'd raised vitriol to both an art form and a lucrative career.

Lindsay's insight had allowed her and Alice to remain close friends.

So much so that she didn't want to share family secrets with just anyone. That was why she hadn't brought a third party to Benjamin's. She also felt she'd be safe there unaccompanied. She saw Tad Thacker sitting alone at the bar. To Lindsay's eye, it looked like he had a glass of ginger ale in front of him.

That made her feel good. If the guy was really trying to help Alice, he wasn't going to let alcohol diminish his capacities. She walked up to within a few feet of him before he noticed her. Then he said, "You came alone."

"I did, and I'll leave quickly if you give me any reason."

He shook his head. "All I want is a little help, if you can do that."

"Let's see."

Tad had reserved a table in a quiet corner. They sat down, and he told her his story. He started by showing Lindsay a photo of Jenny Nyland. She looked at it for several seconds, amazed at how closely the girl from Oregon had resembled Alice. When Tad told her about the bus crash in Italy, tears formed in Lindsay's eyes.

Before their dinner orders arrived, she'd agreed to do anything she could to help him.

***Dumbarton Oaks — Washington, DC***

McGill revisited his bachelor father days and made dinner for Patti and himself: angel-hair pasta with tomatoes and basil. Per custom, he was also making his famous, all around his house, focaccia. Patti was slicing the tomatoes, as had been part of their ritual since she'd first dined with the McGill family at their now-sold home in Evanston, Illinois.

They worked next to each other at the kitchen counter of their far grander home in Washington. McGill's efforts were helped along by a chilled bottle of Yuengling Amber. Patti sipped a glass of Zinfandel.

Vivaldi's *Four Seasons* provided an ethnically compatible musical atmosphere for both the dinner and the couple's companionable silence.

After Patti had finished slicing more tomatoes than they'd need for three helpings apiece, she told McGill, "Galia is seriously displeased with me. Who knows, she might even sell her house."

McGill stopped kneading the dough for the focaccia and looked at her. "You mean the one next door?"

"That's the one."

McGill thought he should feel delighted, or at least relieved, but he suspected there was a trapdoor lurking somewhere nearby. One false step and it would be a long way down. So, treading carefully, he asked, "Was it something I said or did?"

He took a hit of beer just in case it was his fault.

Patti shook her head and said, "This one's on me … even if you suggested I needed to do it. I told Galia she couldn't work for both Frank Morrissey and me. She couldn't use my company as a front while spying for Frank. So I have to take the blame."

McGill took another sip of beer, and asked himself if he should enjoy two bottles that night. He decided to play it by ear. Maybe yes, maybe no. It would depend on the mood at the dinner table. An atmosphere of regret would caution against it; a spirit of resolve would favor it.

In the latter mood, he told Patti, "Credit would be a more apt description than blame."

Patti deflected the compliment. "The oven is ready. You'll have the dough done soon?"

"You can't rush perfection," McGill said, hoping for a grin from Patti and getting one, but just barely.

Then she let McGill know how she really felt. "Imagine if something came between you and Sweetie, and you were likely to see her only rarely, if at all."

Just the thought set McGill back on his heels.

Maybe it would be a two-bottle dinner in any case.

"I'd be lost," McGill said. "Sweetie is family."

"And Galia is the same to me, despite her hard feelings at the moment."

McGill nodded and thought he'd been pretty damn slow on the uptake. It shouldn't have taken him all these years to see the parallel between Sweetie and Galia. A true knucklehead, that was what he'd been.

He finished his beer and, dough still on his fingers, went to the fridge for another bottle. Returning to the kitchen counter, he topped off Patti's wine glass. He kissed his wife and said, "There's only one thing to do. It may take some time, but it will happen eventually, and when it does we have to be ready."

"What are you talking about, Jim?"

"Well, there are two main areas of concern with the plan Frank laid on Galia, aren't there?"

Patti nodded. "That Galia would get imprisoned, hurt or killed, and she'd ruin the reputation of Committed Capital."

"Right. If she has no professional connection to the company, and her estrangement from you becomes known, you'll have no worry about your company taking a hit if Galia gets caught with her knickers down."

"Not a charming image," Patti said, "but go on."

"Okay, so what we need to do then is intercede in the nick of time when Galia's amateur spy-craft fails, as it certainly will."

"Define 'we,' and how we'll manage said timely intercession."

"Before we even get to that, let's see if we agree that neither Galia nor Frank Morrissey will let go of this bonehead idea and move on to more sensible schemes."

"I don't think either of them will, do you?"

"No, so we're agreed on that. The next step, as I see it, is you'll need to have another chat with your sister president, Jean Morrissey. Tell her we'll need someone really good from, say, the State Department's Bureau of Intelligence and Research."

"The INR in the parlance of the intelligence community," Patti said. "Go on."

"The person we'll need, a woman, I think, will need a cover that includes globe-trotting responsibilities."

"So she can shadow Galia anywhere she might go," Patti said.

"Including the ladies' powder room or a health club sauna."

"I was wondering why you suggested a female operative."

"There's another consideration," McGill said. "As much as I love our conversations, I've always felt women speak more easily with one another."

"For the most part," Patti agreed, "but not always. Please continue."

"Anyway, you'll need to speak with Jean Morrissey to have her conscript someone from the INR to be Galia's shadow."

"I can do that. I think she already knows Frank and Galia will continue to think of some *sub rosa* scheme. She wouldn't want something to blow up in her face either. What's next?"

McGill said, "The dough is now ready. I put the focaccia in the oven."

Patti asked. "Do you see the INR person pulling Galia's backside out of the fire?"

McGill closed the oven door, set the timer, and shook his head.

"No. We wouldn't want an official of the U.S. Government getting into trouble either. What the INR person does is provide an assessment of the risk Galia is taking and report to us through a cut-out, say … Welborn Yates. Do you think he'd be up for it?"

"I do. So we learn Galia's taking a serious risk and then what?"

"No, we learn of the risk assessment before Galia goes somewhere dangerous. Then we send a person or a crew skilled in exfiltration in just ahead of her. If necessary, he, she or they snatch Galia and spirit her away in the legendary nick of time."

Patti thought about that for a moment. "If Galia doesn't know about anyone shadowing her, she'll think she's being kidnapped."

"As far as you know," McGill asked, "does she have a bad heart?"

"No, she doesn't."

"Good, then a bone-chilling scare will do her good. Let her have a taste of what she might really have suffered."

"What about the additional exposure the government will have if both Galia and the exfiltration people get caught?" Patti asked.

"Neither they nor Galia will have diplomatic passports," McGill said.

"No? You're thinking, what … mercenaries?"

McGill kept a straight face and said nothing.

After a long beat, Patti said, "All right, I never asked that question, so you never had to lie to me. When I was in the White House, I did authorize some off-the-books operations. I hope you'll never tell a soul. Not even the kids or Sweetie."

"I'll take it to my grave," McGill replied. "But I already know from someone else, whom I won't name, that there are people with government training and skills, now working in the private sector, who most likely could do the job I described: getting Galia's neck out of a wringer."

"That would be good," Patti said. "I like this idea."

"It might not work, but it's better than doing nothing."

"Yes, it is, but do you think Galia would be grateful if we saved her?"

"Her family would, and it's likely she would, too, but there's something even more important from my point of view."

"What's that?" Patti asked.

"*You* will feel better if we tried to help Galia and failed than if we'd done nothing at all."

Patti nodded. One of the main lessons the presidency taught any occupant of the Oval Office was you could only do your best, and then you just had to hope things went your way.

The oven timer rang and McGill took the focaccia out.

It was perfect, as always.

***Benjamin's — Chapel Hill, North Carolina***

The conversation between Tad Thacker and Lindsay Todd reached a critical juncture.

He said, "I'm sure Mr. McGill and his people have considered this, too, but do you think it's possible Alice reached a breaking point with Teagan Tobias, quit her job, and just took off for some sunny clime to decompress?"

Lindsay shook her head. "Alice is too thoughtful to do something that might worry anybody. She'd at least have let me know where she'd gone. Sent me a postcard at a minimum. Maybe even asked if I was free to join her."

Tad nodded. "That's why I thought I should talk to you."

It still creeped Lindsay out just a bit that Tad, a stranger, had done research on her.

But given what had happened to Jenny Nyland, she could forgive that. The guy was just hoping to prevent what might be a second tragedy. She could understand that, even admire it. How many guys possessed even a bit of the spirit of Don Quixote these days?

"So what do you think?" Tad asked. "Does Alice have any other old friends she might be staying with or who might have heard from her?"

"There's one," Lindsay said.

***I-95 — Virginia, Southbound***

After that night's show in Washington, Teag Tobias took I-95 south out of the nation's capital. Before he'd gotten onto the highway, though, he spent 15 minutes driving through town looking to see if someone was tailing him. There had been times when people who had been pissed off by his show had followed him. So had dirtbag reporters for scandal sheets, looking to see if maybe they could catch him banging his grandma or something.

But what really stoked Teag's paranoia that night was another idea: What if McGill had put someone on his tail? If McGill somehow had figured out that Teag was up to no good, say he'd done in Alice, which was part of their agreement after all, well then, McGill might consider the possibility that Teag might lead them straight to Alice. Or where he'd buried her.

That would assume, of course, that McGill suspected Teag of foul play. So far, Teag hadn't seen any sign of that. What he had recognized right from the start was McGill didn't like him at all. That was okay. Teag was a love-him-or-hate-him kind of guy, haters being in the majority.

Teag used a half-dozen techniques he'd either seen on TV or read in mystery novels to reveal and ditch anyone who might be tailing him. By the time he got on I-95 heading south, he thought all the evasion BS had been a waste of time. Washington, as far as he could tell, was an early-to-bed town on most work nights. People turned in at a reasonable hour so they could get up the next morning either to work for the government or try to suck money out of it.

Except for a parade of long-haul truckers, I-95 wasn't that busy either. Some of the bastards in the 18-wheelers were hauling ass like they thought the state cops had better things to do than write speeding tickets. Teag wasn't taking any chances that he might be stopped, though. He was obeying all the rules of the road.

He wanted to be a ghost in the night.

If things ever got to the point where he needed to arrange a power failure for Alice's life-support system, he wanted to be as far away as possible from the scene of the crime. He'd even want a nice period of time to elapse between his final visit to Alice and the moment she took her last breath.

Sure, he wouldn't be able to cover up that he'd known where Alice was all along, but that was no crime. Lying to a private investigator, even James J. McGill, was every citizen's right. Wasn't like P.I.'s were federal agents. It might even come out that he'd paid for Alice's care in her last days, but, hell, his financial generosity would be a mark in his favor.

The irony of it all was that Teag was hoping hard that Alice would somehow recover.

That bastard McGill had spooked him good with his analysis of Teag's show.

You couldn't just rag on everyone *all* the time. He had to show some heart, even if he'd never felt that way about anyone … except, he'd come to realize, Alice. Which was rich because he still had no physical interest in her. Not that she was bad looking. Not at all.

He'd just come to realize that she'd been dealt a shitty hand herself. Somehow, though, she'd found a different way to deal with it. Other than blaming the rest of the world for her troubles. That took a kind of strength he'd come to realize he didn't have.

He simply had no use for anyone who had no use for him.

Thinking of people like himself, he wondered if Alice's kraut sister-in-law had cut off the money to McGill yet. That might get McGill out of his hair real fast. But, no. McGill, from everything he'd read about him the past few days, wasn't the sort to give up. And Teag wasn't the kind of guy who got that lucky.

He exited the highway at Richmond and got to Old Dominion Palliative Care ten minutes later. That was one of the good things about high-end hospice. You paid the freight, visiting hours were whenever you wanted them.

The place was quiet and dimly lighted. Suitable to the time and general mood. Teag checked in and walked softly to Alice's suite. Or Barbara Lipman's, as she was registered under her alias. Besides her room, there was a second sleeping area and a bathroom for anyone who didn't want to leave the nearly-departed's immediate vicinity. The staff had even offered to hang creed-appropriate religious images and icons on the walls, if requested.

Teag had passed on that.

He appreciated, though, that someone had changed the lighting in Alice's room. It now provided a rosy glow. The result was that Alice's face looked almost as if she'd be ready to spring out of bed in the morning.

The illusion of vitality was spoiled when Teag took her hand. It was too cool, as if the hospice machinations could only go so far in simulating actual life.

Nonetheless, Teag said, "Come on now, Alice, let's fool all these bastards. It turns out I really need you."

## CHAPTER 4

***Thursday, November 3, 2017***
***McGill Investigations International — Austin, Texas***

Responding to a text sent the prior evening by James J. McGill — also known as the boss — Maj Olson and Gene Beck were in Gene's office by seven a.m. The phone rang at 7:05. The caller ID didn't identify the company's home office. It read: THE WHITE HOUSE.

Gene and Maj shared a look, but Gene picked up before a second ring sounded.

Gene said, "Madam President?"

A man chuckled and said, "Close but not quite; this is Byron DeWitt calling, along with Jim McGill on the line. Is that all right with you?"

Gene said, "He's the man who signs our paychecks, so it better be."

Two male voices in DC laughed.

Byron said, "I meant, was it all right that the president wasn't the one calling?"

Maj said, "We're reassured that she has more important things to do."

That got another laugh.

"Right," DeWitt said. "Anyway, Mr. McGill called and asked me if I might suggest someone in the DEA who could help you bring a *Señor* Eloy Chavez to American justice. I called a friend who has a friend well placed in the DEA. She told me Chavez is currently number two in the narcotics business south of the border, but just like Avis, he tries harder."

"He's going to take a run at number one?" Maj asked.

McGill provided Maj's name to DeWitt. "Yes, Ms. Olson. It's a terribly cutthroat business in the most literal sense. After hearing from Mr. McGill last night, I learned from a source who must remain nameless that Mr. Chavez has placed great stock in his new hat."

"What?" Gene asked. "He thinks he's the new John Wayne?"

DeWitt said, "Not so much the man as the icon: a heroic figure who can never be bested."

Maj said, "Last night, while we were waiting to hear from Mr. McGill, I watched the movie where John Wayne wore that hat. It ends with him getting shot and killed."

"It sure does," Gene agreed.

DeWitt said, "I saw it, too. Part of the story has villains coming out of the woodwork thinking they can finally take down the big hero. The agreed upon thinking among the DEA upper echelons is that Chavez thinks he's one of the up-and-comers who *can* knock off number one. The hat will only make him think more so. So when he hears it's a knock off and the real one is still in Texas, he will come to grab it, in person. That way he'll be assured, at least in his own mind, that he'll be the victor when he goes back home."

"Why wouldn't he just send someone to get it?" Maj asked, playing the devil's advocate.

McGill spoke up. "You want to take that one, Gene?"

"Sure," Gene said. "The hat, in this case, is his crown. If someone else grabs it, that guy might draw enough followers to his side to take on Chavez and anyone else."

For the benefit of the power duo in Washington, Maj said, "Okay."

To Gene, the only one who could see her, she silently mouthed, "Men."

"Crystal clear to me," Gene told DeWitt and McGill. "But is this going to be a federal power grab or will there be room for a cast of thousands? I ask because our client, Wallace Rhymes, the hat's rightful owner, wants to be involved, and he has a whole lot of friends in state government and law enforcement. Someone messes with Texas, they think it's their fight."

"Understandable," DeWitt agreed. "You'll be hearing from the DEA in the person of Chief of Operations Anne Macklin. Mr. McGill and I briefed her on this situation, and while she believes in the DEA leading the charge she's promised to be collegial in her approach. She feels this is the kind of opportunity that might be one of a kind."

"What's our role here?" Gene asked. "What do Maj and I do?"

"Serve as honest brokers between local people and the feds," McGill said. "That and making sure you don't get shot."

"How about creative input?" Maj asked. "We're the ones who came up with this plan."

There was a click and a momentary silence. Gene and Maj knew a private conversation was taking place. A moment and another click later McGill said, "If you come up with bright new ideas, feel free to offer them."

DeWitt added, "If they're really good ideas, but the powers that be just don't understand them, get back to us. We'll see what we can do. Is that fair?"

Gene and Maj agreed it was.

***Old Dominion Palliative Care — Richmond, Virginia***

For the first time since Alice had zoned out on him and had to be hospitalized, Teag Tobias spent the night with her. Well, in the adjoining room. Part of that was he thought he was just too tired to make the drive back to DC safely. Wouldn't do anybody any good if he ran off the road and hit a tree. Killed himself. If that happened, fate would rewrite the script, and Alice would wake up as good as new.

All the people who thought Teag was a shit would laugh themselves sick.

The haters getting sick part was all right with Teag. The part where he died wasn't.

He yawned, stretched, gave himself a good scratch or two and slowly got out of bed. His reluctance to be more lively owed to the thought that he had to move only a few steps to see whether Alice was still breathing.

He even thought Alice's remains might be gone. Carried away by hospice staffers who'd seen she'd died. He'd been left sleeping as a kindness. That or the place was tacking another day's charges on his tab. Bastards.

Teag's characteristic bile got him moving. Alice was right where he left her. Only the rosy lighting from last night had been extinguished, replaced by morning sunlight pouring through the windows. That did an even better job of making Alice's face seem lifelike. Unable to restrain emotions he'd conceal from the rest of the world, Teag gently stroked Alice's cheek with his right hand.

And, damn, if she hadn't warmed up. Seemed almost normal. He went back for a second pass with his hand. Still warm. He wondered if that was simply the effect of the sun. Teag thought to look at the array of monitors on the other side of the bed.

Alice's body temperature had been hovering just under 96° last night.

Now, it was a solid 98°. He thought that had to be a good sign. Didn't it?

He looked at the monitors for heart rate and blood pressure. They both were stronger, too. Damn, he'd never believed in miracles, but *something* was going on here. He reached out and stroked Alice's cheek a third time. That was when her eyelids fluttered open.

It was just for a second, but he'd swear she'd made visual contact with him.

He grabbed the room phone, hit zero, and yelled at the person who answered, "Get me a doctor right away!"

### *Woodley Park-Zoo Metro Station — Washington, DC*

McGill stepped out of his front door trying to remember the last time he'd regularly taken public transportation to work. He thought it was … when Abbie was a toddler, just starting to walk but still in diapers. She'd caught a persistent cold that evolved into bronchitis, leaving Mom and Dad to worry that it might take an even nastier turn and become the flu.

In those days, any number of children fought their way through a bout of influenza with only home care and over-the-counter remedies. It was something of a middle-class rite of passage before the flu vaccine became routinely administered. Only McGill's parents had lost a child, a baby girl, to the disease. So the virus was regarded with great seriousness and no small alarm in his family.

The departed infant, Emma, had been born two years before McGill. He was five years old when he'd learned that his parents had briefly had a daughter. The subject only came up because he'd asked his mother if heaven was real. Even at that tender age, it seemed to him to be too good to be true. That was when Mom had told him that heaven was where his sister lived.

McGill had forgotten all about heaven for the moment and wanted to know everything about his sister. When he learned she'd died before her first birthday, he flew into a rage. A baby taken so shortly after being born? He couldn't imagine anything more unfair. After that, even though he'd yet to be born, he'd often felt there was something he should've done to save his sister. The fact that he'd arrived too late to do anything sometimes made him weep.

Still, he was well able to do everything that he could to make sure Abbie recovered and thrived. He left the family's only car with Carolyn to speed their little girl to the hospital, should that become necessary. He took a bus and the "L" to the station house.

Even after Abbie had recovered, McGill continued to rely on public transit to get to work. Carolyn was soon pregnant with Ken, and McGill wanted to be sure his wife could get to the doctor without waiting for a bus or a train. It was only after Caitie was born and a thriving two-year-old that the family bought a second car, and he drove to work again.

McGill appreciated the convenience of having his own wheels, but for at least the first year of doing his own driving he missed taking the CTA. There were few uniformed cops who did that, rode to work with the commuting public. He got a lot of smiles and even some handshakes from the other commuters.

It wasn't as if the public was in love with cops, though. There was plenty of antipathy, a good deal of it deserved. Still, when most people saw him get on the bus or an "L" car, and he smiled at them, they felt safer for his presence. Were glad to have him aboard.

That morning in Washington, McGill walked to the closest Metro station. Paying for his ride took a bit of education. He needed to input his departure and arrival stations, grin and bear it that he'd have to pay peak travel time fares, and then purchase a SmarTrip card for his passage. Managing to do all that, he made his way, a *long* way down it seemed to him, to the subway platform.

He'd no sooner arrived than he heard a woman scream. A surge of adrenaline brought him up on his toes. Maybe 100 feet ahead on his right, McGill saw a man tussling with a woman at the edge of the platform. Other nearby commuters quickly began to scream and disperse.

McGill started to run toward the confrontation. Two strides into his approach, he also saw a man in jeopardy. The man was off the platform and on the tracks, attempting to climb back up. The first man, the one wrestling with the woman on the platform, looked as if he might shove her onto the tracks, too.

Christ, McGill thought, that guy had to be a lunatic.

As he ran, he caught sight of an electronic sign saying the next train arriving on those rails was two minutes away. The madman looked as if he would succeed in throwing the woman onto the tracks before then. The old guy who must've been pushed on the tracks, however, was making progress climbing back onto the platform. The attacker switched his attention back to him. He stomped one of the man's hands and kicked him in the chest. The man fell backward.

As McGill raced forward, he saw that the Metro had an electrified third rail just like the Chicago subway. If you hit that thing you'd be dead before the train smashed you to pulp.

McGill's progress was slowed by the mob of people racing toward him, away from the conflict. He had to dodge back and forth between them. His mind whispered to him: *Walter Payton and a little Gale Sayers, too.* Inspired by memories of two of football's greatest runners, he hit the holes in the fleeing mob faster and soon came out on the other side.

That was when he saw a woman carrying an attaché case running toward the scene of the fight from the opposite end of the platform. She had a clear path all the way. It was an open question as to which of them would reach the conflict first, and whether either of them could intervene before the oncoming train arrived.

Then he saw a small boy, maybe seven or so, pop out from under a bench opposite the madman and sink his teeth into the lunatic's right leg. The attacker's hands shot straight up as if he'd been electrocuted himself, maybe saving the woman — the boy's mother? — from being pushed onto the tracks.

The other woman, the one with the attaché case, saw McGill closing in fast. She pointed a finger at herself and then at the madman's head. McGill understood what she'd signaled. She would hit the bastard high. He should hit him low. He nodded to her.

She got there a step ahead of McGill. She didn't just plow into her target. She clipped his head with her attaché case. The blink of an eye later, arms wide, leading with his right shoulder,

McGill slammed into the bastard's midsection, wrapped him up and slammed him to the surface of the platform.

Sometimes martial art skills were what carried the day.

Other times the simple application of roaring brute force was the winner.

McGill was rewarded with the sound of ribs cracking, soft-tissue thudding and a thin shriek of pain before the bad guy went quiet. Getting to his knees, and then his feet, McGill heard the oncoming train slam on its brakes. The grating squeal was horrific.

But the two women had helped the man, an old gent, McGill could now see, up onto the platform just before the train skidded by, throwing sparks. McGill thought to look for the kid who'd bitten the madman. The boy was standing next to the bastard, kicking him in the back as hard as he could.

He stopped when he saw McGill watching him.

McGill gave the assailant a none too gentle kick in the ass.

The kid laughed when he saw that, followed it with another kick of his own, and then burst into tears. He ran to the woman who was hugging the old guy. "Mom! Grandpa!"

Cops were hustling down the escalator now, looked like a platoon of them.

McGill walked over to the woman who'd held the attaché case. She was picking it up off the platform. She looked at McGill and said, "That lady and I got the old guy off the tracks in … hell, it wasn't the nick of time, it was the nick of the nick of time."

Extending a hand to her, McGill said, "Nice work, however close you cut it. I'm Jim McGill."

She shook his hand and said, "Emma Wiley."

McGill's heart almost stopped. "Emma?"

### *Committed Capital — Washington, DC*

Edwina Byington ran into Patti's office in such a state of high commotion she almost gave the former president a heart attack.

Patti jumped up from the chair behind her desk as the blood drained from her face. All she could say was, "Jim or one of our kids?"

"Mr. McGill, ma'am."

Patti's knees buckled. Edwina caught her and managed to direct her back to her chair.

"No, no, ma'am. He's all right. Everyone's all right, but you have to see what he did."

"Something bad?"

"No, ma'am. Something wonderful. Mr. McGill and a woman named Wiley."

Still regaining her balance, weak now from the mercy of hearing she hadn't lost anyone she loved, Patti asked hoarsely. "What? Tell me what happened."

"I'll show you, ma'am. Describing it is beyond me."

There was no television in Patti's office: her choice. But she did have an iPad Pro with a 12.9 inch screen. A silver-haired senior who was proud of keeping up with modern office tools, Edwina pulled up the MSNBC website on the tablet computer, and Patti saw, right from its start, the video that was running on an almost continuous loop at the moment.

The grainy resolution and the flat colors of the scene told Patti she was watching security camera footage, but she recognized her husband immediately, and wondered what in the world he was doing in the subway. The video didn't have a sound track, but she saw the sudden look of alarm on Jim's face and knew he must have heard … something awful, judging by the way he took off running with such fierce purpose.

Patti squeezed the arms of her chair and leaned forward as she saw Jim hurtle like a madman through a crowd of fleeing bystanders. Just as Jim cleared the knot of people, the view maddeningly cut to a woman with an attaché case also sprinting down a subway platform. A second before Patti was about to curse the editing decision of whomever cut away from Jim, she saw both her husband and the woman enter the same frame and the two of them collide with a man so forcefully she was sure they must have killed him.

No, wait, the woman had hit the man with an object she held in her hand and then turned toward the subway tracks.

Patti watched the loop again, and then Edwina paused the video and took the iPad back to its homepage.

Edwina said, "That creature, the one Mr. McGill and the lady clobbered, ma'am? He'd pushed an elderly man onto the Metro tracks and was trying to do the same thing to a woman. A train was approaching. Mr. McGill and the lady saved two lives."

Patti looked at Edwina and smiled through her tears, still at a loss for words.

Before Edwina could elaborate further, the phone on Patti's desk rang.

Edwina looked at the caller ID and said with a straight face, "It's Mr. McGill, ma'am. Shall I put him through?"

***University Hospital — Richmond, Virginia***

Sitting in a lounge at the end of a hallway opposite the room where a team of doctors, each of them seeming to have his own nurse for company, was examining Alice, known to the hospital staff as Barbara Lipman, Teagan Tobias was doing his best to ignore the TV that a worried-looking middle-aged woman was watching. Only minutes ago, Tobias had been evicted from the room where Alice was being examined.

He'd tried to resist, had said he was paying all of their goddamn fees and he'd stay as long as he pleased. That was when a nurse, the toughest looking woman he'd ever seen, had told him, "Get the fuck out of here right now, or I'll put *you* in intensive care." She held a ball-point pen in her hand, and he was sure she'd try to stick it in him somewhere.

Any other time, he'd have put her to the test, but he didn't want Alice's care interrupted so he left. And now the woman who'd been looking at the television was tapping him on the arm and saying,

"Watch this, watch this."

Tobias was about to tell her to leave him the hell alone when he caught sight of James J. McGill running hell bent for leather down what looked like a subway platform. Holy shit, he thought, what was going on?

McGill and a woman coming from the opposite direction absolutely destroyed some cluck standing on the platform. It didn't make any sense to Tobias until the video loop restarted from the beginning with a chyron at the bottom of the screen: *The Henchman Returns, and Now He's Got a Sidekick.*

Now, Tobias' eyes were absolutely glued to the video. The footage didn't have a soundtrack, but McGill must have heard a cry of distress and, bang, he was off to the races. Ran really fast for a guy his age, too.

The way McGill darted in and out between all the chickenshits running the other way was pretty damn amazing, too. Tobias thought McGill's knees, maybe even his ankles or his hips, should have given way when he made some of those cuts. But, no, he just kept right on sprinting, didn't look like he slowed down for a second.

Then he absolutely *crushed* that bastard on the subway platform. The best linebackers in the NFL would be cheering and slapping their knees in approval when they saw that hit. He could almost hear the pro jocks saying, "Now, *that's* the way you do it!"

And the woman who'd helped McGill, she was something else, too. She'd whipped that attaché case around like she was swinging a headsman's axe. She didn't take the guy's head off, but she had to fracture his skull. Then just a few moments later she and McGill were shaking hands.

Congratulating each other on a job well done, Tobias thought.

All of which made Tobias think it was now a good time for him to make himself scarce. Somewhere *he* wouldn't have to worry about McGill. He'd take Alice with him, if she recovered enough to travel. He would have prayed for such an outcome, except he didn't believe in any pleadings like that.

Even if he was wrong about divine intercession, he didn't kid himself that he deserved anything resembling a miracle. The best he could do was hope, and even that was likely a set-up for disappointment. Always had been for him.

He was watching the video loop of McGill for what had to be the tenth time when the tough nurse who'd kicked him out of the treatment room tapped him on the shoulder. Tobias saw that she still had her pen in hand with the metal nib out.

Good for her, he thought, she was no fool.

"Yeah, what?" Tobias asked.

"Your friend, Barbara." Alice's alias.

He thought the hard-ass nurse was going to say Alice had died.

That'd be about right for him. Get his hopes up and …

The nurse put her pen in a pocket and said, "She spoke your name."

***Outside Lindsay Todd's Apartment — Chapel Hill, North Carolina***

Lindsay rose with the first rays of sunrise and went outside to where Tad Thacker reclined asleep behind the steering wheel of his rental car. She rapped gently on the window next to Tad's head. He stirred and shifted position but didn't wake up. It was early on the East Coast, earlier still for someone jet-lagged and whose circadian rhythm was still functioning on Pacific Time.

Nonetheless, she rapped again, not loud enough to jolt him awake but sufficient to get his eyes to open. Lindsay could see that he didn't recognize her immediately. Then as he started to orient himself her face clicked into place. She thought he might have been about to smile, only he winced and put his right hand on the back of his neck. Obviously, his body was starting to complain about where it had spent the night.

He let himself out of the car and straightened up slowly, seeming to experience only minor stiffness except for the pain in the neck.

Lindsay said, "You didn't have to spend all night in your car. You could've gone to a hotel, and I would have called you."

Tad gave a weak grin. "My mother says I'm reasonably smart, but not always sensible."

"Maybe you can work on that second part. Come on in. I'll give you some ibuprofen and coffee. There are muffins I can heat up and an apple if you're hungry. You're also welcome to use the bathroom, if you didn't pee in the shrubbery last night."

Tad looked mortified at the thought, but then he realized a sudden urge was making itself known. "Yes, thank you, I'd like to use your bathroom. The coffee and the food would be welcome, too. And the ibuprofen."

Letting him into her apartment, Lindsay said, "One breakfast special coming up. Bathroom is right down that hall. Kitchen's at the back of the place."

Before going their own ways, Tad asked, "So can you tell me the name of that one friend that Alice might have decided to call on for help?"

"Her name is Elise MacAdams, another college classmate."

"Thanks. If you'll excuse me for just a moment …"

Tad ran to the bathroom. He wanted to relieve that necessity right away. He also wanted to distract Lindsay. She'd no doubt be upset with him if she knew just how much he had learned about her.

Hell, she'd likely kick him out of her apartment.

### *McGill Investigations International — Washington, DC*

Rockelle Bullard, chief of police for the Metropolitan Police Department, gave McGill a ride to his office after he finished talking with the crime scene cops and his wife. He'd asked Patti if he should come to see her in person at Committed Capital.

Patti had asked, "You're not hurt in any way?"

"I wouldn't mind a good massage and long soak in a hot tub, but otherwise I'm all right."

"Good. I can and will make sure you get both of those things. Have you located Alice Janeway since you left home this morning?"

"I've been a little busy," McGill said.

"As the whole world now knows, yes. My point was, if you're well enough to work, you should do so."

"Duty first and foremost, right."

"One other thing."

"Yeah?"

"Use a car service wherever you go next."

McGill laughed and said he would.

The DC chief of police, one of the tougher women McGill had ever known, picked up where his wife had left off. "You feeling all right?"

"I have a tear in my right pant leg," McGill said. "Not a good look for a professional man, but I keep a change of clothes at my office. Also have my own private shower."

Rockelle said, "La-di-da. How's the leg where those pants got ripped?"

"Now that you bring it to my attention, my knee is a little sore."

Rockelle nodded. She'd seen the video of McGill in action on her way to the scene of the crime. "I'm surprised both of your legs aren't sore. I didn't know you, or any middle-aged white man, could move that fast with all those fancy moves."

McGill told her, "I also have an on-key singing voice, and I can do a creditable Nat "King" Cole take-off when I want to."

The chief of police laughed. "I bet you can. You'll have to do a charity performance sometime." She left things there as they arrived at McGill's office building.

He had just finished cleaning up and donning new clothes when he received a call from yet another woman who'd seen the video of his exploits that morning: Dorie McBride, Hollywood super-agent.

"You were magnificent!" she told McGill by way of saying hello.

McGill replied, "Is that you, Mom?"

"What?"

"Just kidding, Dorie. My caller ID told me who's on the line."

"Oh … how old is your mother?"

"She's sworn me to secrecy, but just like you her beauty is timeless."

Dorie laughed. "Irishmen and their blarney."

"It's a big hit with the ladies," McGill agreed. "You have any news for me on Teagan Tobias?"

As someone who never forgot the importance of sticking to business, Dorie shifted gears, "I do. Mr. Tobias is relatively well off when compared to the average American. Wealthy in a minor way when compared to top-tier show business folk. He does well enough in current box office revenue for a one-man stage performer."

"No complaints then?" McGill asked.

"My dear boy, there's always room to complain in show business. While Mr. Tobias is doing sufficiently well in the here and now, his future looks less rosy. Graphing his critical and monetary progress since he started performing, the first three years were a dramatic climb; the next three were less so; the last four he flatlined. The two after that show a shallow drop-off. Projecting ahead, I'd say the next two years will be his last marketable ones. After that, it's 'what ever happened to old what's-his-name?'"

McGill could easily imagine the picture Dorie had painted. "It's a cruel business, performing."

"For most people, yes."

McGill paused a moment before asking, "Do you think that's how it would have gone for Patti, if she'd stayed in acting?"

Dorie took a beat before answering. "It might well have. Being in the public eye is especially cruel for women. When the audience sees a favored actress grow old, they're reminded the same thing is happening to them. With a series of wonderful scripts, though, I think Patricia might well have outlasted most of her peers, but you know the problem with that."

"There's only so much good writing to go around?" McGill asked.

"Exactly."

"Do you think Tobias could extend his career if he got some good, fresh material?"

"It would certainly help his public viability, give him another five good years, maybe even ten if the new approach was timely and had continuing resonance with the public."

"Another five-to-ten years would also mean a lot more money for him, right?"

Dorie told McGill, "We'd be talking eight-figure money, maybe even nine."

***Lindsay Todd's Apartment — Durham, North Carolina***

When Tad Thacker made his way to Lindsay Todd's kitchen table, he found the promised cup of coffee, still steaming, two blueberry muffins, also recently reheated, an apple, a previously unmentioned banana and a bottle of ibuprofen waiting for him. His sore neck was telling him to take the pain-killer first.

"May I have a glass of water, please?" he asked Lindsay.

She accommodated him from the kitchen sink. He washed down three tablets, and measuring his hostess's facial expression asked, "May I sit down and eat?"

"Only if you tell me just how far you've been poking your nose into my friend's life."

"Pretty far, but only for purposes of comparison, nothing predatory."

"You sure about that?"

"Absolutely. I saw Alice only one time, for probably less than two minutes."

Lindsay stayed on her feet for the moment, leaning against the kitchen counter. There was a drawer to her right. Tad was thinking there could well be a knife or two in the drawer that might inflict great bodily harm if used in a hostile fashion. And who knew, in the South, she might even have put a handgun in there.

"Remember last night how I showed you the photo of Jenny Nyland?" Tad asked.

"I do. There was quite a resemblance. At that point in time anyway."

"Yeah," Tad said. "So I got to wondering, in a mostly academic way, how many other things Jenny and Alice had in common. Maybe there were more differences than similarities. My thought was, finding the differences would keep me from obsessing about Alice."

Remaining on her feet, Lindsay asked, "And did you find that was the case?"

"More often than not, yes."

"So you admit snooping into Alice's life."

"I do, from afar. Never intending to make further contact."

"Until now."

Tad shook his head. "All I want is to know that Alice is safe. If she's in some kind of danger, I only want to alert the police. Then I'll go back home and be at peace with myself."

Lindsay joined Tad at the table. "You know that you're in no way responsible for Jenny Nyland's death, don't you?"

Tad said, "I know it, but I don't feel it."

"And you think if Alice is in trouble, and you can help her, that'll change things?"

Tad took a sip of coffee, thinking how to answer. "I don't think anything will ever heal the pain I feel, but if I can help Alice that might be something to balance the pain, be a place in my heart where I can go for some comfort."

Lindsay picked up the banana, peeled it halfway down and broke it in two. She put the remainder back in front of Tad. She took a bite and nodded to herself. "Okay, let's go see Alice's friend Elise MacAdams. She lives up in Virginia Beach."

"If she's not an academic, what does she do?" Tad asked.

"She writes song lyrics," Lindsay said. "Actually makes money from it, too."

Lindsay packed a messenger bag with snacks and bottles of

spring water. She asked Tad if there were any other foodstuffs or drinks he wanted to pick up at Harris Teeter. He said, no, he was good to go. Still had almost a full tank of gas in the car, more than enough to get to their destination.

Lindsay was reaching for the doorknob when the doorbell rang.

She and Tad looked at each other. Lindsay thought it would be ironic if Alice were there, solving their problem and saving a road trip. Tad had Alice in mind, too, but he was silently praying it wouldn't be the cops at the door with news that Alice's remains had been found.

Neither of those notions was on point.

Sweetie and Leo were there.

Sweetie said, "Ms. Todd, Mr. Thacker."

"How do you know who I am?" Lindsay asked.

Sweetie said, "Well, I'm a detective. I work with James J. McGill."

"Me, too," Leo said.

"But the real answer," Sweetie confessed, "is that Mr. Thacker shared his research with us. Your name was at the top of his list."

***McGill Investigations International — Austin, Texas***

"No way, no damn way at all," Kyle Tompkins told Gene Beck and Maj Olson.

They met in Maj's office this time. She had a photograph of herself on a wall breaking the tape as the winner of a high-hurdles event at an Ivy League track meet. The musculature in her arms and legs stood in bold relief. The expression on her face was a combination of fierce exultation and utter exhaustion.

Kyle kept sneaking peeks at it, even as he refused to help with their plan to lure Eloy Chavez to Austin.

Gene had told Maj he was going to come up with a tune to go with that photo, but thus far his muse had yet to comply. He did find a stinging reply to Kyle's obstinate refusal to help. "The boy here is just … a boy. He might grow up to be a man someday, but I wouldn't put money on it."

"Yeah, well," Kyle said, "if I do what the two of you want, I might not get any older at all."

Gene said, "Not real likely you'd get killed over this, but anything's possible."

Kyle nodded. "And those dudes don't just shoot you, they torture you first."

The young journalist sneaked another peek at Maj's photo.

"I think he might like you," Gene told Maj.

She shook her head. "It's not my bod or even my victory that interests him."

"What is it then?" Gene asked.

"Kyle is wondering where that photo ran, who published it. If it was just the *Daily Spectator* — the student newspaper at Columbia — that would be no big deal. But I'm sure Kyle knows Columbia has a great journalism school that places its graduates into big newspapers and broadcasters across the country. On top of that, Ivy League athletics actually matter to readers in the Northeast. So maybe that photo of me got some big play, along with an accompanying story."

"That's real cool for you," Gene said, "but how's it help Kyle?"

Maj said, "He's wondering if I might have any big-time media contacts, people to whom I might introduce him."

Gene slapped his knee and laughed. "Did you hear that, Kyle? She said, 'to whom.' Even the jocks up there in the Ivy League know better than to dangle a preposition."

Kyle gritted his teeth, put his hands on the arms of his chair and looked as if he might head for the exit. Until …

Maj said, "The photo ran in *The New York Times.* So did the accompanying story."

Kyle settled back into his chair.

"Someone with your research skill could have found that out easily enough, but what you'd have a harder time finding would be the unpublished phone number of the editor who worked with me on my book, *Stealing the Chief.* He not only told me he'd want to see any other story idea I might have, but also to let him know if I might happen across any other writer with a bright idea. But, you know, I just might write the story of John Wayne's lost cowboy hat myself."

Kyle looked like he might throttle Maj, but then he remembered all those muscles in her photo. That and Gene wouldn't sit still for an assault on his partner. Between the two of them, they'd shred him.

He sank back into his chair.

Gene had another dig he might have thrown Kyle's way, but he knew when enough was enough.

Kyle looked at Maj, "It'll be all right with you if I jack up my life insurance policy?"

"Sure. Prudent financial planning is always a good idea."

"Ha-ha. If I get killed for doing this, I'm gonna come back and haunt the both of you. The worse I die, the worse it'll be for you, too."

"You okay with that, Gene?" Maj asked.

"I'll man up as best I can."

"We're good here, Kyle. Now, you can write the blog post, in your own words and style of course, but the gist of it has to be —"

"That Eloy Chavez is a prize chump, strutting around in a knockoff of John Wayne's hat thinking it's the real thing, never guessing that it's a phony, just like him. That and the real hat is right here in Austin, and there's going to be a big party to celebrate the hat being right where it belongs. Stop in and see what you're missing, dummy, if you've got the *cojones*."

Gene said, "Don't forget that Solana Fuentes thought she'd stolen the real thing. Her late father had thought it was real when he surrendered it to Chavez, too."

"We have to protect that family as best we can," Maj told him.

Kyle shook his head. "Yeah, sure, *them* you look out for."

Gene wagged a finger and said, "Watch that preposition, Kyle."

The reporter was tempted to say, "Asshole," but he'd done some research on Gene and gotten hints the investigator could be highly dangerous himself.

Maj calmed him with the assurance: "You do your part with style, and we bring it off successfully, you'll be able to write your own ticket for your next job."

The young journalist was still scared.

But he was starting to see the reward might be worth the risk.

***The Brooklyn Bridge — New York City***

Detective Lily Kealoha couldn't take any time off from her job to help Deke Ky delve into the early life and times of Teagan Tobias, but she was working the overnight shift that day and said she'd be happy to stay awake a few more hours to earn the $500 fee Deke was offering. She picked him up at the Omni Berkshire in Midtown at 8:15 A.M and headed to lower Manhattan and the Brooklyn Bridge.

The overwhelming majority of commuters was inbound to Manhattan; the outbound traffic was merely heavy and moved steadily.

"We could've taken the subway to Brooklyn," Lily told Deke, "but to an island girl like me the idea of riding in a tunnel under a body of water like the East River seems like tempting fate. One big crack in the concrete and look out below."

"So you wouldn't advocate for a subway line between the Hawaiian Islands?" he asked.

Lily laughed heartily. "You'd have to dig *real* deep to do that, and then you'd probably hit lava flows along the way."

"So, not too practical an idea?"

"Not hardly." She glanced over at her passenger.

"You're *hapa,* aren't you?"

"I'm what?" Deke asked.

"Means mixed heritage, like me. The first time I saw you, last year, I thought: Asian. Then I noticed those blue eyes of yours, and being the detective I am, I thought *hapa.* Asian, white and black, right? Your family name, it sounds Vietnamese to me."

"It is. Mom is Eurasian, Vietnamese and French. Dad is African-American, a former G.I."

Lily nodded. "Well, all your ancestors did a real nice job coming up with you. I'm three-quarters native Hawaiian and one-quarter Dutch. You ask me, there are some real nice blends waiting to happen among all God's children. Don't know why some people get so concerned about mixed breeding."

"Yeah, and that racial purity stuff can result in real narrow minds."

Lily laughed again, and to Deke it was starting to sound like music.

She asked, "Would it be politically incorrect for me to think you got your sense of humor from your father?"

Deke wasn't even sure he had a sense of humor. "If you mean the wisecracks, I think that's something I picked up working for James J. McGill the last nine years."

"Yeah? Well, maybe you can tell me about that sometime." The following silence drew a look from Lily. She said, "Or not."

Deke sighed. "He's not a bad guy. Actually, he's a good man, but he made it all but impossible for me to protect him when I was with the Secret Service … and my mother had once told me I'd better be willing to sacrifice my life for him."

Traffic slowed to a stop as they neared the Brooklyn side of the bridge. Lily looked at Deke. "She really *said* that?"

"Yeah, well, Mom was a crook and probably a spy for Hanoi, too."

"Holy shit. I've got to hear these stories. We've got to exchange phone numbers if one of us can't visit the other soon."

Keeping a smile off his face, but feeling very good about things, Deke said, "We can do that." Then the sense of discipline at the core of his life reasserted itself. "So what can you tell me about this retired cop we're going to see?"

"His name is Gianni Calendri, former street cop and former desk sergeant, won a small fortune right after he retired with a lotto ticket that hit on all six numbers."

"You're kidding."

"No. It wasn't one of those giant pots. In fact, he hit it right after someone else got a *really* big payday. Dago John's jackpot was … well, it started at $40 million, but he took the one-time payment, and after taxes were taken out, I don't know the exact number he got, but I'm pretty sure it was still in eight figures. He bought the building where his diner is and a place for him and his wife to live. So with New York City real estate prices, he probably has $1.98 left over."

Deke grinned, but his mind had fixed on something else.

"The guy doesn't mind being called dago?"

Lily shook her head, as traffic started to move again. "He *insists* on it. It was his father's name, too. His dad was in the Navy at Pearl Harbor when the Japanese attacked. He helped rescue several shipmates, and then one of the enemy planes took off his right leg below the knee with a burst of gunfire. He was saved by other sailors, and wound up winning the Navy Cross. He was put in for the Medal of Honor, but that didn't happen."

"The Navy Cross is plenty impressive, but still the name …"

"It caught up with this Dago John when he joined the Navy in the '60s. Turned out the captain of his ship was the son of an officer who'd served with the original Dago John. When he saw that one of his crewmen was named Gianni Calendri, he asked if his father had served at Pearl Harbor. Hearing yes for the answer, the captain told the story to the whole crew through the ship's P.A. system. From that moment on, the son became the new Dago John. It was a badge of honor, not an ethnic slur. And here we are now."

Deke looked up and saw a sign saying "Day-Go John's Diner."

Pulling into a parking space, Lily said, "As you can see, a concession to political correctness has been made, but only in the spelling, not the spirit."

### *Committed Capital — Washington, DC*

Patti met McGill at the doors to the elevator and kissed him in front of God and everyone who worked for Committed Capital. The entire crew had been invited up to the top floor. A cheer went up as McGill stepped off the elevator. Whether it was for the kiss, McGill's heroics or both, it was impossible to say.

McGill smiled and waved to the onlookers.

To Patti, he said, "I couldn't help myself. I had to see you. Must be a side-effect of adrenaline. Pretty amazing how quickly you organized the reception party."

She took his arm in hers and walked him toward her office, the smiling crowd parting as they advanced. McGill gave Edwina Byington a wink as he passed her desk. She responded with an upraised thumb and a grin.

The last person McGill noticed as he entered his wife's office was Daphna Levy, Patti's Secret Service agent. She wasn't overtly congratulatory, but she did manage a tiny nod of approval. McGill returned the gesture in equal measure, one pro to another.

Once Patti closed the door to her office behind them, she embraced McGill and clung to him. He began to think they might stay right where they were indefinitely, but he'd been married long enough not to even think of interrupting. Besides, he was enjoying the contact.

Finally, Patti said, "Abbie is on her way over. Ken called, but your phone went to voicemail. Caitie heard from Ken and wants to know if she should come home from Paris. She left a message on your phone, too. I told Ken and Caitie you'd get back to them. Oh, and Carolyn called, too. She reassured me you'd be fine."

McGill smiled, thinking how his first wife had ended their marriage because she'd feared that McGill's job as a cop would get him killed. Now, a life-or-death incident in the subway was no big deal. Perspective was everything.

"Mind if we take a seat?" McGill asked. "You can sit on my lap, if you like."

Patti leaned back and told him. “Don’t think that I wouldn’t.”

But she didn’t. They sat side by side on the sofa in Patti’s office.

“Start at the beginning,” she said. “What were you doing in a Metro station?”

“Going to work.”

Patti shook her head. “I know Leo and Sweetie are using your car, but why didn’t you take a taxi?”

“Because I’m a man of the people,” McGill suggested.

That got him a sock on the chest. “Tell me the truth, and no joking.”

“Well … it seemed to be the right thing to do at the moment. I used to take the CTA to work in Chicago for a few years when I was a uniformed officer. And if I hadn’t been at that Metro station this morning, things likely wouldn’t have worked out so well. So it was a good impulse, choosing public transportation.”

“Wouldn’t that woman with the briefcase have managed all right by herself?”

“Well, she clocked the crazy guy a good one … broke his neck, in fact, according to what I heard a paramedic say.”

Patti winced.

“But she couldn’t have known that at the time, and if she’d stayed with the bad guy even another few seconds, the old man on the train tracks probably wouldn’t have been yanked to safety.”

Patti said, “She felt free to do that because you knocked the man down like he was a rag doll?”

“Yeah.” McGill paused before adding, “I did some spinal damage to him, also.”

Patti leaned in and embraced McGill, kissed his cheek. “How are you feeling? In your heart, I mean.”

He put an arm around Patti and thought for a minute. “Well, last year I shot and killed a sick old lady. That bothered me more than this one. Today, I felt I literally had no choice. I heard a woman scream, and at the start, at least, I thought I was the only one who was responding. By the time I saw I had help, I was already committed by momentum.”

"You couldn't have pulled up short?" Patti asked.

McGill paused to reflect. "By momentum, I mean a high-speed mental and emotional commitment as well as physical velocity. No, I couldn't have stopped."

Patti kissed McGill. "I'm all for your emotional commitments."

"I've always suspected as much." Then McGill let out a sigh.

"What? A sudden pang of regret just barged in?"

"A regret, yes, but not sudden."

Patti said. "What's wrong?"

"I haven't found Alice Janeway yet. "

"Aren't missing persons cases sometimes difficult or even impossible to solve? I seem to recall Jimmy Hoffa is still unaccounted for."

"Yeah. James *Riddle* Hoffa. There's an ironic name for a guy who vanishes without a trace. I don't want Alice to follow in his ghostly footsteps. On top of that, as predicted by Teagan Tobias, the client's wife called me and said her husband would no longer be paying for my services."

"How could Tobias know that? Does he have a relationship with the woman?"

Just the thought jolted McGill, but he relaxed and shook his head. "I don't think so. He said Alice badmouthed her sister-in-law. Painted her as manipulative and greedy."

"Never a pleasant combination," Patti said.

"Frau Janeway is also terse. Didn't take her more than 20 seconds to cancel her husband's agreement with me."

"Can she do that?"

McGill shrugged "Under German law? I have no idea. For that matter, I don't know if Marlon is still alive. He looked awful on Skype, more awful than most people look on Skype. He also pretty much said he wanted to speak to his sister before he died of dengue fever."

"Oh my, that is bad. From what I've heard, few people last long with that, and fewer still actually recover. Something like that might trouble even a saintly spouse."

"Which is not how she was described at her best."

"You're not going to drop the case, are you?"

McGill shook his head. "No. As you heard, Sweetie and Leo are in North Carolina now, looking to contact some of Alice's old friends. That was where she grew up. Deke, and possibly Detective Lily Kealoha of the NYPD, are looking into Teagan Tobias' formative years to see if that might suggest an avenue of investigation."

"Good, I was going to suggest that. You never know if he might be holding back something that might embarrass him."

McGill raised his eyebrows. "Someone in show biz has a skeleton in his closet?"

Patti shrugged. "I have a whole boneyard in mine, but I'm not going to tell you what my dirty little secrets are until you no longer find me desirable."

McGill laughed. "I don't think either of us will live long enough to see that day."

Patti gave him a quick kiss. "All right, you have your minions going busily about their business. What's *your* next move?"

McGill got to his feet and pulled Patti up to stand with him.

"Until I get a bright idea …"

"Yes?"

"I'll wait right here to see Abbie, call the other two offspring, and then I'll go out and buy a new car."

"Sounds like a good use of time for a chief executive."

McGill grinned. "We're some pair, you and me."

Patti kissed McGill and said, "So tell me, did you and your new partner in derring-do, the woman with the briefcase, exchange business cards? Should we all get together for a celebratory drink?"

"We did exchange cards, and a drink is a fine idea, once Alice is found."

"So, what's the Metro lady's name?" Patti asked.

"Emma Wylie." McGill took a beat before adding, "I don't think, in all the time we've known each other, that I've ever told you about my sister."

Patti smiled. "You don't have a sister. We'd have met long ago."

"Well, that's the thing," McGill told her, "I didn't get to meet her either."

He told her the story of the child his parents had lost before he was born.

Patti squeezed his hand in sympathy and kissed his cheek.

"Oh, Jim, I'm so sorry."

"Me, too. But when Emma Wylie told me her name this morning, I just had to wonder: Would my sister, Emma, have had the same impulse to help a stranger that Emma Wylie did? Might she have grown up to be brave like that? I kind of think so. I even wonder if some spirits — some souls — are just too strong not to find a way to stay in this world or at least make a momentary return and give someone else a nudge in the right direction."

That notion made Patti's eyes mist over. "Should I keep watch for Andy?

"You never know."

Before the discussion could go any further, Edwina came on the intercom and said, "Miss Abigail is here."

***Day-go John's Diner — Brooklyn***

The diner was one of those places that had a couple hundred photographs on the walls. Breaking with the usual tradition, the faces in the frames didn't belong to celebrities. They were mostly NYPD cops, some in uniform, others in plain clothes. The interesting thing was, someone had gone to the trouble of finding an image of what each subject had looked like as a kid as well as an adult. In some instances, there were more than two photos showing a larger sequence of a life's progress. Dago John had six images of himself on one wall.

The only likeness of a person known to the general public was that of the 99th mayor of New York City, Fiorello La Guardia. The little mayor stood proudly next to the original Dago John when he'd just come home from Hawaii, minus half of his right leg.

The photo was inscribed and signed by the mayor. "You make us all proud, Gianni."

Lily pointed that one out to Deke as soon as they stepped inside. The place was packed with a breakfast crowd, many of them present-day cops. Lily received more than a few nods of recognition, and at least four looks, by Deke's count, that spoke of more than collegial interest.

Deke also had the feeling just about everyone in the place pegged him as a fed.

Then Dago John stepped out of the crowd, beamed at Lily, made a shaka gesture with a raised thumb and an extended pinkie and said, *"Aloha nui loa, Lily."* Warmest regards, Lily.

*"Mahalo,* Gianni," Lily said, embracing him and kissing each cheek.

Deke got the feeling that was a cross-cultural thing: the kisses. He also noticed she hadn't called the man Dago John.

Stepping back, she introduced Deke. "This is my friend Donald Ky. Everyone calls him Deke."

"Dago John," the man said, extending his hand and asking. "FBI or Secret Service?"

Deke shook the man's hand, "Secret Service, retired. Private investigator now."

Dago John looked at Lily as a memory clicked into place. "Didn't you tell me once that this guy works with McGill's outfit? He was one of the people who came here last year when —"

"They took down that female assassin who was going after Mr. McGill, yeah," Lily said.

The diner owner patted Deke's shoulder. "You must have some stories to tell."

"Saving them for my memoirs," Deke said with a straight face.

"Terrific. Maybe Lily can get me a signed copy. Let's go into my private dining room where we can hear ourselves think." He led them into a separate space in the back with four round tables that could have seated another two dozen people. A tray of pastries sat on one of the tables. Cups and saucers were available for coffee.

Glasses and a pitcher of orange juice rested on a side table along with a coffee urn.

"Help yourselves to whatever you'd like to drink. We can get some tea, if you want that."

The diner owner sat at a table and waited for his guests to help themselves. Lily filled a cup with coffee. Deke chose a glass of orange juice. While they were getting their drinks, Lily nodded to a nearby spot on the wall.

There were dozens more photos in the back room, but the two Lily had indicated were of her. The first was her graduation photo from the police academy; the other was of her wearing a grass skirt at about age eight. She was a knockout in each.

In a quiet voice, she told Deke, "Dago John visits the Pearl Harbor Memorial every year. When he heard a Hawaiian recruit had joined the NYPD, he made a point of introducing himself. He's a really good guy."

Deke nodded, and they joined the diner owner at his table.

Dago John got straight to the point, asking Deke. "Lily tells me you want to get some background on Teagan Tobias, is that right?"

"Yes, it is."

"You're looking for a missing woman?"

"I'm one of the people looking. We're not sure if she's missing or just got angry and quit her job without saying so."

"Yeah, there are people who do that. Usually not before they pick up their last paycheck, though. Did you check that?"

"Can't say, honestly. I was just brought in on the case to come up here and get some idea of who Teagan Tobias really is."

Dago John looked at Deke and then Lily, saw they were sitting closer together than a simple professional acquaintance would call for. He was fine with that. Cops needed companionship as much as anyone else. Oftentimes, more.

He just wanted to understand the situation.

Then he said, "Okay, so what you really want to know is whether Teagan Tobias ever did anything to bring him to the attention of the NYPD. Fact is, I had occasion to question him myself."

Both Deke and Lily leaned forward with interest.

"For what reason?" Deke asked.

"It was a school thing, high school. Two guys talking tough. No blows struck at the time and no real reason for hostility, other than they just didn't like one another."

Deke asked, "So they were both white, both straight, and they weren't interested in the same girl?"

Dago John smiled. "I asked young Teagan pretty much those same questions. I even wondered if it might be a religious thing, but they were both Methodists. He also denied any other reason for conflict."

"What about size difference?" Lily asked. "Sometimes big kids just feel entitled to pick on smaller kids."

Dago John pointed a finger at her and said, "Bingo. At least, that was my working theory. Nicholas Pell wasn't real tall but he was thickset, and I found out that he had a reputation for pushing smaller kids around. He didn't do that for any particular reason that I could find, except to amuse himself. Only Teagan, as some kids told me, didn't cower properly. He called the bully Nicky the Prick to his face. Also called him the Brick Shithouse because of his body odor."

"And that didn't start a fight?" Deke asked.

"Well, I also heard a story that Teagan carried a very sharp knife. You know, back in the days before everyone had a gun. That might have been a deterrent. But then I talked to young Mr. Tobias and got another story."

"Which was?" Lily asked.

"Well, according to the kid himself, he challenged Shithouse to a fight in a vacant lot up in the Bronx near 138th Street. Only the bigger kid never showed."

Lily asked, "Why the hell go way up there in the first place?"

Deke, unfamiliar with the city's geography, turned to her. "That's not right around the corner?"

"Not even close," she said.

"Yeah, well," Dago John said, "it did have its advantages. The crime stats up there weren't anything the police commissioner bragged about then or now. Two young guys going at it might not even rate a call to the cops. Plus, you've got the Hudson River fairly close, if you needed to dump a body."

"Pell got killed?" Deke asked.

Dago John shrugged. "That remains an open question. What's certain is nobody's seen Nicky the Prick since those long-ago high school days."

Lily said, "Tobias had to be the guy you liked for —"

"Can't call it a murder, sweetheart. Wasn't any body. Not so much as a drop of blood or a stray hair left behind. For a chunky guy, the Brick Shithouse just went poof! Disappeared into thin air. Not that the air around town was very thin back then."

"You checked Tobias' knife, though," Deke said.

"Confiscated it, in fact, even though it was a fixed blade."

"As opposed to what," Deke asked, "a folding blade?"

"Yeah," Lily said. "Any kind of folding-blade knife is automatically considered a weapon here, and it's illegal to carry one or even have it in your home. With a fixed blade, you're good to go at four inches or less."

"So Teagan Tobias brought a four-inch blade to school?" Deke asked.

Dago John nodded. "Sharp as hell, too. Seeing that, and guessing the kid maybe even had some idea of how to use it, I started to wonder why the school bully messed with him at all. We seized the knife for 'purposes of laboratory analysis.' Or so we told young Teagan."

"You were trying to scare him," Deke said. "Hope he might crack and see if he'd try to cop a plea."

"Tell you where to find the body, too," Lily added.

"Yeah, that's what we hoped. Kid acted like he had brass balls, though. Told us to test the hell out of the knife. Just give it back when we were done. Like he didn't have a worry in the world."

"Turned out he didn't, right?" Lily asked.

"Little shit never got charged with anything," Dago John said, "but just for spite I told him the lab lost his damn knife. He didn't say a word back to me, but I knew he was thinking: 'Fuck you, too.'"

"Do you really think Tobias killed Pell?" Deke asked.

"Not that I'd ever say outside this room. He's a semi-big-shot in show-biz now, isn't he? And me, I actually have some money of my own I'd like to keep, not get sued out of. But just between us … I don't believe in coincidences. Do you?"

Deke shook his head.

"What I will tell you straight out is I think that story about a fight in the Bronx was pure bullshit. Something to get us looking in another direction. Whatever happened, it went down right around here in Brooklyn. The kid's home and mine. That's what galls me the most: Not being able to figure out what happened on my own turf."

Deke could sympathize. Then he had a thought.

"Does the NYPD still have that knife?"

Dago John smiled and said, "Funny you should ask."

***Chihuahua State — Mexico***

The death rate in the northern border state of Mexico was comparable to that of a war zone: 31 people had been killed in seven hours on a recent day. Another 23 murders had occurred in the other states across the country in the previous 24 hours. The national news reported that the two youngest victims of the massacre were 14 and 15 years old. People were shot dead on the streets, in their shops and even in their homes. They were the ones who died quickly. Others were tortured and decapitated.

Eloy Chavez had removed himself from the center of the bloodbath, Ciudad Juárez. His estate in the countryside resembled a military base more than a residence. The perimeter was strung with electrified barbed wire. Outside of that was a mined no-go zone. If anyone got past those obstacles, three armored personnel carriers were waiting for them.

Gun emplacements rose at the four corners of his home and featured .50 caliber machine guns. It was rumored, but had not yet been put to the test, that Chavez had purchased black-market FIM-92 Stinger missile launchers, a shoulder-fired weapon that could bring down helicopters or be reconfigured to take out a wide variety of land vehicles.

For all his military hardware and armed men, Chavez knew he was in a fight to the death in the drug war raging in that part of his country. When you went after the king, you either killed him or wound up dead yourself. If you were taken alive, your death would be long in coming and horribly painful with your gruesome remains made public as an object lesson to others.

Given all his precautions, Chavez was not in the best of moods to receive bad news.

His first lieutenant, Fermin Gomez, was equally reluctant to provide it. Especially as the boss was wearing the cowboy hat that supposedly had been the property of some old gringo movie star. Fermin was still young, and he preferred videos of naked young *chicas,* not movies about old white men. Even so, he had to deliver his message. Otherwise, if the boss learned of what was said from another, he might be gunned down on the spot.

Of course, the same thing might happen now.

Still, he handed his iPad to the boss with the bad news blog on the screen. "Something you should see, *jefe.*"

Chavez glanced at the iPad and frowned. "You read it to me, Fermin. My English is never good when my mood is black."

Gomez took the iPad back, trying not to seem reluctant. If he was in the midst of reading, he might not even see the boss pull his gun on him. But what else could he do except obey? In one of Chavez's *black moods,* he might shoot someone for farting out loud in his house.

It had happened before.

So Gomez decided the thing to do would be to read a few words at a time, glance up to see if his life was in danger, and hurl the iPad at the boss, if necessary. Then draw his own gun.

Before he even began reading, Gomez said, "This story comes from Texas, *jefe*. Austin."

With a cynical laugh, Chavez said, "More about how the *yanquis* are winning the war on drugs?"

"No, *señor*. It is about your new hat."

Chavez's face darkened beneath its brim. "The *americanos* are going to try to take it back from me? Let them come. They will only be more targets for our men to kill." He laughed. "Unless they send their whole army and take what little land they left us the first time."

"They don't intend to send anyone, boss."

Suspicious now, Chavez asked, "No? Why not?"

Gomez took a quick glance at his lord and master. At the moment, he didn't have a pistol tucked into the waistband of his pants. He might have one at the small of his back. He almost certainly had the one he carried in his boot. For Chavez, sticking that gun in the top of his right boot, under his jeans, was simply a part of getting dressed for the day.

But if the boss went either to his back or a leg for a gun, that would give Gomez time to draw his own weapon. Clearing his throat, Gomez began to speak.

"This is from a blog we watch to see what the Texans in their state capital might be planning. Today they talk about you personally." Gomez saw Chavez frown even more deeply, but he kept going. "The writer is a man named Kyle Tompkins."

Chavez said, "I don't know him. How does he know of me? From news stories?"

"No, *señor*. He knows you from your new hat."

"What?" Anger spread across Chavez's face. "He will never have it. I will never give it back."

"That is not his concern, *jefe*. You want me to go on?"

His jaws clenched, Chavez nodded.

Doing his best to clarify, Gomez said, "These are Tompkins' words, *señor*, not mine."

"Read!" Chavez demanded.

"'Nobody ever beats John Wayne, not in the end. Not even after he's been dead for going on 40 years. You even mess with the man's legend, you're just begging for trouble, and misfortune is what you're guaranteed to get. I'll let you know shortly who the Duke has put in his place, but —'"

"Who is this Duke and what does the name mean?"

"*El Duque,* a nobleman. Wayne's nickname."

Chavez gestured for Gomez to continue.

"'But now I'll explain how this whole situation came about. A local stockbroker, Wallace Rhymes, bought the hat John Wayne wore in his final film, *The Shootist.* The hat has become almost as iconic as the actor. It's a beauty that not just anyone could wear.'"

Chavez nodded, a glow in his eyes now.

"'You put it on the wrong man, and he'd look like a jester pretending to a role far exceeding his abilities.'"

"Hah," Chavez laughed and slapped his leg. "Just as I thought when I saw that peasant Fuentes wearing my hat. The hat begged me to take it from him."

The weight of Gomez's apprehension grew. The boss was not going like how this story turned out. Nevertheless, he continued reading.

"'You put the hat on the right man, though, and he looks like a king."

Chavez smiled broadly and clenched his right hand into a fist.

"'Despite being a multi-millionaire, Wallace Rhymes has an innate sense of personal modesty. He wore John Wayne's hat only on very special occasions. As he grew older, he came to worry about what to do with the hat. He thought, incorrectly, that none of his four children had any interest in inheriting the hat from him. In fact, his sons, rodeo champion Cole Rhymes and identical twin brother, Clint, would love to have it.'"

"Too damn bad, gringos," Chavez said. "It's mine now."

This was getting worse and worse, Gomez thought. Still, he continued.

"'As it turned out, Wallace Rhymes' housekeeper, Solana Fuentes thought her father, Ernesto, would also like it. Ernesto had worked for Wallace Rhymes as his jack-of-all-trades, tending to house maintenance and groundskeeping. After working on the Rhymes' property for over 30 years, Ernesto had saved enough money to buy a small spread of his own back home in Mexico. His daughter, Solana, however, still works for Wallace Rhymes as his housekeeper.

"Thinking, as Rhymes did, that no one in her employer's family wanted John Wayne's hat, Solana decided it would make a fitting gift to her father, reflecting his new status as a property owner, a landed man."

Chavez sat on a sofa, laughed and slapped his knee. "*¡Maravillosa!*"

Fermin Gomez wondered if he should kill the boss now. While he was distracted and could die happy. Gomez couldn't quite bring himself to do it.

"'Wanting to protect herself, though, Solana ordered a duplicate hat made for the Rhymes children she assumed had no interest in the real thing. She took the precaution of using a first-class hat maker to render the copy of John Wayne's hat. She didn't want anyone to catch on to the switch before she could make a graceful exit from the family home. Presumably with a nice bequest from her employer's estate.'"

Chavez nodded in agreement with the soundness of the woman's thinking.

"'Solana shipped the hat to her father, Ernesto, who loved it. He'd never felt more grand in his lifetime, but things soon took a turn for the worse. Much worse. Word of the hat's arrival in Mexico soon reached the ears of big-time drug thug, Eloy Chavez.'"

Gomez had dared to use a precise translation of *el jefe's* description, and the boss narrowed his eyes and said, "*¡Cabrón!*"

Hurrying on now, Gomez read, "'Chavez soon showed up at Ernesto Fuentes' house and demanded to have the hat for himself. He threatened to kill Ernesto and take the hat from him anyway, if that was the way Ernesto wanted things. Ernesto meekly surrendered the hat, even congratulated Chavez on the way it looked on him. That was enough to appease the creep, and Ernesto got to live a while longer.'"

"I should have shot that peasant just for target practice," Chavez said.

While the boss was lost in that pleasant reverie, Gomez took a seat in an easy chair opposite Chavez on his sofa. He discreetly slipped his pistol out of its holster and left it out of sight but close to hand where he could grab it in a hurry.

"'Ernesto Fuentes died shortly after losing the hat. It was said he died of a broken heart, but a doctor said the cause was an aneurysm. The truth was, according to his two sons living in Mexico, Solana, his daughter, had made a mistake. The knockoff was so good to an unschooled eye that she sent the duplicate to Mexico instead of the real thing. Ernesto, though, knew this, but he wasn't about to spoil his daughter's gift. Nor was he going to die for a knockoff. Instead, he got the last laugh.

"'So, Mr. Drug Boss, down there in Mexico, enjoy your *Juan* Wayne hat. If you ever lose it, you can get another one for $495.00 with free shipping.'"

If ever there was a time Chavez was going to shoot him for delivering bad news, now would be the time, Fermin Gomez thought.

But the boss just sat where he was, unmoving, staring at a wall but thinking about who knew what.

Still taking a big chance, Gomez added, "There is a photo here of the man who owns the real hat. He is wearing it and smiling. The writer says anyone who wants to see the real thing can come to a music club in Austin called Hell's Belle on this Saturday night."

Chavez extended his hand, and Gomez put the iPad in it.

The drug boss looked at a photo of Wallace Rhymes wearing the hat, smiling, and giving Chavez the finger.

Chavez softly laid the iPad on a sofa cushion.

He took the hat off his head and laid it atop the tablet computer.

He said to Gomez, "We will go to Texas. I will take the real hat, as I took this one from that damn peasant. Then I will put the false one on the old *americano's* head and shoot him between his eyes. We will see if he's still smiling then."

***Chick's Beach — Virginia Beach, Virginia***

Leo pulled McGill's Chevy into the driveway of Elise MacAdams' beach cottage. He and Sweetie were in the front seats. Lindsay Todd and Tad Thacker sat in back. Tad had turned in his rental car at the RDU Airport in North Carolina. Leo had agreed to drop Tad off at another car rental location if the two parties chose to go their separate ways before they reached Washington, DC.

Two seconds after Leo brought the car to a stop and killed the engine, a pair of black Labs bulled aside the cottage's front screen door and bounded toward the vehicle. The animals presented an imminent threat to lick to death any intruder who confronted them. A more serious concern appeared in the form of a barefoot young woman wearing running shorts and a shiny, sleeveless shirt bearing a large blue 9. She casually held a shotgun in her right hand.

As the crew in the car stepped out of the vehicle, the young woman with the firearm called out, "Any damn Yankees among you?"

In his best down-home drawl, Leo said, "Not me, ma'am."

He went down to one knee to gather both gaily dancing dogs into his embrace.

Sweetie raised her hand. "Yeah, I qualify."

Tad gave Lindsay a questioning look.

She smiled, gave him a pat on the shoulder and said, "Elise, being from south New Jersey hardly makes you a ridge runner."

"Hey," Elise said, grinning, "I grew up south of Philly, which is practically in Maryland, which is right next to Virginia, where I went to UV as an undergrad, and just south of that is North Carolina, where I got my master's degree at UNC. I'm as southern as … I care to be."

"Right," Lindsay said, "when you're not shopping on Fifth Avenue or Rodeo Drive."

She stepped forward and gave her old friend a hug, Elise put the shotgun aside to return the embrace. Lindsay asked, "May my friends and I come inside?"

"Sure. Fun time's over. I've been worrying ever since you called. Come on in."

She picked up the shotgun and opened the screen door for the others. Leo said he'd stay outside and keep an eye on the dogs, and more importantly McGill's car. Sweetie, Lindsay and Tad stepped inside. Elise gave Tad a quick look of appraisal, trying to discern his standing with Lindsay.

Sweetie, on the other hand, started with a quick scan of her new surroundings. The place was fairly small but very nicely furnished. In the years Sweetie had spent living with Putnam, she'd come to accept, and even appreciate, that there was nothing wrong with having a nice place to live and other small luxuries — as long as you regularly practiced compassion to those less fortunate than yourself.

What struck Sweetie as more significant than the high-end merchandise were three awards sitting on a shelf in the living room. She went over for a look. Two of the awards were for artistic achievement: a Grammy and a CMA award for best song of the year, *Can't Get There from Here.* Lyrics by Elise MacAdams. The third award was for a major donation to the Breast Cancer Research Foundation.

Elise saw where Sweetie was looking and said, "That's the one that means the most to me."

Sweetie turned to look at her hostess.

"Come on," Elise said. "Let's go into the kitchen and have a cup of something hot and sweet. We can all talk about Alice while we're at it."

Elise offered her guests a choice of coffee, tea or cocoa. She got a taker for each. Lindsay took the coffee, Sweetie the tea and Tad the cocoa. Elise joined Tad in his choice. They sat around a circular table in the kitchen.

"That guy out front," Elise said, "he used to drive NASCAR, didn't he?"

Sweetie nodded. "He did."

"Won a couple of races, didn't he?"

"Three." Sweetie named them. "You're a racing fan?"

"My brother is. He had magazines and posters all over his room. His sanctuary, where he hid out from his eight sisters. But enough about me. Let's talk about Alice." Turning to Tad, she asked, "Are you someone special to her?"

Tad shook his head. "Just someone who'd like to help."

Lindsay told him, "It's okay. Tell Elise what you told me, if you feel like it."

Tad took a breath and closed his eyes for a moment. Then he looked at Elise and saw she wanted to hear. So he told her his story, wondering as he finished if she might grab the shotgun leaning against the wall behind her and order him out of her house.

Instead, she said, "My sympathy for your loss, Mr. Thacker."

What she didn't say was Tad's story made her think of the title for a new song: *The Best Friend I Never Had.*

"Thank you," he said.

Turning to Sweetie, Elise said, "You are or were a cop. My hot-rodding big brother was one, so I know the vibe."

Sweetie explained how Teag Tobias had come to Jim McGill, looking to find Alice.

"Okay, then," Elise said, "we're all looking for Alice. She and I were pretty good friends, so I wouldn't have been surprised if she came to see me, if she needed help or even just wanted to crash here for a while. After I got the call from Lindsay this morning, I went for a long, long run up the beach to see if Alice had decided she'd rather have a nice hotel room, if she'd come to town. I checked out a dozen or so places where I thought she might stay. Of course, with Airbnb places sprouting like mushrooms these days, she could've gone that way, too, and I'd never know. So, basically,

I've got zip."

Sweetie said, "Eliminating possibilities can be a help, too."

Elise nodded. "Yeah, that's something my brother told me. You going to follow the next logical stops along that path?"

"What do you mean?" Lindsay asked.

Sweetie said, "Elise means checking hospital admissions and new arrivals at the morgues in the area. We checked between Georgia and DC and came up empty."

"Well then," Elise said. Looking at Lindsay, she asked, "Do you know if Alice was having any health problems that might've landed her in someone's spare bedroom instead of a hospital?"

Lindsay only shrugged and shook her head.

All three women at the table turned their heads to look at Tad.

"What?" he asked. "I don't know about any minor illnesses. I wasn't having Alice followed."

"That's too bad," Elise said. "I know some people who know some other people. I think I can cover most of the hospitals from Maryland through New Jersey, in case Alice got that far. I don't know anyone in Kentucky, but I've got the eastern half of this state covered, too."

"That's something," Lindsay said, "but that leaves the rest of the country, and maybe the whole world."

Tad nodded, looking anything but hopeful.

"Well, I can check out the rest of my old girl's network, too," Elise said. "I never knew how many great friends I'd had back at UNC until I gained my smidge of fame. Present company excepted," she added putting a hand on one of Lindsay's.

"Yeah, thanks," Lindsay told her, rolling her eyes.

Elise said, "There is one more thing to consider, though it's not hardly a comfort."

"What's that?" Sweetie asked.

"Well, Alice was here a couple of years back. She told me this would be a nice place to settle in, grow old, and pass on to whatever reward you'd earned in your life. So, maybe even then Alice was feeling intuitive, or sickly."

Leaving the others in the kitchen, and Leo still playing with the dogs, Sweetie went out to the Chevy and called McGill.

He answered the phone by saying, "You've seen the video, too?"

"What video?"

"Then you haven't seen it."

"Okay, I haven't seen whatever it is you're talking about. You want to tell me, so we can move this conversation forward?"

McGill told her about the incident at the Metro station.

Sweetie's voice brightened. "You saved someone's life? That's wonderful."

"Technically, I assisted in saving two lives, but, yeah, it feels pretty good and also makes me feel a bit negligent."

"How do you think things would have gone *without* you?" Sweetie asked.

McGill took a long moment to consider, finally saying, "Maybe one life saved and one life lost. Possibly two lives lost."

"There you go. How many people save a life or two on their way to work in the morning?"

"I'm glad not many are called upon to make the attempt," McGill said. "On the other side of the ledger, I just heard that Nestor Vasilis, the guy who caused all the trouble, will never use his arms or legs again because of all the damage done to his spine."

"Quadriplegic?"

"Yeah."

Sweetie sighed. "You didn't intend that, did you?"

"No."

"Then —"

"I also kicked him after he was down. That's on the video, too."

"Why did you do that?"

McGill told her about the young boy, the grandson of the man who'd been pushed onto the tracks. "The kid bit Vasilis on the back of a leg, distracting him, giving Emma Wylie and me the time to take him down. Once Vasilis was down, the kid started kicking him."

Sweetie heard all that, but her focus had shifted. "Emma, huh?"

"Yeah." Unlike Patti, Sweetie had heard of Emma — after a long, hard night on the job back in Chicago, and then too many beers on McGill's part.

Returning to the previous point of discussion, Sweetie asked, "So how does the kid's presence and example figure into *you* kicking a guy who was down?"

"The kid was taking out his anger on Vasilis. It seemed to me to be an entirely reasonable, even therapeutic, thing to do. So, in the spirit of the moment, I allowed myself one kick, too."

"I want to criticize that," Sweetie said, "but I can't find it in my heart to do so. You'll have to pardon the following pun, but I feel there's a kicker coming."

McGill told her, "You're absolutely right. Rockelle Bullard just called to let me know about Vasilis's condition. Then she told me the SOB has a lawyer, his uncle, I think, at the hospital. The uncle told Rockelle he's going to sue both the kid and me for kicking the guy while he was down and no longer a threat to anyone."

Sweetie took a beat to think. "Did you kick him in the spine?"

"No. I watched the video again after Rockelle called. I got him in the ribs. So did the kid. But I don't think technicalities will keep the suit from being filed."

"You're probably right. What about Emma Wiley? Is she going to be sued, too? From what you told me, you hit the guy right at his waist. She clocked his head. That sounds more like a neck-breaker to me."

McGill said, "I don't know the extent to which either of us is responsible for the damage, but I'm not going to try to lay off the blame on her."

"Of course, not … You think she might try to lay it off on you?"

McGill was speechless for several seconds before saying, "No, I don't think so."

"Good. So what you do is counter-sue the shyster for abuse of process."

McGill produced a dry laugh. "Putnam taught you that?"

"Among many other things. I also think you'll have public opinion on your side, and a judge, whatever his or her supposed impartiality, won't want to catch holy hell for ruling against you. Just think, if you put the old guy, his daughter and his grandson on the stand, how is the bad guy's lawyer going to attack them. He even tries, he'll be cutting his own throat."

"Thanks for cheering me up, Margaret."

"What's a chief ethics officer for? You ready to get back to the Janeway case now?"

"Yeah, I was thinking of going to look for a new car before Rockelle called, but now I'm back on track. We've got to find Alice before we all have regrets."

"Agreed. I'm starting to get a bad feeling about all of this. I don't think Alice is just off on a jaunt somewhere."

"Why's that?" McGill asked.

Sweetie told him about Alice speaking of Virginia Beach as a nice place to die.

"That kind of thing makes me leery," she said. "Young people aren't supposed to talk about dying that way. I didn't. Did you?"

McGill said, "No."

Sweetie told McGill about Elise MacAdams reaching out to her friends in eastern Virginia, see if any of them had heard a report of an injured or ill woman that made the local news.

McGill said, "That's a start, but you and I know a lot of people who know a lot of people, too. Alice was last seen in Atlanta after Teag's final show down there. We checked the hospitals and morgues in Atlanta and DC, the logical places to look if she flew or had plans to fly from there to the show's next stop. But if Alice got into a car intending to drive from Georgia to Washington, then we've got to consider looking for accidents and/or road fatalities in Georgia, South Carolina, North Carolina and Virginia. And who the heck knows, maybe she avoided I-95 and took the scenic route. We haven't tried looking at small-town hospitals and morgues. "

Sweetie sighed. "Yeah, and state bureaucracies being what

they are, it might take a long while to check on the local fender-benders and minor injuries. Shouldn't be as many road fatalities; those should stand out more readily."

"Small comfort there," McGill said. "We'll just have to work every personal contact we have. See if we can turn up *something*."

"Putnam knows a lot of people up and down the Eastern Seaboard," Sweetie said. "I could ask him for help."

"Good. I won't argue with my chief ethics officer. Hey, I just thought of something."

"Yeah?"

"I'm going to call Yves Pruet in Paris. See if Alice's brother in Germany is still alive, if not kicking. Maybe he can dredge up a memory of where the Janeway family traveled in years gone by."

"Couldn't hurt," Sweetie said. "I'll get Leo back behind the wheel, and we'll see you soon."

"Look forward to it," McGill said.

***McGill Investigations International — Washington, DC***

McGill was in his office reading Tad Thacker's file on Alice Janeway and thinking Thacker had done an amazing job of profiling someone he'd only seen once and briefly, using secondary source material. It made McGill think the firm should hire a researcher. Someone who could tap both traditional tomes and online databases. Compiling biographical profiles and other data would give the field investigators a big head-start. Make the whole operation more efficient.

He was still sifting through Tad Thacker's handiwork when Esme Thrice knocked on his door. When Esme came in, she had Deke with her. He was just back from New York. Both Esme and Deke came bearing food. Esme had a thin crust pizza sent from Canale: plain cheese for McGill, mushrooms and onions on her half. Deke was carrying takeout from 2nd Avenue Deli: roast beef and roast turkey sandwiches and a cucumber salad. Everyone decided to share. To keep clear heads and given the food on McGill's desk, they all drank A&W Root Beer from the company's soft-drink stock.

McGill told Deke, "I was just about to ask Esme what she thinks a young woman like Alice Janeway might do when confronted by a roadblock to her professional advancement."

Deke nodded around a mouthful of roast turkey. He thought it a worthy topic to consider.

Esme said, "The first thing, traditionally, is you'd do what anybody would do: look for a better job while holding onto the one you have. But that would require continuing to show up at your old job, and Alice didn't do that. So, looking back at my old job with Monty Kipp, the one thing he wanted me never to do was to go to work for one of his TV rivals. He tried to get me to sign a non-compete agreement. I told him no way, but I wonder if Alice signed one."

McGill said, "I'll call Dorie McBride. She should be able to find out. She's already given me some info on Tobias. Said his appeal is waning. Dorie should be able to find out if Alice is moving up in show biz or just moving on."

Esme said, "If Alice quit in a huff, it'd be good to know if she'd been careful about saving her money. I've always operated that way. It gives you the freedom to tell people where to stick their non-compete agreements. Or hunker down and figure out your next move."

"Maybe Alice got a new phone number?" McGill offered.

"Definite possibility," Esme said.

"New apartment?" McGill asked.

"You'd need more money for that, but if you'd been a really good saver, could be. If you were lucky enough to own a place, it could be a reason to sell and buy somewhere else."

McGill said, "Tobias provided us with Alice's home address. We can check online to see if the place is up for sale. Anything else for us to consider, Esme?"

"Well, if Alice was anywhere near normally sociable, chances are she had at least one good friend among the other employees, if not a total confidant then at least a griping buddy. Find that person and you might learn something important."

"Man or woman?" McGill asked.

"Could be either," Esme said.

That response brought Haskell Carver to McGill's mind. Maybe an obligation of friendship had made him reluctant to tell McGill everything he knew. Of course, the wise thing to do would be to check out all the other names on Teagan Tobias' payroll. See if there was anyone else with whom Alice might have shared a secret.

He made a note to himself to do that.

Turning to Deke, McGill asked, "How'd things go in New York?"

Deke provided a summary of what he'd learned.

McGill's first focus was the obvious one. "A guy who thought he could muscle young Teagan disappeared? Never to be seen or heard from again?"

"That's right," Deke said.

"That's *scary,*" Esme added. "Especially, the part about the knife."

"It should be here tomorrow, the knife," Deke said. "The NYPD let me have it, after I promised we'd return it to Tobias. I sent it FedEx express delivery to our building here, so I wouldn't have any hassle trying to carry it on a plane."

McGill nodded. "Good choice."

Esme said to him, "You're not going to give the knife back."

"Remains to be seen how we use it," McGill said, "but it might be useful one way or another."

Deke nodded and said, "One thing Lily and Dago John definitely agreed on was the idea that the fight up in the Bronx was a fake-out. Whatever happened to this bully, Nicholas Pell, it happened right there in Brooklyn where both of them lived."

McGill agreed, and had a further thought.

"The story about how Tobias got into show-biz in the first

place, the confrontation with his boss at the ad agency, let's find out whatever became of that guy. You know, see if he's still present and accounted for."

Both Deke and Esme gave McGill a look.

He said, "Hey, maybe it's nothing, or maybe people who get on the wrong side of Tobias have the unfortunate habit of vanishing."

"If that's the case," Deke said, "why would he help us find Alice?"

McGill said, "Another mystery to solve."

Esme produced an unexpected laugh.

"What," McGill said, "you don't think we can find her?"

She shook her head. "Of course, we can. I was just imagining things boomeranging, and Teagan Tobias ending up with pie all over his face. That'd be so cool."

McGill and Deke looked at each other.

Esme's team spirit made both of them smile.

***Paxton-Carter Theater — Washington, DC***

Sitting in his dressing room backstage, Teagan Tobias just couldn't help himself. He'd lost count of how many times he'd watched various presentations of the video of McGill's heroics in the Metro that morning. Every station on TV and every site on the Web that he visited all had the same footage: the images recorded by the train station's security cameras. Several of the media outlets had edited the footage differently to fit their time slots or senses of drama, but it was all the same thing over and over again.

Teag was amazed, at first, that nobody had whipped out a cell phone to catch all the drama and possibly a person or two mashed to a bloody pulp by the train. So far, though, nobody had come forward to sell their video to the media or even post it on their own websites. That told Teag something truly amazing. The people in that Metro station had been more motivated by their horror than the possibility of achieving their 15 minutes of fame and a possible windfall of thousands of dollars.

Even so, in the midst of all that craven flight, McGill and that woman, Emma Wiley, hadn't hesitated a second. They flat-out raced toward the source of danger. Spat in its ugly face, metaphorically speaking. The more Teag watched the two of them do that, the more he wondered how each of them had come equipped with such reckless bravery.

Were there truly such beings as heroes?

To walk down the streets of any major city in the world, you wouldn't think so. Most of the people you saw were just trying to rise to the challenge of getting through their daily grind. But then there were these two lionhearts in the DC Metro and … why the hell was McGill taking public transportation anyway? Without any Secret Service protection. It didn't make sense to Teag.

It was almost as if … shit, it was hard for him just to form the thought.

What if McGill had simply been playing his part in some grand design? Acknowledging that even as a possibility made Teag shudder. If there was some higher power cranking out pages for unwitting players on a vast stage … Well, who was to say McGill wasn't meant not only to find out where Alice was, but also discover more about Teag than he ever wanted anyone to learn?

Teag could, of course, just tell McGill he'd found Alice. She'd experienced a medical crisis, which was the truth, and he'd arranged the best medical help money could buy, also true. Would that be enough to get McGill to stop his investigation, though?

He might keep going just to fill in every last detail, completely satisfy his own curiosity.

No, it wasn't a question of maybe. That was *exactly* what he would do.

Teag had recorded the most complete video of the event in the Metro he had seen. He ran it again and stopped where the action cut from McGill to the woman, Emma Wiley. She'd declined to do any interviews yet, just as McGill had. Still, Teag would bet he could find her, where she worked and lived by searching the

Internet.

If necessary, he could go on the Dark Web and hire someone to find her.

The point being, if Teag told McGill *adios*, and then, poof, Emma Wiley disappeared, well, McGill might go looking to solve a new mystery rather than continue to poke around one that had been resolved.

Yeah, Teag thought, the combination of those two things could be what'd save his ass.

***Hell's Belle — Austin, Texas***

Drug Enforcement Agency Chief of Operations Anne Macklin walked into the bar all by her lonesome. That hadn't kept Wallace Rhymes' daughter, Catherine Clarke, from looking out the front window and seeing one of the federal government's black SUVs parked outside. Catherine crooked a shoulder as a shield and held out three fingers against her chest, indicating to her compatriots in the bar the number of federal agents waiting in reserve, ready to rush to their boss' aid should she find the locals to be either truculent or simply stubborn.

As it was, the group waiting to meet the poohbah from DC would have had the feds outnumbered even if the guys in the SUV dropped in. Ever so quietly, Gene began to whistle the theme music from *A Fistful of Dollars.* Maj gave him a gentle poke in the ribs. Now wasn't the time to think of starting a gunfight.

Maybe later, if Eloy Chavez showed up and things went wrong.

Macklin defused any potential tension by offering a bright and seemingly genuine smile to Gene, Maj, Wallace Rhymes, all four of his children, journalist Kyle Tompkins and Conrad Winstead, deputy assistant director of the Texas Rangers. The reception committee, aside from Catherine, was sitting at the bar and looking Macklin's way.

She nodded to Catherine and said, "A round for the house,

please, and one for yourself."

"Anything for the gents outside?" Catherine asked, letting Macklin know her reinforcements had been spotted and taken into account.

"Sure, why not? Ginger ale or cola, your choice."

"The federal government's picking up this tab?" Catherine asked. "I hear it's running a steep deficit already."

Macklin grinned and said, "The government is in hock, but this expenditure is coming out of my pocket, and I'm good for it, Ms. Clarke." She slapped her credit card on the bar.

Catherine laughed and looked at the crew on the barstools. "The lady knows my name. She obviously does her homework."

The bar owner pulled three bottles of Coke out of an ice-filled cooler, popped the tops and took the drinks outside.

Gene, Maj and then the others all stood up and shook the hand Macklin extended to them. She knew each person's name and got the pronunciations right without any hesitation. She even complimented Gene on the two hit songs he'd composed.

"Being a Boston girl," she told Gene, "I don't listen to much country music, but I do like your tunes." She then whistled a measure from his biggest seller in a respectable fashion.

Gene said, "Okay, I'm all in with whatever this lady wants to do."

Speaking for herself and the others, Maj added, "The rest of us will have to come to a meeting of the minds."

Catherine heard that comment as she reentered the bar. "Let's push a few tables together, so we can all talk comfortably." Addressing Macklin, she added, "I locked the front door to keep the public out, but I gave your guys a key if they need to come in, use the men's room or whatever."

"Works for me," Macklin said. "I'll have a Lone Star, by the way. I'm not driving."

With that example set, everyone else had a beer, too. Three round tables were abutted as well as their shapes and the available space allowed. Chairs were filled so that Macklin had the one closest to the door to the street.

"In case you need to make a break for it," Cole Rhymes told her.

"I'll try to hold my own," she replied, "but why don't all of you tell me about any plans you have in mind?"

"We plan to get my hat back," Wallace Rhymes said.

"As peacefully as possible," Conrad Winstead added. "Ideally, nobody gets killed or shot, even if that doesn't make for a good newspaper story."

The last half of that statement was directed at Kyle Tompkins.

He flashed a grin and a peace sign at Winstead.

"I'm good with all of that," Macklin said, "and I genuinely appreciate the opportunity you've created to put Eloy Chavez away. The DEA has wanted to bag that bastard for a long time. When I was told of what you have going on down here, I jumped up and cheered."

Ignoring Winstead's hope for a peaceful resolution, Wallace Rhymes asked, "How'd you feel if I put a round right between Chavez's eyes?"

"Seems a bit stiff for stealing a hat," Macklin said, "even for Texas."

"The hat's one thing," Rhymes said. "Taking it away from Ernesto Fuentes, it sounds to me like the bastard crushed my old friend's soul. Ernesto died soon afterward. His remains are being shipped back here to be buried on my land."

Macklin said, "My condolences, Mr. Rhymes. In your place, I'd probably feel much the same. I can tell you, though, from what I've heard, serving a life sentence in a federal super-max prison might well be a fate worse than death. I wouldn't be surprised if Director Winstead agreed with me on that."

The Texas Ranger chief nodded, "I'd like to shoot this bastard myself, Wallace, but I have to go along with Ms. Macklin. If it was me looking at a sentence where I'd spend the rest of my life getting out of my cell for only one hour a day, getting all my meals passed to me through a port in the cell door, having my every move watched by a TV camera, but never having absolutely anybody I love to talk to me … man, I'd shoot myself before I ever let that happen."

Wallace thought about that and said, "You make a good point, Conrad. If that's the way things are in one of those prisons, you know what I'd like? I'd like to watch the bastard fall apart bit by bit. Wouldn't have to be every day. Maybe once a month, just to see him get ever more desperate and finally go wild-eyed crazy."

Henry Rhymes put a hand on his father's arm. "You say that now, Dad, but you'd get sick of it real fast."

"Just once then," Wallace persisted. "Let me see him in the little corner of hell where they put him, and I'll imagine the rest." He turned to Macklin. "You think they'd let me do that?"

She took a beat to think about it. "I don't know. It doesn't seem unreasonable to me, but it would have to be done with great discretion. Chavez is responsible for many more deaths than just Ernesto Fuentes'. I don't think such an opportunity could be applied broadly. It'd start to be regarded as a zoo visit."

Rhymes laughed harshly. "Maybe it should."

Macklin said, "Maybe, but it would never fly politically. I will ask, though, that you get a chance, just as a special favor, but it would have to be kept quiet by everyone here. That includes you, Mr. Tompkins."

As a matter of professional pride, Kyle was about to object, until he saw everyone else in the room giving him a hard stare. "Okay, okay, I agree. I'll have more than enough other good stuff to write."

"Good," Macklin said. "What's next?"

After a moment's silence, Catherine said, "If everybody else is feeling shy, what we talked about before you arrived was the Rangers should take Chavez into custody. They can hand him over to you, but they should make the arrest."

Anne Macklin sat back in her chair. For the first time since entering the bar, her eyes narrowed and her jaw tightened. After an interval long enough for everyone but her to take a hit of their beer, she said, "That depends."

"On what, ma'am," Winstead asked in an even tone.

"Well, I have the feeling that you plan to bust Eloy Chavez right here. Am I right about that?" she asked.

All the others nodded.

"Colorful," the DEA boss said. "It would add to local legends for both the law officers and Ms. Clarke's bar here. Only … what if things don't go according to plan? My ass would get barbecued right along with yours. I don't mind taking chances when I'm running the show, but when other people are calling the shots …" She shook her head, "I get very edgy."

Winstead said, "Just about everyone who'll be here will be an armed Texas Ranger, not in uniform, of course. Plain clothes will be the drill."

"Sure, that makes sense, but are you telling me that none of the civilians here now will be here then?"

"I damn well will be here," Wallace Rhymes said. "I *won't* be kept away from that."

Macklin said, "If you allow civilians to be here, Mr. Deputy Assistant Director, that's on your head. If you allow them to be armed, you've got *rocks* in your head. I don't care if this is Texas."

Catherine put a hand on her father's shoulder, keeping him quiet for the moment.

That gave Winstead the opening to say, "They won't be armed if they want to be here." He turned to Wallace before the old man could get started. "Take it or leave it, Wallace. Only the Rangers will be armed, and casual customers will be turned away at the door."

"You'll still be taking a big risk," Macklin told him, "but I'm not going to try to big-foot you."

"Glad to hear it," Winstead told her. "That's real refreshing coming from the federal government."

The DEA boss laughed. "That statement is in effect only if I'm not fired before Mr. Chavez hits town. If I'm replaced, '*Que sera*.'"

Gene said, "If you've been replaced, we won't blame you."

The others nodded, even Wallace, grudgingly.

"There are two other things, I'll insist on," Macklin said.

"And they are?" Winstead asked.

"If Chavez is dumb enough to fly into town, the DEA will bust him at the airport. If he otherwise makes his presence obvious outside this lovely establishment, we will also take him down. And if he gets all the way inside here, well, I'll probably need a cowboy hat to blend in, because I'll be here, too."

Everyone at the table, even the grumpy old man, seemed amused.

"What?" Macklin asked.

Maj said, "*Everyone* here will be wearing a cowboy hat."

Gene added, "Each one of 'em looking just like John Wayne's hat."

### *In Traffic — Washington, DC*

McGill brought work — Tad Thacker's file — home with him from the office. Per his custom of the past several years, Leo was driving him home in his armored black Chevy. Sweetie shared the backseat with him. She was giving him a quick rundown of her travels with Leo.

"Both Lindsay Todd and Elise MacAdams told us it would be unlike Alice just to take off on her own for a personal holiday without letting someone know where she was going," Sweetie said.

"That or send some postcards to friends, if she did go somewhere," Leo added.

"Right," Sweetie confirmed.

McGill asked, "Did anyone say or even hint that Alice has a boyfriend, particularly a new one?"

"I asked about that," Sweetie said. "No luck. On another relevant matter, Leo knows a guy from his racing days who knows a senior man in the Georgia State Patrol. He told us that in the week following the closing of Tobias' show in Atlanta, no woman of Alice's age and description was either injured or killed in a highway accident in Georgia. He checked with a friend in Florida in case she drove south, but that didn't turn up anything either. The Georgia friend said he'll check with South Carolina tomorrow. We'll have to find other contacts in North Carolina and Virginia."

"Well, at least we're narrowing things down a little," McGill said. "Good work, Sweetie. My thanks to you and your friend, Leo."

"Sure thing, boss."

McGill filled them in on Deke's trip to New York City.

Sweetie seized on the item that caught her attention in a big way. "Tobias was hassling with some jerk in high school, and then that guy vanishes in a puff of smoke?"

"I don't think there were any theatrics involved," McGill said. "The guy was simply never seen again, starting on the day after he was supposed to have a fight with Tobias."

"Did the New York cops try to verify that Tobias was where he said he was and not somewhere else?" Sweetie asked.

McGill said, "I called Detective Kealoha to ask just that. She got in touch with the retired cop in Brooklyn who told her and Deke the story in the first place. His account is Nicholas Pell, the kid who disappeared, didn't have attentive parents. He wasn't reported missing until a week after the date of the supposed fight. It was only through the high school classmates of both boys that the NYPD even learned of the fight, if there was one."

"Did Tobias tell the cops that he showed up for the fight?" Leo asked.

"He did. He said he waited for an hour and then went home."

Sweetie said, "I don't suppose the NYPD turned up any witnesses who saw him up there in the Bronx."

"They did not. Tobias said he was wearing a dark hoodie, jeans and black sneakers. He said he was leaning against an empty building next to a vacant lot. It was evening and getting dark."

"How convenient," Sweetie said.

Leo replied, "Yeah, Ms. Sweeney, but you got to hand it to the kid. Who's gonna approach someone lookin' like Teag said he did for any reason, 'specially with night comin' on. If it's a made-up story, it's a good one."

"All the more so if you tried to disprove it a week after the supposed fact," McGill said. "Who's going to remember a stranger they passed on the street seven days ago?"

"Nobody in the world," Sweetie said, "not unless the other person's hair was on fire." She looked for a moment as if she might break her taboo on the use of vulgar language, but she didn't. "If Teagan Tobias, as a kid, was smart enough to get away with murder, you know what that probably means."

"That he didn't stop with his first victim," McGill said. "If Nicholas Pell *was* his first victim."

A thought struck McGill and he fell silent for a moment. "I just remembered something. Patti shared a newspaper story with me about how Tobias got the money to start his showbiz career. He sued the ad agency where he worked after his boss tried to beat him up. Tobias got the better of the other guy without even throwing a punch. He also had witnesses that he was the aggrieved party."

"Okay," Sweetie said. "He's smart and he can slip a punch. How does that fit in with everything else?"

McGill said, "Like this: Alice seems to have vanished; Nicholas Pell disappeared, too. And, now, Deke is looking into Tobias' old boss at the ad agency. Either of you think he's still around?

Leo shook his head. "Unh-uh."

Sweetie whispered, "Dear God."

***Dumbarton Oaks — Washington, DC***

"Do you think we should have a cook?" Patti asked.

She'd arrived at the new McGill house ten minutes after Leo had dropped McGill at home and headed off to take Sweetie back to her place.

McGill had just taken two roasted chicken breasts, left over from the night before, from the refrigerator. He was going to finely slice the poultry, stack it on artisanal Italian bread, slice some tomatoes and onions and put out any condiments either of them might care to add. He'd have a bottle of Beck's Sapphire beer, and Patti would have a glass of whatever wine she cared to pair with last night's main course.

"Don't I handle most of the food prep around here?" McGill asked. "I think my bachelor-father cooking skills have been coming back quite nicely."

Patti said, "You are a prince, and your cooking is surprisingly good for a man of action."

McGill laughed. "Yeah, well, I have to compensate since I can no longer leap tall buildings at a single bound."

"That's all right. Capes and bodystockings have gone out of fashion, not that I would mind if you wanted to give that look a try."

McGill squeezed a dollop of French's mustard on a fingertip and applied it to his lips. He kissed Patti and said, "Now, where else would you find a chef whose kisses taste that good?"

"I don't know," Patti said. "I might have to interview extensively."

"Hah! You'd have to give up your day job. However, there are times when I don't feel like either cooking or dining out. So, what would you think of having a chef or two, male or female, on call. People versed in different cuisines who wouldn't mind whipping something up for a retired public servant and her spouse on proper notice. I also hear that there are services these days that will pick up meals from restaurants and deliver them still hot."

"You mean you're taking your nose out of the *Chicago Tribune's* sports section these days?"

"Only when I must. Tonight, for instance, I brought home a report on the life and times of Alice Janeway, as compiled by the guy we detectives formerly considered to be the poor woman's possible stalker."

Patti thought about that as she pulled a bottle of Pinot Blanc from the wine cooler. McGill constructed a sandwich for each of them, Patti getting Grey Poupon mustard instead of French's. He could've used that for the kiss, but he didn't want the missus to swoon.

Pouring a glass of wine for herself, Patti asked, "The formerly suspected creep has cleared his name?"

McGill told her Tad Thacker's story, and Sweetie's opinion of him, as gained from their road-trip together.

Patti nodded. "Sweetie is an excellent judge of character."

The two of them sat at the kitchen table and toasted each other's health.

"Anyway," McGill told Patti, "I've got my after-dinner reading to do. I'm hoping to get a better idea of what might have happened to Alice."

"That doesn't sound hopeful, a pre-destined outcome."

McGill sighed. "Consensus is building, between the gang at the office and me, that something or someone unfortunate has crossed paths with Alice. We don't think she's just off on her own."

"You have any inkling of a suspect?"

McGill told her what he'd heard from Dorie McBride about Tobias' presently plateaued and soon to decline career prospects.

McGill said, "I've been running that through my mind for hours now. The prospect of an approaching failure never cheers anyone. If Alice felt creatively stymied by Tobias, and she, too, sensed the bottom was about to fall out of *Every Last Bastard in the World*, mightn't she look for new prospects? Esme Thrice seems to think that's a possibility, and she's a young professional who might empathize better with Alice than a grizzled detective."

Patti ran a hand through McGill's hair. "You're starting to go silver, not gray. It's quite distinguished looking."

"Don't get me excited, not yet," McGill said.

"I'll try to control myself. So you're starting to think Tobias did … what?"

"That's part of the problem. We're not sure exactly what he might have done."

McGill told Patti of the disappearance of Nicholas Pell in New York.

"And now Alice has gone missing," McGill said. "All of which led me to wonder, just before coming home, how that guy who got Tobias fired from his ad job is doing these days."

"Oh, my," Patti said. "Do you really think he could be that evil?"

McGill shrugged. "Could be I'm way off base, but I still have to check it out. I don't remember you mentioning the ad boss' name to me."

"I don't think I did. Give me just a minute."

She got up and took her phone from her purse on the kitchen counter. She tapped keys with the kind of speed McGill had never been able to manage. By the time she sat down again, she had a name: "Harrison Richards."

"What else you got on him?" McGill asked.

Patti expanded her search. "Well … he's from New York City. His father was also in advertising but as an account executive not a creative person. Richards, the son, was married and divorced. No mention of children. Oh, here's something. That incident with Teagan Tobias? Richards was let go from his job six months after the ad agency that had employed him settled their suit with Tobias, an amount this account notes to be a substantial sum."

"Anything else on him?" McGill asked.

After a minute of searching, Patti shook her head. "There's nothing any of the New York papers have. Don't see anything from other major advertising outposts either." She put her phone down. "Jim, this doesn't mean Richards has disappeared, too. He could just be living outside an area of media notice."

McGill said, "Mmm-hmm."

Not wanting to let her husband dwell on the matter, at least for the moment, Patti gave him something else to think about. "I heard today that Galia has found a new job."

That effectively commanded McGill's attention. "Not with you, you mean?"

"No, not with me. The company that hired her is called Strategic Evaluation Services. They do political and economic risk analysis for high-tech companies looking to set up manufacturing facilities overseas."

"So, the opposite of your plan to create such jobs here at home," McGill said.

"Yes, exactly."

"Do you think of Galia's move to that particular company as a jab at you?"

Patti said, "I told myself no, at first, but the denial didn't last long."

"Is the job just a cover for Galia to do the snooping she wanted you to front for her?"

"I don't know."

McGill said, "I could look to see if Frank Morrissey has left any fingerprints on this."

Patti shook her head. "No, don't. This is a sensitive matter, to put it mildly. If Jean is on top of things, she'll see what's happening. It will be her call what to do next."

"Before things get messy?" McGill asked.

"I sincerely hope so."

The former first couple finished their sandwiches and drinks. McGill washed the few dirty dishes that needed attention. After KP duties were done, McGill had his reading to do. That and make a phone call to Detective Lily Kealoha in New York City. She still had some free time before her NYPD shift started.

Not long after dinner, Patti gave McGill a kiss and indulged in a pleasure almost never afforded to any responsible Chief Executive of the United States. She went to bed early in the hope of catching up on needed rest. McGill never argued with such a move, and he rarely tried to interest his drowsing wife in a moment of conjugal companionship, even if that might make her rest more blissful.

He did, however, accede to that possibility if she rolled over to his side of the bed.

What else would a good man do?

At that moment, though, McGill had repaired to his home office, a space reconfigured to resemble as closely as possible his Hideaway in the White House. His long leather sofa was there, of course, as were the other fixtures he'd brought along. The flooring and lighting in the room had been altered to resemble his former space. The view out the windows, looking at the garden in the backyard, was even better than the one he'd had at the White House.

Added to all that, Patti had insisted on tucking a small, discreet fridge in a corner of the room. It was stocked with his current favorite beers, bottled waters and light snacks, the proximity of which would save him the steps of going to the kitchen.

Blessing, the former White House head butler, was still with them, of course, but these days he served in an on-call basis. That left Blessing with far more time to spend with his children and grandchildren while still receiving a full-time salary.

McGill took a chilled bottle of San Pellegrino, his favorite sparkling water of the moment, and a handful of Dove dark chocolates from the fridge. He sat on his sofa, his snacks at hand on an end table, the file Tad Thacker had given him at his side. He took out his phone and called Lily Kealoha in New York City.

The NYPD detective answered on the second ring. "Mr. McGill, this is a surprise. Did Deke forget to ask me something?"

"It wasn't a question of forgetting, Lily. More of a new idea that came to mind."

"I like it," she said. "New ideas are how cases get solved. Sometimes, anyway."

"Well, in this case, it's more a question of understanding who I'm dealing with."

"That's good, too."

McGill told her the tale of Teagan Tobias and Harrison Richards and their tussle at the New York ad agency. "What I'm wondering, Lily, is if Mr. Richards has ever popped up on the NYPD's radar."

"Not on mine. If he showed up on the department's at large, it'd be helpful to know in which borough you might think we'd find him."

"As I understand it, he was a semi-big shot in the ad business. So my guess would be Manhattan."

"Let me make a couple of quick calls before I go to work. If I don't get something right away, it'll have to wait until I'm off duty again. You good with that?"

"Completely. If you can find anything, bill us another five hundred dollars."

Lily laughed. "You keep throwing money at me like that, I might have to ask if you're hiring."

"Have you reached pension eligibility yet?" McGill asked.

"Two more years."

"Wait until then. I'm assuming people will still need our services, and we can talk."

"Sounds good. I'll see what I can do in the meantime."

They said their goodbyes and McGill turned to Tad Thacker's file on Alice Janeway. It struck him that the dossier began with photos of Alice as an infant. He started to wonder how the Oregon-based environmental engineer had come up with those. It took him only a moment, though, to come up with the answer: social media.

These days, people posted everything but their colonoscopy videos online.

Some heedless souls might even share those, and McGill's own children would have laughed at him for not coming up with where the photos originated immediately. That was when he noticed that Thacker, thoughtfully, had noted the source of his material: Flickr.

McGill wrote a note to himself to ask his children to keep him up to date on internet trends. The speed with which these new forms of communications arose, gained popularity, faded and died lay beyond his grasp. He'd have to pay Abbie, Ken and Caitie for their help, of course, but that was only fair.

The pictures of Alice as a grinning, toothless infant touched McGill's heart. Hardened it as well. He thought: *Teagan Tobias, you better not have harmed this young woman.*

He pushed through the file, saw more photos of a growing

Alice. He followed her progress through elementary school with images of her report cards. Straight-A's, year after year. Thacker put a footnote in at the bottom of the fifth-grade scholastic evaluation: *This school makes its students earn their grades. Checked with the state evaluation of school's own performance.*

Adjacent to a junior high photo of Alice, Thacker had written: *This was the age when I first met Jenny Nyland. The resemblance breaks my heart.*

McGill felt sympathy for Thacker, but he also grew suspicious. Yes, the information he had from Keely Powell indicated that Thacker hadn't been stalking Alice. Not in person, anyway. But how many times had Thacker turned to this dossier for comfort? Chances were he had compiled much more information on Alice than had been available to gather on Jenny.

After all, Thacker's first true love had died before the advent of social media.

McGill would be dumbfounded if Jenny Nyland's family or friends had posthumously posted more than a simple, dignified headshot of a young girl who had died in a bus crash. Then again, drawing on his cop experiences, McGill knew there was no end to the way people could confound expectations.

Random turns of fate could be equally perverse. Leafing through Alice's medical history — and knowing that Tad Thacker must have hacked this material, given the HIPPA Privacy Rule — McGill saw that as an early teenager Alice had suffered a bout of encephalitis caused by a mosquito bite during a trip to Florida.

McGill pulled up a summary of encephalitis on his phone. In most cases, the inflammation of the brain caused either no symptoms or those of a mild flu-like state: headache, fever, muscle and joint aches, and fatigue. In more severe cases, however, things could get much worse: hallucinations, seizures, paralysis and loss of consciousness, among others.

Alice had fallen unconscious and been non-responsive for a week. A doctor's note said: *Death appears to be imminent.*

Dying wasn't what fate or some other higher power had in

mind, though. Just as Alice was about to be given up as lost, something within her rallied. She opened her eyes while a nurse was present and in a rasping voice asked, "Where am I?"

A subsequent chart notation read: Patient's immune system refused to quit.

That made McGill remember how his son Ken had been to the brink and came back. He had to blink tears from his eyes. He whispered to himself, "Hang in there again, Alice. We're going to find you."

McGill kept reading and with every page he turned the conviction grew that Tad Thacker, while behaving legally, for the most part, and publicly appropriately, had never lost his obsession with Alice. It seemed to McGill to be a desperate way to live, but how many people were there who became obsessed with a person simply because of the movies he or she had made or the songs they'd recorded?

He didn't want to know the actual numbers.

He didn't try to kid himself that it was uncommon.

Before McGill could reach the end of the file, sleep claimed him, and reflex made him stretch out on the couch. No alarm on his phone had been set, but a call woke him anyway. It was the middle of the night, for him. For Detective Lily Kealoha, it was lunchtime.

In a soft, tentative voice, Lily said, "Mr. McGill, did I wake you?"

"Yeah, but that's okay. I was trying to read through the night, a case file, but I'm not as young as I used to be."

"Nobody is," Lily told him with a small laugh.

"Yeah, anyway, you've got something, right?"

"I did. I'm on a break, and I thought I should tell you in case I got caught up in something before I clocked out. I kinda hoped I'd get voicemail."

"It's okay, really. What did you find?"

"Harrison Richards is the subject of a missing-person report."

A chill ran through McGill. He shifted himself into a sitting position.

"Who made the report? Any particulars?"

"His sister, Angela, called Manhattan South. Harrison was supposed to meet her up in Hartford, Connecticut where she lives. After Harrison lost his ad job here in the city, he couldn't find a job at another ad agency. His sister had a friend at a big insurance company in Hartford. They needed someone in their ad department. The friend was willing to give Harrison an interview and seemed understanding that he'd been provoked by Teagan Tobias. Only Harrison never showed for the interview, and when Angela couldn't reach him by phone, text or email, she came to the city. She had a key to his apartment and let herself in."

"He wasn't there," McGill said.

"No, he wasn't, but his passport, his luggage and most of his clothes were. His rent was paid for a month in advance, so there was no reason to evict him."

Understanding the situation now, McGill said, "And there was no sign of a violent struggle."

"None. The neighbors said they hadn't even heard a raised voice."

"Sonofabitch," McGill said.

"That's pretty much the way the detectives who worked the case feel, too. They were real interested when I asked them about it. They'd love to hear from you."

"I'll call you with anything I find out. You can pass it along, earn some goodwill."

"Thanks. Anything you want to share now?"

"Yes. This has to be related to the Nicholas Pell disappearance."

"Damn!" Lily said. "That was exactly what I had in mind, and you know what? Teagan Tobias is involved here, too."

"How? How is he involved?"

"After Harrison Richards lost his ad agency job and couldn't find another one in town, he got himself a lawyer and filed two suits, one against his former agency and the other —"

"Against Tobias," McGill said.

"Yeah. Tobias got served while he was between shows."

"You have the date on that, Lily?"

She gave it to him. "Tobias got handed notice of the suit at Teterboro. You know what that is, right?"

"General aviation airport in New Jersey, just outside Manhattan. Where the private jet crowd goes to take off and land."

"Yeah, exactly. Tobias was on his way down to the Caribbean for a vacation, and the word is when he got told he was being sued, he said, 'Fuck it,' and took off anyway."

"Let me guess," McGill said. "He returned exactly on schedule."

"You got it."

McGill thought for a moment. "But there's nothing to say he didn't make another quick trip in between. Using another aircraft, a different name, and landing at a different airport. Hell, maybe even at a private landing strip."

Lily said, "Now, that last bit, the landing strip, that was one the detectives here hadn't thought of. At least that they told me."

"You hang out with the president of the United States for eight years, you get a glimpse of what really big money can buy."

"I'll pass along that idea, anyway, okay?"

"Let's hold off for the moment." Getting in gear now, McGill added, "My guess is if Tobias left pale and white, he came back with a good tan."

"Damn, you nailed that, too."

"What the tan tells us," McGill said, "is if Tobias is behind Richards disappearance, and I bet we both think he is, then he made a quick turnaround, came back north, took care of business and still had time to go back south and sun himself."

Lily said, "If he did that, it'd narrow the window of time for him to get his dirty work done."

"Yeah, and he'd do it in a way that wouldn't leave any tracks."

"But what'd he do with…"

McGill was sure Lily was about to say Harrison Richards' body, but he let her work things out for herself. It didn't take long.

She said. "All Tobias would have had to do was lure Richards onto the private plane he took back to the Mainland. Then he could kill Richards and fly right back to the Caribbean and dump Richards' body in the ocean somewhere along the way. If he did that far enough away from land, the body would never wash up. It'd sink to the bottom or get eaten by marine carnivores. I heard stories about things like that growing up in Hawaii. Except out there people used their boats to dump bodies, but an airplane would work, too."

"Yes, it would," McGill said. "Lily, the reason I ask you to hold off sharing any of this for a while is we don't want it to get back to Tobias."

"Okay, but let me know when I can say something, will you?"

"I will, and thanks for the good work. I'll have your fee sent today."

"That'd be great. You have the bank and account numbers you'll need?"

"You gave them to Deke, didn't you?"

After a beat of silence, she said, "Well, yeah, I did."

McGill suspected Lily might have shared her personal phone number, too. "Okay, then," he said, "we're good, and thanks again."

McGill decided to add a bonus $500 on top of the agreed-upon fee.

After all, even if she didn't realize it yet, Lily had just given McGill an idea of how Tobias might've gotten rid of Nicholas Pell's body. Maybe, even as a kid, Teag had known somebody who had a boat — wouldn't even have to be a very big one — and wouldn't mind doing a bit of dirty work. After all, there was a whole lot of water around New York City.

McGill pulled up the time on his phone: 3:36 a.m.

That'd be 8:36 a.m. in Paris.

He hadn't gotten around to calling the Paris office yesterday, but someone should be there by now. He tapped the contact number on his phone. Gabbi Casale answered on the first ring.

"*Salut. C'est bien toi, mon chef?*" Good morning. You're well, boss?

"I am, Mademoiselle Casale. I was wondering if you or Yves

Pruet might try calling Marlon Janeway. His wife said she was cutting off any further payment to us and …"

McGill caught the vibe as if it had bounced off a satellite and chilled him on landing in DC. "He died, didn't he?"

Gabbi told him, "I got the call not ten minutes ago. Not from the wife, from Mr. Janeway's personal attorney."

"Damn," McGill said.

"Yeah. It's a real shame he didn't get to talk to his sister again, but he should have tried harder while he still could. We're still good to go on the investigation, though."

"I intended to," McGill said, "but what do you mean?"

"Mr. Janeway's lawyer, who's in Switzerland, by the way, says Mr. Janeway put money away for what he called contingencies."

"Which would include us?"

"Yes. He also put aside a million dollars, or its equivalent in Swiss francs, for Alice. Apparently, he understood his wife's … greed. There's even a poison pill in his will. If Erika Janeway contests any of the bequests to people other than herself, she gets nothing."

"There were people other than his children and Alice?" McGill asked.

"Apparently, Mr. Janeway had a longtime mistress of whom he was quite fond. She got a million, too."

"A Swiss lawyer told you that?"

"Of course not. Yves and Odo did a little discreet snooping. They came up with that just before you called. They're still looking into something right now. What the lawyer said was to please let him know if Erika tries to claw back any of the money he left for Alice or for us to find her. He'll put the fear of going broke into her."

"What about the children?" McGill asked.

"They're young adults now, and they'll be covered by money coming from the lawyer not from Mama. By the way, you did some nice work in that Metro station."

McGill said, "Thanks."

"Sorry you weren't able to find Alice before her brother died."

"Me, too."

"You will find her before too long, right?"

"Honestly, Gabbi, it might well be another very close call."

***University Hospital — Richmond, Virginia***

Teagan Tobias canceled another show after he got a call from Alice's attending physician. "Barbara is awake and speaking. She'd like to talk with you. But she is somewhat disoriented. She's calling herself Alice."

"That's her stage name," Teag lied glibly.

"She's an actress?"

"Aspiring, but talented."

The doctor bought it or at least didn't argue.

As someone who definitely did not believe in miracles, Teag was a bit off balance and lapsed into a silence long enough for the doctor to ask, "Are you still there, Mr. Tobias?"

"I am, yeah. Sorry. I was just at a loss for words. Is Alice all right? Is she going to be … normal?"

Now, there was quiet on the doctor's end of the call.

Just before Teag could ask if he was still there, the doctor responded. "I honestly don't know. Going by her vital signs, it would seem there's no reason she shouldn't recover completely. But we don't have a medical history on this patient. We did hear that you brought her to us from a hospice facility, so that's a worry. We've seen patients who defy long odds, but I've never personally experienced someone rebounding from the brink of death to stable good health. To be frank, I don't know what we should expect to come next. I'd suggest that, while exercising prudence and obeying the traffic laws, you should get here as quickly as you can. Assuming you wish to speak with Alice."

"Yes, I damn well do."

The doctor gave Teag Alice's room number. "If you can give me a call when you're about ten minutes out, I'll meet you there."

"You're not going to stay with Alice?" Teag asked, surprise clear in his voice.

"A nurse will be with her until both you and I get to the room. It would be helpful to us if you can provide any of Alice's medical history."

"Yeah, I'll see what I can find, but why can't you stay with her?"

"Other patients also need me."

Teag almost blurted, "Screw them," only he knew that idea wouldn't fly.

"Okay, I'll get there as fast as I can."

"In one piece," the doctor said.

"Yeah, right."

Teag was tempted to call Haskell to drive him down to Richmond, but he didn't want to let anyone else know Alice's whereabouts. What if Alice relapsed, if that was what you'd call it. She might even die before he got there. That'd be a real kick to the head. On the other hand, if she died on her own in the hospital, he wouldn't have to arrange her death.

Of course, if he reached Alice in time to speak with her, and then she went back into a coma, that'd be pretty damn bad, too. How could he know whether she might wake up again and whether she'd be normal if she did?

In the darkest corner of his shriveled soul, Teag found a speck of pitch-black humor. Maybe the right thing to do would be a murder-suicide. Kill her. Croak himself, too. Put the both of them out of their misery. He didn't believe in any kind of a hereafter, so he wasn't worried about Alice going to heaven while he burned in hell. What put him off of that idea was the slim hope that Alice would be okay again, and the two of them could have some good years together.

He could continue to be the cynical hard-ass: expect the worst from the world and get it. She'd look for rainbows and love songs and get them. Which would drive him crazy, making the audience laugh its collective ass off.

That would be a shift in his act, of course, but he already

knew his work was getting stale. McGill and the softening box-office receipts told him so. It was a hell of a thing when people stopped seeing the fun of sticking it to someone else who'd stuck it to you.

Then again, Alice might have come into his life at just the right time to save his ass. While he didn't believe in salvation, he had no doubt dumb luck existed. It showed up every time some cluck won a big lottery jackpot.

He'd get to the hospital in time to talk with her and they'd go from there.

That was just what happened, too. Seemed to Teag like he'd gotten lucky.

Alice was reclining in her partially raised hospital bed. Her eyes were open and she saw him the moment he stepped into her room. She even managed to give Teag a small smile. He gave her a wink in reply. The doctor was there along with a nurse. He gave the medical people a quick nod, stepped past them and took Alice's hands in his.

Staying in character, he told her, "Some people will do anything for attention."

He immediately regretted his words. What if they were the last ones she ever heard?

Or told him she was taking a job with someone else.

Neither of those things happened.

Her voice hoarse from lack of use, Alice said, "I've got a new idea for the show."

That cracked up Teag, and the doctor and nurse as well.

For that one moment, Teag couldn't remember being any happier.

He asked the doctor and the nurse if he might have a moment alone with his friend.

The doctor nodded and whispered to him, "Call immediately if you need help."

Teag nodded and even smiled.

Alice told him what she'd come up with, and it was similar to his idea, only more outrageous. She'd start out playing the Pollyanna, and he'd be the curmudgeon. Little by little, though, each personality would rub off on the other. By the end of the show, they'd completely reverse roles. The idea of playing a nice guy absolutely floored Teag, left him speechless.

Then Alice refocused the conversation. "Teag, what the hell happened to me?"

"You collapsed," he told her. "We were in my hotel room, talking, just standing there schmoozing and you started to crumple. I barely caught you before you hit the floor."

Tears formed in Alice's eyes. "Is this the encephalitis again? Did I get another damn mosquito bite?"

"No, no mosquitoes. I talked to a doc when you were admitted the first time, and I talked to the one who was here just now. They both said the same thing: your blackout and your comeback, they were both idiopathic."

Alice looked liked she'd heard the word before but couldn't summon the meaning.

Teag saw her lack of comprehension and told her: "Means they don't have a clue, either time."

Alice began to shiver. "I'm scared. What might happen to me next?"

He sat on the side of the bed and took her hands in his. "It was me, I'd curse and rage. We never talked about praying, you and me, but if you believe that way, that might be a good thing to do."

Alice thought about that and asked, "What happened when I was unconscious?"

"You were in the hospital, and it looked like the end. So I had you moved to a hospice facility."

Tears rolled down Alice's cheeks. "It was that bad?"

"Yeah."

That reality brought the tears to a halt. After a moment, Alice asked, "Did you think about doing what we promised each other?"

He nodded.

"But you didn't."

"No, I didn't want to break my promise, but I thought I should give it enough time to … to make sure I wasn't being hasty."

To Teag's surprised, Alice laughed. "Hasty, that's a good one." Doing a terrible English accent, she added, "Let's not be hasty here, guvnor, the old girl might wake up yet."

Teag laughed at the dark humor. "Yeah, well, we can laugh *now*."

As if taking a cue, Alice stopped laughing. In a quiet voice, she asked, "If things had gotten to the point where you honestly thought enough was enough … would you have been able to honor our agreement?"

Teag nodded, and in a sober voice said, "Yeah, Alice, I would have."

Tears reappearing, she said, "It still might come to that."

"You never know," Teag agreed. "That being the case, let's get the hell out of here."

## CHAPTER 5

***Friday, November 4, 2017***
***McGill Investigations International — Washington, DC***

When he got to the office, McGill asked Sweetie to step into his office. The moment the door was closed and they were both seated, he asked, "You remember Deke's story about the kid named Nicholas Pell vanishing."

"Yeah."

"And I raised the notion about Tobias' ad agency boss being at risk."

Sweetie did the math in nothing flat. "Oh, God help us. That really happened to him, too?"

He nodded. He told Sweetie about talking with Detective Lily Kealoha and how she found out about Harrison Richards filing a suit against Tobias, only to disappear soon thereafter.

McGill said, "I led Lily to consider the possibility of Richards being lured into a private plane by Tobias, and then dumped into the ocean. She said she'd heard similar stories growing up in Hawaii. Only the people there used boats to dispose of the bodies. It took a while, but that led me to think: What if a young Tobias had a friend with access to a boat? He wouldn't have had to dump Nicholas Pell into a local river where the body might wash up along the shore. They could go out onto the ocean a few miles and toss Nicky over the side, never to be seen again."

Sweetie could only shake her head, in lament not disagreement. She felt sure McGill had things exactly right.

"You're going to ask Detective Kealoha to follow up?" she asked.

McGill shook his head. "I remember the times I worked the night shift. I hated it when anything less than vital woke me up when I was sleeping through the day."

"I remember that, too. So, you're going to let her sleep and then call?"

"No, I went downstairs this morning and borrowed a business card that Deke got from retired NYPD Sergeant Gianni Calendri. I'm going to give him a call when we're done talking."

Sweetie started to ask, "You think Alice ..."

McGill held up a hand. "Let's not go there, not yet. Better to think that Alice *is* still breathing, and we're going to keep her that way."

"Right," Sweetie said.

Then McGill shared the sad news of Marlon Janeway's passing.

***Chihuahua, Mexico***

Eloy Chavez, wearing what he now thought of as his faux John Wayne hat, lifted off from the helipad adjacent to his home in the pre-dawn darkness. His aircraft of choice that morning was an Airbus AS365 N3+. The machine might be flown by either a single pilot or with a co-pilot. A careful man, Chavez always made sure there were two aviators at the controls. The helicopter could hold a maximum of 11 passengers in the configuration that came from the manufacturer.

Chavez had his chopper modified to hold only four passengers: himself, his wife and their two children. The weight savings had allowed him to add a 30-millimeter chain gun and air-to-air missile launchers to his ride. If he were attacked by either ground forces or another aircraft, he would be able to respond with nearly the weaponry of an attack helicopter.

In addition to its firepower, Chavez's helicopter had custom-designed rotor blades that substantially quieted its sounds of operation. The drug boss had been impressed by how the U.S. special forces had used relatively quiet helicopters in the attack that killed Osama Bin Laden. On the other hand, the thought that someone — the military of his own country, the yanquis, or even rivals in the drug trade — might silently come for him one night had given him an occasional nightmare.

His sleep became peaceful once again only after he'd posted men with black-market Stinger missiles to watch the sky over his house in the hours of darkness.

The flight that morning was meant to be peaceful, silent and all but invisible, and it succeeded in all those goals. Chavez disembarked from his helicopter at a dock on the Sea of Cortez. There was ferry service from Guaymas to Santa Rosalia in Baja California, but Chavez had even more enemies in Mexico than among all the americanos. He cruised to Baja California in a relatively small but extremely well-armed yacht.

In Santa Rosalia, Chavez boarded a Gulfstream G650. The executive jet could transport as many as 18 passengers, fly 7,000 nautical miles nonstop and reach a speed of over 600 miles per hour. Again, though, Chavez was the only passenger. He had eschewed even the presence of a cabin attendant. He could get his own drinks and snacks. He would have only the two pilots in the cockpit for company. His hat rested on the seat next to him.

Chavez's airplane pilots, like all the others facilitating his travels, were lavishly well paid, and they knew without a doubt how hideous their deaths would be if they ever betrayed the boss. The flight took off within minutes of Chavez's arrival. The sun was just coming up as the plane climbed to cruising altitude.

Chavez reclined his seat and settled in for the flight to Vancouver, British Columbia that would take just under four hours. A more direct flight path would have saved time, but Chavez would fly out over the Pacific to Canada, avoiding American airspace altogether. Doing that meant his plane wouldn't have to comply with the *americanos'* Secure Flight program that matched passenger information to watch lists maintained by the U.S. federal government.

The original purpose of Secure Flight was to thwart terrorists, but the *yanquis* were equally happy to capture men of Chavez's profession as well. Even though Chavez was flying under an assumed name, using a Paraguayan passport to enter Canada and had cut his normally long hair, shaved his beard but not his mustache and inserted soft contact lenses to change his eye color to hazel, the drug boss still was not going to enter the enemy's airspace from the south.

He would do so from the north, flying into the U.S from Canada.

He'd use a Spanish passport to do that, after adding gray to his hair and mustache.

He would fly to Oklahoma City and drive to Austin, Texas from there.

The ten men he'd chosen to join him in Austin, skilled in mayhem but all of them expendable, would come across the border from Mexico to Texas in the usual ways. If Chavez lost one or two of them in transit, so be it. They all knew the risks, imprisonment or death, and their families would be well compensated.

The pilots found clear air for a smooth flight north. The sun continued its climb in the sky. Chavez lowered the shade on the window next to his seat. He helped himself to a shot of Casa Noble tequila and drifted off to sleep.

Dreaming of taking back John Wayne's hat.

Watching Wallace Rhymes die wearing the hat on the seat next to him.

***McGill Investigations International — Washington, DC***

"Dago John," said a voice with a thick New Yawk accent.

In his DC office, McGill replied, "Sergeant Calendri, this is

Jim McGill calling."

Real surprise filled the reply. "Son of a gun. I saw your company name come up on my phone, but I thought it was Deke Ky calling. Hey, you know, I voted for your wife both times."

"I never get tired of hearing that, Sergeant."

"I bet. You're some lucky guy, landing a lady like her."

"It amazes me, too. Do you have a minute to talk?"

"Absolutely. Hold on just a minute while I go to my office. It's pretty noisy here in the diner."

"Sure."

McGill could hear a babble of voices and the clatter of knives and forks on china in the background. He also heard Dago John say in a not-so-quiet whisper, "You know who I got on the phone here? James J. McGill. Yeah, that one. No, really."

There were doubters and the retired sergeant told them where they could stick their disbelief. Then things got quiet, and Dago John rejoined the conversation. "Okay, Mr. McGill, what can I do for you? Hey, by the way, I saw the video of you and that lady laying out that nutcase in your subway down there in DC. Made me proud to see a brother officer handle a situation like that."

"Thank you. Ms. Wiley handled herself with distinction, too."

"That lady? She sure did. So what can I do for you? Anything you want that won't get me locked up, I'll be happy to do."

"Actually, Sergeant, I'm hoping I might be of some help to you."

There was a pause before Dago John said, "How's that?"

"Did you ever hear of a man named Harrison Richards? He used to live and work in Manhattan."

"Mr. McGill—"

"Please call me Jim."

"Okay, Jim. If Dago John doesn't work for you, I also answer to Gianni."

"I think I'll go with the second one, Gianni."

"That's fine. To answer your question, I hardly ever get over to Manhattan and haven't for years. If I'm not here in Brooklyn, I've gone someplace warm. So I don't recall the name Harrison Richards.

Mustn't have made any headlines in the *Post*."

McGill said, "Mr. Richards was an advertising executive. He got into a fight with Teagan Tobias, who worked for him."

"Oh shit," Dago John, "what happened to the poor bastard? Richards, I mean."

"He disappeared," McGill said, "right after he filed a lawsuit against Tobias."

"Damn, when was this?"

"Quite some time ago," McGill said. "Right after Tobias started to get a big name."

"And this is connected to the woman you're looking for?"

"We hope not, but it has to be considered a possibility."

"Yeah, it would."

"Detective Kealoha and I were talking. I speculated maybe Tobias conned Richards into getting on a plane with him, and then dumped Richards in the ocean. Lily said when she was growing up in Hawaii she'd heard stories of people dumping bodies off of boats into the Pacific. You know what that made me think?"

Long retired or not, Dago John knew immediately. "Tobias found someone with a boat to get rid of Nicholas Pell. Damn. I waited what seems like half my life for that kid's body to surface in a river around here. I never thought Tobias could dump him way out in the ocean. He was just a teenager back then. His parents had two cars, but no boat I ever heard of."

"How about a friend of his?" McGill asked. "Or even a friend of a friend."

"Yeah. Now, you've got me thinking. It's gotta be something like that. There are other places you could put a body it wouldn't be found, the foundation of a building that's going up, or under the support for a new bridge, but out in the ocean would be the easiest."

McGill said, "I know you've been retired a long time, Gianni, but do you know any NYPD detectives who might be willing to take a look? See if they can run down any of Tobias' childhood friends, find out if maybe some family connection had access to a boat. Wouldn't even have had to be a long trip on the water. The ocean gets deep fast, doesn't it?"

A former Navy man, Dago John knew the answer. "Not so much off the East Coast. The West Coast, yeah. But around here you can go out five, ten miles and have water not much more than a hundred feet deep."

"Huh," McGill said. "Even so, there's a *lot* of ocean out there."

"No question about that. Without some kind of clue, you'd never find out where the kid's body went in the water. By now, of course, you'd be lucky even to find bones with tidal movement shifting them all to hell and gone."

"Yeah, I guess so," McGill said. "I was thinking more of finding an accomplice anyway. If my idea has any chance of success, I was pinning it on somebody helping Tobias. Some reckless kid who'd think it'd be exciting to get rid of a body. Maybe even a kid Nicholas Pell had pushed around a time or two."

Dago John replied. "I like that division of labor. It has a nice fit. Tobias could've made a pitch like: 'I'll kill him; you dump him.'"

"It's an approach to start looking for someone, anyway," McGill said.

"Yeah, I know a retired detective who I can ask for help with this. I'd work it with him, and if it looks like we've found something promising, we'll take it to the department. Get some guys on it who aren't collecting their pensions yet."

"That'd be good."

"Of course, like everything else with this guy Tobias, it's gonna be a long shot."

McGill said, "You mean an accomplice might've moved far away or died of natural causes."

"That or Tobias did him in, too."

McGill sighed. "Yeah, that's possible."

"Maybe even probable," Dago John said, "but you know what? Overall, I'm starting to feel lucky here. Like it's time some good cops caught up with that little shit, Tobias. Hey, I just had a thought."

"What?" McGill asked.

"Well, did your guy, Deke Ky, tell you one of Nicholas Pell's nicknames was The Brick Shithouse? Because he had bad B.O. or something."

"I must've missed that detail," McGill said.

"Well, it's true. It's also a fact that there's an area of ocean off Long Island that's called the 12 Mile Dump. New York City started dumping its sewage waste there when George Washington was in diapers. I think I read once the amount of sludge, crap and whatnot got up to six million tons per year."

"Dear God," McGill said.

"Yeah, and it went on for years and years, until the late 1980s, I think. Whole area is toxic as hell. You think a couple of kids who knew about the place would think it'd be just the spot to dump The Brick Shithouse?"

"You know, Gianni, I think that'd be exactly the place."

"I don't know if we could get divers to go down there. People are definitely warned to stay out of the water. God forbid you should try to fish there. But maybe you could send some robot down to take a look. Or one of those mini-subs."

"Wouldn't tidal movement be at work there, too?" McGill asked.

"Sure. Maybe it's just my imagination, though, but I could see human remains being stuck in that muck a lot longer than most places. Anyway, I'm glad you called. I feel more charged up right now than I have in years. In fact, if I felt any better, I'd have to hurry home and surprise the missus."

McGill laughed. "Happy to help any way I can."

"Right. Listen, I'm going to get the ball rolling right away. I'll call you if we have any luck."

McGill said, "Thank you, Gianni. Good hunting."

The moment he put his phone down, Esme buzzed him.

"Deke would like to see you, Jim."

"Send him in."

McGill gave Deke a quick summary of his conversation with

Dago John.

"Good to hear things are moving forward," Deke said.

Then he put a small package on McGill's desk.

"What's that?"

"That is the knife the New York cops took from Teagan Tobias when he was a kid."

McGill opened the package and picked up the knife. It had a slim four-inch blade and a black rubber handle for a secure grip. McGill skimmed the blade's edge with his fingertips. It was as sharp as if it had just come off a whetstone.

Deke said, "Just the thing to slip between somebody's ribs, huh?"

McGill held the knife up to the light. "The NYPD said there were no blood traces."

Deke gave a cynical laugh. "Doesn't mean Tobias didn't have another knife."

***Hell's Belle — Austin, Texas***

DEA Chief of Operations Anne Macklin did a visual survey of the bar in the light of day. Not that the sun ever penetrated past the first barstool. Alternating current electricity and incandescent light bulbs still ruled within those four walls. Macklin looked at the long, narrow room some more and shook her head.

The establishment's owner, Catherine Clarke, said, "What? You don't like my decor?"

Also present were Gene Beck, Maj Olson, Wallace Rhymes, and Conrad Winstead, deputy assistant director of the Texas Rangers. They were all getting the uneasy feeling the boss fed was going to back out on the agreement she'd made the night before — and they were right.

Knew it before Macklin said another word.

"You just wait one minute, Ms. Macklin," Rhymes said. "If you think you can commandeer this operation, you'd better think twice. This is Texas."

Macklin gave him a polite smile. "I haven't forgotten that for a second, sir. What I'm seeing here, though, is a cramped space where people might get shot not only by intent but also by mishap. I wouldn't want any of the good guys to get plugged, would you?"

Rhymes didn't want any unintended victims; that was plain on his face.

Still, he didn't yield without a struggle. "Texas Rangers shoot plenty damn straight."

"Director Winstead?" Macklin asked.

The Ranger chief turned to Rhymes. "We're very good, Wallace, but we're also entirely human. Besides all that, there isn't a marksman in the world who can make his shot curve around a good guy and hit the bad guy standing behind him. Director Macklin is right. In a space this confined, crowded with people, getting a clear shot, if one was called for, could be very difficult. I lost more than a few hours sleep last night thinking about that problem."

Rhymes didn't quite gnash his teeth, but his jaw tightened.

Gene took advantage of the opening to add, "Besides all the practical considerations, I've got a feeling here I used to get in the Air Force. Higher powers are taking an interest, and if not a direct order, they've given Ms. Macklin a strong suggestion."

The DEA chief smiled. "Suggestions were not on the menu. It was, as Mr. Beck suggests, a time to snap to attention, salute and follow orders smartly."

Rhymes was still skeptical. "You didn't guide your superiors' thinking just a bit?"

"Sir, I described the situation as I understand it. They took it from there."

Catherine Clarke asked, "Just how high are we talking about here, the height from which these orders came?"

"Ms. Clarke," Macklin said, "they don't come any higher."

Gene Beck whistled the opening notes of *Hail to the Chief.*

And Macklin nodded.

Winstead asked, "Does this mean my people are out?"

"No, Director Winstead, barring any misfortune, the Texas Rangers will make the arrest of Eloy Chavez. Assuming he shows up."

Maj said, "Smart woman, the president."

Winstead seemed appreciative; Rhymes was accepting.

"Mr. Chavez, I assume, will be charged with state offenses," Macklin said.

"He will," Winstead said.

"After that, the DEA will take custody of him, federal charges will be added, and any chance of Mr. Chavez ever again seeing the light of day as a free man will be nil."

"Your people will be accompanying my people once we take Chavez into custody?" Winstead asked.

Macklin smiled disingenuously. "Yes, we will. Did I forget to mention that?"

"You did," Winstead said. "How will our respective people be deployed?"

"Yours will be at the heart of things. Mine will be at the perimeter. With one exception."

"What's that?" Gene asked.

"My people will also be onstage."

"Doing what?" Catherine asked.

Macklin smiled again. "Playing music. They'll be the band."

Gene smiled, "G-men cranking tunes. That's cool … if they're any good."

"They are," Macklin told him.

Maj asked, "So if we're not using Hell's Belle, where does the show go on?"

Macklin said, "We're looking for a place right now. The plan is, make it an inviting outdoor venue, easy for Chavez to enter, impossible for him to get out. Somewhere we can grab as many of his men before they can even enter the musical area and, in general, minimize the chance of any of our people suffering a loss of life."

Wallace Rhymes smiled for the first time. "I got just the place."

"Where?" Macklin asked.

Catherine Clarke explained, "What Daddy meant to say, Ms. Macklin, is the party should be held at his ranch."

***Air Canada — En Route Vancouver, BC to Oklahoma City, OK***

Eloy Chavez booked two front row first-class seats on the commercial flight to the United States. He wanted enough room in the overhead bin to make sure his damn knock-off John Wayne hat didn't get mangled by some *pendejo's* carry-on bag. He also wanted an empty seat next to him to lessen the chance another passenger might try to strike up a conversation.

That part of his plan worked. Another proved insufficient.

Damn his luck, one of the first-class cabin attendants was an attractive *puertorricaña.* Puerto Rican. She engaged him in Spanish as he boarded, telling him she had married a Canadian fellow and moved north. It would be her pleasure to speak with him in their common native tongue. That was bad enough, but the woman also sounded educated, and with her access to complimentary air transportation, it was easy for Chavez to imagine she might have visited Spain, and knew what Castilian Spanish sounded like.

Its rhythms, intonations and even its infernal lisping were nothing like Mexican Spanish. People like Chavez attempted a Castilian accent only as a matter of ridicule, an insult to a man's masculinity most often. If Chavez spoke with the damn woman for more than a moment, it would be a dead giveaway that he wasn't who he was pretending to be.

The idea of losing himself among the flood of other people entering the U.S. from Canada would be wrecked. So he coughed on the woman, only partially shielding his mouth with his hand.

In a barely audible, hoarse voice, he said, *"Lo siento mucho. Necesito dormir. No seré ningún problema."* I'm very sorry. I need to sleep. I won't be any trouble.

Chavez stashed his hat in the overhead bin, collapsed onto his window seat, buckled in and closed his eyes. He coughed again, but only once. He didn't want to be put off the plane because of illness. Being delayed might ruin all his plans.

His men, most of them anyway, would be in Texas on time. If he wasn't also punctual, they would begin to wonder if something had gone wrong. Had the boss been arrested or even killed? Just the possibilities would make them worry. His fate would also likely be theirs: spending decades in a *yanqui* prison or sneaking back home only to be slaughtered by a new boss who suspected their loyalty.

Goddamnit, Chavez thought, how could he have foreseen a puertorricaña marrying a Canadian and being the person hired to attend his needs? It was … a sign that he was doomed? Chavez felt beads of sweat pop out on his forehead. He knew immediately that wasn't good; it would only make him seem more ill.

He almost wiped the sweat away with a sleeve of his suit coat. While no one would ever criticize the social gaffes of a drug boss, now was not the time to pull out a gun, that he didn't have anyway, and kill the fool who should have known better. No, he had to remember the role he was playing: a rich Spaniard who wasn't feeling his best.

Instead of using his sleeve, Chavez reached into his coat and withdrew a handkerchief. He was careful not to swab his forehead but dab at it gently and return the pocket square to its proper place. Then he did his best to keep his breathing slow and steady, calm himself. After what seemed like an eternity he heard the pilot announce that the flight crew should be seated for takeoff.

Moments later, he felt the rush of the plane accelerating and the weightless moment when it first left the earth. Chavez felt sure the aircraft would not turn back unless something drastic happened. Airlines despised disruptions to their schedules. So did the passengers. Chavez thought he would offer only the occasional subdued cough to keep his pretense intact and the cabin attendant at a distance.

So he was startled when she wrapped a blanket around him.

His eyes popped open and she said, *"Para la protección contra el frío."* To keep the cold away.

Chavez hadn't realized until that moment that he'd been sleeping and shivering. The blanket not only warmed him, it was also wonderfully soft and calming. He drew it closer and felt himself drifting back into sleep.

Before he dozed, he managed to say, *"Gracias."*

In a clearly Mexican accent.

***McGill Investigations International — Washington, DC***

"Jim, I have a Ms. Lindsay Todd on the line," Esme Thrice said. "She says she has information regarding a Mr. Tad Thacker for you."

Even with short hours of sleep, McGill had woken that morning with a spring in his step. There was nothing like a loving embrace to produce restorative vigor. Make you feel like you were somewhere in your prime if not exactly like a kid again. Leo had the Chevy parked at the front door when he'd stepped out to meet the day. So there would be no adventures on the Metro that morning.

"Please put her through, Esme," McGill said.

The connection was made and McGill said hello and gave his name.

"Mr. McGill, I'm calling you at Tad's request. He asked me to give you something."

"His file on Teagan Tobias?"

The surprise in the young woman's voice was clear. "How did you know?"

"I read Mr. Thacker's summary on Alice Janeway's life last night. Have you seen it?"

After a moment's hesitation, Lindsay said, "Yes."

"Have you read it?" McGill asked.

"I have."

"What did you think of it?"

She said, "It made me think of the work I put in to earn my Ph.D. Tad's research is thorough and detailed. All of his sources and methods are cited. His reasoning and conclusions are clear and persuasive. To me, anyway."

McGill said, "I feel the same way, but I think his coursework is incomplete."

"In what way?" Lindsay asked.

"Seems to me a complete study of the subject should also include an in-depth examination of the important people in Alice's life, beyond the members of her immediate family. I don't see Mr. Thacker regarding that consideration as unimportant, do you?"

"No," Lindsay said.

"So I was wondering where Mr. Thacker's study of Teagan Tobias was. Certainly, Mr. Thacker would want to know if Tobias was treating Alice well."

"I have that information," Lindsay said. "Tad asked me to give it to you."

"Did you read it?"

"Not yet, but I made a copy for myself."

McGill made a guess. "You're hoping that things will turn out right fairly soon, and you won't need to snoop on your friend."

"Yes, exactly."

"You realize that you might not want to read it even if things go wrong?"

"I've thought of that, too. I also considered that I might feel an obligation to read it … to understand what might have happened to a very good friend."

McGill decided not to say that some acts of cruelty were simply incomprehensible.

The best you could hope for was that there would be answers in the hereafter.

"I need to get back home soon, Mr. McGill. I have classes to teach on Monday. Would you be able to pick up the file within the next hour?" She told him she was staying at a hotel not far from his office.

"I'll be right over," McGill said. "Won't be longer than 20 minutes. How are you getting home?"

"Amtrak. I thought about flying, but I want more time to think things through. Say a prayer or two that Alice will be all right."

"I can drop you off at Union Station, if you like," McGill said.

"That would be very kind of you. I'll meet you in the lobby. Let's make it 30 minutes."

"Sure. May I ask a couple more questions."

"Of course."

"Did Mr. Thacker tell you where he was going?"

"No."

"At a guess, would you say Mr. Thacker might respond violently if he learned something unfortunate happened to Alice?"

A moment of silence followed, and then Lindsay said, "Do you mean, would he take it out on Teagan Tobias if he hurt Alice … or did something even worse?"

McGill heard the tremor in Lindsay's voice as she completed her question.

"Yes, that's what I mean."

"Mr. McGill, Tad told me he didn't want me with him today, so I wouldn't share in any legal liability for what he might do. What does that tell you?"

It told McGill everything he needed to know.

Tad Thacker was ready to kill to avenge Alice, if she was dead.

Symbolically, to make an Italian bus driver pay for his crime, too.

And to hope McGill would step up if Teagan Tobias got the better of him.

### *Traversing Washington, DC*

McGill and Leo picked up Lindsay Todd at the Kimpton Hotel Palomar. A doorman, under Leo's watchful eye, put her suitcase in the trunk. Leo took it from there, tipping the hotel employee and telling him, "I've got it from here, pal."

He ushered Lindsay into the backseat next to McGill, and got back behind the wheel.

"Union Station, right, boss?"

McGill looked at Lindsay for confirmation. She nodded. Leo saw the affirmation in his rearview mirror and eased into the flow of traffic.

"Thank you, Mr. McGill," Lindsay said.

"Glad to help."

She didn't doubt his sincerity but asked, nonetheless, "You want something from me, don't you? Something you didn't want to talk about on the phone."

McGill nodded. "Professional paranoia. You never know who might be listening in on a phone call these days. Cell phones only make it easier."

"Your car can't be tapped?"

Leo coughed up a small laugh.

"I'll take that as a no," Lindsay said.

"It would be orders of magnitude more difficult," McGill said.

Leo added, "Confessions could be heard in this car."

"He means the sacramental kind," McGill said.

"And your driver has been ordained?"

Both McGill and Leo liked that one.

"Only by Richard Petty," McGill told her, "but Leo can keep a secret as well as any priest I've ever known."

Lindsay sighed and said, "I really don't know anything more than I've already told you." She reached into her purse, the size of a small attaché case, and took out a sheaf of papers bound by metal brads. "Here's your copy of Tad's dossier on Teagan Tobias."

"Thank you." McGill took the document and let it rest on his lap. "What I'd like to ask you probably hasn't been set down in writing. I'd like to get your impression of Tad Thacker. How stable he is, how driven he is, how he might react in a tight situation."

Lindsay met McGill's eyes. "Boiled down, you'd like to know if he's crazy."

"Okay," McGill said, "we can start with that."

"What I think is … Tad has been emotionally scarred in a way he'll never completely get past. He both grieves and rages at himself that he didn't find some way to go on that trip to Italy with Jenny Nyland. He looks at that as the greatest failing of his life. He told me he's sure he would have either saved Jenny or died trying. Either outcome would have been preferable to the guilt he suffers every day."

"He told you this?" McGill asked.

"Yes, he wanted me to understand him. He also showed me a photo of Jenny he carries in his wallet. The resemblance between her and Alice is remarkable. Given that, I was impressed by how he managed to restrain himself from bothering Alice after that first impulsive encounter."

McGill said, "So Tad realizes that Alice is not Jenny come back to life? She's her own, distinct person."

"Yes, he knows that. He's come to take comfort in the knowledge that there are other wonderful people in the world, at least one of whom looks a lot like the dear friend he lost. He used that knowledge to begin healing his heart, but he never expects to reach completion. That's what he told me."

McGill sat back and thought about that. "So at least in some measure, the poor guy was on the mend when one of my colleagues and a local cop showed up and started questioning him."

"Yes, exactly. That's what he told me. He also said he wasn't going to let another opportunity to help someone pass him by."

"Not just someone," McGill said, "but a living reminder of how he thinks he failed before."

Lindsay smiled and shook her head. "I was brought up religious, Mr. McGill, but I've grown up to be a rational thinker. In this situation, though, I'm starting to think of myself as a bit player in a larger tragedy scripted by fate."

McGill gave her hand a gentle squeeze. "You and me both."

Leo pulled up at the curb in front of Union Station.

Lindsay told McGill, "I'm pretty sure your role's bigger than mine."

McGill felt the same way, but he only asked, "Do you know if Tad has a gun?"

"Not yet," Lindsay said.

"Meaning he intends to?" McGill asked.

"He checked online what the requirements for buying a gun in Virginia are. There's no waiting period. If you're 21 or older, you can buy a handgun. You simply submit to a background check. If you don't have a criminal record, you're cleared to buy in a matter of minutes. You only have to be 18 to buy a rifle. Tad said he'd get around to making his purchase later. I think the delay had to do with considering me again, distancing me from anything that might happen."

McGill had one last question for Lindsay. "Do you think Tad would actually shoot Teagan Tobias, if he has hurt Alice?"

Lindsay nodded. "Him or anyone else he even considered a threat to Alice."

Gabbi Casale called McGill while he and Leo were still on the way back to the office.

She said, "The Swiss lawyer handling Marlon Janeway's estate?"

"Yeah?" McGill replied.

"He emailed some papers to us, and one of them is particularly interesting. It seems Marlon knew, and the lawyer being Swiss isn't saying how, that Alice has rented an apartment in West Hollywood. Lease starts January 1, 2018."

McGill replied, "Please tell me you got a phone number and Alice answered."

"No, but I called the rental agent, and she said the deal was done a month ago and the necessary deposit was sent express mail. Alice is good to move in on the first day of the year if she wants."

McGill thanked Gabbi for the information and immediately

called Dorie McBride in Los Angeles. He didn't have to wait five seconds before his call was put through, and the agent told him, "I could get you a three-picture deal right now."

McGill said, "I've never acted in my life."

"You never conned street criminals when you worked patrol?"

"That's different."

"How?"

"There was no script. It was all improv."

"But it was *effective* improv, wasn't it, and that's all you need to start. You wouldn't even have to fight your way through an Austrian accent like Arnold did."

"Dorie, one McGill, my youngest child, is enough of a family contribution to the cinematic arts."

A dramatic sigh was followed by, "Oh, very well. What can *I* do for *you?*"

"Have you ever heard of the name Alice Janeway?"

Before Dorie answered, McGill heard the tippety-taps of a keyboard being struck. "Oh, this is interesting. She just signed a deal with Jack Hillerman."

"And he is?"

"A very successful show-runner who landed a big new deal with Netflix. Three streaming series over the next five years."

"That's pretty substantial?" McGill asked.

"If they're any good, it's a very important move. Alice Janeway is going to be the lead writer on what's billed as an edgy adult romantic comedy. A production note, oh, this is delicious. It says Hillerman wanted to talk with Teagan Tobias about doing a project together, but Tobias sent Alice to express his regrets. Tobias wasn't interested. Hillerman and Alice got to talking and the rest is … well, that remains to be seen, but Alice got herself a job out of the meeting."

McGill asked, "Would there be any way for you to find out if Alice Janeway is actually in L.A. right now?"

"I have eyes and ears everywhere, but you know I'm just so busy."

"Should I ask Patti to call you?"

"That would be a very low trick to pull."

McGill said, "I'm trying to find out whether a woman's life might be in danger, Dorie."

"You're telling the truth now?"

McGill said, "Yes, I'm really not that good an actor."

***Will Rogers World Airport — Oklahoma City, Oklahoma***

*"Adios, Señor Martinez,"* cabin attendant Luciana Rodriguez said to Eloy Chavez with a smile, using his alias. It would have been a perfunctory farewell, the same as any other deplaning passenger might receive, except for its ever so slight tone of mockery and a point of pronunciation.

Luciana had given the terminal "z" in Martinez the "th" sound used in Castilian Spanish. Martineth. That might have been a simple sign of respect for the passenger's purported nationality, had it not been for the whisper of wised-up jest in Luciana's voice.

You're Spanish? Yeah, right.

Eloy Chavez, with his hat in his left hand, got the point of the gibe immediately, and he didn't think it was funny at all. He fixed Luciana with a glare that had been the last thing seen by many of the people Chavez had killed. For just a second both of them thought Luciana would be added to that list. Her legs began to buckle.

Then a loud male voice from the back of the cabin piped up. "Hey, let's keep things moving. I have a hockey game to play."

That was followed by a cheer and a chorus of other voices urging forward progress.

The Mexican drug boss had no choice but to get moving. He did look back over his shoulder at Luciana, though. Scaring her even more, he held up his right hand, thumb and index finger forming the shape of a gun. He brought the thumb forward decisively, a shot fired.

Some of the passengers immediately behind Chavez also recognized the gesture and were not amused. Even so, their pace slowed, wondering if the gesture had been possibly aimed at them, or maybe at the hockey player in back, or someone in between. In any case, Eloy Chavez had a gap of several paces between himself and the closest following passenger as he stepped out of the jetway and entered the airport, placing what he thought was the fake John Wayne hat on his head.

That was all it took to blend in with many of the other men and some of the women who occupied the airport. After all, the nicknames of the Oklahoma State University athletic teams were the Cowboys and Cowgirls, and it was football season. Chavez was both pleased and annoyed that he received many compliments on his hat as he walked down the concourse.

He realized that he'd come close to losing control as he'd left the plane, and he couldn't afford that. He repressed his anger, started to accept the compliments that came his way with good graces. He even smiled at an elderly *latina* woman in a wheelchair who beamed at him and said, *"Magnifico."*

*"Muchas gracias, señora,"* Chavez replied with a small bow.

Chavez had pre-cleared his entry into the country at the U.S. Customs and Border Protection station in Canada. The *yanquis* had no problem with visitors who held Spanish passports. The Anglo security people on duty hadn't quibbled with his accent.

Damn that *puta* of a flight attendant, he thought.

He considered the possibility of having someone discover who she was, where she lived and kill her. Only that would confirm that he wasn't who he'd pretended to be when he got on the plane. Then he'd have more people looking to kill him than he already had.

As much as he hated to let an insult go unanswered, Chavez tried to forget the incident.

A limo met him outside the terminal. He got into the backseat as the chauffeur held the door open for him. Getting behind the wheel, the man said, *"Bienvenido, jefe."*

Chavez nodded in acknowledgment, and the driver put the

limo in motion.

Before they crossed the state line into Texas, Chavez and the driver would change places. Chavez would don a chauffeur's uniform and drive. The man now behind the wheel would change into a business suit and become the privileged character riding in the back.

Chavez would drive within the speed limit and be a very courteous motorist to everyone else on the road. He would give no cop any reason to stop the car, not that they were ever likely to stop a limousine. If they did, though, chances were excellent they wouldn't look too hard at the poor working man in the driver's seat. He was just an employee, not worth bothering about.

That was the plan, anyway.

When they got to the motel in Austin where Chavez and his men would meet, *el jefe* would make another costume change and put the damn fake hat on his head. Still, it was a very handsome imitation; even yanqui strangers thought he looked good in it. He'd look even better and more powerful once he killed the old bastard who'd mocked him, and put the real hat on his head.

Working to counter that fine scheme, Luciana Rodriguez had slipped into the cockpit right after Chavez had deplaned, leaving the remaining passengers to exit without fond farewells. She persuaded the captain and first officer that something was seriously wrong with the passenger calling himself Martinez. He certainly wasn't Spanish, his passport was probably a fake, and he'd looked like he might have killed her right there on the plane if he'd had the opportunity.

Both flight officers knew Luciana wasn't given to over-dramatizing.

She'd held things together on some of the hairiest flights any of them had ever flown.

So, taking her at her word, and being a good neighbor to the U.S., the captain alerted the Transportation Security Administration office at the airport. When the TSA couldn't find anyone matching Chavez's description on the airport premises, they passed the word on to the FBI.

It took additional time for the FBI to share the news with the Drug Enforcement Agency.

***Paxton-Carter Theater — Washington, DC***

McGill changed his plans on the way back to the office and had Leo drive him to the theater where Teagan Tobias was performing. He didn't want to see Tobias; he didn't think the star of the show would even be at the theater that early in the day. McGill wanted to talk with Haskell Carver. The head bodyguard might be on hand to make sure everything was in order at the site where his boss would be onstage that night.

That was the way the Secret Service would handle things, McGill thought.

Of course, once the feds approved a location's security, they would leave people there to maintain it. So, if Haskell wasn't on hand, maybe one of his people would be and could put a call through to the security chief for McGill.

As Leo smoothly wove through traffic like the other vehicles were standing still, he said to McGill, "You know one of the things I miss about you and Mrs. McGill not living in the White House anymore, boss?"

"What's that?" McGill asked.

"Losing that little gizmo I had that let me turn red lights green."

That piece of technology had indeed been surrendered. Patti had said it would be inappropriate for a private citizen to have one. Jean Morrissey might have let McGill keep it, if requested, but Patti had said if word got out, everybody would want one, and if the devices were widely distributed, automotive traffic would get worse and more dangerous.

McGill hadn't argued, shrugging off the loss.

Now, he told Leo, "Your ability to time green lights has always seemed almost supernatural to me, anyway."

Leo grinned, McGill catching his merriment in the rear-view mirror.

"I am pretty good, boss, but I'm still human."

McGill caught the subtext: If Leo was human, so was McGill. "Have you been talking to Patti?"

"Mrs. McGill called me. You know I'd never bother her on my own."

"Yeah, I do know that. So, what did she ask you to do?"

"Just ask you a question: How would you feel about having Special Agent Daphna Levy as your full-time bodyguard?"

"Leaving Ace Cole to watch over Patti?"

"No, she knows that'd mean you and Cole would still have too many occasions to grind on each other. She said she'd find someone new."

McGill thought about that. "I think I can get along with Daphna. I don't think she'd get too frustrated working with me. But what's puzzling me right now is this is the kind of thing Patti and I usually discuss directly."

Leo said, "She called when you got out of the car to walk Ms. Todd to the train station. Mrs. McGill did want to speak with you herself, but she felt the conversation might get lengthy and she'd just heard from President Morrissey who asked could she drop by the White House at her earliest convenience."

McGill blinked. "Leo, it's a good thing you're not a reporter because you sure know how to bury the lede."

"Bury what?" Leo asked.

"Never mind," McGill told him. "I don't suppose Patti hinted at why she was summoned by the president."

"No, boss, she didn't say. She only asked me to sound you out about Daphna Levy. I tried to do that in a way we could both understand."

McGill said, "And you did it well." Changing the subject, he added, "I'm thinking about asking GM to build another Chevy like this one for my personal use."

Leo nodded. "That'd be a fine machine. Cost you a bundle, but

I don't see that as a problem."

"No, it wouldn't be."

Leo pulled into a slot in front of the theater where Teagan Tobias' name was on the marquee. Leo's ability to find legal parking spaces eclipsed even his timing of green lights.

Nonetheless, he asked McGill, "You don't intend to do *all* your driving, do you, boss?"

"Not until I'm as good as you," McGill said.

Leo smiled broadly.

There was nothing like job security to make someone happy.

***The White House — Washington, DC***

Patti stepped into the Oval Office for the first time since she'd left the presidency. She half-expected she might long for the power and prestige she'd relinquished. What the heck, Franklin Delano Roosevelt had been elected as the chief executive four times. She might have had three terms, if it hadn't been for that pesky 22nd Amendment. Her flight of fancy died the moment she saw Jean Morrissey.

Jean looked like she'd aged a year in just the past two days. Doing a quick review of newspaper headlines, Patti couldn't come up with either a political battle or a foreign crisis that should have caused the president so much stress. Then again, presidents were privy to a raft of awful realities that few others could even imagine. There was never a shortage of crises at the White House.

Patti was glad, now, that she'd left the presidency behind.

Jean stepped out from behind her desk and wearing a wan smile shook Patti's hand. Then, with just the two of them in the room, she embraced her predecessor in office.

As Jean stepped back, Patti asked, "Are things really that bad, whatever is going on? Byron's all right, isn't he?"

Jean smiled broadly now and nodded. "I should feel so good. He keeps meeting and exceeding benchmarks in his recovery.

You hear how people normally use only a small fraction of their brains? Well, whatever parts he lost, the reserves are filling in brilliantly."

"That's wonderful."

Jean gestured to Patti to have a seat on a nearby sofa and sat in an adjacent armchair.

"Would you like some tea or coffee?" the president asked. "Or maybe a double-knock of whiskey."

"Oh, my," Patti said, "are things as bad as all that?"

"Frank is getting married."

Frank Morrissey, the president's brother and chief of staff, was gay.

"You think that will be a problem?" Patti asked. "A gay wedding in the White House."

Jean said, "Not if I approved of the other man. Wouldn't bother me at all. If anyone else didn't like it, tough luck for them."

"But you don't like Frank's fiancé?" Patti asked.

"He's a louse."

Keeping a straight face, Patti asked, "But more than a little attractive?"

Jean nodded. "Gerald would be too good-looking, only he used to play lacrosse in college and got his nose busted a couple of times. The result is he now looks rugged and striking."

"Okay, I can picture that," Patti said, "but I never thought of Frank as someone who would fall head over heels for just any handsome face. Is your objection also a matter of, what, personality?"

"Honesty or a lack thereof," Jean said. "Gerald can pretend to be charming. He also has a bachelor's degree in business from the University of Georgia and a law degree from Tufts."

"Practical education from good schools," Patti said.

"Yes, but Gerald didn't go to work for a big company or a top-drawer law firm. He set himself up as an investment advisor, a money manager."

Patti had no trouble guessing what was coming. "Oh, no, don't tell me."

"I don't need to, do I?" Jean said. "Due to a number of *irregularities,* Gerald found himself in court and was looking at time behind bars. Only he made good for all the clients he was accused of defrauding. Paid everyone back down to the last dollar. Because of that he was given a two-year suspended sentence, never spent a day incarcerated."

"Frank told you all that?" Patti asked.

"He told me *none* of that."

Patti winced.

Jean said, "I didn't trust Gerald from the get-go. I had him investigated by some people I know back in Minnesota. That was how I found out about his troubles. I had been thinking of asking a certain James J. McGill to do the job, but I didn't want to cause any awkward feelings. I'm still undecided whether to ask my Minnesota friends to find out the source of Gerald's stay-out-of-jail funds."

Patti said, "My advice? If your friends are good, careful and completely trustworthy, have them look into that matter and hold whatever they find in reserve. If it becomes necessary for you to know, you'll have it in hand. If you never need it, let it gather dust in some dark corner. And, by the way, thank you for leaving Jim out of it."

"You're welcome, and I like your advice. But now I have another problem. I told Frank an hour ago what I'd found out about Gerald. I said he could keep his job or his boyfriend but not both. Frank didn't care for my ultimatum. He quit his job. Stormed right out. So, I'm going to need a new chief of staff immediately."

Patti said, "I'm so sorry for you, Jean, but I don't see how …"

*It's my place to find a new chief of staff for you,* Patti was about to say. But then she understood exactly what Jean was thinking.

"Oh, no," Patti said. "You can't have Galia in mind."

The president nodded. "I can."

"Do you know about —"

"The cockamamie scheme she and Frank were considering?"

"Yes, that."

"I would have put a stop to that before it ever started," Jean said. "That wasn't the right job for Galia at all. But she was a *killer* chief of staff, and there are no term-limits on that position."

There was no disputing any of those points, Patti thought.

And she certainly didn't want Galia to be any angrier at her than she already was.

Which she certainly would be if she learned Patti had given her a bad rap.

So all Patti said was, "Make sure you have a good, long talk with Galia before you decide."

The president said, "I was hoping for an endorsement, but you raise a good point."

***Brooklyn, New York and the 12 Mile Dump***

Immediately after talking with McGill, Dago John called Feldman and Donnegan, the two retired NYPD detectives who'd worked the disappearance of Nicholas Pell. They'd both slowed down a bit since retiring but they were far from restricted to rocking chairs, and both of them were still cops down to their DNA. They took deep satisfaction in the cases they'd closed successfully, and the ones that eluded them continued to be as painful as passing broken glass.

When Dago John got both of them on a conference call and told them of McGill's idea that Nicky Pell's body had been dumped in the ocean, the two detectives reacted defensively.

"Gee," said Donnegan, "dump a body in the ocean. I don't know that anybody's ever thought of that one before. Come on, DJ, you and McGill should be able to do better than that."

Feldman had less of a penchant to crack wise, but he still said, "We did think of that, Gianni, but the kid had no means to pull it off. We thought Tobias might have tossed the kid in the Hudson River, but even that wouldn't have been easy. Nicholas Pell was a load."

"Listen," Dago John said to the two detectives, "is this thing still eating at you like it is at me or have you let go of all those cases that used to keep you up at night?"

"Fuck you, DJ, there's still plenty of cases that keep me up," Donnegan said.

"And he often calls me when he can't sleep," Feldman added, "not that I mind because I'm usually awake, too."

"So what do you think?" Dago John asked. "Did either of you ever ask at the high school where both Tobias and Pell were students if Tobias had a friend with a boat in his family? You know, someone who might also help shoulder the load of dumping a heavy body."

Both Feldman and Donnegan went silent.

"Guys?" Dago John said, wondering if either of them was still on the line.

Donnegan finally said, "All right, here's the thing: It honest-to-God never occurred to me a little prick like Teagan Tobias could have *any* friends."

"Me either," Feldman admitted.

"I'll make that unanimous," Dago John said. "Still, since McGill brought up the possibility, I've got to check it out. I called you guys out of courtesy. If you want to come along, you're welcome; if you don't, you get no grief from me."

"What do we do if we actually find something?" Feldman asked.

"We pin it down as tight as we can, and then we turn it over to the cops we trust the most who are still on the city's payroll," Dago John said. "What we get is the satisfaction of knowing we're not all the way out to pasture yet."

"That and a better night's sleep," Donnegan said. "But what about any expenses we might incur. You know, more than gasoline money. I mean, if we're talking renting a boat or something here ..."

Dago John laughed. "Either of you guys win the lottery lately?"

The two detectives only laughed.

"Okay, then, I'll front the money."

***

Barry Carstairs, the former principal of the former Morris Meyers High School, now Meyers College Prep, answered the bell when the three retired cops, who'd phoned him earlier, appeared at his door. They'd said they had just a couple of questions for him. That, and Carstair's wife having a headache were reasons enough not to invite them in.

Each of the ex-cops knew from personal experience that pleading an ailing spouse was a perfectly legit excuse for a lapse of hospitality. They stood on the front steps to the house without rancor. Since this was Dago John's baby, he got to start the questioning.

"Mr. Carstairs, do you remember a student of yours named Teagan Tobias?" he asked.

"Sure do, the little prick."

The three ex-cops looked at each other. Each wondered if the former educator had been so plain-spoken while on the job. They collectively decided, no he wasn't, while not saying a word.

Carstairs saw he was being judged, and he explained himself.

"Do you know what that smart-ass bastard said about me at commencement, the second after I handed him his diploma and congratulated him?"

All three visitors shook their heads.

"He turned to the auditorium full of graduating seniors and their families and, like he was the MC of some show, announces: 'Mr. Carstairs almost but not quite reminds me of Jonathan Winters. He's fat and freaky, but he's not funny.'"

Now that the man brought it up, the ex-cops could see a resemblance to the late comedian, and he didn't come off as a barrel of laughs.

"What pissed me off more than that, he got a big laugh from the audience. Students and families both. I was probably the inspiration for the little prick's show biz career."

Dago John thought he knew how to play things. "We're sorry for what had to be a really bad moment, Mr. Carstairs. Would you know if anyone among those students that night was a particularly good friend of Teagan Tobias? Somebody who might have a boat in his family."

Carstairs shook his head. "As far as I know, he didn't have any friends, and if he died friendless, that'd make *me* laugh."

So that put the kibosh on McGill's angle, but Dago John had thought of another approach on the way to the erstwhile educator's house. "How about this then: Do you remember the names of any students who were especially bullied by a student named Nicholas Pell?"

"Another prick," Carstairs said, "only this time a bigger one. Yeah, I know some names on this one. You got something to write with?"

Dago John had brought a pen and a notepad. He took them out of a pocket.

Carstairs gave him ten names off the top of his head. He didn't know if any of them still lived in Brooklyn or had relocated elsewhere. But he said, "These poor kids weren't high achievers. Chances are they didn't go far, figuratively or literally. You know, unless gentrification displaced them."

It hadn't.

Gary Llewelyn was the third victim of Nicholas Pell's bullying they visited, and just in the nick of time, as it turned out. He was dying of cystic fibrosis and was waiting for a visit from a parish priest to hear his last confession. "So I'll have a chance in hell of going to heaven," Llewelyn told the three ex-cops in a thready voice.

"What do you have to confess?" Donnegan asked.

Feldman raised a hand before Llewelyn could answer. He took out his phone, set it to video, and asked, "Mr. Llewelyn, do we have your permission to record this conversation?"

"Yes."

Feldman gave the particulars of the situation: time, location and identities of those present.

"Go ahead, sir," Feldman said. "Tell us, if you wish, what you have to confess."

Llewelyn gave a raspy laugh. "I was going to say I killed someone, Nicky, the Brick Shithouse, Pell. But I didn't really do that."

"What did you do?" Dago John asked.

"No, no," Donnegan said, "the first question is who, if anyone, did kill Nicholas Pell?"

"Teagan Tobias killed Shithouse."

"That being Nicholas Pell," Feldman asked for the purpose of clarity.

"One and the same," Llewelyn agreed with a small nod.

"How did Teagan Tobias kill Nicholas Pell?" Donnegan asked.

"Slit his throat. Got old Shithouse to throw a punch at him, sidestepped it, and, zip, quick as a wink, opened his throat with one swipe of his knife."

Dago John got back to his original question. "If Tobias killed Pell, what did you do? Why were you present at all?'

All three ex-cops could see Llewelyn was revisiting his memory of that moment.

A smile crept across his lips. He'd have to do better than that, Dago John thought, when he talked to his priest. You were supposed to be *sorry* for your sins.

"What did I do?" Llewelyn asked. "After Nicky fell like the sack of shit he was, I took the knife Teag handed to me and I stabbed Shithouse until my arm got tired. That was part of my deal with Teag. The other part was I took my dad's boat out on the ocean, so Teag and I could dump the body."

"Why did your father have a boat?" Feldman asked.

"He was a captain at NYC Ferry. He loved being out on the water. Taught me everything I needed to know about helming our 25-foot bay cruiser."

Dago John thought he saw a flaw in Llewelyn's story. "Were you strong enough back then to help Teagan Tobias get Nicky Pell's body into your father's boat?"

"No."

"So Tobias carried the load all by himself?" Donnegan asked, doubt clear in his voice.

"No."

"So who was the third man?" Feldman asked.

"My father."

The three ex-cops looked at each other. Donnegan asked, "He didn't participate in the murder, before, during or after?"

"Shithouse was dead before Dad got involved. Teag and I were having trouble getting the body on board. Dad was supposed to be home at the time, but he liked to visit his boat at odd hours, to tinker with it or just look at it. That night he found out what we'd done. Teag was real nervous until Dad helped get the body on his boat. After that, he was part of the crew."

"Your father is dead, isn't he?" Dago John asked.

"Yeah."

"Where'd you dump the body?" Feldman asked.

"The 12 Mile Dump. Seemed like the right place. Ashes to ashes. Shit to shit."

"You weigh the body down?" Dago John asked.

"Yeah, that was Dad's suggestion."

"Your father have anything to say about what you and Teag Tobias did?" Donnegan asked.

"He knew that Shithouse was bullying me. I think he would have done something himself if the situation had kept up. That was part of the reason I agreed to help Teag."

"Tobias came to you?" Feldman said.

"Yeah, and he didn't need to ask twice. I was all in the moment I heard what he had in mind. After my dad found out what we'd done, he didn't have a bad word for either Teag or me. He only told Teag not to involve me in anything ever again. Teag was cool with that."

"You don't mind telling us about Tobias now?" Donnegan asked.

"I do, but it's time for me to come clean. I'll have to tell my priest about this, too. Looking back, though, I keep thinking we should have come up with some other idea. Maybe just working Shithouse over with baseball bats or something. Making sure he never walked without canes again."

"Would that have satisfied you?" Dago John asked.

"I don't know, but I doubt it would have felt as good as plunging that knife into him while he was still warm."

Feldman sighed.

Donnegan said, "I'll go see if that priest is coming."

Dago John had one last question, "You know approximately where you dumped the body."

Llewelyn gave him a thin smile. "I can give you the exact coordinates from memory."

And he did.

***Paxton-Carter Theater — Washington, DC***

There was a doorbell next to the far left entry door to the theater. McGill rang twice without getting a response. When he tried the door, though, he found it was unlocked. McGill looked over to Leo, who was on station behind the wheel of the Chevy. McGill flashed him a thumbs-up. Leo, a Reform Jew, responded ecumenically by making the Sign of the Cross.

That both got a laugh from McGill and reminded him that a lot of people met their Maker when they least expected it. Now was not the time to get careless. For all McGill knew, Teagan Tobias had come to the theater early and might be sharpening a knife he kept handy. The theater was a bit of a drive from the ocean, but the Potomac River was pretty close, if Tobias wanted to make another body disappear.

Keeping his senses sharp, McGill didn't see anyone in the theater's lobby, in the main floor seating area or on the stage. There might have been someone lurking in one of the shadowed wings, but McGill was listening as hard as he was looking, and he didn't get the feeling of anyone else being present.

As he approached the orchestra pit, McGill turned to look at the balcony. The lighting up there was minimal. Dark corners hid seats where someone might lurk unseen. The only comfort he could take now was a shot from that distance and at that angle wouldn't be easy. Nonetheless, he hurried backstage.

The lighting there was good, and he saw Haskell Carver sitting on a folding chair with no one else in sight. Haskell looked up when he heard McGill approach. The expression on the security boss's face was anything but happy. McGill stopped several feet away from him. The last thing you wanted to do with someone in a bad mood was crowd him.

Especially someone Haskell's size.

Small talk also wasn't a good idea. So McGill got right to the point, "Tobias cancel another show?"

In a chill tone, Haskell responded, "Canceled the rest of this run."

McGill didn't like the possible implications of that.

"Where's he heading next?"

"Supposed to be Chicago, but he canceled that, too."

Sonofabitch, McGill thought. "Does he have any other dates scheduled?"

"Not anymore. The way he told us, he needs some time off. Don't see how he's gonna have that with all the people who'll be suing him, but that sure as hell isn't my problem now."

Drawing the obvious inference, McGill asked, "Did he fire you and your people?"

Haskell nodded. "Us and everybody else. No notice. Just a month's severance pay and 'See ya later.'"

"Sorry to hear that," McGill said. "Did he tell you he heard from Alice?"

That caught Haskell by surprise. "No. Did you hear something?"

McGill shook his head.

"So that's why you came by, to ask him where she is? You think he even knows?"

"I think he might, either know where she is, or where she went."

McGill could only hope Alice hadn't gone for a final dip in the ocean.

Haskel leaned forward, making his chair creak from the strain. "You think he'd tell you?"

"I can be persuasive," McGill said.

Haskell understood the implication. He'd seen the video of McGill in the subway. As a former NFL player himself, Haskell had *loved* the hit McGill had put on that bastard.

Still, he said, "Teag kept me and the other guys around to see he didn't get muscled."

"I know, but I got the feeling from you that you like Alice. Wouldn't want to see anything bad happen to her."

Haskell nodded. "That's right. Alice was someone special. She started out real mild mannered, but she got to the point where she was the only one who could talk back to Teag and get away with it. Whenever that happened, we'd all do chest bumps with our fists. Do it so Teag couldn't see. It was our way of giving Alice a standing ovation."

McGill grinned. Did a chest bump of his own.

Haskell asked, "Why would anything bad happen to Alice?"

McGill hesitated just for a second, and then he told Haskell about Nicholas Pell and Harrison Richards. "I didn't come here to see Tobias; I want to talk with you."

Haskell got to his feet, frowning, fists clenched. "About what?"

McGill put up a hand to forestall an unintended clash.

He said, "I don't think you had anything to do with whatever has or hasn't happened to Alice. I just want to ask if you have any idea where Tobias might go when he wants to get away from everything. Simply put, where would he go to hide?"

Haskell relaxed and said, "Maybe I'll get to that in a second. First, tell me what you think. Is Alice all right or not?"

McGill sighed. "I honestly don't know."

"You want me to help you look for her?"

"How about I call you if I need some help?"

"You're trying to keep me out of whatever you're going to do?"

"I am. That might be frustrating now, but better for everyone in the end."

"Better how?"

McGill said, "I'd be satisfied to see Tobias locked up. If he's done something bad to Alice, you might yank his head off."

Haskell liked that image, and he laughed.

"See," McGill said. "You laugh now, but when the dust settles, you'd be the one behind bars. Maybe on Death Row."

That was a sobering thought for the big man.

He nodded and told McGill, "Teag does have some spots mapped out around the country, places where some of the other guys and I could take him to hide."

"He ever say why he might need to do that?" McGill asked.

Haskel shrugged. "You read the online comments he gets, a lot of it is just trolls, but there are others … those people sound serious about doing the man harm, and now I can't rightly blame them."

The big man gave McGill three locations that spanned the country from east to west where Teagan Tobias might go to seek refuge. He only asked that McGill let him know how things turned out in return for the information. McGill agreed.

Getting back into the Chevy, McGill asked Leo, "You done saying your rosary?"

Leo grinned. "Haven't gone that far yet."

McGill said, "Let's go back to the office. I want to talk with Sweetie and Deke."

***McGill Investigations International — Washington, DC***

Along with its other amenities, the headquarters building of the detective agency had a small gym: his and hers locker rooms, sauna, steam and massage rooms, a half-court basketball layout, assorted strength machines and free weights. The feeling of the place was a mix of yuppie indulgence and a mini-YMCA.

After McGill arrived at his place of business, he went to the men's locker room instead of his office. He called Sweetie and

Deke and asked them to join him. Then he changed into a DePaul Blue Demons T-shirt, gym shorts and sneakers. Exiting the locker room, carrying a gym bag, he saw not only Sweetie and Deke. Esme and Dikki Missirian were there, too.

Word had obviously been passed that the boss was up to something too good to miss.

Dikki observed, "You still look quite fit, Jim."

Sweetie added, "For an old guy, he means. You're not thinking of training for a marathon or doing something else that's foolish?"

McGill replied with a question of his own. "As chief ethics officer, Sweetie, would you say it's either inappropriate or simply bad for business if I got into a fight with a celebrity?"

No one in the room had any doubt who that celebrity might be.

Still, Sweetie told him, "I'm not a big fan of moral relativism, but it would probably depend on who the celebrity is. Someone who's widely loved, you'd probably do better not to go beyond using kid gloves. Someone who's not kindly regarded would give you more latitude."

McGill said, "I thought as much."

"We're talking about Teagan Tobias here?" Sweetie asked.

"We are."

"Are you going to involve firearms, or are we talking a hand-to-hand confrontation?"

"Might be a knife-fight," McGill said.

Sweetie said, "Well, then, allow me to change my mind. Someone pulls a knife on you, and you have a gun, you use it. Aim for center mass. No trick shots at the hand holding the knife."

"Yeah, I'm done with trick shots," McGill said.

"Maybe you should just let the NYPD handle things," Deke said.

"Have you heard something?" McGill asked.

"Detective Kealoha called just before we all got together here. Gianni Calendri and two retired detective friends found an accomplice who helped Teagan Tobias kill that high school bully back in the day. Well, technically, Tobias killed the kid, and his pal helped him to get rid of the body. The accomplice's father even helped out."

McGill said, "Will this guy testify in court?"

Deke shook his head. "He made a literal deathbed confession, but the former detectives got it all on video."

"The accomplice's father?" McGill asked.

"Long gone."

McGill said, "Did they dump the kid's body in the ocean?"

Deke nodded. "Some area called 12 Mile Dump. Just like Gianni thought."

"Have they recovered any remains?"

"Working on it. The New York D.A. wants to see if they find anything before he files any charges."

McGill nodded. "Tobias has canceled the rest of his run in DC and the next stop in Chicago. If the information I got earlier today about where he might be holed up is right, the New York D.A. will need an extradition order to get him back. But this is a good start."

"So you're not going to do anything foolhardy here?" Sweetie asked.

"We still have to find Alice and make sure she isn't in harm's way," McGill said.

Sweetie couldn't argue with that, so she asked, "What's in the gym bag?"

"Let me ask one question first," McGill said. Looking at Deke, he asked, "How did Tobias kill the kid who was bothering him?"

"The accomplice said he used a knife. Slit the guy's throat. Then he let his pal stab the body until his arm got tired."

McGill nodded. "When Tobias' boss at the ad agency went at him, Tobias didn't have to throw a punch to come out on top. So he's quick, maybe a naturally skilled fighter, and he likes knives."

Sweetie saw where McGill was going. "Good God, Jim, are you serious?"

"Only as a last resort, but it's always wise to be prepared."

He opened the gym bag and took out two knives with fixed

six-inch blades. The blades were made of rubber, but for training purposes they were entirely adequate. He tossed one to Deke, who caught it neatly.

McGill smiled and told Deke, "Think of all the times you felt I was the world's biggest pain in the ass."

That was all Deke needed. He charged McGill.

***Dumbarton Oaks — Washington, DC***

When Patti got home that evening, Special Agent Daphna Levy did her usual brisk top-to-bottom search of the house. No malefactors lurked anywhere on the premises. The house had a state of the art security system wired into both the Secret Service and the Metro PD, but Daphna operated under the presumption that any electronic system could be hacked and defeated.

She trusted the well-being of Patricia McGill to no one but herself.

Even so, Daphna asked Patti, "Will Mr. McGill be home soon?"

"Possibly, but as you know, he doesn't keep normal office hours."

Daphna tried but couldn't quite keep a frown off her face. She discarded her pique as quickly as it had appeared, but that was already too late. The former president both saw and understood the source of Daphna's displeasure.

"I'm sorry," Daphna said. "It's not my place to judge, and it's not professional."

The special agent wouldn't have been surprised if she was told her services were no longer required. After all, Mr. McGill had given Ace Cole the boot. She'd heard Ace had been reassigned to investigating a counterfeit gift-card ring. Maybe the two of them could work together again. Keep the country safe from bogus Starbucks cards.

Apropos of that dark thought, Patti asked, "Do you like working with me, Daphna?"

"Yes, ma'am, I certainly do. It's just sometimes —"

"Mr. McGill can be a handful."

"Yes, ma'am."

"And you wish both of us would conform to the protocols the Secret Service applies to most of the people it protects. Such as having dedicated personnel to watch both us and our home around the clock."

"Yes, ma'am."

"Would you like to live that way?"

"No, ma'am."

"As a federal officer yourself, do you think, after you retire, you might push back against any security demands other people might try to impose on you?"

The very idea stiffened Daphna's spine and her attitude. "I'm better prepared than —" That was where she caught herself, realizing James J. McGill had been a cop for as long a time as she'd been alive. He'd also managed to stay in one piece through a two-term presidency. Using just one Secret Service agent.

She revised her intended statement. "Better prepared than most people, but I have to concede that with Mr. McGill's police experience he has earned … a significant degree of latitude."

Patti beamed at Daphna. "That was very nicely put. So, tell me, how would you feel about being Jim's full-time shadow instead of watching over me?"

Daphna had served as McGill's personal bullet-catcher in rotation with Ace. He hadn't put himself in a single life-threatening situation while she was with him, but it was still easier on her when she went back to guarding the former president. Patricia McGill was naturally inclined to be more agreeable to the precautionary guidance the Secret Service gave her. James J. McGill went his own way, and she not only had to keep up, she also needed to be out front when necessary.

Worse still, his work involved physical danger as a routine possibility.

Not that she was fearful. The timid need not apply to the Secret

Service.

It was Mr. McGill's unpredictability that concerned her.

The idea that he might lead her into a situation for which she hadn't been trained or had the instinct to respond to properly … well, that was just unacceptable.

Even so, she gave Patti the only response available to her if she wanted to keep her job and her self-respect. "I'd be delighted, ma'am, if Mr. McGill would like that."

Patti said, "Good. I'll talk to him tonight then. We'll let you know in the morning."

"Yes, ma'am. Good night."

Patti opened the house's front door for the special agent and closed it behind her. She was well aware that Daphna had taken her time answering the question about working with Jim. Patti didn't hold it against her. Rather, she considered it a mark of both intelligence and character.

Patti's only concern about the situation was the closeness in age between Daphna Levy and Abbie McGill. In a violent circumstance, she worried that her husband's natural impulse might make him take a bullet for the young woman, instead of the other way around.

With that cheerful thought in mind, Patti heard the house phone ring. As she went to answer it, she saw the caller ID displayed only a number, not a name. The number was enough; Patti recognized it as belonging to Galia Mindel.

She picked up the phone and clicked the answer button.

"Good evening, Galia."

"Good evening, Madam President."

Patti didn't need, had never asked people to use her honorary title. With Galia at that moment, she let it stand. "Is there something I can do for you, Galia?"

"I just wanted you to be the first to know, ma'am, that I've accepted President Morrissey's offer to become her new chief of staff."

That was quick, Patti thought.

"If that makes you happy, Galia, then I'm happy, too."

"It does please me. Gives me a sense of renewed purpose. I want to thank you for recommending me to President Morrissey."

"Think nothing of it," Patti said.

Especially since she hadn't made any such recommendation. Still, Patti understood what Jean Morrissey had done. She'd forestalled any rupture between Patti and Galia. So if Jean wanted to call on Patti to handle a task, either ceremonial or political, Galia would be less likely to push back against the decision.

"There is one other thing I should mention," Galia said.

"Please do."

"Since I want there to be no question of President Morrissey needing any outside coaching, I'll be selling my house in Dumbarton Oaks. So it won't look like I'm a conduit either way, for the president or for you, ma'am."

"Very wise, Galia. I'm sure you'll do a wonderful job for Jean."

And won't Jim be glad to have you live elsewhere, Patti thought.

McGill came home an hour later with a red welt on his left cheek. Being the keen observer that she was, Patti took notice. Then again, she could hardly miss the discoloration on her beloved's face while giving him a welcome home kiss.

Once that felicity was completed, she said, "Are you going to make me ask?"

McGill didn't pretend not to know the point of the question.

Still, he offered, "Shaving cut?"

"Only if you're using garden shears these day, and I might have noticed that."

"Okay, if it's the truth you want, Deke got me with a rubber knife."

Patti knew better than to doubt McGill on that response, and she conjured the image in her mind. "Stop me if I'm wrong, but I have to think you had your own rubber knife. Did you hurt Deke?"

"Gutted him from navel to breastbone. Or a reasonable facsimile thereof."

"Please tell me this was just an exercise in overflowing testosterone."

"More like practice makes perfect."

Patti took her husband's hand, led him to the staircase leading to the second floor. She sat on the third step and pulled McGill down next to her. Looking him straight in the eye, she said, "Over the years, I've had any number of nightmares that involve, you, me and many other people. I think some writer could have a smash bestselling book titled 'Bad Dreams in the Lincoln Bedroom.' If the book was a collection of sleeping torments from an assortment of presidents, it might be a perennial chart-topper, with people waiting eagerly for new editions."

McGill nodded. "Might give Stephen King a run for his money."

"Commercial possibilities aside, I've been trying to sleep more peacefully since leaving public service. I'm happy to say I've succeeded more often than not. I hardly ever find myself in desperate, imaginary situations anymore."

"Glad to hear that," McGill told her.

"I even have fewer bad dreams about our kids these days."

"That's also very good, but I have the suspicion there's still one guy who disturbs your REM sleep."

Patti nodded. "Really, Jim? You think you might get into a knife fight? If you were still a cop, would you even consider such a thing?"

McGill hadn't considered things in that context. "If I were still in uniform, I'd have my sidearm, Taser, mace, billy club, maybe a shotgun or carbine in the trunk of my car. There were times I did carry a folding knife, but I only used it to open envelopes."

"So what made you drag Deke into a mock knife-fight?"

"If I tell you, it might lead to uneasy sleep."

"I'll risk it."

Taking her at her word, McGill told Patti how Teagan Tobias had killed Nicholas Pell.

And how his accomplice, Gary Llewelyn, had vented his fury on the bully.

Patti said, "That's brutal and horrible in every respect. Still, I have a very basic question. If you can find Teagan Tobias, and if he's holding Alice Janeway captive, why wouldn't you call the police to make an arrest?"

"I might."

"Might?"

McGill just looked at Patti, giving her a moment to think.

That was all it took. She even knew the appropriate phrase: "Exigent circumstances."

An emergency situation requiring swift action to prevent imminent danger to life.

"Uh-huh, that's one," McGill said.

Sharing McGill's mindset now, Patti added, "Another circumstance might be avoiding a hostage situation. Cops arrive like a thunderstorm not ninjas."

"Yeah," McGill said. "Trying to negotiate with a hostage-taker is supposed to work eight or nine times out of ten, if you can believe the statistics. What I've never understood, though, is how the people who fail can live with themselves. I don't think I could."

Patti took a deep breath and let it out slowly. "All right, I can see where you might feel the need to intervene personally. Even so, I still don't understand why you'd choose a knife for either a means of defense or attack. Did you ever think Tobias might have an accomplice, the way he did when he was a teenager?"

That notion hadn't occurred to McGill. He gave it some thought. "No, I don't think so. He needed Gary Llewelyn's boat back then. I don't think he'll need help now."

"So you wouldn't have to silently take down a third party before confronting Tobias. If that's the case, why use or even bring a knife? Wouldn't a handgun be more effective? You know, like the old joke about bringing a knife to a gunfight."

A gun did have the advantage, McGill thought, but only if you had the gun out, aimed and ready to fire. A quick opponent holding a knife and standing within 15 feet of an adversary could kill him before a holstered gun could be drawn, aimed and fired.

McGill chose not to inform Patti of that. Her point was still valid in many cases. A shooter with a gun at the ready should prevail over someone with a knife.

"You want me to leave my knife at home?" McGill asked.

"Only if you think it would be more of a distraction than a help. What I'd really like, of course, is for you to avoid harm altogether. Unless you think you have absolutely no choice, call the cops. Let them do their job."

That raised another question for McGill. Whom did he trust more to get the outcome he wanted? He didn't share that with Patti, but he was sure she already knew the answer.

He just said, "Okay."

"Will you be leaving early for … wherever you're going?" Patti asked.

"No. Leo's outside right now. I just wanted to come home, pack a few things and …" Say goodbye, McGill had in mind. He quickly edited that thought for one that sounded less final. "Say I'll be back before you know it."

Patti stood and pulled him into her embrace. "You'd damn well better be."

McGill kissed his wife, packed three days changes of clothes, and kissed Patti again on the way out. He'd left his personal Benchmade knife at home. But he'd taken the one Deke had given him: Teagan Tobias' knife, the blade the NYPD had taken from him.

***Shenandoah National Park, Virginia***

Tad Thacker pitched his tent in the woods. Spending a night outdoors was something he'd done since he was a boy. His father had been a lumber company executive. Dad had first taken him to see a stand of trees being cut down when he was five years old. When Tad had witnessed his first Oregon White Oak fall, he'd burst into tears. When his father asked what was wrong, Tad responded that the tree had "died."

He was only somewhat comforted when his father told him new trees were planted to replace the ones that were harvested. That was only the responsible thing to do, his father said. The only commercially sustainable thing, also, but Dad hadn't gotten into that concept until later. As Tad grew older and saw all of the uses to which wood was put, he understood that much of everyday life depended on trees being cut down for people to use.

Dad pointed out that their house, from its floors to its roof, was largely constructed of wood, including the doors, walls, and window frames. So were the kitchen cabinets and furniture. Without cutting down trees, Dad said, people would still be living in caves and tents.

Tad came to accept that reality as he grew older, and while he never wanted to live in a cave, he didn't mind sleeping outdoors in an artificial-fiber tent. Pitching a tent in a forest, in fact, was blissful for him. He'd never camped out in an Eastern U.S. forest before, but he'd done his homework. He'd learned there were black bears, venomous snakes and maybe even some cougars in the Shenandoah National Park.

After having dinner, he'd stored his food supplies in bear-resistant sacks, and hung them on the branch of a tree a hundred feet from where he'd set up his tent. Following the park's "leave no trace" policy, he buried his excrement an equal distance in the opposite direction. If a predator still poked a nose in his tent, Tad was newly and well armed.

He'd made a stop at a gun shop in Reston, Virginia and bought a Weatherby Mark V Accumark rifle: a weapon used to hunt grizzly bears. Equipped with a Leupold scope and .340 Weatherby ammo, it could stop one of the apex predators in its tracks at 300 yards.

Tad thought a round from the hunting rifle might cut Teagan Tobias in two.

For close-in work, he'd purchased a Sig Sauer P226, the handgun the Navy Seals used.

And, if hostilities got within arm's length, he'd also bought an Al Mare SERE special operations knife.

To see in the dark, Tad purchased Pulsar Night Vision Goggles.

He'd become a one-man strike force because he'd learned Teagan Tobias had purchased a house outside the small town of Woodstock, Virginia, in the shadows of the national park. Hiding among the trees, using the scope on his rifle, he could maneuver to get a 270-degree view of any unshaded window in Tobias' house.

After Tad had been ejected from the Portland theater the second time he'd gone to see Tobias perform, he'd told himself he needed to forget about Alice Janeway. His resolve had lasted less than two days. He'd decided that even if Alice wasn't Jenny, she almost certainly was a nice person.

On the other hand, he'd bet that Tobias was pretty much the same SOB he played onstage. That being Tad's opinion, he'd decided he better learn everything about the performer that he could. To prevent anything bad happening to Alice, if things came to that.

So he'd studied Tobias in minute detail. Read every biographical and professional reference he could find online. Learned his parents' names and that he didn't have any siblings. While Tobias didn't have a brother or sister, he did have some aunts and uncles. When Tad looked into where Tobias lived, he found that he had a duplex in Cambridge, Massachusetts and a loft in downtown L.A.

Titles to property were public records. So finding those addresses hadn't been hard.

Some people might have stopped looking at that point, but Tad felt that Tobias had a sneaky side to his personality. So he used Tobias' mother's maiden name in another search. He came up with dozens of results, but they were all in decidedly un-showbiz locations: Iowa, West Virginia, North Dakota, and other places like that. Views of the addresses on Google Earth showed small dwellings for people of humble means.

Tad was about to give up on his extended search when he remembered one of Tobias' aunts, his mother's sister. Maybe, Tad thought, a slick guy would go a step beyond using Mom's maiden name for a cover and use his aunt's name. That seemed like a reasonable guess.

So Tad checked public property records of Mary Emerson and found satellite photos of three nice houses where he thought a guy with a good chunk of money might hide out. He'd never found proof-positive that any of those residences actually belonged to Tobias, but he felt comfortable with the assumptions he'd made.

He liked his hunches even better after learning that Alice had last been seen at Tobias' show in Atlanta, shortly before the performer's next show opened in Washington, DC. The driving distance between the nation's capital and Woodstock, Virginia was less than 100 miles. Hardly a long drive.

So, Woodstock was the first place Tad went to look after leaving DC.

And now, peering through the scope on his rifle, he saw the man himself.

Teagan Tobias stood in the light coming through a second-floor window.

Perfectly outlined and well within range of his bear-killing weapon.

***City Limits Motel — Austin, Texas***

After showering off the fatigue and body odor of his long trip, Eloy Chavez stepped out of the bathroom clad only in a towel. His unit was at the far end of the 1.5-star motel that he and his men had rented for their exclusive use. They'd peacefully evicted the inhabitants of the three occupied units with bribes of a few hundred dollars each. The manager had been given a thousand dollars to take the rest of the weekend off. The gang from Mexico had the place to themselves.

Chavez's lieutenant, Fermin Gomez, sat on the edge of the room's only bed, a twin, not even a queen. The threadbare coverlet looked like it hadn't been new since Elvis died. Some of the smudges on it looked like laundered and dried but not removed blood. Made Chavez wonder if someone had breathed his last on this bed.

From the looks of the place, more than one person might have expired there.

While Gomez remained fixated on his laptop computer, the boss used the thin towel from the bathroom to dry his crotch. He asked his second in command, "You bring any baby powder? I forgot mine."

Still not looking up, Gomez said, "Over there. The drawer under the TV."

The television looked like it came from the '70s, too. Big hulking monster, had an antenna, not even a cable hook-up. No porn movies here tonight, *amigo,* Chavez thought to himself. Gomez had turned the motel's "No Rooms Available" sign on once the manager had left. Chavez thought that was a mark of how careful Gomez could be, but it was also probably unnecessary.

On a mild night like this one, Chavez thought, it was likely most people would prefer to sleep outdoors than in this dump. Still, the room had a door, walls and curtains on the windows. Some business you just couldn't go about in public. Chavez found the powder and applied it liberally to his crotch and underarms. He felt much better, wrapped the towel back around his waist and sat next to Gomez.

He gazed at the image on the computer screen.

"That is the man's property?" Chavez asked. "A live picture?"

"Yes."

"How big?"

Gomez did the conversion from 100 acres in his head. "A little more than 40 hectares."

Chavez made a scoffing sound. "And this is supposed to be a rich man? This *pendejo,* Wallace Rhymes."

Taking the risk of pissing off the boss, Gomez put things into perspective for Chavez, because that was what he always did. His willingness to talk straight might well get him killed someday, he knew, but in the meantime, he was making enough money to provide for his children and grandchildren even if they all lived to be to a hundred.

"The next largest landholding in this area is one-tenth that size. Also, the land here is much more expensive than in Mexico. This man's land by itself would cost more than two million dollars. His house would double that amount, perhaps even triple it."

"So six million at most." Chavez shook his head unimpressed. "That is not so much money."

"*Jefe,* we are not talking the kind of money you have, but this is only a small part of Rhymes' holdings. His company buys and sells stocks for tens of thousands of people. He makes money on every transaction. A Texas business magazine I found estimated his fortune at over $200 million, and that was four years ago."

Even a drug dealer didn't sneer at a nine-figure sum.

So, Chavez tried another angle. "So, he's a rich old fool, but a fool he is to mock me."

"That worries me, too, *jefe*. He was indeed witless to provoke you. He could have let you think you had the real John Wayne hat when he knew he had the real one. But he didn't. He insulted you instead. I have to ask myself why he would do this. I can't find any other time he acted this way."

"One mistake is all a man needs to cause his own death," Chavez said.

Gomez thought he knew that only too well, but still he said, "I have had one other idea, *señor*."

Still unhappy with the last one, Chavez growled, "What?"

Gomez took a deep breath, let it out and said, "What if the hat you have is the real one, and Rhymes is trying to trick you with an imitation?"

"*Hijo de puta,*" Chavez growled, jumping to his feet.

He stormed back and forth in front of the bed, making Gomez think he should have kept his mouth shut. Then Chavez plopped back down on the bed, making old bedsprings groan. The drug boss jabbed the computer screen with a finger.

"How high is our drone flying?"

"Two thousand feet. Too high for anyone on the ground to see at night."

"Can they hear it?"

Gomez shook his head.

"Can you bring the image closer?"

The second-in-command zoomed in on the house, but the result wasn't intimate enough for Chavez. "Fly the thing lower."

Gomez brought the tiny aircraft down a thousand feet. "Any lower and they might hear the machine, *señor*."

The image now, with the zoom still in place, was close enough for Chavez.

Addressing Wallace Rhymes' house, he said, "You think you have me, old man? *Chinga tu madre.* I will not only have the true hat, I will have your head."

Chavez ripped the towel from his waist and stepped into a pair of pants, not bothering about any underwear.

"What are we going to do?" Gomez asked.

Jamming his arms into a shirt, Chavez smiled like a wolf about to devour a lamb.

"What we are going to do, Gomez, is we are going to find, buy or steal a hat that looks very much like that one." Chavez pointed to the hat on the dresser next to the television that may or may not have once belonged to John Wayne. "Then we are going to set that new hat on fire and post a video online of it burning. We will see how that old *bastardo* Rhymes likes that. The way he reacts will tell us what to do next."

Gomez closed the laptop, stood and extended a hand to Chavez.

"*¡Magnifico, señor!*"

He wasn't just sucking up to the boss as they shook hands.

Gomez thought it was a brilliant counterstroke.

It also saved him from showing Chavez the new blog post in the local paper that made fun of him. That truly might have been his end.

Looking around in disgust at the motel room, Chavez told

Gomez, "Leave the men here. You and I will go somewhere much nicer. You will make the arrangements; I will slip in behind you."

Gomez nodded and quickly brought up a hotel search site.

He was glad to be leaving the motel, but still considered it an unnecessary risk.

Corporal Ennis Williamson, a patrol officer in the Northeast Area Command of the Austin Police Department, laughed out loud when he drove past the sign: City Limits Motel. He'd seen the name of the place more times than he could remember in his two years on the job. What made him laugh was the part of the sign he'd never seen lit up before: *No Rooms Available.*

Yeah, right.

When that dump was even one-third full, it was a banner night.

Still, there did seem to be an unusually large number of cars in the parking lot. Nothing fancy except … had that been a black limo way at the far end? The light wasn't too good way in back. He'd only gotten a glimpse, and he was dog tired at the end of his shift.

He'd leave a note for the next patrol car out.

Maybe something was going on at City Limits Motel.

They could decide if they wanted to take a closer look.

## CHAPTER 6

***Saturday, November 5, 2017***
***Police Department — Woodstock, Virginia***

The police department in town occupied a two-story brick building. To McGill's eye, it looked to be quite a respectable cop-shop for a hamlet with just over 5,000 residents. Leaving Leo in the Chevy parked at the curb out front, McGill walked to the front door. The lights were on inside but the glass door was locked. That problem was addressed by an adjacent doorbell.

Ring for help, McGill thought.

Quaint enough to make him smile.

He rang the bell and waited. Looking through the door, he saw a photo pinned to a corkboard. A chief of police in a white shirt and dark tie stood in the midst of seven cops in dark blue uniforms. All of the cops were white, and only one of them was a woman. The youngest one.

She was also the one working the weekend night shift. Her name tag read: HENDRIX.

Presumably, Officer Hendrix could call for help if the citizenry turned unruly.

She gave McGill a serious scan, checking him from head to toe for any weapons or other means of mayhem. Say, knuckles scarred from unlicensed fisticuffs. When she got back to looking at his face, she seemed to recognize him. His face had appeared in mass and social media with fair regularity during his and Patti's White House years. A small nod indicated she came to the conclusion that a celebrity of sorts had appeared at her duty post.

Nonetheless, she pressed an intercom button and blandly asked, "Help you, sir?"

"Yes, Officer Hendrix, my name's Jim McGill, formerly of the Chicago Police Department."

He thought it better to establish a common bond than try to throw his weight around.

"Yes, sir. I believe I've noticed you a time or two from TV and the newspapers. Those accounts mentioned your police service, among other things. Haven't come to town to apply for a job, have you?"

McGill grinned. He liked the way Hendrix had said that with a straight face.

"You mean with your department? No. I'm already collecting two police pensions. Three would just be greedy."

That got a smile from her and made the young cop seem more like a teenager than the mid-20s she probably was.

"So how may I help you? You need a recommendation of a place to put up for the night?"

McGill shook his head. "I was wondering if I might have a word with your chief. I know it's late, but I'm looking for a missing person I believe to be in or near your town, and it's a situation where she might be in danger."

"What kind of danger?" Hendrix asked.

"The kind where the person she's with is thought to have murdered at least one person and possibly two."

"How do you mean 'thought to?'"

Good question, McGill thought. "The accusation regarding the first homicide came from a deathbed confession of an accomplice. The second individual, who had a fight with this person, disappeared. As in never to be seen again."

The pink highlights in Hendrix's cheeks disappeared, leaving her face a chalky white.

"The chief is out of town," she said. "He and the mayor are in Richmond lobbying the legislature for some additional funding."

"Who's the next ranking officer?" McGill asked.

"Lieutenant Nicholls, but he's down in South Carolina. His daughter just had a baby yesterday."

"Well," McGill said, "I'd ask who your sergeant is only I get the feeling this is a slow time of year for your department, and he might be unavailable, too."

Hendrix nodded, feeling somewhat ashamed now. "He's in Florida fishing."

"Okay. Is there any other officer in town whose experience you'd trust more than your own?"

"There are three guys with more time in uniform but, believe me, I can outthink them before I even open my eyes in the morning."

"Well, then," McGill said, "would you like to accompany me or see how fast someone from the State Police can get here?"

Hendrix didn't miss McGill's point. "You mean you're going somewhere hereabouts, and I can come along or stay right where I am?"

"I do."

"What if I took you into custody?"

"On what charge?"

"I can think of something. Would you resist?"

"No. What'd I'd do is sue you out of your job and your department out of existence. And if the person I'm looking for suffered because of the delay, you'd have to live with that even more than I would. Not to mention no police department anywhere else would ever hire you."

In a quiet voice, Hendrix told McGill, "I was just asking. I'll be right back. I've got to get the keys to my car and send a text that I'm out on patrol. Won't be a minute. Just wait for me, okay?"

McGill nodded, feeling like a bully.

He would have felt a lot worse, though, if his inaction led to Alice's …

No, he didn't even want to think like that.

***Teagan Tobias' Hideaway House — Woodstock, Virginia***

While Teag had always thought of Alice as *nice*-looking, he'd never considered her physically compelling. Not that there was anything wrong with her figure. She was neither plump nor scrawny. Her skin didn't glow but it was unblemished. Her hair did reflect light nicely, but its color was a uniform medium brown. No highlights.

Summing things up, Alice was somebody you'd be happy to have as your sister.

Only she was more than that. She was smart, fairly funny, and had the tenacity of a bulldog. All of that did have some appeal. So, okay, maybe she deserved more than simple sibling affection. Ought to be thought of as more than someone who could competently carry out the directions he gave her.

Alice had been eager to contribute to the creative end of his performances since she first went to work for him. Hell, even before that probably. She first showed up for his shows in Raleigh, coming to every performance in the week-long run there. Even back then, when he played college towns and smaller cities, ticket prices were substantial. Paying to see multiple performances in a row, in seats down in front, was a substantial investment for anyone who wasn't a trust-fund kid.

That kind of interest was what led him to allow her to come backstage after the final show of the run in Raleigh. For one thing, he wanted to see if she was right in the head or a potential stalker. People wouldn't ordinarily think of a woman as being dangerous in that role, but, what the hell, a woman could buy a gun as easily as a guy. Gender equity and all that.

Once he started talking to Alice, though, he saw she wasn't

some screw-loose crazy. She was simply someone who really related to what he had to say. Got even some of his slyest, quickest digs and darts that slipped right by most people. Only she didn't seem to have any of the burning anger that was the pilot light of his life.

He'd pretty much said as much when they'd met that first time.

He asked, "What is it you get out of my act?"

"I get that it *isn't* an act, and it teaches me to be ready for whatever comes my way."

That had made Teag smile. He'd never thought of himself as a self-defense instructor, but, yeah, he could see that reasoning. It made him feel good. He also liked that she knew his performances grew out of personal experience not just glib observations of society at large.

He asked, "What do you do for a living?"

"I teach high school social studies. I'm saving money. I might work toward getting a Ph.D., or I might not. I'm not sure. I want something more than I have, but I don't know what."

That was when Teag committed an unprecedented act of generosity. He wrote out a check to reimburse Alice for the cost of coming to see him all week. He knew the amount down to the penny, including tax and the ticket vendor fees.

Alice started to get misty-eyed, but Teag held up a hand.

"None of that. I'm thinking I might have a job for you, if you're organized, good with numbers and scheduling, also if you can deal cordially with people I wouldn't put up with for a second. But if you're the emotional type, you have no business being around me."

In response to all that, Alice tried to look tough.

Teag laughed.

And Alice growled.

That only made him laugh harder, and ask if she'd work for a salary that was half again more than what she'd made as a teacher. And that was how they got together. Problem was, after her first year or so with the show, Alice would drop little *insights,* as she called them, dashed off on Post-It Notes, on how he might tweak his act: add a line she wrote, cut a line he wrote.

That might have been enough, from the very first suggestion, to get her canned. Only she was so damn efficient at the rest of her job, and the rest of the crew absolutely loved her, that Teag didn't want to lose her.

He only said, "Alice, you do this one more time, I'm going to strangle you."

She'd knock off giving him any suggestions for a few months, and then she'd start again. She couldn't help herself. What bothered him the most was when she came up with *good* ideas. He couldn't bring himself to use them, damnit, because he'd have to start giving her some measure of creative credit. Meaning he would no longer be the sole genius behind his act.

He couldn't have that, not at all.

What he did with Alice's ideas, though, was keep them. Locked away. If she ever did go back to school or just got tired of being on the road most of the year, he'd wait a few months after she'd left and then start using her material.

Let her *prove* she'd come up with the ideas, if she made a fuss after she left.

Only she never did leave, except for almost dying recently.

And, to Teag's immense surprise, that changed the way he felt about Alice. He'd never gone anywhere near having sex with Alice. If a woman allowed you that intimacy, she'd come to think she could make claims on you. Teag was determined that he would always be the only one to chart his own course. He had to concede, though, that exposure to the world of show biz and the denizens therein had clued Alice in on how to be more stylish.

She still wasn't a hot babe by any means, but she'd overlain her country girl innocence with a sense of élan that would make most guys, including Teag, look twice. Even so, he didn't so much as hint at the idea of going to bed with her. Professionally, Alice was already close to being his mate. He wouldn't give her cause to think she had even more influence.

What had developed between them was a willingness to share personal confidences. Alice had told Teag about the time a mosquito bite almost killed her. She'd also told him about her parents dying, leaving a brother who lived overseas as her only family. Teag had said he didn't have any siblings, and he'd wished his parents had died sooner than they did.

"If my parents had croaked, maybe I could have sued somebody for an unnatural death," he told Alice. "Something I could have walked away from with some loot."

Then he laughed and added, "Oh, well, they gave me a shitty outlook on life that seems to be paying off pretty well."

That was the only time Alice kissed him. On a cheek, not the lips. It was a gesture of compassion, not romance. Teag had never known anything like it. There were times when he was alone that he could still feel that kiss. In some of those moments, he felt like a young boy again, finally getting some emotional warmth from another person.

Even that was a joke on him. What was he going to do if he wanted to repeat the experience? Ask Alice for another kiss just like the last one? And then they could hold hands and skip off to the malt shop and ask for one milkshake with two straws?

Yeah, right.

What they did when they learned that each of them was basically alone in the world was to extend powers of attorney to one another. Not for financial matters but for medical decisions. Having already been in a coma once, Alice had told Teag she didn't want any extreme measures taken simply to preserve her body by mechanical means.

Teag wanted Alice to do the same for him if he became a zombie.

He also wanted one more thing: "When I'm officially dead, see to it that my body is donated to some medical school for dissection. I want to see if anybody can figure out how I lived so long without having a heart."

He laughed at his own joke.

Alice replied, "Maybe you don't need one. Piss and vinegar might circulate all on their own."

That stopped Teag cold, made him wish he'd thought of that line.

For the first time, he started to think maybe he should let Alice write some small part of the next show.

"Hey, I was just kidding," she told him.

"Yeah, I know. I'm just bitter with envy. I wish I'd come up with that line."

When Alice went into her recent coma, his heart almost stopped for real. He thought there had to be a limit on the number of times someone could incur a near-death experience without the Reaper finally saying, "Enough of this shit, you're mine."

So when he went into her bedroom that night in his Virginia hideaway to check on her, and she woke up and recognized him, appeared to be well oriented, he sat on the bed next to her. When she smiled at him, he felt warm in a way that brought back the feeling of her kiss.

"You know," he said, "I think it's finally time you started to write the show with me, and get an onstage role, too. Not that we'll ever be Ozzie and Harriet or even Burns and Allen."

He thought that last bit was weak, but the good news might have gotten a smile at least.

Instead, Alice looked stricken, and a chill went through Teag.

He thought maybe she was about to relapse. One last time.

What she told him, though, was even worse.

She took his hands and said, "Oh, Teag, I'd love to, but I can't."

"What, you don't think you'll be healthy enough?"

"God, I hope so, but …"

"But what?"

"I … I've taken another job. In L.A. I start in January."

Teag began to blink quickly, like his brain was flashing a semaphore at him. He eased his hands out of hers and stood up. Looking down at Alice, he said in an unusually quiet voice, "Well … good luck. I'll take you to DC in the morning. Get you a hotel room or check you into a hospital. Whatever you think is better. If you're feeling up to it, maybe you should fly out to the Coast right away. Hope everything works out for you."

Tears formed in Alice's eyes. "I'm sorry, Teag. I just thought —"

He held up a hand. "No need to explain. You'll do great."

He left the room and closed the door behind him.

Wondering how he'd ever let himself become such a chump.

And where he could dump Alice's body.

***Northeast Area Command***
***Austin Police Department — Austin, Texas***

Tired or not, the urgent advisory poster on the locker room message board stopped Corporal Ennis Williamson in his tracks. The side-by-side photos of "Mexican Drug Boss Eloy Chavez" and "Airline Passenger Using Alias Esteban Martinez" were riveting. Williamson was good with faces. He saw them in detail, and rarely forgot anyone he'd seen more than once.

Looking at these two photos, he had no doubt they were the same man. The guy in the hat was cleaned up and closely shaved, but he had the same brow, eyes, nose, mouth and chin as the other dude. Unless Williamson was looking at identical twins … no, it wasn't that. Even the facial wrinkle patterns in the two photos were the same. Shit, identical twins didn't match that closely.

Reading the information beneath the pictures, the man in the hat had landed in Oklahoma City and might be headed to Texas. At the bottom of the poster was a smaller photo of a limo that the guy in the hat had used to leave the Oklahoma airport.

That was when things clicked for Corporal Williamson. He thought he'd seen a black limo at the City Limits Motel. On the way back to the office, he started to wonder if he'd imagined seeing a big fancy car at a dump like the motel. Now, he didn't doubt himself at all. He knew he had something hot. Information that might get him bumped up in rank.

At the bottom of the alert was the command: *Report any sighting to your commanding officer immediately. We will alert the FBI.* Naturally enough, some cop had drawn a line through the

FBI reference. No self-respecting cop held the feds in high esteem.

Unless he had one in the family.

Ennis Williamson's cousin Marquez worked for the DEA — which really should be the federal agency to bring in a drug boss anyway. The corporal went to a quiet corner of the locker room and called his cousin. Not with his personal phone but a burner he used mostly to chat up his girlfriends.

Marquez answered grumpily, "Do you know what the hell time it is, whoever the hell you are?"

"It's me, Ennis, and it's time to get your lazy ass out of bed, if you want to become a hero. And, cuz, you are gonna *owe* me."

Ennis filled in Marquez about Eloy Chavez coming to town and said he was going to give the DEA a ten-minute head start. Then he was going to let the Austin PD in on the game.

Marquez got moving so fast he didn't bother with goodbye.

***Kyle Tompkins' Apartment — Austin, Texas***

The columnist for the *Austin Journal,* born in 1989, was part of the Millennial Generation. He hated that. Wouldn't have wanted to be a Gen-Xer, either. The Baby Boomers he regarded with mixed emotions. No damn way he'd have wanted to get his ass shipped over to Vietnam. Man, those poor guys who got drafted and sent over to some damn jungle to get shot at by invisible little people, he had nothing but sympathy for them.

Aside from that, though, he thought growing up in the 1960s would have been the coolest thing ever. Okay, the two Kennedys and Dr. King getting killed, those were horrible things, too. Still, the country was starting, finally, to move away from all that Jim Crow bullshit. Civil rights and voting rights became law. The music, damn, in his mind there was never a greater time for American music. So much of it came from every possible direction. Then there was the arrival of the birth control pill. Holy shit. Free love. Or at least the chance to get *some* nookie.

Yeah, there were all the illegal drugs, too, but he'd never felt that pull.

A cute girl, a warm room where you could get together, and a new album to put on the turntable every week, that was his idea of heaven. You could also add to all of the above that the '60s were the years when alternative newspapers came into vogue. They were social media decades before everybody had a personal computer or a smartphone. Kyle thought he'd have fit right in writing for one of the old hell-and-consciousness-raising publications. Say, *Rolling Stone* or *The Seed.* Wouldn't that have been too cool?

The way things had turned out for him, though, he was working for a publication he considered to be just okay at a rate of pay that was marginal at best. He didn't have a casual girlfriend much less a significant other. He had actually gotten tired of listening to most of the old tunes. And next year, damn it, he'd turn thirty.

Still, if it turned out he'd written the blog post and done the podcast that lured Eloy Chavez into the country, helped to get one of the biggest drug lords in Mexico locked up for life in an American penitentiary … well, shit, if he couldn't capitalize professionally on that coup, he would deserve neither fame nor fortune.

Only … what if Chavez slipped the trap? Got away. Learned who'd been responsible for suckering him into coming to the U.S. Those drug guys, they weren't forgiving types. The more agony they inflicted on their enemies, the better they liked it.

So that night, instead of listening to tunes old or new, Kyle had a pair of shortwave receivers tuned into the Austin PD and DEA frequencies. The combined transmissions tended to garble one another, and were giving Kyle a more than a mild headache, but he wasn't listening for content. He was paying attention to tone. He figured if there were news of Eloy Chavez being spotted, there would be a real sense of urgency in the voice of anyone broadcasting the news.

Then he'd lower the volume of one receiver and pay attention to the other.

That was just what he did a minute later when the DEA

signal carried an urgent message that Chavez and his crew might be holed up at a dumpy motel called the City Limits. The news that the drug boss had taken the bait Kyle had written made his mind glow and his sphincter tighten. For a moment he couldn't decide: Go to the motel to see what happened or stay safe right where he was.

He decided he wouldn't ever be able to live with himself if he wimped out.

He had to observe. He had to write. That meant he had to go.

Which he did, right after calling Gene Beck and Maj Olson.

Hoping they could provide some cover for him, if he needed it.

***12 Mile Dump — Atlantic Ocean***

The water, appropriately, was dead calm. Couldn't ask for better when you were looking for immersed human remains. It was the dead of night, but both the boat and the three divers had their own lights. The overtime rates for the boat, its crew and the guys down in the water were ungodly, but Dago John didn't mind. He was actually way ahead of the game with his lottery winnings, not down to his last few dollars as Lily Kealoha had averred.

The first thing he'd done, even before telling his wife he'd won the jackpot, was to hook up with a guy he knew from his own school days. Bobby Kaufman had both a law degree and a CPA. His specialty was wealth management. Bobby had been delighted his old friend had hit it rich and didn't have any cockamamie ideas about splurging with his money.

Well, Bobby hadn't been thrilled with the idea of John opening a diner, but that had turned out to be a winner, earning money from the day the doors opened. The house John bought had tripled in value and the rest of his stash was invested in ways that would make Warren Buffett smile. So if Dago John wanted to take a flyer on trying to solve a decades-old murder, there were worse ways to spend discretionary funds.

He wouldn't have opted to spend the overtime pay for the boat and the divers if the weather forecast hadn't said conditions would be going to hell in a hand-basket in about 12 hours. Temperatures would plunge, gale force winds would blow and the ocean would be an all-encompassing peril. Dago John and Detectives Feldman and Donnegan all had the same feeling: They were going to find whatever remained of Nicholas Pell that night or they never would.

The three ex-cops stared down at the water until their cervical spines creaked.

"Jesus, we're all too old for shit like this," Donnegan complained.

Feldman raised his head enough to complete a nod. "Moses would be inclined to agree."

Dago John said, "Hey, they're coming up. All three of 'em."

The divers' lights first appeared as pinpoints in the black water and grew progressively larger and brighter. It was only when the divers broke the surface, though, that the cops, the captain and the crew all saw they had brought the majority of a skeleton with them, and one of them held up what looked like a scrap of metal. It was about the size of a name bracelet.

Turned out that was just what it was.

The homemade kind.

Crudely etched into its surface were the words: Brick Shithouse.

***Teagan Tobias' Hideaway House — Woodstock, Virginia***

Teag walked into his kitchen deep in thought, trying to work out the best way to get Alice's body into deep water. That was the way he'd disposed of bodies since he was a kid, and it had never failed him. Yeah, Alice was still alive, but that was only a technicality. Then again, maybe it'd be a better idea to keep her breathing until they got close to wherever he'd dump her. You never knew when some highway cop might stop you. Having a body in the trunk —

He jumped a foot into the air.

A guy stood just inside the kitchen door to the backyard.

The sonofabitch had a semi-auto handgun pointed right at him.

"You want money?" Teag said, starting to regain his composure. "Take it. I've got a few grand in the house. It's all yours. I'll get it for you."

The guy shook his head, and Teag didn't like that at all.

If he didn't want money …

"Where's Alice?" the guy said.

That dumbfounded Teag. The best response he could manage was, "Huh?"

"Alice, where is she? God help you, if you've hurt her."

The guy's tone was not just threatening, it was worried. This jerk had feelings for Alice, but who the hell was he? Teag had never seen him before … and then the light dawned.

"Are you the guy from Oregon? The one who came backstage with a ring?"

Holding a gun on him or not, the guy still flushed with embarrassment.

"Yeah, that was you," Teag said. "Listen, I never got to meet you, but I thought that was pretty cool, what you did."

"Bullshit."

"No, no, really. I mean, there was *no* way it was going to work. You don't just pop up out of nowhere and expect a woman to say, 'Sure, I'll marry a perfect stranger.' But crazy as it was, it still took real stones and, I think, a sense of romance to give it a try."

Teag saw the guy relax just a bit. Not enough to make a move yet, but things were heading in the right direction. He said, "Alice is upstairs. She hasn't been feeling too well lately, but she's getting better. I was just heating up some water to make her some tea."

That was true. A blue flame rose under a water-filled pot on the stove.

On a counter nearby was a teapot. Other cookware, dishes and utensils were neatly stacked in a dish-drain adjacent to a double sink. The orderliness of it all, Teag hoped, would show signs of good character to the dope with the gun.

What he really wanted, though, was to get his hands on one of the sharp kitchen knives in the dish-drain. From the distance of a few feet, he'd take his chances with a knife against the clown's gun. He'd killed people before. He wouldn't hesitate to do it again.

He'd bet the idiot in front of him hadn't ended anyone's life and would have a moment of indecision before acting. A second of delay would be all it would take. Teag would slit his throat. Still, it would make a mess that would have to be cleaned up and mean another body to dump. The thought of all the extra work annoyed Teag.

A flicker of anger appeared in his eyes and the guy caught it.

"I want to see Alice now," he said.

"Can I bring her some tea, before we go?"

"No, take me to her now, or I'll gut-shoot you."

Teag raised his hands in a gesture of surrender. "Okay, okay. Don't shoot. Alice is upstairs. We'll go see her right now."

Teag turned and took the first step toward the stairs leading to the second floor.

His mind raced, thinking of where he might duck into another room and be out of the line of fire just long enough to counter-attack. Even though self-preservation was foremost in his mind, he couldn't stop himself from asking another thought that popped into his head.

"Hey," he said, "you didn't bring Alice another ring, did you?"

Leo Levy cut the Chevy's engine, turned off the headlights, and the black car coasted silently through the night for a quarter-mile before easing to a stop in front of the house at the edge of the national forest. Woodstock Police Officer Hendrix, whose first name, she'd reluctantly revealed, was Camille, had agreed to travel in McGill's car once she'd learned Leo had driven the NASCAR circuit and had won the Chevy Rock & Roll 400 in Richmond.

She did insist on sitting shotgun.

McGill was okay with that.

Before either she or McGill got out of the car, Hendrix told McGill, "You will follow my instructions to the letter."

He replied, "I sometimes have trouble remembering the alphabet."

Seeing that strict discipline was going to be problematic, Hendrix asserted, "I'm going to be the first through the front door."

Hendrix was wearing body armor; McGill wasn't. He conceded the point. "Okay."

Trying her luck, she added, "You will follow wherever I go."

"How long have you been on the job, Officer?" McGill asked.

She didn't want to answer and only reluctantly said, "Eighteen months."

"I have 25 years police experience," McGill said. "You ever shoot anyone or been shot at?"

Without saying so, Hendrix invoked her right to remain silent.

"How about this?" McGill asked. "Each of us does what he or she thinks best, we try not to shoot each other, and we bring this situation to a conclusion that reflects well on both of us, if at all possible."

She gave McGill a tight nod and got out of the car, taking care to close the door quietly.

McGill gave her points for that, and more to Leo for making sure the dome light hadn't gone on. He told his old friend, "If you hear any shooting, call the State Police. If someone who isn't either Officer Hendrix or me comes out of the house with a gun in hand, tell him to drop it. If he doesn't obey immediately, shoot him. With as many rounds as necessary."

"You got it, boss," Leo said.

McGill added, "I know this might strain your professional ethics, Leo, but take cover behind the Chevy before any shootout begins. Better the car should suffer than you."

"If the car gets hurt, I'll feel the pain, too, but okay."

Officer Hendrix grew impatient and started approaching the house before McGill was out of the car. When she got to the door and turned to look for him, he was nowhere in sight.

Teag's understated, almost gracious, concession to Alice's revelation that she'd be leaving his show had surprised her. More than that, it had also made her uneasy. After all, she'd all but forced her way into getting a job with him. He'd gotten her the medical attention to bring her back from whatever damn medical misadventure had knocked her on her ass this time. And when she says she's going to work elsewhere, he genially accepts that news? Even tells her it might be a good idea to head to L.A. right away?

That wasn't the Teag Tobias she'd come to know.

The change of character struck her as … ominous?

And then she thought she heard two voices coming from downstairs. She didn't know what time it was, but a glance at the window made clear it was full dark. So who'd come calling? For that matter, where exactly was she?

The question of whether she'd heard two voices downstairs was definitively answered when she heard a man yell, "You asshole, get moving or I'll shoot you right now."

The voice was male, but it wasn't Teag's.

The words themselves were terrifying, but as a memory was keyed in Alice's mind, she became even more frightened. She'd heard that other voice only once before and briefly, but its source came rushing back to her: *The crazy guy with the ring in Portland.*

She pushed herself out of bed and looked for a place to hide.

Teag Tobias climbed the stairs to the second floor, thinking maybe this was his lucky day after all. He knew if he'd held a gun on some jerk who well and truly pissed him off, he'd have punched the bastard's ticket then and there. What had the nimrod from Oregon done? Given him and fate a chance to turn things around, that was what.

Teag wasn't going to distract himself by trying to talk to the chump. He was looking as hard as he could for some opportunity to improve his odds of surviving, and what he saw when he got to the second-floor landing made him smile with wicked pleasure. Alice was no longer in bed where he'd left her. He directed a quick glance at the narrow space between the open bedroom door and the adjacent wall.

That was where she was hiding. Behind the door. His eyes met one of hers.

She was scared speechless. As well she should be.

Teag leaped forward and pulled Alice out from behind the door. He clutched her in front of him, one arm around her shoulders, the other arm across her waist. The only thing wrong with Teag's strategy was the dip-shit from Oregon didn't know how to play his part. Instead of being daunted and submissive in light of his fantasy girlfriend's peril, he popped off a round that cleared Alice's head and took the lobe off of Teag's left ear.

Teag's reaction was immediate and logical, but also unpredictable. If his human shield was inadequate to do its job, he had to get rid of it fast. He thrust Alice hard at the would-be hero. The guy caught her all right, kept her upright, but he wasn't expecting Teag to charge right in behind Alice.

Turning sideways, Teag clasped the barrel of the nitwit's pistol in his left hand and grabbed the guy's wrist with his right hand. He gave the gun a quick twist upward. The weapon's trigger guard broke the wannabe rescuer's finger. He howled as Teag snatched the weapon from him and took two steps backward.

Haskell Carver had taught Teag the gun disarm.

He'd said Teag would never know when he might need it.

Haskell had also told him, "You grab someone's gun, you use it. You don't chat."

That was Teag's intention, but the hayseed had one last act of valor in him.

He pulled Alice behind him and stepped forward to take the bullet, and that's just what he got, smack in the middle of his chest. There were no heroics after that, just the laws of physics and limits of human anatomy. The Oregon hero flew backward and collapsed in the second floor hallway. Stepping out of the bedroom, Teag didn't see Alice but knew she couldn't have gone far. He was about to look for her when someone began pounding on the front door.

A woman's shrill voice shouted, "Police, open the door! Open the goddamn door, or I'll break it down!"

She seemed sincere, Teag thought, only her threat would have been more effective if she didn't sound like a teenager who was about to burst into tears. He started down the stairs. As soon as he got an angle he liked, he started shooting through the door. The gunshots were loud as hell, but he thought he heard a body falling.

He kept firing until the magazine was empty just to make sure.

Then he climbed the stairs to get his tactical-ops knife from his bedroom.

McGill had gone around to the back of the house. If Officer Hendrix's presence at the front door was going to scare someone into running, he'd be there to stop the getaway. Of course, there was no saying that someone who'd decided to run wouldn't also be violent in his escape attempt; that was always a possibility. McGill had his semi-auto in hand with the safety off.

He took a quick peek through a lighted window. He didn't see anyone but recognized the room as a kitchen, even noticed a gas flame on under a pot. People sometimes left things simmering on a stove while they were out of the room, but this was just one pan not a part of a larger meal being prepared. McGill got the feeling someone had been in the kitchen, got distracted, and left the room.

He took another look, this one longer and from a different window.

He neither saw anyone in the kitchen nor heard any nearby sound.

He tried the door leading into the kitchen and found it unlocked. He hoped, as he always did when making an entry into a place where someone might be waiting with a gun, that there were such things as guardian angels. He prayed that his was at the top of his game.

McGill went in low, fast and quiet, only to find no one else was present.

The pan on the stove held what looked like furiously boiling water.

He wondered what the heck Officer Hendrix was doing.

She should have made her presence known by now.

On impulse, McGill took out the knife that had been seized from Teagan Tobias years ago and placed it on the kitchen table in the middle of the room. He didn't know for sure, but he had a feeling the knife might serve as a distraction or maybe even a lure.

That was when McGill heard the first gunshot, the sound of a body falling, Hendrix's high-pitched self-identification as a police officer and her demand that the front door be opened. That was followed by a volley of gunfire. McGill felt sure the shots had come from within the house, not from Camille Hendrix.

Mother of God, he thought, had he gotten the young officer killed?

The idea must have dazed him for a moment because the next thing he knew Teagan Tobias was standing in the doorway between the kitchen and what looked to be a dining room. Tobias didn't have a gun, but he held a knife with a wicked-looking black blade in his hand …

And then he saw the knife McGill had put on the table.

Recognized it, and for just a second Tobias was the one in shock.

With his gun already in hand, McGill took a step backward and continued to ease back as Tobias moved forward to the table. He looked up at McGill and his gun. Tobias smiled, having recognized that McGill had retreated. Maybe he wasn't such a big hero after all.

Moving with impressive quickness, Tobias' hand shot out and grabbed his old blade off the table. Now, he had a lethal knife in each hand. He began to move the blades up and down, like a drummer establishing a rhythm. The movement was slow and even now, but there might be a rapid-fire paradiddle coming up.

That was the thing about knives; they could be hypnotic.

It was possible to attack from numerous angles.

And if someone had two of them in his hands and was even slightly ambidextrous, it would be almost impossible to keep from getting cut, slashed or stabbed. Unless, of course, you had a gun ready to fire. Which McGill did.

Only the big hero, Tobias could see, kept backing up.

Hey, who knew, maybe a knife was the only thing that scared him, and two of them, maybe he'd be wetting himself soon. Or not. McGill stopped giving ground. The gap between them was no more than ten feet now. McGill might get one shot off before Tobias got to him. Might even hit him, but if it wasn't a kill shot …

That was when Tobias understood that McGill hadn't been retreating; the bastard had been sucking him in. Sonofabitch. Quick as wink, McGill half-turned, without ever taking his gun off Tobias, and picked up the pot of boiling water from the stove.

There was no question what he was going to do with that.

For just a heartbeat Tobias couldn't decide whether to turn and run or charge McGill and try to get at least one blade into his gut and rip it upward. He decided to attack, but it was already too late. McGill flung the boiling water at Tobias.

He saw the scalding liquid leave the pan, tried to both turn away and duck.

He was too late. The searing water hit the right side of his face and neck. The pain was so intense it dropped him to his knees. He couldn't even find the breath to scream. For a moment, he teetered between insanity and unconsciousness.

McGill decided the choice for him.

He stepped up behind Tobias and slammed the bottom of the pan against his head.

Then a loud bang, not another gunshot, but still alarming, made McGill jump.

He realized he'd just heard a door being broken down.

And Leo yelled, "You all right, boss?"

"Yes," McGill called out. "What about Officer Hendrix?"

"Still breathing. Caught what looks like four or five rounds in her armor."

"You call the state police?"

"Them and an ambulance for the officer."

Looking down at Teag, McGill said, "Better make that two ambulances."

That was when a woman's voice called out, "Is it safe to come downstairs?"

McGill hurried to the front of the house. He looked up the stairway, and that was when he got his first look at Alice Janeway.

"Yes," he told her. "It's not pretty, but it is safe. How are you, Alice?"

Her face crumpled and she began to weep.

"The man who saved me was killed."

***City Limits Motel — Austin, Texas***

Gene Beck and Kyle Tompkins arrived at the same vantage point on the sidewalk opposite the U-shaped parking lot of the motel within ten seconds of each other. Both of them beat the forces of law and order by just under a minute. Kyle had a name tag clipped to a shirt pocket. His profession — *Journalist* — and employer — *Austin Journal,* were also noted. Gene wore an old untucked USAF desert camouflage shirt that noted his last name over stonewashed jeans and Asics Roadhawk running shoes.

The feds beat the locals to the motel by two car-lengths. That was, the DEA's first two SUVs entered in sequence followed by alternating vehicles from the Austin PD, the DEA, the Texas Rangers and so on. The fact that nobody locked bumpers with anybody else was impressive in itself. But when the assorted feds and cops knocked down the doors to every unit in the fleabag motel at the same time, it was almost balletic.

Moments later, without a shot being fired, the good guys

started bringing the bad guys out of their rooms, not only in handcuffs but also wearing leg shackles. None of the prisoners put up a struggle as they were deposited into police vans, formerly known by the politically incorrect as paddy wagons.

Despite neither Gene nor Kyle having uttered a disparaging word, two lawmen, one local cop and one federal agent, both of whom might be sons of Erin from the looks of them, crossed the street to have a word with the two onlookers now that substantive matters had been concluded.

"Put that thing away," the fed told Kyle.

Not wanting to trust the light-gathering ability of his phone, Kyle had shot the whole sequence of events at the motel with a Sony Hi-Def Camcorder. Kyle did as he was told without objection.

Only slightly mollified, the fed looked at Kyle's name tag.

He turned to the local cop and asked, "*Austin Journal?*"

"Freebie weekly," the cop said with a slight sneer in his voice. Turning his attention to Gene, the cop asked, "You still active duty?"

Gene shook his head. "Not for a while now."

"What'd you do when you were in?"

"Bike chaser, among other things."

"What?" the fed asked.

The cop knew. "He jumped out of airplanes, after throwing his motorbike out first."

Both the fed and Kyle looked at Gene, trying to assess his truthfulness.

The cop finally asked Gene, "What're you and your friend doing here, other than shooting video?"

"Is it okay to reach into my shirt pocket?" Gene asked.

Both lawmen looked at his shirt and saw no threatening bulge. Nonetheless, the fed said, "Nice and easy."

Gene followed his direction and took out two business cards.

One from DEA Chief of Operations Anne Macklin and the other from Conrad Winstead, deputy assistant director of the Texas Rangers.

The fed eyed the cards first and passed them along to the local.

Gene said, "My colleagues and I thought of a gag to lure Eloy Chavez up here to Austin. We did that with the approval of the two people whose cards I just gave you. If you haven't gotten that word yet, feel free to make some phone calls."

The fed and the cop looked at each other.

The fed said to Kyle, "Chief Macklin said you could film this?"

"Didn't say I couldn't," Kyle responded.

Gene added, "The only thing we saw was you and your people pulling off your operation slick as a whistle. The only thing that video will show is your people are top notch."

The two lawmen looked at each other again.

"What?" Gene asked.

Didn't take him the blink of an eye to figure things out.

"Eloy Chavez wasn't in there with the others?" Gene asked.

"Oh, shit," Kyle said, thinking his worst fear was coming true.

The fed told Gene, "Nobody we picked up just now looks anything like our photos of Eloy Chavez."

"Damn, damn, damn," Kyle said.

"My feelings exactly," the cop said.

Gene asked, "Any of those boys you grabbed have a real pretty cowboy hat with him?"

Both lawmen shook their heads.

Gene thought about things for a second and asked the fed. "How high-tech are these drug gangs supposed to be?"

"They're getting pretty damn good," the fed said with disgust. "One of the hired hands said they were using a drone."

"A drone?" Gene asked.

"Hell, why not?" the cop said. "Half the kids in this country have drones."

Gene asked, "Was this one the kind that launches missiles?"

The cop went pale. "Jesus, I hope not."

He looked at his counterpart, who said, "I can't say I know for sure, but the current opinion is no missiles. Not yet."

"Small damn comfort," the cop said.

The fed said to Gene, "Why the hell are you asking about all this?"

"Well, it might just be a process of elimination, but maybe I know where Eloy Chavez might show up. Himself in person, I mean."

"Where's that?" the cop wanted to know.

Gene said, "My client's house, out in Georgetown."

"You say you've got clients, you say you've got colleagues," the fed said. "You've got our bosses' business cards. Who the hell do you work for, anyway?"

Gene told him. "James J. McGill."

That explained things sufficiently for the fed and cop to go back to hauling off the gang of men they'd just arrested. They'd kept the cards Gene had shown them. Maybe they thought they could get Gene on a theft of stationery charge.

Gene called Maj. She was at Wallace Rhymes' place in Georgetown, guarding the client. Also keeping him from doing anything impetuous. He let her know that Chavez's crew had been arrested, but the kingpin was still on the loose. Told her to keep an eye out for an enemy drone overhead, too.

Then he used his phone to go to Google.

Glancing over Gene's shoulder, Kyle asked, "What're you looking for?"

Gene said, "Closest five-star hotel. Accommodations a drug-boss might enjoy."

Kyle smiled and nodded. "Wonder if those guys will think of that?"

He gestured at the caravan of departing law enforcement and their prisoners.

Gene said, "If they don't, we'll tell them eventually."

***Interstate 35 Northbound — Passing Pflugerville, Texas***

Eloy Chavez sat behind the wheel of a Maserati Gran Turismo. His lieutenant, Fermin Gomez, had rented it for him, using a Centurion Card bearing the name of a resort owner who fronted for Chavez back home. The drug boss never set foot on the car rental lot. At the time, he was enjoying two scoops of pecan buttered rum ice cream at Prohibition Creamery.

Chavez had to hand it to the *yanquis.* When it came to indulging themselves, they were hard to beat. Feeling generous after his waitress complimented him on his beautiful hat, he doubled his usual extravagant tip and even bought two scoops of whisky chocolate ice cream to go for Gomez. His lieutenant got to eat while Chavez drove.

He was pleased with the car Gomez had found, swapping out their limo for something a bit less conspicuous. The Maserati was yet another sign that if you were truly wealthy, there was no place like the United States to satisfy your every whim. Getting onto highway 35, as the car directed him, Chavez asked Gomez, "No one asked to see what was in your suitcase?"

A small arsenal of weapons was the cargo.

"No, señor. They were only too happy to put it in the car's trunk for me."

"Good. People who understand they were born to serve others are a blessing."

Gomez kept his mouth shut about that observation, knowing the boss included him in the servile number. For that matter, so were the boss's parents. Reminding *el jefe* that he wasn't the descendant of royalty, however, would likely be a fatal mistake.

For the moment, Gomez contented himself eating the best ice cream he'd ever tasted.

Cruising along the interstate highway, Chavez said, "The car tells me we should arrive in 20 minutes."

"At present speed, yes."

"This car can go so much faster, can't it? But look at all the cars passing us right now."

"This is their country, *señor.* Most, I think, are licensed to drive here."

Chavez wasn't licensed to drive anywhere. At home, there was no cop who would even think of stopping any car he was driving.

Then again, he traveled in an armored column in Mexico. Sometimes he even had his helicopter overhead for air support.

"A new idea has just occurred to me, Gomez."

"Yes, *jefe?*"

"What do you think it would take for Mexico to reclaim Texas?"

Gomez couldn't help himself. He answered honestly. "More nuclear weapons than the *yanquis* have. And then the patience to wait until all the radiation goes away."

Chavez scowled at such defeatist thinking.

"Well, I tell you this, *amigo,*" he said, "we have all the weapons we need right now to take over one little rancho in this state and get that damn hat I alone should have."

"*Sí, señor.* Also to kill the old man who mocked you."

That little detail produced two results. Chavez laughed with delight and he pushed the gas pedal down hard. The Maserati roared like a rocket. Passed all other vehicles on the road like they were parked with their motors off.

"Gomez, these *pendejos* thought they could lure me into their trap at the cantina they talked about. But now I will take them by surprise. Make that old gringo beg for mercy before I shoot him."

Possibly, Gomez thought. If they didn't get into a pitched battle with the highway police first. The car had crossed 100 miles per hour more quickly than Gomez would have thought possible, and its speed was still increasing. Maybe they wouldn't need the *americanos* to kill them. One little mistake behind the wheel by the boss would do it.

Not that Gomez was about to do anything to distract el *jefe.*

He placed the now empty ice cream container between his feet and took out his iPhone.

He made the connection with the drone circling above Wallace Rhymes' property.

The view from its camera showed no lights on in the house.

Sleep soundly, Gomez mentally instructed everyone there.

At least until we have our guns pointed at you.

Neither Gomez nor Chavez noticed a car with its lights out keeping pace a half-mile behind them. Gene Beck wasn't the driver Leo Levy was, but he wasn't half-bad either. In fact, he was whistling a new tune that came to him just as his car hit 120 mph.

***Wallace Rhymes' House — Georgetown, Texas***

Maj Olson was a crack shot, one of those people with the intuitive feel, exceptional eyesight and fine motor control to make hitting a bull's-eye or other distant target duck soup. Added to her natural ability, Gene Beck had provided her with a weapon no civilian was supposed to have: an M4A1 carbine. It was a fully automatic assault rifle of the type used by U.S. special operations units.

Gene had told Maj that he washed out of the USAF Combat Control Team training, but only because a unit psychologist thought he whistled too much. Might have given away his position unintentionally, without even being aware of what he was doing.

Gene had told Maj that evaluation was pure BS. He always knew when he was whistling. He'd even developed a technique he called silent whistling: forming the mouth and tongue shapes to produce a sound but dialing back the respiratory power until the result was less than a whisper. Gene knew in his mind, of course, what the tune would sound like at a regular volume, but anyone else would have had to be in his back pocket to hear even a note of music.

Maj had sympathized with Gene's predicament, and she understood the need for secrecy when Gene said he'd found another opportunity to put his hard-won skills to use for the benefit of the country. Had to be as a covert intelligence officer or a contract mercenary, she thought. She never asked for details, but she wasn't surprised when Gene asked her one day if she'd like to fire the M4A1.

There was no end to the open space in Texas to do all sorts of target shooting. Maj hadn't cared for the full-auto shooting. She thought of it as a meat-grinder with an ear-splitting racket. She did appreciate the weapon's single-shot accuracy and range. Equipped with an advanced combat optical gunsight and an effective range of 500-600 meters, Maj thought the weapon made hitting a long-distance target easy as pie.

Of course, if the target was moving and you were shooting at night, that increased the challenge, made things a bit more interesting. Even so, five minutes before Eloy Chavez arrived at the Rhymes' house, Maj shot down the drone circling overhead with her first shot.

The weapon wasn't silenced, but a single rifle shot in the wide-open spaces of Texas was not likely to draw much attention from distant neighbors or the cops. She and Wallace Rhymes had discussed whether they should enlist a police presence at the property. Rhymes had sent his four adult children back to their homes. His housekeeper, Solana Fuentes, was at a hotel in town. Rhymes had said Maj could leave, too, if she wanted. He could still take care of himself, he asserted. He backed up the claim by taking in hand a Sharps rifle that had once been used to hunt bison, but its .50 caliber cartridge looked like it could bring down an elephant.

Maj chose to stay, and she and Rhymes worked out a new strategy to bag Chavez.

Chavez braked sharply, even though the Maserati's computer guide had told him the driveway to his destination was just a few feet ahead on the left. Gomez, busy frowning at the absence of the drone's-eye view on his iPhone, was caught unaware and hurled forward against his seatbelt. His phone flew from his hand, landing in the footwell.

"*¡Mierda!*" he yelped.

Chavez only laughed, but not at his companion's discomfiture.

"No, no, *amigo*. Look, there. We have won already."

Remembering his place in the scheme of things, Gomez dutifully looked in the direction the boss was pointing. He saw immediately what had made Chavez so cheerful. Dangling from a post at the entrance to the driveway was … John Wayne's hat?

"You see, Gomez, even what passes for a rich *yanqui* these days knows better than to anger me. It's true that this man has mocked me, but now he seeks to escape my wrath. What do you think we should do now, my friend?"

Gomez wanted to say, "Take the hat and go, while we still can." Still, he knew the correct answer was, "Whatever you think is best, *jefe*." Only he saw something that did not allow him to be properly submissive. He had to say, "Boss, look over there, further up the path to the house."

Chavez did so, and what he saw made him grind his teeth.

The damn *yanquis* were trying to play him for a fool.

Maybe 50 feet further on from the entrance, under an adjacent light, dangling from another post, was a second hat. It looked exactly like the first one. So which one, Chavez was forced to wonder, was the real hat? The one with the movie-star magic. The hat that would allow him to rule for years after he returned home wearing it. Telling stories of having humbled and killed the old man and eluding the *americanos*' lawmen.

Chavez saw only one answer to the problem. Seize both hats and make the insolent old bastard tell him which was the real one. After learning the answer, Chavez would make the gringo suffer worse than any of his previous victims. The stories of those torments would also add to Chavez's legend and power.

He and Gomez saw there were three more hats on the way to the house.

Chavez regarded each of them as a further insult.

He all but frothed at the mouth as he stopped the Maserati in front of the house.

Seeing yet another hat sitting on the doorstep, the drug boss could no longer contain himself. He got out of the car and used his handgun to shoot this hat full of holes. Then he reached back into the car and pulled the trunk release. He would get his assault rifle now and show this *pendejo* no mercy. He'd forget slow torture and blow him to pieces.

Chavez's fury was such that he failed to notice Gomez standing on the other side of the Maserati with his eyes wide and his hands raised in surrender. Chavez tossed his pistol into the trunk and was about to reach for the bag where his heavy weapons were stashed when a woman's voice told him, "That's far enough."

She repeated her warning in Spanish. *"Eso es suficiente."*

What cut through Chavez's rage was the calmness of the woman's voice.

He'd been warned. That was the only chance he'd get. Whatever happened next was on him. He turned and saw a woman pointing her assault rifle at him. She could cut him to pieces if he made one wrong move. A man to the woman's right had another rifle pointed at Gomez.

Both the man and the woman wore hats identical to the one on Chavez's head.

Their rebuke was clear: In Texas, everyone was John Wayne.

Chavez did the only thing he'd dare do to show his contempt. He took the hat off his own head and slammed it to the pavement in front of him. He was about to smash it with his upraised right foot when Wallace Rhymes bashed the side of Chavez's head with the butt of his Sharps rifle. The blow knocked the drug boss to one side where he crumpled unconscious to the ground.

Rhymes looked at the fallen drug boss and said, "Ernesto Fuentes sends his regards."

Then he picked up John Wayne's hat, took off the imitation and put the real thing on his head.

Anne Macklin, DEA Chief of Operations, and Conrad Winstead, deputy assistant director of the Texas Rangers made their way to

Wallace Rhymes' house fifteen minutes later. They and their minions arrived in two helicopters: a Blackhawk transport and an Apache attack helicopter. Having arrived late to the party, they probably wanted to show off their muscle. Once it was clear there would be no need for the Apache's M230 chain gun or Hellfire missiles, the attack chopper was sent back to its base.

In the best American tradition, the federal and state lawmen and women had brought two lawyers with them, along with a videographer and medical personnel. Eloy Chavez was treated for a concussion, and then he and Fermin Gomez were read their rights in English and Spanish and bundled aboard the Blackhawk.

Winstead had the pleasure of escorting the prisoners back to Austin where Chavez would be hospitalized in a secure ward and Gomez would be locked in a one-man cell. Chief of Operations Macklin stayed behind to get the story of what had happened at the ranch.

Wallace Rhymes pointed to Maj and told her, "This bright young woman came up with what my forebears back in New England would call a wicked smart idea. We had a bunch of nice cowboy hats on hand. We'd planned to use them another way tomorrow, but she said why not put them to use tonight?"

He described how the hats were set out to draw Chavez into the property, make him think he might never know which hat was the real one, and get him upset and looking the wrong way.

Macklin smiled and said, "I like it."

She shook Maj's hand in congratulations.

Maj said, "Gene gave me the heads-up. The sense of urgency sparked the idea. Necessity being the mother of invention and all that."

Macklin looked at Gene, who'd arrived moments after Chavez had been laid low. "How'd you find Chavez?"

He explained his five-star hotel notion. "I got lucky and caught sight of Chavez and his pal coming out of the hotel. Followed them to Prohibition Creamery. Chavez went in for a treat, so I followed the other guy to a car-rental place. From there, I fell in place behind them on I-35 and followed them out here."

"You didn't think to call the DEA or the Rangers on the way?" Macklin asked.

Gene said, "Yeah, I did, but once the pursuit got to over 100 miles per hour, and trying to be sneaky about it, I didn't think I should further divide my attention."

Gene had already whispered into Maj's ear how he'd come up with a new song during the chase.

Macklin said, "All right. No harm, no foul. You two did a fine job. Nobody shot, only one bad guy hurt." Turning to Rhymes, though, she said, "You, sir, I'm not so sure you needed to bash in a man's head. The EMTs said it looks like Mr. Chavez's skull was fractured."

Rhymes was unrepentant, "After what he did to my old friend Ernesto, he's lucky I didn't shoot his head clean off."

The DEA boss chose not to argue that point.

She knew no prosecutor in Texas, state or federal, would ever bring charges against Wallace Rhymes. That position would likely be the same in all 49 other states. Rhymes would be seen as one of the heroes in this story. Trying to say otherwise might be a career ender.

So Macklin vented her objection indirectly.

Hooking a thumb at Rhymes, she asked Maj, "So how'd you get that old goat to go along with your plan to use all those hats as bait?"

Maj forestalled a rebuttal from Rhymes to Macklin's characterization of him with a gently raised hand. Then she said, "I just told him what should have been obvious to all of us from the start."

"What's that?"

Maj said, "It's not the hat that makes the man; it's the man that makes the hat."

## CHAPTER 7

***Sunday, November 6, 2017***
***Widow Kip's Country Inn — Woodstock, Virginia***

By the time McGill and Leo got done talking with the Virginia State Police, it was early Sunday morning. Officer Camille Hendrix had been airlifted to MedStar Georgetown University Hospital in Washington, DC. Hendrix had been hit by five gunshots. All of them, after going through the front door of the house, hit her armored vest. None managed to penetrate it. All the shots, however, gave her chest a brutal pounding.

She experienced ventricular fibrillation, a type of arrhythmia that can cause cardiac arrest and death. Leo was credited with being the hero of the moment. McGill's Chevy had a defibrillator in the trunk. It was intended to be used on him, should the need ever arise, and both Leo and Deke Ky had been trained in its use. Acting with a speed worthy of his driving skills, Leo had shocked Camille Hendrix's heart back into a normal rhythm on the first try.

The EMTs credited Leo's swift response with saving the officer's life.

From that day forward, Leo's money was no good in Woodstock. Anything he'd ordinarily buy in town was on the house. Emails and tweets from police departments around the country lauded his quick thinking and decisive action.

NASCAR drivers from A to Z hailed him.

Leo's self-effacing response — "I only did what was right." — drew further praise.

For McGill's part, the state cops had no problem with what he'd done: scalding and concussing Teagan Tobias. Shortly after finishing his interview with the state cops, and not wanting to wake Patti, McGill called Sweetie. He apologized for waking her and gave her the whole story of what had happened up to that point.

Teagan Tobias was taken to University Hospital in Charlottesville. His facial scarring would be extensive and terribly painful for a long time. He'd been charged with the attempted murder of a police officer and the aggravated murder of Tad Thacker.

On top of that, the Brooklyn District Attorney's Office filed a murder charge against Tobias in the death of Nicholas Pell. Virginia had the death penalty; New York did not. The officials in the two states conferred and agreed that Virginia should try Tobias first; if anything went awry with that proceeding, he would be extradited to New York for trial there.

Alice Janeway called Lindsay Todd to thank her old friend for her help. She promised to get back in touch as soon as she could. Then Alice accompanied the body of Tad Thacker back to Portland, Oregon. At his memorial service, she met Tad's parents and several of Jenny Nyland's relatives, all of whom were stunned and moved to tears by her resemblance to their departed family member. When everyone heard of how Tad had saved Alice's life, they wept even more, but to a person, they were certain that if there was any reward for living a good life, Tad and Jenny must be together at last.

Alice moved on to Los Angeles, found a good doctor to monitor her health, and invited her brother's children to come visit her. It was the least she could do after Marlon had left her a million dollars in his will. Erika Janeway thought of suing to recover the money, but after Alice gave it to the Saint Jude Children's Research Hospital, the greedy widow was told a suit would never succeed.

Alice started working on a comedy show with a wry but not cruel view of life. In a podcast interview, she was asked if she thought Teagan Tobias would like any of her new material. She said, "You mean the guy who tried to kill me? Well, if I'm any good at all, I'll come up with something that'll get him to die laughing."

Taking Maj Olson's words to heart — that the man makes the hat — Wallace Rhymes sent John Wayne's hat out to be cleaned and donated it to the Smithsonian Institution. The night after Eloy Chavez's arrest, a party was held at Hell's Belle, where music and beer abounded, and everybody wore the hat of his or her choice. Unlike all the others, Kyle Tompkins limited himself to one chilled bottle of Lone Star, sat at the end of the bar with a view of the room and began making notes for what would become his first best-selling book.

McGill got word of the outcome of the Texas case from Sweetie when he woke up shortly after a long nap at the bed-and-breakfast establishment to which the local cops had taken him. Being a trained observer, he spotted the note that had been slipped under his door.

It said that breakfast hours had come and gone, but just this once, for favors rendered to the town, room service would be provided whenever he liked. Just hit #21 on his room phone. His growling stomach told him it was an offer too good to refuse. He made the call and asked what was on the menu.

He was given four choices and said, "How about a little of all of the above?"

Fifteen minutes, he was told.

That was just long enough for a quick shave and shower. He'd slipped back into yesterday's clothes when there was a knock at the door. He took a twenty-dollar bill out of his wallet, figuring management could offer a free feed, but employees should always be compensated.

McGill opened the door with his money in hand, and saw Patti had brought his breakfast.

He said, "Changed career paths, have you?"

She stepped into the room. "Only for you. Only occasionally. And I don't need a tip, thanks."

She set the tray down on a table in the sitting area of the room. Didn't spill a drop of orange juice or coffee. Some people were blessed with an array of talents. McGill sat opposite the chair where his better half had tidily arranged herself.

"Have you been waiting long for me to wake up?" he asked.

"Not too long. After driving here, I checked in to see where you were and what was what. Then I took a walk around town. Even went to see where all the action was last night. There were still a few uniformed officers around with their technical counterparts. They let me take a look from the outside of the house. I think they recognized me."

McGill reviewed his wife's summary, and was struck by her account.

"Wait a minute," he said. "Did *you* drive here?"

"I did."

"With Daphna Levy?"

"By myself."

McGill searched his memory. "I don't *ever* remember seeing you drive."

"That's because you didn't know me in my wild and crazy years. I can even use a stick shift."

McGill looked for deeper meaning. "Is all this implicit criticism of me, myself?"

"You mean because you've basically rejected having Secret

Service protection? No, I'm not criticizing that. I was thinking, rather, of the freedom you've reclaimed for yourself. I came to envy that quite soon. So when Sweetie called to tell me what went on with you here, I asked Daphna whether the Secret Service knew of any threat to my life between Washington and Woodstock on this particular morning. When she said no, I checked and, would you believe, some dear person, Edwina most likely, has been renewing my driver's license for me. I was good to go. So I did."

"In whose car?" McGill asked.

"Special Agent Levy was kind enough to let me borrow hers, a BMW 230i coupe. Oh, Jim, I can't tell you how liberating it was to take that sleek little car out on the road. I felt so free. I had to keep myself from speeding a half-dozen times."

McGill beamed. Patti had been a mature adult when he first met her. Now, he could see what she must have looked like in her early 20s. Teasing her, he asked, "So you managed to avoid any moving violations?"

Patti got up and crossed to the room's door on the hallway.

She made sure it was locked.

Looking back at McGill she said, "I'll handle the movement, you signal any violations."

McGill grinned and replied, "You know, way back when, I wrote very few traffic tickets."

## ABOUT THE AUTHOR

Joseph Flynn has been published both traditionally — Signet Books, Bantam Books and Variance Publishing — and through his own imprint, Stray Dog Press, Inc. Both major media reviews and reader reviews have praised his work. Booklist said, "Flynn is an excellent storyteller." *The Chicago Tribune* said, "Flynn [is] a master of high-octane plotting." The most repeated reader comment is: Write faster, we want more.

You may read free excerpts of Joe's books by visiting his website at: *www.josephflynn.com*.

www.ingramcontent.com/pod-product-compliance
Lightning Source LLC
Chambersburg PA
CBHW071224250626
47163CB00001B/94
*9780997450057*